*This low-priced Bantam Book
has been completely reset in a type face
designed for easy reading, and was printed
from new plates. It contains the complete
text of the original hard-cover edition.*
NOT ONE WORD HAS BEEN OMITTED.

BEAUVALLET
*A Bantam Book / published by arrangement with
E. P. Dutton, Inc.*

PRINTING HISTORY
First published 1929
Dutton edition published February 1968
Bantam Book / October 1969
2nd printing ... February 1970
3rd printing .... June 1970
4th printing .... July 1975
5th printing ... February 1983

ISBN 0-553-22934-6

blished simultaneously in the United States and Canada

*n Books are published by Bantam Books, Inc. Its trade-
consisting of the words "Bantam Books" and the por-
of a rooster, is Registered in U.S. Patent and Trademark
and in other countries. Marca Registrada. Bantam
Inc., 666 Fifth Avenue, New York, New York 10103.*

PRINTED IN THE UNITED STATES OF AMERICA

H   14 13 12 11 10 9 8 7 6 5

PIRATE'S PRISONER

"Lady," Beauvallet began, his voice softening, "for once I do not jest. Hear my solemn promise! I will make you an Englishwoman before a year is gone by. And so seal my bond." He bent his handsome head quickly, and kissed her lips before she could stop him.

Dominica brushed her hand across her lips, as though she would brush his kiss away. "How dared you—!" she choked. "Hold me—kiss me! Oh, base! It's to insult me!"

"Hold, child. I would wed you. Did I not say it?"

"You will never wed me!" she defied him. "You are ungenerous, base! You hold me prisoner, and you do as you will with me!"

"Nay, nay, there's no talk of prisoners or gaolers, Dominica, but only of a man and a maid." He bent, and kissed her fingers. "There! let it be forgot—until I kiss you again."

"That will be never, señor."

GEORGETTE
HEYER
BEAUVALLET

BANTAM BO
TORONTO · NEW YORK ·

To
F.D.H.

BEAUVALLET

◁ Chapter I ▷

THE deck was a shambles. Men lay dead and dying; there was split woodwork, a welter of broken mizzen and sagging sail, dust and grime, and the reek of powder. A ball screamed through the rigging overhead; another tore the sea into wild foam beneath the galleon's stern. She seemed to stagger, to reel, to list heavily to port. From his quarterdeck Don Juan de Narvaez gave a sharp order; his lieutenant went running down the companion into the waist of the ship.

Soldiers crowded there in steel breastplates and chased morions. They had halberds and pikes, and some held long double-edged swords. They looked out to sea, to where the smaller ship came steadily on, the Red Cross of St. George flying at her mainmast head. They were sure now that it would end in a hand to hand fight; they were even glad of it: they knew themselves to be the finest soldiers in Christendom. What chance could these bold English have against them at close quarters? The English ship had held off beyond reach of the Spanish guns this past hour, ceaselessly bombarding the *Santa Maria* with her longer-reached cannons. The soldiers in the waist did not know how serious was the damage she had wreaked, but they were fretting and nervous from their impotence, and their forced inaction. Now the English ship drew nearer, the wind filling her white sails, and bearing her on like a bird through the scudding waves.

Don Juan watched her come, and saw his guns belch

1

fire upon her. But she was close, and there was little damage done, full half of the Spanish guns shooting above her from the over-tall sides of the galleon. The *Venture*—and he knew now beyond all doubt that it was the *Venture* herself—bore down upon them undaunted.

She came up alongside, discharging her fire into the galleon's waist, and passed on unscathed. Drawing a little ahead of the Spaniard she wore suddenly, came sailing across the galleon's bows, and raked her cruelly fore and aft.

The *Santa Maria* was riddled and groaning; there was panic aboard, and a hopeless confusion. Don Juan knew his ship was crippled and cursed softly in his beard. But he had cool courage enough, and he knew how to rally his men. The *Venture* was coming round, and it was evident that she meant to grapple the larger galleon now. Well, therein lay hope. Let her come: the *Santa Maria* was doomed, but aboard the *Venture* was El Beauvallet—Beauvallet the mocker of Spain, the freebooter, the madman! His capture would be worth even the loss of so noble a galleon as the *Santa Maria*: ay, and more than that! There was not a Spanish admiral who had not that capture for his ambition. Don Juan drew in his breath on the thought. El Beauvallet who bit his thumb at Spain! If it should fall to his lot to take this man of a charmed life prisoner for King Philip he thought he would ask no more of life.

It had been with this in mind that Don Juan had challenged the ship when she hove into sight that afternoon. He had known that El Beauvallet was sailing in these waters; at Santiago he had seen Perinat who had sailed forth to punish the *Venture* not a fortnight ago. Perinat had come back to Santiago in his own long boat, biting his nails, a beaten man. He had talked wildly of witchcraft, of a devil of a man who threw back his head and laughed. Don Juan had sneered at that. The bungler Perinat!

Now it seemed that he too stood in danger of having bungled. He had thrown down the gauntlet to Beauvallet, who never refused a challenge, and Beauvallet had picked it up, and flirted his dainty craft forward through the sparkling sea.

There had been some desire to show a lady what a Narvaez could accomplish. Don Juan chewed his lip, and knew a pang of remorse. Below, in the panelled stateroom, was no less a personage than Don Manuel de Rada y Sylva, late Governor of Santiago, with his daughter Dominica. Don Juan knew only too well in what peril they now stood. But when it came to hand to hand fighting the tables might still be turned.

The soldiers were armed and ready in the waist and on the forecastle. There were gunners, grimed and stained with sweat, standing by their culverins; the brief panic had been swiftly quelled. Let the *Venture* come!

She was near, standing the fire from the long basiliscos; she drew nearer, and through the smoke one might see the men on her with boarding axes and swords, ready for the order to board the Spaniard. Then, suddenly, there was a crack and a roar, the bursting flame and the black smoke of a score of swivel-guns on her decks, all trained upon the waist of the *Santa Maria.* There was havoc wrought among the Spanish soldiery; cries, groans, and oaths rent the air, and swiftly, while havoc lasted, the *Venture* crept up, and grappled the tall galleon.

Men swarmed up the sides, using their boarding axes to form scaling ladders. From the spritsail yard they sprang down upon the deck of the *Santa Maria*, daggers between their teeth, and long swords in hand. No might of Spanish soldiery, maimed as it was by the wicked fire, could stop them. They came on, and the fight was desperate over the slippery decks: sword to sword, slash and cut, and the quick stab of daggers.

Don Juan stood at the head of the companion, sword in hand, a tall figure in breastplate and tassets of fluted steel. He sought in the press for a leader amongst the boarders, but could see none in that hurly-burly.

It was hard fighting, frenzied fighting, over wounded and dead, with ever and again the crack of a dag fired at close range. The pandemonium was intense; no single voice could be distinguished amongst the hubbub of groans, shouted orders, sharp cries, and clash of arms. One could not tell for a while who had the advantage: the fight swayed and eddied, and the *Santa Maria* lay helpless under all.

A man seemed to spring up out of the mob below, and gained the companion. A moment he stood with his foot upon the first step, looking up at Don Juan, a red sword in his hand, a cloak twisted about his left arm, and a black pointed beard upthrust. A chased morion shaded the upper part of his face, but Don Juan saw white teeth agleam, and crouched for the stroke that should send this stranger to perdition. "Down, *perro!*" he snarled.

The stranger laughed, and answered him in pure Castilian. "Nay, señor, the dog comes up."

Don Juan peered to see more closely into the upturned face. "Come up and die, dog," he said softly, "for I think you are he whom I seek."

"All Spain seems to seek me, señor," answered the stranger merrily. "But who shall slay Nick Beauvallet? Will you try?"

He came up the first steps in a bound, and his sword took Don Juan's in a strong parry that beat it aside for a moment. He brought his cloak swirling into swift play, and entangled Don Juan's sword in it. He was up on the quarterdeck in a flash, even as Don Juan, livid, shook his sword free of the cloak. The two blades rang together, but Don Juan knew that he had met his master. He was forced back and back across the deck to the bulwarks, fighting grimly every inch of the way.

Cruzada, his lieutenant, came running from the poop-deck. Beauvallet saw, and made a quick end. His great sword whirled aloft, cleaved downwards, hissing through the air, and shattered the pauldron over Don Juan's shoulder. Don Juan sank, half-stunned, to his knees, and his sword clattered to the deck. Beauvallet turned, panting, to meet Cruzada.

But there were Englishmen on the quarterdeck now, hard upon the heels of their leader, and from all sides came cries from the Spaniards for quarter. Beauvallet's sword held Cruzada in check. "Yield, señor, yield," he said. "I hold your general prisoner."

"But yet I may slay you, pirate!" gasped Cruzada.

"Curb ambition, child," Beauvallet said. "Here, Daw, Russet, Curlew! Overpower me this springald. Softly, lads, softly!"

Cruzada found himself surrounded, and cried out in

fury. Rough hands seized him from behind, and dragged him back; he saw Beauvallet leaning on his sword, and cursed him wildly for a coward and a poltroon.

Beauvallet chuckled at that. "Grow a beard, child, and meet me when it's grown. Mr. Dangerfield!" His lieutenant was at hand. "Have a guard about the worthy señor," said Beauvallet, and indicated Don Juan by a brief nod. He bent, picked up Don Juan's sword, and was off, light-footed, down the companion into the waist of the ship.

Don Juan recovered his senses to find himself unarmed, and El Beauvallet gone. He came staggering to his feet, an English hand at his elbow, and was aware of a fair boy confronting him. "You are my prisoner, señor," said Richard Dangerfield, in halting Spanish. "The day is lost."

The sweat in Don Juan's eyes; he brushed it away, and could see the truth of this statement. All over the galleon his men were laying down their arms. The rage and anguish that convulsed him were wiped suddenly from his face. By a supreme effort he recovered his *sosiego,* and stood straight and looked impassively as should befit his breeding. He achieved a bow. "I am in your hands, señor."

Over the quarterdeck towards the poop men were hurrying already in search of plunder. Some three or four stout fellows went clattering down the companion that led to the staterooms. They came upon a sight to astonish them. Backed against the wall, with hands laid along the panelling to either side of her stood a lady, a lady all cream and rose and ebony. Cream her skin, and rose her lips, ebony the lustrous hair confined under a net of gold. Her eyes were dark and large under languorous lids, the brows delicately marked, the nose short and proud, the full lips curved and ripe. She wore a gown of purple camlet, worked cunningly with a pattern of gold thread, with a kirtle of armazine to fall from the veriest hint of a farthingale. Behind her head reared up a high ruff of lace sewn with crystals. It framed a face piquant and lovely. The square of her bodice was cut low across her breast; a jewel lay upon the white skin, rising and falling with her quickened breath.

The foremost of the invaders stood in an amazed

stare, but recovered before those behind him might push forward. "A wench!" he cried on a coarse laugh. "A rare wench, as I live!"

His fellows came crowding to get a sight of this miracle. There were sparks of anger in the lady's eyes, and, at the back of them, fear.

A man rose from a high-backed chair by the table, a man of middle age, enfeebled by the West Indian climate. Latent fever had him in its grip; it might be seen in his overbright eyes, and in the intermittent ague that shook him. He wore a long furred gown, and a close cap, and he leaned heavily upon a stick. There was a priest of the Franciscan order beside him, cowled darkly, but the holy man paid no heed to anything but his beads, over which he muttered ceaselessly. The other man went with an infirm step to stand before his daughter, shielding her from curious eyes. "I demand to be taken before your commander!" he said in the Spanish tongue. "I am Don Manuel de Rada y Sylva, late Governor of the island of Santiago."

It is doubtful whether much of this was intelligible to the English seamen. A couple advanced into the stateroom and put Don Manuel aside. "Hold off, old greybeard!" William Hick advised him, and put a dirty hand under the lady's chin. "The pretty chuck! Buss me, sweeting!"

There came instead the sound of a ringing slap. William Hick started back with a rueful hand clapped to his cheek. "Oh, a shrew!"

John Daw caught the lady about her trim waist, clipping one of her arms to her side. The other fighting hand was imprisoned in his huge paw. "Softly, my cosset, softly!" he chuckled, and gave her a hearty kiss. "That's the way to use, lads!"

Don Manuel, held between two men, cried out. "Unhand her, fellow! Your commander! I demand to see your commander!"

They caught at the last word, and it sobered them a little. "Ay, hail 'em before the General. It's safer." John Daw pushed Hick aside, who was fingering the jewel about the girl's neck. "Let be! Do you want Mad Nick after you? Come lass, on deck with you!"

The lady was forced, resisting to the door. She did not know what they were going to do with her, and struggled wildly, throwing herself back against their pulling hands. It did not serve. "The curst wench!" growled Hick, still smarting from the blow she had dealt him. He snatched her up into his arms and bore her up the companion to the poop-deck.

There were others gathered there, others who greeted the appearance of this frightened, wrathful lady with amazement and some ribaldry. She was set on her feet, and straightway fell upon Hick like a wild-cat. She ignored a warning cry from her father, brought under ward on to the deck, and hit out at Hick, stamped with her heel on a large foot, scratched at a bearded face. She was seized and held fast, each wrist in custody of a grinning sailor. One of them chucked her under the chin, and laughed hugely to see her throw up her head. "Little turtle-dove, pretty love-bird!" said John Daw, essaying satire.

There were men crowded all about her, wondering, jesting, feasting their eyes. A lip was smacked; there was a knowing wink and a bawdy joke. The lady shrank.

Then, all at once, a ringing voice authoritatively from beyond the group that encircled her. "God's death! What's this? Give way there!"

Two men went staggering aside, spun apart by an iron hand on the shoulder of each. The lady looked fearfully into the face of El Beauvallet.

He had cast aside his morion, and his close black hair showed, curling neatly over his head. Under straight brows she saw fine eyes, the blue of the sea with the sunlight on the water. They were bright eyes and keen, vivid under the black lashes; laughing eyes, watchful yet careless.

The laugh was stayed in them now as he checked in his impatient stride. He stood staring; a mobile eyebrow flew up comically; Sir Nicholas Beauvallet appeared incredulous, and blinked at this unexpected vision.

His glance, quick moving, took in next the lady's captors, and the stilled laughter went right out of his eyes. He was swift in action, too swift for Hick, still stupidly grasping one of the lady's wrists. A clenched fist shot out and took Master Hick neatly on the point of the jaw. Master Hick fell a-sprawl on the deck. "Cullions! Dawcocks!"

said Beauvallet terribly, and swung round to deal in kind with John Daw.

But Master Daw had hurriedly released the wrist he held, and was making off as quickly as he could. He was sped on his way by a shrewd kick to the rearward. Beauvallet turned to the lady. "A million pardons, señora!" he said, as though here were no great matter.

The lady was forced to admit him to be a personable fellow, and she found his smile irresistible. She bit back an answering gleam: one would not smile friendly upon an English freebooter. "Unhand my father, señor!" she commanded, mighty haughty.

The tone seemed to amuse Beauvallet; his shoulders shook appreciatively. He looked round for sign of my lady's parent, and saw him standing between guards who straightway let him go, and stepped back in something of a hurry.

Don Manuel was shaken, and ashen pale. He spoke breathlessly. "I demand instantly to see the commander!"

"A million more pardons!" Beauvallet responded. "Behold the commander, Nicholas Beauvallet, at your service!"

The lady exclaimed at that. "I knew it! You are El Beauvallet!"

Beauvallet turned to her; the eyebrow was raised again, and the eyes themselves were twinkling. "Himself, señora. Wholly at your feet."

"I," said Don Manuel stiffly, "am Don Manuel de Rada y Sylva. You address my daughter, Dona Dominica. I demand to know the meaning of this outrage."

"Outrage?" said Beauvallet, honestly puzzled. "What outrage, señor?"

Don Manuel flushed, and pointed a shaking finger to the shambles forward. "You need ask, señor?"

"The fight! Why, to say truth, noble señor, I had thought that this ship opened fire upon me," said Beauvallet pleasantly. "And I was never one to refuse a challenge."

"Where," demanded Dona Dominica, "is Don Juan de Narvaez?"

"Under guard, señora, until he goes aboard his own long boat."

"You beat him! You, with that little ship!"

Beauvallet laughed out at that. "I, with that little ship," he bowed.

"What of us?" Don Manuel interrupted.

Sir Nicholas looked rueful, ran a hand through his crisp hair. "You have me there, señor," he confessed. "What a-plague are you doing aboard this vessel?"

"I conceive that to be none of your business, señor. If you must know I am on my way home from Santiago to Spain."

"Why, an evil chance," said Beauvallet sympathetically. "What folly possessed that numskull of a commander of yours to open fire on me?"

"Don Juan did his duty, señor," said Don Manuel haughtily.

"Alack then, that virtue has not been better rewarded," said Sir Nicholas lightly. "And what am I to do with you?" He bit his finger, pondering the question. "There is of course the long boat. She puts off as soon as may be for the island of Dominica. It lies some three miles to the north of us. Do you choose to go aboard her?"

Dona Dominica took a quick step forward. Since her fears were lulled her temper rose. This careless manner was not to be borne. She broke into impassioned speech, shooting her words at Beauvallet. "Is that all you can say? Sea-robber! Hateful pirate! Is it nothing to you that we must put back to the Indies and wait perhaps months for another ship? Oh nothing, nothing! You see where my father stands, a sick man, and you care nothing that you expose him to such rough usage. Base, wicked robber! What do you care! Nothing! I could spit on you for a vile English freebooter!" She ended on a sob of rage, and stamped her foot at him.

"Good lack!" said Beauvallet, staring down into that exquisite face of fury. A smile of amusement and of admiration crept into his eyes. It caused Dona Dominica to lose the last shreds of her temper. What would you? She was a maid all fire and spirit. She struck at him, and he caught her hand and held it, pulled her closer, and looked down into her face with eyes a-twinkle. "I cry pardon, señora. We will amend all." He turned his head and sent a shout ringing for his lieutenant.

"Loose me!" Dominica said, and tried to pull her hand away. "Loose me!"

"Why, you would scratch me if I did," Beauvallet said, teasing.

It was not to be borne. The lady's eyes fell, and encountered the hilt of a dagger in Beauvallet's belt. She raised them again, held his in a defiant stare, and stole her hand to the dagger's hilt.

Sir Nicholas looked quickly down, saw what she would be at, and laughed. "Brave lass!" He let her go, let her draw out his dagger, and flung wide his arms. "Come then! Have at me!"

She stepped back, uncertain and bewildered, wondering what manner of man was this who could mock at death itself. "If you touch me I will kill you," she said through her teeth.

Still he came on, twinkling, daring her. She drew back until the bulwarks stayed her.

"Now strike!" invited Beauvallet. "I'll swear you have the stomach for it!"

"My daughter!" Don Manuel was aghast. "Give back that knife! I command you! Señor, be good enough to stand back."

Beauvallet turned away from the lady. It seemed he gave no second thought to the dangerous weapon she held. He waited for Dangerfield to come up, standing with his hands tucked negligently into his belt.

"Sir, you called me?"

Beauvallet indicated Don Manuel and his daughter with a comprehensive sweep of his hand. "Convey Don Manuel de Rada y Sylva and his daughter aboard the *Venture*," he said, in Spanish.

Don Manuel started; Dominica gave a gasp. "Is it a jest, señor?" Don Manuel demanded.

"In God's Name, why should I jest?"

"You make us prisoners?"

"Nay, I bid you be my guests, señor. I said I would amend all."

The lady broke out again. "You mock us! You shall not take us aboard your ship. We will not go!"

Beauvallet set his hands on his hips. The mobile eyebrow went up again. "How now? First you will and then you will not. You tell me I am a dog to hinder your return to Spain, and curse me roundly for a rogue. Well, I have said I will amend the fault: I will convey you to Spain with all speed. What ails you then?"

"Take us to Spain?" said Don Manuel uncomprehendingly.

"You cannot!" cried Dominica, incredulous. "You dare not!"

"Dare not? God's Son, I am Nick Beauvallet!" said Sir Nicholas, amazed. "Dared I sail into Vigo a year back, and lay all waste? What should stop me?"

She flung up her hands, and the dagger flashed in the sunlight. "Oh, now I know that they named you well who named you Mad Beauvallet!"

"You have it wrong," Beauvallet said, jesting. "Mad Nicholas is the name they call me. I make you free of it, señora."

Don Manuel interposed. "Señor, I do not understand you. I cannot believe you speak in good faith."

"The best in the world, señor. Is an Englishman's word good enough?"

Don Manuel knew not how to answer. It was left for his daughter to say No, very hotly. All she got by that was a quick look, and a slight laugh.

Across the deck came Don Juan de Narvaez, stately even in defeat. He bowed low to Don Manuel, lower still to Dona Dominica, and ignored Beauvallet. "Señor, the boat waits. Permit me to escort you."

"Get you aboard, Señor Punctilio," said Sir Nicholas. "Don Manuel sails with me."

"No!" said Dominica. But it is very certain that she meant yes.

"I have no desire to jest with you, señor," Don Juan said coldly. "Don Manuel de Rada naturally sails with me."

A long finger beckoned to Don Juan's guard. "Escort Don Juan to the long boat," said Sir Nicholas.

"I do not stir from here without Don Manuel and his daughter," said Narvaez, and struck an attitude.

"Take him away," said Sir Nicholas, bored. "God speed

you, señor." Narvaez was led away, protesting. "Señora, be pleased to go aboard the *Venture*. Diccon, have their traps conveyed at once."

Dominica braved him, to see what might come of it. "I will not go!" She clenched the dagger. "Constrain me at your peril!"

"A challenge?" inquired Beauvallet. "Oh, rash! I told you that I never refused a challenge." He bore down upon her, and dodged, laughing, the dagger's point. He caught her wrist, and had his other arm firmly clipped about her waist. "Cry peace, sweetheart," he said, and took the dagger from her, and restored it to its sheath. "Come!" he said, tossed her up in his arms, and strode off with her to the quarterdeck.

Dominica forebore resistance. It would be useless, she knew, and her dignity would suffer. She permitted herself to be carried off, and liked the manner of it. They did not use such ready methods in Spain. There was great strength in the arm that upheld her, and the very carelessness of the man intrigued one. A strange, mad fellow, with an odd directness. One would know more of him.

She was carried down the companion into the waist, where the men were busy with the treasure—China silks, and linen-cloths, ingots of gold, bars of silver, and spices from the islands. "Robber!" said Dominica softly.

He chuckled. It was annoying. To the bulwarks he went, and she wondered how he would manage now. But he did it easily enough, with a hand on the shrouds, and a leap up. He stood poised a moment. "Welcome aboard the *Venture*, sweetheart!" he said audaciously, and climbed down with her safe tucked in his arm to his own poop-deck below.

She was set on her feet, ruffled and speechless, and saw her father being helped carefully down the side of the tall galleon. Don Manuel appeared to be both bewildered and amused.

"See them well bestowed, Diccon," Beauvallet bade the fair youth, and went back the way he had come.

"Will it please you to come below, señora?" Dangerfield said shyly, and bowed to them both. "Your chests will be here anon."

Don Manuel smiled a little wryly. "I think the man is

either mad—or else—an odd, whimsical fellow, my daughter," he remarked. "We shall doubtless learn which in time."

Chapter II

DONA DOMINICA was escorted below decks, and led to a fair cabin which she guessed to be the home of Master Dangerfield, hurriedly evicted. She was left there alone, while Master Dangerfield took her father on to yet another cabin. She took stock of her surroundings, and was pleased to approve. There were mellow walls, oak-panelled, a cushioned seat under the porthole, a table with carved legs, a joint-stool, a fine Flanders chest, a cupboard against the bulkhead, and the bunk.

There was presently a discreet scratching on the door. She bade enter, and a small man with an inquisitive nose and very bravely curling mustachios insinuated his head into the room. Dona Dominica regarded him in silence. A pair of shrewd grey eyes smiled deprecatingly. "Permit that I bring your chests, señora," said the newcomer in perfect Spanish. "Also your ladyship's woman."

"Maria!" called out Dominica joyfully.

The door was opened farther to admit a plump creature who flew to her, and sobbed, and laughed. "Señorita; They have not harmed you!" She fell to patting Dominica's hands, and kissing them.

"But where were you all this time?" Dominica asked.

"They locked me in the cabin, señorita! Miguel de Vasso it was! Serve him right that he took a grievous knock on the head! But you?"

"I am safe," Dominica answered. "But what will happen to us I know not. The world's upside down, I believe."

The man with the mustachios came into the room and

revealed a spare figure garbed in sober brown fustian. "Have no fear, señora," said this worthy cheerfully. "You sail upon the *Venture,* and we do not harm women. Faith of an Englishman!"

"Who are you?" Dominica asked.

"I," said the thin man, puffing out his chest, "am no less a person, señora, than Sir Nicholas Beauvallet's own familiar servant, Joshua Dimmock, at your orders. Ho, there! bring on the baggage!" This was addressed to someone without. In a moment two younkers appeared laden, and dumped down their burdens upon the floor. They lingered, gaping at the lady, but Joshua waved his hands at them. "Hence, get hence, numskulls!" He hustled them out, and shut the door upon them. "Please you, noble lady, I will dispose." He looked upon the mountain of baggage, laid a finger to his nose, skipped to the cupboard, and flung it open. The raiment of Master Dangerfield was exposed to Maria's titters. Joshua swooped, came away with an armful of doublets and hose, and cast them into the alleyway outside the cabin. "Ho there! Avoid me these trappings!" he commanded, and the two women heard footsteps coming quickly in obedience to the summons. Joshua returned to the cupboard and swept it bare, flung out the boots and pantoffles that stood ranged upon its floor, and stepped back to observe with pride the barrenness of his creating. "So!" The chest caught his eye; he went to it in a rush, lifted the lid, and clicked his tongue in impatience. He seemed to dive into it head first.

Dominica sat down on the cushioned seat to watch the surprising gyrations of Master Dimmock. Maria knelt by her, clasping a hand still in both of hers, and giggled under her breath. An indignant voice was uplifted in the alleyway. "Who cast them here? That coystrill! Dimmock, Joshua Dimmock, may the black vomit seize you! Master Dangerfield's fine Venice hosen to lie in the dust! Come out, ye skinny rogue!"

Joshua emerged from the chest with an armful of shirts and netherstocks. The door was rudely opened; Master Dangerfield's servant sought to make a hasty entrance, but was met on the threshold by Joshua, who thrust the pile of linen into his arms, and drove him out. "Avoid them!

Avoid, fool! The noble lady hath this cabin. By the General's orders, mark you! Hold your peace, wastrel! The Venice hose! What's that to me? Make order there! Pick up that handruff, that boot, those stocks! There are more shirts to come. Await me!" He came back, spread his hands, and shrugged expressive shoulders. "Heed naught, señora. A hapless fool. Master Dangerfield's man. We shall have all in order presently."

"I should not wish to turn Master Dangerfield from his cabin," Dominica said. "Is there none other might house me?"

"Most noble lady! Waste no moment's thought upon it!" Joshua said, shocked. "Master Dangerfield, forsooth! A likely gentleman, I allow, but a mere lad from the nursery. This mountain of raiment! Ho, the young men! all alike! I dare swear a full score of shirts. Sir Nicholas himself owns not so many." He threw the rest of Master Dangerfield's wardrobe out of the cabin, and shut the door smartly upon the protests of Master Dangerfield's man.

Dominica watched the disposal of her baggage about the room. "I must suppose you a man of worth," she said, gently satirical.

"You may say so, indeed, señora. I am the servant of Sir Nicholas. I have the ear. I am obeyed. Thus it is to be the lackey of a great man, lady," Joshua answered complacently.

"Oh, is this Sir Nicholas a great man by your reckoning?"

"None greater, lady," said Joshua promptly. "I have served him these fifteen years, and seen none to equal him. And I have been about the world, mark you! Ay, we have done some junketting to and fro. I allow you Sir Francis Drake to be a man well enough, but lacking in some small matters wherein we have the advantage of him. His birth, for example, will not rank with ours. By no means! Raleigh? Pshaw! he lacks our ready wit: we laugh in his sour countenance! Howard? A fig for him! I say no more, and leave you to judge. That popinjay, Leicester? Bah! A man of no weight. We, and we alone have never failed in our undertakings. And why, you ask? Very simply, señora: we reck not! The Queen's grace said it with her own august lips. 'God's Death,' quoth she—her favourite oath, mark you!—'God's Death, Sir Nicholas, you should take *Reck Not* to be your watchword!' With reason, most gracious lady! Certain we reck not. We bite our glove in challenge to whosoever ye will. We take what we will: Beauvallet's way!"

Maria sniffed, and cocked up her pert nose. Joshua looked severely. "Mark it, mistress! I speak for both: we reck not."

"He is a bold man," Dominica said, half to herself.

Joshua beamed upon her. "You speak sooth, señora. Bold! Ay, a very panther. We laugh at fear. That's for lesser men. I shall uncord these bundles, gracious lady, so it please you."

"What is he? What is his birth?" Dominica asked. "Is he base or noble?"

Joshua bent a frown of some dignity upon her. "Would I serve one who was of base birth, señora? No! We are very nobly born. The knighthood was not needed to mark our degree. An honour granted upon our return from Drake's voyage round the world. I allow it to have been due, but we needed it not. Sir Nicholas stands heir to a barony, no less!"

"So!" said Dominica with interest.

"Ay, and indeed. He is own brother to Lord Beauvallet. A solid man, señora, lacking our wits, maybe, but a comfortable wise lord. He looks askance at all this trafficking upon the high seas." Joshua forgot for a moment his rôle of admiring and faithful servant. "Well he may! Rolling up and down the world, never at rest—it is not fit! We are no longer boys to delight in harebrained schemes and chancy ventures. But what would you? A madness is in us; we must always be up and about, nosing out danger." He rolled up the cords he had untied. "I leave you, señora. Ha! we cast off!" He hopped to the porthole, and peered out. "In good time: that hulk is done. I go now to see the noble señor safely housed. By your leave, señora!"

"Where is my father?" Dominica asked.

"Hard by, señora. You may rap on this bulkhead, and he will hear. Mistress—" he looked austerely at Maria—"see to the noble lady!"

"Impudence!" Maria cried. But the door had shut behind Joshua Dimmock.

"An oddity," said Dominica. "Well—like master, like man." She went to the port, and stood on tiptoe to look out. The waves were hissing round the sides of the *Venture*. "I cannot see our ship. That man said she was done." She came away from the port. "And so here we are, upon an English ship, and in an enemy's power. What shall come of it, I wonder?" She did not seem to be disturbed.

"Let them dare to touch you!" Maria said, arms akimbo. "I am not locked in my cabin twice, señorita!" She abandoned the fierce attitude, and began to unpack my lady's baggage. She shook out a gown of stiff crimson brocade, and sighed over it. "Alas, the broidered taffety that I had in my mind for you to wear this night!" she lamented.

Dominica smiled secretly. "I will wear it," she said.

Maria stared. "Your finest gown to be wasted on a party of English pirates! Now if it were Don Juan——"

Dominica was impatient suddenly. "Don Juan! A fool! A beaten braggart! He strutted, and swore he would sink this ship to the bottom of the sea, and take the great Beauvallet a prisoner to Spain! I hate a man to be beaten! Lay out the gown, girl. I will wear it, and the rubies too."

"Never say so, señorita!" cried Maria in genuine horror. "I have your jewels safe hid in my bosom. They would tear them from your neck!"

"The rubies!" Dominica repeated. "We are here as the guests of El Beauvallet, and I vow we will play the part right royally!"

There was a soft scratching on the door, and Don Manuel looked in. "Well, my child?" he said, and looked around him with approval.

Dona Dominica waved her hand. "As you see, señor, I am very well. And you?"

He nodded, and came to sit beside her. "They house us snugly enough. There is a strange creature giving orders to my man at this moment. He says he is El Beauvallet's lackey. I do not understand these English servants, and the license they have. The creature talks without pause."

He drew his gown about his knees. "We labour with the unexpected," he complained, and looked gravely at his daughter. "The commander bids us to supper. We shall not forget, Dominica, that we sail as guests upon this ship."

"No," said Dominica doubtfully.

"We shall use Sir Nicholas with courtesy," added Don Manuel.

"Yes, señor," said Dominica, more doubtfully still.

An hour later Joshua came once more to her door. Supper awaited her, he said, and bowed her down the alleyway to the stateroom. She went regally, and rubies glowed on her bosom. The dull red of her stiff gown made her skin appear the whiter; she carried a fan of feathers in her hand, and had a wired ruff of lace sewn over with jewels behind her head.

The stateroom was low-pitched, lit by two lamps hung on chains from the thick beams above. On the bulkhead opposite the door arms were emblazoned, arms crossed with the bar sinister, and with a scroll round the base, bearing the legend *Sans Peur*. A table was spread in the middle of the room, and there were high-backed chairs of Spanish make set round it. Beside one of these was standing Master Dangerfield, point-de-vice in a bombasted doublet of grograine, and the famous Venice hosen. He bowed and blushed when he saw Dominica, and was eager to set a chair for her.

She had no quarrel with Dangerfield; she smiled upon him, enslaved him straightway, and sat her down at the table, unconcernedly fanning herself.

There was a cheerful voice uplifted without, a strong masculine voice that had a ringing quality. One might always know when Sir Nicholas Beauvallet approached.

He came in, apparently cracking some jest, escorting Don Manuel.

Dominica surveyed him through her lashes. Even in dinted armour, with his hair damp with sweat, and his hands grimed with powder he had appeared to her personable. She saw him now transformed.

He wore a purple doublet, slashed and paned, with great sleeves slit to show stitched linen beneath. A high collar clipped his throat about, and had a little starched ruff atop. Over it jutted his beard: none of your spade beards this, but a rare stiletto, black as his close hair. He affected the round French hosen, puffed about the thighs, and the netherstocks known in England as Lord Leicester's since only a man with as good a leg as his might reasonably wear them. There were rosettes upon his shoon, and knotted garters, rich with silver lace, below his knees. Starched handruffs were turned back from his wrists; he wore a jewel on one long finger, and about his neck a golden chain with a scented pomander hanging from it.

He entered, and his quick glance took in Dominica at the table. He swept her a bow and showed his even white teeth in a smile that was boyish and swift, and curiously infectious. "Well, met, señora! Has my rogue seen to your comfort? A chair for Don Manuel, Diccon!" The room seemed to be full of Sir Nicholas Beauvallet, a forceful presence.

"I am ashamed to have stolen Señor Dangerfield's cabin from him," Dominica said, with a pretty smile bestowed upon Richard.

He stammered a disclaimer. It was an honour, a privilege. Dominica, choosing to ignore Beauvallet at the head of the table, pursued a halting conversation with Dangerfield, exerting herself to captivate. No difficult task this: the lad looked with eyes of shy admiration already.

"A strange, whimsical fellow ordered everything, señor," she said. "I cry pardon: it was not I threw your traps out on to the alleyway! I hope the master was not so incensed as was the man?"

Dangerfield smiled. "Ay, that would be Joshua, señora. My man's a fool, a dolt. He is greatly enraged against Joshua. You must understand, señora, that Joshua is an original. I dare say he boasted to you of Sir Nicholas' exploits—always coupling himself with his master?"

Dominica had nothing to say to this. Dangerfield plodded on. "It is his way, but I believe he is the only one of our company who takes it upon himself to censure his master. To the world he says that Sir Nicholas is second only to God; to Sir Nicholas' self he says——" he broke off, and turned a laughing, quizzical look on his chief.

Sir Nicholas turned his head; Dominica had not

thought that he was attending. "Ah, to Sir Nicholas' self he says what Sir Nicholas' dignity will not permit him to repeat," said Beauvallet, smiling. He turned back to Don Manuel, who had broken off in the middle of a sentence.

"Your servant did not seem to hold him in so great esteem as he holds himself, señor," said Dominica.

"Ah, no, señora, but then he threw my clothes out into the alley."

"I doubt it was dusty," Dominica said demurely.

"Do not let Sir Nicholas hear you say that, señora," Dangerfield answered gaily.

By a half smile that was certainly not conjured up by her father's conversation Dominica saw that Sir Nicholas was still attending.

Meat was set before the lady, breast of mutton served with a sauce flavored with saffron. There was a pasty beside, and a compost of quinces. She fell to, and continued to talk to Master Dangerfield.

Don Manuel tried more than once to catch his daughter's eye, but he failed, and was forced to pursue his conversation with Sir Nicholas. "You have a well-found vessel, señor," he remarked courteously.

"My own, señor." Beauvallet picked up a flagon of wine. "I have here an Alicante wine, señor, or a Burgundy, if you should prefer it. Or there is Rhenish. Say but the word!"

"You are too good, señor. The Alicante wine, I thank you." He observed that his cup was of Moorish ware, much used in Spain, and raised his brows at it. Delicately he forebore comment.

"You remark my cups, señor?" said Beauvallet, lacking a like delicacy. "They come out of Andalusia." He saw a slight stiffening on the part of his guest, and his eyes twinkled. "Nay, nay, señor, they never were upon a Spanish galleon. I bought them upon my travels, years ago."

He threw Don Manuel into some discomfort. Don Manuel made haste to turn the subject. "You know my country, señor?"

"Why, yes, a little," Beauvallet acknowledged. He looked at Dominica's averted face. "May I give you wine, señora?"

So rapt in conversation with Dangerfield was the lady

that it seemed she did not hear. Beauvallet watched her a
moment in some amusement, then turned to Don Manuel.
"Do you suppose, señor, that your daughter will take wine
from my hands?"

"Dominica, you are addressed!" Don Manuel said
sharply.

She gave an admirable start, and turned. "Señor?" She
encountered Beauvallet's eyes, brimful with laughter.
"Your pardon, señor?" He held out a cup in his long
fingers. She took it from him, and turned it in her hand.
"Ah, did this come from the *Santa Maria*?" she asked,
mighty innocent.

Don Manuel blushed for his daughter's manners, and
made a deprecatory sound. But Beauvallet's shoulders
shook. "I had these quite honestly, señora."

Dominica appeared surprised.

Supper wore on its way. Don Manuel, shocked at the
perversity of his daughter in bestowing all her attention on
Dangerfield, began to talk to the young man himself, and
successfully ousted Dominica from the conversation. She
bit her lip with vexation, and became absorbed in the
contemplation of a dish of marchpane. At her left hand
Beauvallet lay back in his chair, and played idly with his
pomander. Dominica stole a sidelong glance at him, found
his eyes upon her, wickedly teasing under the down-
dropped lids, and flushed hotly. She began to nibble at a
piece of marchpane.

Sir Nicholas let fall his pomander, and sat straight in
his chair. His hand went to his belt; he drew his dagger
from the sheath. It was a rich piece, with a hilt of wrought
gold and a thin, flashing blade. He leaned forward, and
presented the hilt to the lady. "I make you a present of it,
señora," he said in a humble voice.

Dominica flung up her head at that, and tried to push
the dagger away. "I do not want it."

"Oh, but surely!"

"You are pleased to mock me, señor. I have no need of
your dagger."

"But you would like so much to kill me," Sir Nicholas
said softly.

Dominica looked at him indignantly. He was abominable, and to make matters the more insupportable he had a

smile that set a poor maid's heart in a flutter. "You laugh at me. Take your fill of it, señor: I shall not heed your sneers," she said.

"I?" Beauvallet said, and shot out a hand to grasp her wrist. "Now look me boldly in the face and tell me if I sneer at you!"

Dominica looked instead towards her father, but he had turned his shoulder, and was descanting to Master Dangerfield upon the works of Livy.

"Come!" insisted the tormentor. "What, afraid?"

Stung, she looked up. Defiance gleamed in her eyes. Sir Nicholas kept his steadily upon her, raised her hand to his lips, kissed it fleetingly, and held it still. "You will know me better some day," he said.

"I've no ambition for it," Dominica answered, but without truth.

"Have you not? Have you not indeed?" His fingers tightened about her wrist; there was a brilliant look of inquiry before he let her go. It disturbed her oddly; the man had no right to such bright, challenging eyes.

A silence fell between them. Don Manuel, absorbed in his topic, had passed on to the poet Horace, and was inflicting quotations upon Master Dangerfield.

"What came to Don Juan, señor?" asked Dominica, finding the silence oppressive.

"I suppose him to be steering for the island of your name, señora," Sir Nicholas replied, and cracked a nut between finger and thumb. The problems besetting Don Juan seemed to hold no interest for him.

"And Señor Cruzada? And the rest?"

"I did not send him alone, señora," said Beauvallet, one eyebrow lifting humorously. "I suppose Señor Cruzada, whomsoever he may be, to be of his company."

The lady selected another fragment of marchpane from the dish, and refused an offer of Hippocras to drink with it. She looked pensive. "You give quarter, you English?"

"God's Life, did you suppose otherwise?"

"I did not know, señor. They tell strange tales of you in the Indies."

"It seems so indeed." He looked amused. "Am I said to burn, torture, and slay, señora?"

She met his gaze gravely. "You are a hardy man, señor. There are those who say you use witchcraft."

He flung back his head and laughed out at that. Don Manuel was startled, and broke off in a middle of a line, to the relief of Master Dangerfield, a-nod over his wine. "The only craft I use is sea-craft, señora," Beauvallet said. "I wear no charms, but I was born, so they tell me, when Venus and Jupiter were in conjunction. A happy omen! All honour to them!" He raised his cup to these planets, and drank to them.

"Alchemy is a snare, as also astrology," said Don Manuel sternly. "I regard the tenets of Paracelsus as pernicious, señor, but I believe they are much studied and thought of in England. A creed both absurd and heretical! Why, I have heard a man doubt that his neighbour was born under the sign of Sagittarius for no better reason than that he had a ruddy cheek, or a chestnut beard. Likewise you will meet those who will not stir beyond their doors without they have a piece of coral about them, or a sapphire to give them courage, or some other such toys, fit only for children or infidels. Then you will hear talk of the sky's division into Houses, this one governing such-and-such a thing, and that some other. A silly conceit, obtaining credulity of the foolish." Thus Don Manuel disposed of Paracelsus, very summarily.

⌒◁ Chapter III ▷⌒

THE second day was very bright, with a hot sun beating down upon the sea, and a stiff breeze blowing to fill the sails. Don Manuel remained below on his bunk, worn and shaken by the agitations and exertions of the previous day. He made a poor breakfast of sops dipped in wine, and sent his daughter from him. He shook with fever, and complained of the headache. Hovering assiduously about him was his own man, Bartolomeo, but he had also Joshua Dimmock to attend to his wants. This was done mighty expertly. Joshua discoursed learnedly on several fevers, and, not sharing Don Manuel's views on the Chaldean creed, prescribed the wearing of some chips from a gallows as a certain cure. These he produced from somewhere about his person, and expatiated fervently upon their magical properties. Don Manuel waved them testily aside, but consented to drink a strong cordial, which, he was assured, came straight from the stillroom of my Lady Beauvallet herself, a dame well-versed in these mysteries.

"A sure potion, señor, as I have proved," Joshua told him, "containing julep and angelica, a handful of juniper berries, and betony, as also mithridate (so I believe), not to mention wormwood, which the world knows to be very potent against all manner of fevers. The whole, noble señor, steeped in a spirit of wine by my lady's own hands, and sealed up tightly, as you perceive. Deign only to test of its values!"

Don Manuel drank off the cordial, and was assured of a speedy recovery. But Joshua shook his head secretly over the case, and told Sir Nicholas, in his private ear, that he carried a dying man aboard the *Venture*.

"I know it," Beauvallet said briefly. "If I read well the signs the *cameras de sangre* is in him."

"I observed it, sir. A glance, you would say. His man— a lank, melancholic fool if ever I saw one!—stands prating of quotidian fevers, but no, quoth I, say rather the *cameras de sangre*, dolt. I shall poke out the folds of the ruff, please you, sir." He performed this office for Sir Nicholas, and stood back to regard his handiwork. The poking-stick was levelled at Sir Nicholas next by way of emphasis. "Moreover, master, and mark you well! it is not to be considered a favourable omen. By no means! A death portends disaster. I do not speak of such willy-nilly deaths as might chance in battle. That is understood. A lingering sickness is another and quite different matter. We must set the worthy señor ashore with all speed."

"How now! What's this, rogue?" demanded Beauvallet, lying back in his chair. "Set him ashore where and for what?"

"I judge the Canaries to be a convenient spot, sir. The reason is made clear: he must die upon land—or at least upon another ship than ours. We need not concern ourselves with that." He ducked quickly to avoid a boot hurled at his head.

"Cullion!" Beauvallet apostrophised him. "Curb that prattling cheat of yours! We set the gentleman ashore in Spain. Mark that!"

Joshua picked up the boot, and knelt to help Sir Nicholas put it on, no whit abashed. "I shall take leave to say, master, that this is to put our heads in a noose again."

"Be sure yours will end there one day," said Sir Nicholas cheerfully.

"As to that, sir, *I* do not go roystering up and down the world, sacking and plundering," replied Joshua, entirely without venom. "A gentle thrust, sir and we have the boot on. So!" He smoothed a wrinkle from the soft Cordovan leather, and held ready the second boot. "You are to understand, sir, that it is no matter to me, for it was clearly proved in the reading of my horoscope that I should die snug in my bed. It would be well to have your horoscope cast, master, that we may know what to beware of."

"Beware your bed, dizzard, and get you hence!" Beauvallet recommended. "You tempt me overmuch." He made a short, suggestive movement of his arched foot.

"That, master," said Joshua philosophically, "is as may be, and at your worship's pleasure. I do not gainsay you have the right. But I shall take leave to say withal that this junketting upon the high seas with a wench aboard—nay two——"

"What?" Beauvallet roared, and jerked himself upright in his chair.

Joshua's shrewd grey eyes widened. "Oho! Pardon, sir, a lady was the word. But it's all the same, by your leave, or rather worse, if the wind sits in that quarter with you. However, I say nothing. But it's against all custom and proper usage, and I misdoubt me an evil chance may befall."

Beauvallet fell to stroking his pointed beard, seeing him at which significant trick Joshua backed strategically to the door. "An evil chance will without any doubt at all shortly befall you, my friend," said Sir Nicholas, and came to his feet, "At the toe of my boot!"

"If that is your humour, sir, I withdraw with all speed," said Joshua promptly, and retired nimbly.

Beauvallet swung out in his wake, and went up on deck to oversee an inventory of the *Santa Maria*'s cargo in the waist.

Thus Dona Dominica, when she came up on deck to take the air, chanced upon a sight that made her curl her lip, and lift her chin. She wandered to the quarter-deck and stood looking down into the waist, where bales of cloth were lying, and where ingots were being weighed upon a rough scale. Master Dangerfield had a sheet of paper and an inkhorn upon an upturned cask, and wrote carefully thereon while a stout, hairy fellow called weights and numbers. Near him, upon another cask, lounged Beauvallet with a hand on his hip, and a booted leg swinging. His attention was held by what was going forward about him; he did not observe my lady upon the deck above.

You are to know that this seeming piracy was a sort of licensed affair, a guerilla warfare waged upon King Philip II of Spain, who certainly provoked it. Englishmen had a lively hatred of Spain, induced by a variety of causes. There was, many years ago, the affair of Sir John Hawkins at San Juan de Ulloa, an instance of Spanish treachery that would not soon be forgot; there was grim persecution at work in the Low Countries which must make any honest man's blood boil; and a Holy Inquisition in Spain that had swallowed up in hideous manner many stout sailormen captured on English vessels. If you wished to seek farther you had only to observe the way Spain used towards the natives of the Indies. It should suffice you. On top of all there was the abundant pride of Spain, who chose to think herself mistress of the Old World and the New. It remained for Elizabeth, Queen of England by God's Grace, to abate this overweening conceit. In this she was ably assisted by such men as Drake, bluff, roaring man, and Beauvallet, his friend; Frobisher and Gilbert; Davis and the Hawkins, father, sons, and grandson. They put forth into Spanish waters without misgiving and harried King Philip mightily. They laboured under a belief—

and you could not rid them of it—that one Englishman
was worth a round dozen of Spaniards. Events proved
them to be justified in their belief.

Nicholas Beauvallet, a younger son, spent the restless-
ness of his youth in wanderings upon the Continent, as
befitted his station. He left his England a boy overflowing
with such a spirit of dare-devilry that his father and his
elder brother prophesied it would lead him to disaster. He
came back to it a man seasoned and tried, but it was not
to be seen that the dare-devilry had departed from him. His
brother, succeeding to their father's room, shook a grave
head and called him Italianate, a ruffler, a veritable
swashbuckler, and wondered that he would not be still.
Nicholas refused to fulfil his family's expectations. He
must be off on his adventures again. He went to sea; he
made some little noise about the New World, and in due
course accompanied Drake on his voyage round the
world. With that master mariner he passed the Straits of
Magellan, saw the sack of Valparaiso, reached the far
Pelew Islands, and Mindanao, and came home round the
perilous Cape of Storms, bronzed of face, and hard of
muscle, and rich beyond the dreams of man.

This was well enough, no doubt, but Gerard Beauvallet, a sober man judged it time to be done with such
traffickings. Nicholas had won an honourable knighthood;
let him settle down now, choose a suitable bride, and
provide the heirs that came not to my Lady Beauvallet.
Instead of this, incorrigible Nicholas had sailed away,
after the briefest of intervals, this time in a ship of his
own. So far from conducting himself like a respectable
landowner, such as his brother wished him to be, he
seemed to be concerned only to make a strong noise about
the world. This he did with complete success. There was
only one Drake, but also there was only one Beauvallet.
The Spaniards coupled the two names together, but made
of Beauvallet a kind of devil. Drake performed the impossible in the only possible way; the Spaniards said that El
Beauvallet performed it in an impossible way, and feared
him accordingly. As for his own men, they held him in
some affection, and believed firmly in his luck and his
genius. They thought him clearly mad, but his madness
was profitable, and they had long ceased to wonder at

anything he might take it into his head to do. They might be trusted to follow where he led, knowing by experience that he would not lead them to disaster. His master, Patrick Howe, of beared mien, would wag a solemn finger. "Look you, we win because our Nick cannot fail. He is bird-eyed for opportunity, and blind to danger, and he laughs his way out of every peril we come to. Mad? Ay, you may say so."

The truth was that Sir Nicholas would swoop lightning-swift into some hare-brained emprise and be off again victorious while you stood agape at his hardihood.

Thus with his sweeping off of Dona Dominica, before she had time to fetch her breath. And all with no more than a careless snap of the fingers, as it were. Oh, a hardy fellow, God wot!

Dominica thought of all this as she stood looking down at him now, and since Beauvallet paid no heed to her, nor ever looked up towards the deck where she stood she presently gave vent to a scornful little laugh, and remarked to the chasing clouds:—"A merchant, counting stolen goods!"

Beauvallet looked quickly up. The sun was on his uncovered head, and in his blue eyes; he put up a hand to shade them. "My Lady Disdain! Give you a thousand good-morrows!"

"The morrow will not be good while I am upon such a ship as this," she said provocatively.

"Now what's amiss?" demanded Sir Nicholas, and sprang down from the cask. "What ails the ship?"

He was halfway up the companion, which was maybe what she wanted, but she would not have him know that. "Pray you, stay below amongst your gains, señor."

He was beside her on the deck now, swung a leg over the rail, and sat there like some careless boy. "What's amiss?" he repeated. "More dust in the alleyway?"

She gave the smallest of sniffs. "There is this amiss, señor, that this is a pirate vessel, and you are mine enemy!"

"That in your teeth, my lass!" he said gaily. "I am no enemy of yours."

She tried to look witheringly upon him, but it seemed to

have no effect. "You are the declared enemy of all Spaniards, señor, and well I know it."

"But I have it in mind, sweetheart, to make an Englishwoman of you," said Beauvallet frankly.

She was fairly taken aback. She gasped, flushed, and clenched her little hands.

"Now where's that dagger?" said Beauvallet, watching her in some amusement.

She flounced round on her heel, and swept away to the poop. She was outraged and speechless, but she could still wonder whether he would follow. She need have been in no doubt. He let her gain the poop, out of sight of his men, and came up with her there. He set his hands on her shoulders, and twisted her around to face him. The teasing light went out of his eyes, and his voice was softened. "Lady, you called me a mocker, but for once I do not jest. Hear my solemn promise! I will make you an Englishwoman before a year is gone by. And so seal my bond." He bent his handsome head quickly, and kissed her lips before she could stop him.

She cried out indignantly, and her hands flew to avenge the insult. But he had her measure, and was ready for the swift reprisal. She found her hands caught and imprisoned, and his face close above hers, smiling down into her angry eyes. "Will you rate me for a knave, or pity me for a poor mad fellow?" said Sir Nicholas, teasing again.

"I hate you!" she said, and spoke with some passion. "I despise you, and I hate you!"

He let her go. "Hate me? But why?"

She brushed her hand across her lips, as though she would brush his kiss away. "How dared you——!" she choked. "Hold me—kiss me! Oh, base! It's to insult me!" She fled towards the companion leading down to the staterooms.

He was before her, barring the way. "Hold, child! Here's some tangle. I would wed you. Did I not say it?"

She stamped, tried to push past him, and failed. "You will never wed me!" she defied him. "You are ungenerous, base! You hold me prisoner, and do as you will with me!"

He had her fast indeed, with his hands gripping her arms above the elbows. He shook her slightly. "Nay, nay, there's no talk of prisoners or of gaolers, Dominica, but only of a man and a maid. What harm have I done you?"

"You forced me! You dared to kiss me, and held me powerless!"

"I cry pardon. But you may stab me with mine own dagger, sweeting. See, it is ready to your hand. A swift, sure revenge! No? What will you have me do, then?" His hands slid down her arms to her wrists; he bent, and kissed her fingers. "There! let it be forgot—until I kiss you again." That was said with a quick whimsical glance, daringly irrepressible.

"That will be never, señor."

"And so she flings down her gauntlet. I pick it up, my lady, and will give you a Spanish proverb for answer:— *Vivir para ver!*"

"You will scarcely wed me by force," she retorted. "Even you!"

He considered the point. "True, child, that were too easy a course."

"I warrant you would not find it so!"

"Marry, is it yet another challenge?" he inquired.

She drew back a pace. "You would not!"

"Nay, have I not said I will not? Be at ease, ye shall have a royal wooing."

"And where will you woo me?" she asked scornfully. "My home is in the very heart of Spain, I'd have you know."

"Be sure I shall follow you there," he promised, and laughed to see her face of incredulous wonder.

"Braggart! Oh, idle boaster! How should you dare?"

"Look for me in Spain before a year is out," he answered. "My hand upon it."

"There is a Holy Inquisition in Spain, señor," she reminded him.

"There is, señora," he said rather grimly, and produced from out his doublet a book bound in leather. "And it is like to have you in its clutches if you keep such dangerous stuff as this about you, my lass," he said.

She turned pale, and clasped her hands nervously at her

bosom. "Where found you that?" The breath caught in her throat.

"In your cabin aboard the *Santa Maria,* child. If that is the mind you are in the sooner I have you safe out of Spain the better for you." He gave the book into her hands. "Hide it close, or sail with me to England."

"Do not tell my father!" she said urgently.

"Why, can you not trust me? Oh, unkind!"

"I suppose it is no affair of yours, señor," she said, recovering her dignity. "I thank you for my book. Now let me pass."

"I have a name, child. I believe I made you free of it."

She swept a curtsey. "Oh, I thank you—Sir Nicholas Beauvallet!" she mocked, and fled past him down the companion.

◅ Chapter IV ▻

DONA DOMINICA thought it imperative that Beauvallet's impudence should be suitably punished, and took it upon herself to perform this pious office. Master Dangerfield was a tool ready to her hand; she sought him out, cast a thrall about that susceptible lad, and flirted with him, somewhat to his embarrassment. She brought her long eyelashes into play, the minx, was all honey to him, and flattered the vanity of the youthful male. She used a distant courtesy towards Beauvallet, listened when he spoke to her, folded meek hands in her lap, and turned back to Master Dangerfield at the first chance. Beauvallet had stately curtseys and cool impersonalities from her; she let it be clearly seen that Dangerfield could have if he chose a hand to kiss, her smiles, and her chatter. Master Dangerfield was duly grateful, but showed a lamentable tendency to set her high upon a pedestal. At another time this might have pleased her, but she had now no mind to play the goddess. She was at pains to show Master Dangerfield that he might dare to venture a little farther.

But all this strategy failed of its object. Dona Dominica, out of the tail of her eye, saw with indignation the frank amusement of Sir Nicholas. Beauvallet stood back and watched the play with a laughing, an appreciative eye. The lady redoubled her efforts.

She was forced to admit Dangerfield dull sport, and chid herself for hankering after the livelier company of his General. With him one met the unexpected; there was a spice of risk to savour the game, an element of adventure to whet the appetite. She would come up with Dangerfield on the deck, stand at his side and ask him questions innumerable upon the sailing of a ship, and appear to listen rapt to his conscientious answers. But all the time she had a quick ear and a vigilant eye for Sir Nicholas, and when she heard his ringing voice, or saw him come with his quick light step across the deck she would feel her pulses beat the faster, and dread a rising blush. Nor could she ever withstand the force in him that compelled her to meet his look. She might fight against it, but soon or late she must steal a glance towards him, and find his eyes brimful of laughter, upon her, his hands lightly laid on his hips, his feet firmly planted and wide apart, mockery in his every line.

Since pride forbade her to give him her company she found a certain solace in talking of him to his lieutenant. Master Dangerfield was willing enough, but he was shocked to hear what an ill opinion she had of the hero. He could allow that Sir Nicholas had maybe too boisterous and reckless a way to suit a lady's taste, but when Dominica poured more scorn upon Beauvallet the boy was moved to protest. It was likely that she wanted this.

"I marvel that you breed such ruffling bullies in England, señor," she said, nose in air.

"A bully?" Dangerfield echoed. "Sir Nicholas? Why, I believe you must not say so aboard this ship, señora."

"Oh, I am not afraid!" Dominica declared.

"You have little need to be, señora. But you speak to Sir Nicholas' lieutenant. Maybe we who serve under him know better."

At that she opened her eyes very wide. "What, are you all besotted then? Do you like the man so well?"

He smiled down at her. "Most men like him, señora. He is very much—a man, you see."

"Very much a braggart," she corrected, curling her lip.

"No, señora, indeed. I allow he has the manner. But I have never known him promise what he has not performed. If you knew him better——"

"Oh, spare me, señor! Wish me no better knowledge of your bully."

"Maybe he is too swift for you. He goes too straight towards his goal for a lady's taste, and uses no subtleties."

She pounced on that, and put the question that had long hovered on her tongue. "I take it your English ladies think as I think, señor?"

"Nay, I believe they like him very well," Dangerfield replied, smiling a little. "Too well for his desires."

Dominica saw the smile. "I make no doubt he is a great trifler."

Dangerfield shook his head. "Nay, he is merry in his dealings, but I believe he will stay for no woman."

Dominica spent a moment pondering that. Dangerfield plodded on painstakingly. "I would not have you think though that he holds women in poor esteem, señora. Indeed, I think he is gentle with your sex."

"Gentle!" the lady ejaculated. "I marvel you can say so! A rough fellow I have found him! A boisterous, rough fellow!"

"You have naught to fear from him, señora," Dangerfield said seriously. "On my honour, he would not offer hurt to one weaker than himself."

Dominica was affronted. "I fear him? Señor, know that I do not fear him or anyone!" she announced fiercely.

"Brave lass!" applauded a voice behind her. Dominica jumped, and turned to see Beauvallet lounging against the bulwarks. He held out his hand invitingly. "Then since you have no fear of him, come and talk with the boisterous, rough fellow."

Master Dangerfield beat a discreet retreat, and basely

left the lady alone. She tapped a slender foot on the deck. "I do not wish to talk with you, señor."

"I am not a señor, child."

"True, Sir Nicholas."

"Come!" he insisted, and his eyes were bright and searching.

"Not at your bidding, Sir Nicholas," said Dominica haughtily.

"At my most humble prayer!" But his look belied his words.

"I thank you, I am very well where I am," Dominica said, and turned her shoulder.

"The mountain would not. Well, there was a sequel." He was at her side in two steps, and instinctively she drew back in some kind of enjoyable alarm. He frowned quickly at that, and set his hands on her shoulders. "Why do you shrink? Do you think I would offer you hurt indeed?"

"No—that is, I do not know at all, señor, and nor do I care!"

"Brave words, but still you shrank. What, do you know so little of me even now? You shall be better acquainted with me, I promise you."

"You are hurting me! Let me go!"

He held her slightly away from him, and seemed to puzzle over her. "How do I hurt you? By holding you thus?"

"Your fingers grip me well-nigh to the bone," said Dominica crossly.

He smiled. "I am not gripping you at all, sweetheart, and well you know it."

"Let me go!"

"But if I do you will run away," he pointed out.

"I wonder that you desire to talk to one who—who hates you!"

"Not I, child. But you do not hate me."

"I do! I do!"

"God's Death, then, why do you play poor Diccon on your line to tease me?"

That was too much for the lady. She hit him, full across his smiling mouth.

It was no sooner done that she knew a frightened leap of the heart, an instant regret, for he swooped quickly, caught her hands fast in his, and locked them behind her back. She looked up, in part afraid, in part defiant, and saw him laughing still.

"Now what do you think you deserve of me?" Beauvallet asked.

She had recourse to her strongest weapon, and burst into tears. She was set free on the instant.

"Sweetheart, sweetheart!" Beauvallet said remorsefully. "Here's no matter for tears! What, am I so grim an ogre? I did but tease you, child. Look up! Nay, but smile! See, I will kiss the very hem of your gown! Only do not weep!" He was on his knee before her; she looked down through her tears at his bent head, more shaken still, and heard footsteps coming up the companion leading from the waist of the ship. She touched Beauvallet's crisp hair fleetingly. "Oh, do not! One comes—get up, get up!"

He sprang up as his Master appeared at the head of the companion, and stepped quickly forward to shield Dominica from this worthy's notice.

It was easily possible now for her to escape below decks. Sir Nicholas' attention was held by his Master; the way lay open to her. Dona Dominica walked to the bulwarks, and carefully dried her eyes, and stood looking out to sea.

In a minute or two the Master's retreating steps sounded, and a lighter footfall, nearer at hand. Beauvallet's fingers covered hers as they lay on the rail. "Forgive the rough, boisterous fellow!" he begged.

The tone won her; a dimple peeped, and was gone. "You use me monstrously," complained Dominica.

"But you do not hate me?"

She left that unanswered. "I cannot find it in me to envy the lady you take to wife," she said.

"Nay, how should you?"

She looked sharply up at that, blushed, and turned her face away. "I do not know how the English ladies can bear with you, señor."

He looked merrily down at her. "Why, I have not called upon them to bear with me, señora."

She faced him suddenly. "You will scarce have me believe you have not trifled often and often!" she said hotly. "No doubt ye deem women of small account!"

"I do not deem you of small account, child."

She smiled disdainfully. "You are mightily apt. Do you use this manner with the English ladies, pray?"

"Nay, sweetheart, this is the manner I use," Sir Nicholas answered, and promptly kissed her.

Dominica choked, pushed him violently away, and fled down the companion to her cabin. She found her woman there, and was at once conscious of a heightened colour, and ruffled hair. Maria, noting these portents and the storm in her mistress' eyes, set her arms akimbo and looked fiercely. "That bully!" she said darkly. "He has insulted you, señorita? He dared to lay his hand on you?"

Dominica was biting her handkerchief; her eyes looked this way and that, and at the end she laughed uneasily. "He kissed me," she said.

"I will tear the eyes from his head!" vowed Maria, and made for the door.

"Silly wench! Fond fool! Stay still!" Dominica commanded.

"You shall not again stir forth without me to be your duenna, señorita," promised Maria.

Dominica stamped her foot. "Oh, blind! I wanted him to kiss me!"

Maria's jaw dropped. "Señorita!"

Dominica gave a tiny laugh. "He swears he will come into Spain to seek me. If he but dared!"

"Not even an Englishman would be fool enough, señorita."

"Alack, no!" Dominica sighed. "But if he did—oh, I become infected with his madness!" She lifted the tiny mirror that hung at her girdle, and frowned at her own reflection. A pat here and a twist there, and she had her curls demure again under the net. She let fall the mirror, blushed to see Maria still wondering at her, and was off to visit her father.

She found Joshua Dimmock in the cabin, vociferous in defence of his gallows' chips, which he believed, privately,

might serve at least to stave off Don Manuel's death until
he was set safe ashore.

Don Manuel looked wearily at his daughter. "Is there
none to rid me of this fool?" he said.

Joshua tried the effect of coaxing. "See, señor, I have
them safe tied in a sachet. I bought them of a very holy
man, versed in these matters. If you would but wear them
about your neck I might vouch for a certain cure."

"Bartolomeo, set wide that door," commanded Don
Manuel. "Now, fellow, depart from me!"

"Most gracious señor——"

Bartolomeo fell back from the open doorway, bowing.
A voice that to Dominica's fancy seemed to hold all the
sunshine and the salt wind of fine days at sea smote her
ears. "What's this?"

Sir Nicholas stood on the threshold.

Don Manuel raised himself on his elbow. "Señor, in
good time! Rid me of your knave there, and his damnable
chips from a gallows!"

Beauvallet came quickly in, saw Joshua standing aggrieved by the side of the bunk, and caught him by the
nape of the neck, and with no more ado hurled him forth.
He kicked the door to behind him, and stood looking
down at Don Manuel. "Is there aught else I may do for
you, señor? You have but to name it."

Don Manuel lay back against the pillows and smiled
wrily. "You are short in your dealings, señor."

"But to the point, you'll allow. I am come to see how
you do this morning. The fever still hath you in its
hold?"

"A little." Don Manuel frowned a warning. Beauvallet
turned his head to observe the reason of this. Dominica
was standing stiffly by the table.

It seemed this abominable man must be everywhere at
once. One's own cabin was the only safe retreat. She
moved stately to the door. Bartolomeo went to open it,
but was put aside by a careless hand. Sir Nicholas held
the door wide, and my lady went out with a quickened
step.

"You, too, Bartolomeo," Don Manuel said, and lay
watching Beauvallet. He fetched a stifled sigh. This hand-

some man with his springing step and alert carriage seemed to the sick gentleman the very embodiment of life and health.

Beauvallet came to the bunk, and pulled a joint-stool forward, and sat down upon it. "You want to speak with me, señor?"

"I want to speak with you." Don Manuel plucked at the sheet that covered him. "Señor, since first you brought us aboard this ship you have not again spoken of our disposal."

Beauvallet raised his brows quickly. "I thought I had made myself plain, señor. I shall set you ashore on the northern coast of Spain."

Don Manuel tried to read the face before him; the blue eyes looked straightly; under the near mustachio the mouth was firm and humorous. If Beauvallet had secrets he hid them well under a frank exterior. "Am I to believe you serious, señor?"

"Never more so, upon my honour. Wherefore all this pother over a very simple matter?"

"Is it, then, so simple to put into a Spanish port, señor?"

"To say truth, señor, your countrymen have not yet learned the trick of capturing Nick Beauvallet. God send them a better education, cry you!"

Don Manuel spoke gravely. "Señor, you are an enemy—a dangerous enemy—to my country, yet, believe me, I should be sorry to see you taken."

"A thousand thanks, señor. You will certainly not see it. I was born in a fortunate hour."

"I have had enough of portents and omens, señor, from your servant. I make bold to say that if you set us ashore in Spain you place your life in jeopardy. And for what? It is madness! I can find no other name for it."

The firm lips parted; there was a gleam of white teeth. "Call it Beauvallet's way, señor."

Don Manuel said nothing, but lay still, watching his captor and host. After a minute he spoke again. "You are a strange man, señor. For many years I have heard wild tales of you, and believed, perhaps, a quarter of them. You constrain me to lend ear to the wildest of them." He paused, but Beauvallet only smiled again. "If, indeed, you speak in good faith I stand infinitely beholden to you. Yet you might act in the best of faith and fail of such a foolhardy endeavour."

Sir Nicholas swung his pomander on the end of its chain. "God rest you, señor: I shall not fail."

"I pray in this instance you may not. It does not need for me to tell you that my days are numbered. I would end them in Spain, señor."

Beauvallet held up his hand. "My oath on it, señor. You shall end them there," he said gently.

Don Manuel stirred restlessly. "I must set my house in order. I leave my daughter alone in the world. There is my sister. But the child had traffickings with Lutherans, and I misdoubt me——" He broke off, sighing.

Beauvallet came to his feet. "Señor, give me ear a minute!"

Don Manuel looked up at him, and saw him serious for once. "I attend, señor."

"When I approach my chosen goal, señor, I march straight. That you may have heard of me. Let it go. I make you privy now to a new goal I have sworn to reach, a fair prize. The day will come, Don Manuel, when I shall take your daughter to wife."

Don Manuel's eyes fluttered a moment. "Do you tell me, señor, that you love my daughter?" he asked sternly.

"Madly, señor, I make no doubt you would say."

Don Manuel looked more sternly still. "And she? No, it is not possible!"

"Why, as to that, señor, I do not know. I am not over-apt with maids. She will love me one day."

"Señor, be plain with me. What is this riddle you propound?"

"None, señor. Here is only the plain truth. I might bear Dominica away to England, and thus constrain her——"

"You would not!" Don Manuel cried out sharply.

"Nay, I constrain no maid against her will, be assured. But you will allow it to be clearly within my power." He paused, and his eyes questioned.

Don Manuel watched the swing of the golden pomander from long fingers, looked higher, and met the imperative gaze. "We are in your hands I know full well," he said evenly.

Beauvallet nodded. "But that easy course is not the one I will take, señor. Nor am I one to enact the part of ravisher, of betrayer. I will take you to Spain, and there leave you. But, señor—and mark me well! for what I swear I will do that I shall certainly do, though the sun die and the moon fall, and the earth be wholly overset!—I shall come later into Spain, and seek out your daughter, and ride away with her on my saddlebow!" His voice seemed to fill the room, vibrating with some leaping passion. A moment he looked down at Don Manuel with a glint in his eyes, and his beard jutting outwards with his lifted chin. Then the fire left him as suddenly as it had sprung up, and he laughed softly, and the glitter went out of his eyes. "Judge you by this, señor, if I do truly love her as you would have her loved!"

There was silence. Don Manuel turned his head away on the pillow and brushed the sheet with one restless hand. "Señor," he said at last, "if you were not an enemy and a heretic, I would choose to give my daughter to just such a one as you." He smiled faintly at the quick surprise in Beauvallet's face. "Ay, señor, but you are both these things, and it is impossible. Impossible!"

"Señor, a word I do not know. I have warned you. Take what precaution you will, but whether you are quick or dead, I shall have your daughter, in spite of anything you may do."

"Sir Nicholas, you have a brave spirit, and that I like in you. I have no need to take precautions, for you could never penetrate into Spain."

"God be my witness, señor, I shall penetrate."

"You must needs be foresworn, señor. At sea you may be a match for us, but how might you dare face all Spain in Spain itself?"

"I shall certainly dare, señor," said Sir Nicholas calmly.

Don Manuel seemed to shrug his shoulders. "I see, señor, there is to be no ho with you. You may be but an idle boaster, or a madman, as they say—I know not. I could wish you were a Spaniard. There is no more to say."

⌒◀ Chapter V ▶⌒

DON MANUEL took an early opportunity of finding out, as he imagined, what were his daughter's feelings. He asked her without preamble how she liked Sir Nicholas. God knows what the poor gentleman thought to get from her.

"Very ill, señor," said she.

"I fear me," said Don Manuel, closely watching her, "that he likes you too well, child."

Dominica perceived that she was being tested, and achieved a scornful laugh. "Unhappy man! But it's an impertinence."

Don Manuel was entirely satisfied. Liking Beauvallet well enough himself he could even be sorry that his daughter had conceived so vehement a distaste for him. "I am sorry that he is what he is," he said. "I could find it in me to like a man of his mettle."

"A boaster," said Dominica, softly scornful.

"One would say so indeed. But before we set sail, Dominica, methought you made some sort of a hero of him in your mind. You were always eager to hear tell of his deeds."

"I had not met him then, señor," Dominica answered primly.

Don Manuel smiled. "Well, he is a wild fellow. I am glad you have sense enough to see it. But use him gently, child, for we stand somewhat beholden to him. He swears to set us ashore in Spain, and *madre de dios!* I believe he will do it, though how I know not."

The upshot of all this was to make Dominica curious to know Beauvallet's plans. She tackled Master Dangerfield about it that very evening as he played cards with her in the stateroom, and demanded to know what his general had in mind. Master Dangerfield professed ignorance, and was not believed. "What!" said my lady, incredulous. "I am not to suppose you are not in his confidence, señor, surely! It is just that you will not tell me."

"Upon my oath, señora, no!" Dangerfield assured her. "Sir Nicholas keeps his counsel. Ask your question of him: he will tell you, I doubt not."

"Oh, I desire to have no traffic with him," said my lady, and applied herself to the cards again.

There came soon enough what she had hoped to hear: a bluff voice, a brisk tread, a laugh echoing along the alleyway. The door was flung open; Beauvallet came in, with a word tossed over his shoulder for someone outside. "Save you lady!" quoth he. "Diccon, there is a trifle of business calls you. Give me your cards; I will endeavour."

Dangerfield gave up his cards at once, and bowed excuses to the lady. As always, Beauvallet left her without a word to say. Truth to tell she was glad to have him in Dangerfield's stead, but why could he not ask her permission?

He sat down in Dangerfield's chair; Dangerfield, with his hand on the door, paused to say, smiling: "Dona Dominica hath all the luck, sir, as you shall find."

"And you none, Diccon. I may believe it. But I will back myself against her. Away with you." He flicked a card out from his hand, and smiled across the table at Dominica. "To the death, lady!"

Dona Dominica played to his lead in silence. He won the encounter at length. She bit her lip, but took it with a good grace. "Yes, señor, you win." She watched him playing with the cards, and folded her hands. "I shall not pit my skill against yours."

Sir Nicholas put down the pack. "Then let us talk a little," he said. "It likes me much better. How does Don Manuel find himself?"

A shadow crossed her face. "I think him very sick, señor. I have to thank you for sending your surgeon to visit him."

"No need of that."

"My father tells me," Dominica said, "that you have sworn to set us ashore in Spain. Pray, how may you accomplish that?"

"Very simply," Sir Nicholas replied. He held his pomander to his nose, and over it his eyes twinkled at her.

"Well, señor, and how?" She was impatient. "I've no desire to witness another fight at sea."

"Nor shall you, fondling. What, do you suppose that Nick Beauvallet would expose you to the risks Narvaez courted? Shame on you!"

"Señor, are you so mad as to suppose that you can sail into a Spanish port without a shot being fired?"

"By no means, child. If I did so foolish a thing I might expect a veritable hailstorm of shot about my head." He threw one leg over the other, and continued to sniff at his pomander.

"I see, señor, you have no mind to confide in me," said Dominica stiffly.

His shoulders shook. "Do I not answer your questions? You would know more? Then ask me prettily, O my Lady Disdain!"

Her eyes fell; she tried a change of front to see what might come of it. "You have the right to flout me, señor. I am aware that I stand beholden to you. Yet I think you might use me kindlier."

The pomander fell. "Good lack!" said Beauvallet, startled. "What's this?" He uncrossed his legs and stretched a hand to her across the table. "Let there be no such talk betwixt us two, child. Yet stand in no way beholden to me. Say that I do what I do to please myself, and cry a truce!" The smile crept into his eyes. "Do I flout you? Now I had thought that was your part."

"I am helpless in your hands, señor," said Dominica mournfully. "If it pleases you to make a mock of me you may do so without hindrance."

This failed somewhat of its purpose. "Child, in a little I shall be constrained to set you on my knee and kiss you," said Beauvallet.

"I am helpless," she repeated, and would not look up.

A quick frown came. He rose from his chair and came to kneel beside hers. "Now what's your meaning, Dominica? Are you so cowed, so submissive?" He caught a glimpse of the flash in her eyes, and laughed. "Oh, pretty cheat!" he said softly. "If I dared to touch you you would be swift to strike."

Her lip quivered irrepressibly; she looked through her lashes. He took her hand and kissed it. "Well, what is it you would have me tell you?" he asked.

"If you please," she said meekly, "where will you set us ashore?"

"Some few miles to the west of Santander, sweetheart. There is a smuggling village there will receive us peaceably."

"Smugglers!" She looked up. "Oh, so you are that, too? I might have known."

"Nay, nay, acquit me," he smiled. "Look scorn instead upon my fat boatswain. He is the blame. He was for many years in the trade, and I believe knows every smuggling port in Europe. We may sail softly in under cover of night, set you ashore, and be gone again before dawn."

There was a pause. Dominica looked up at the arms on the wall, and said slowly: "And so ends the adventure."

Sir Nicholas rose to his feet again. "Do you think so, indeed?"

She was grave. "In spite of brave words, señor, I think so. Once in Spain I shall be free—free of you!"

He set his hand on his hip; his other hand played with his beard. She should have been wary, but she did not know him so well as did his men. "Lady," said Beauvallet, and she jumped at the note of strong purpose in his voice, "the first of my name, the founder of my house, had, so we read, another watchword than that." His hand flew out and pointed to the scroll beneath his arms. "There is an old chronicle writ by one Alan, afterwards Earl of Montlice, wherein we learn that Simon, the first Baron of Beauvallet, took as his motto these words: *'I have not, but still I hold.'* " His voice rang out, and died again.

"Well, señor?" faltered Dominica.

"I have you not yet, but be sure I hold you," said Beauvallet.

She rallied. "This is folly."

"Sweet folly."

"I do not believe that you would dare set foot in Spain."

"God's Death, do you not? But if I dare, indeed?"

She looked down at her clasped hands.

"Come! If I dare? If I reach you in Spain, and claim you then? What answer shall I have?"

She was flushed, and her breast rose and fell fast. "Ah, if there were a man brave enough to dare so much for love——!"

"He stands before you. What will you give him?"

She got up, a hand at her bosom. "If he dares so much—I should have to give—myself, señor."

"Remember that promise!" he warned her. "You shall be called upon to redeem it before a year is out."

She looked fearfully at him. "But how? how?"

"Dear heart," said Beauvallet frankly, "I do not know, but I shall certainly find a way."

"Oh, an idle boast!" she cried, and went quickly to the door. His voice stayed her; she paused and looked back over her shoulder. "Well, señor, what more?"

"My pledge," Beauvallet said, and slipped a ring from his finger. "Keep Beauvallet's ring until Beauvallet comes to claim it."

She took it, half unwillingly. "What need of this?"

"No need, but to remind you, maybe. Keep it close."

It had his arms engraven upon it, a gold piece, heavy and cunningly wrought. "I will keep it always," she said, "to remind me of—a madman."

He smiled. "Oh, not always, sweetheart! A pledge is sometimes redeemed—even by a madman."

"Not this one," she said on a sigh, and went out.

It seemed to her in the days that followed that Spain drew near all too soon. They had fair weather, and for the most part a favourable wind to bear them home. The Canaries were reached in good time, and Dominica saw adventure's end in sight. She was gentler now with her impetuous wooer, but aloof still, refusing to believe him. She let him teach her English words, and lisped them after him prettily. She forbore to entangle Master Dangerfield in her wiles: time was too short and romance too sweet. Maybe she would have been glad enough, saving only her father's presence, to be borne off to England, a conqueror's prize, but if she had doubted Beauvallet's good faith at first these doubts were soon lulled. He meant certainly to take her to Spain. She had both a sigh and a smile for that, but it is certain that she honoured him for it. For the rest she might not know what to believe. The man talked in a heroic vein, and seemed to be undisturbed by any doubt of his own omnipotence. He would have a poor maid believe him little less than God. Well, one was not so poor a maid as that. Maybe it pleased his strange, braggart fancy to cut a fine figure; surely he would forget just so soon as he set foot on English soil.

Dona Dominica had to admit her heart assailed dangerously. A certain smile haunted her dreams, and would not be banished. Yet he was a hardy rogue, surely. She could not say what there was in him to seize her fancy; he used no courtier tricks, no elegant subtleties. You would have no dropped knee, no sighs, no fashionable languishings from Beauvallet. He would have an arm about a maid's waist before she was aware, snatch a kiss, and be off again on his adventures. Oh, merry ruffler! He was too direct, thought my lady, too swift, employed no gentle arts in his wooing. She played with the idea that he was like a strong wind, vigorous, salt-tanged. He had no repose; he must be here and there, restless, so charged with vitality that it almost seemed to brim over. See, too, his challenging eyes, wickedly inviting under the down-drooped lids! Shame! Shame that one should know an answering leap of the heart! He would swing past along the deck, a hand on his hip, careless, heedless; one was bound to watch him, willy-nilly. He might stop beside his Master a brief while; his quick, gay speech would be borne back to one in snatches on the wind; one would see him fling out a pointing hand, give a decisive shake to his neat black head, some jest to set the Master chuckling, and be off down the companion to mingle amongst his men.

It seemed they held him in some esteem, no little awe. No good came of an attempt to trifle with Sir Nicholas Beauvallet. He was a leader to love, but one to fear withal. Dona Dominica, catching at new-learned English words, heard stray comments, enough to show her what Beauvallet's men thought of him. They thought him a rare jest, she gathered, and pondered over the strange mentality of these English, who spent their time in laughing. They did not behave thus in Spain.

And Spain, with its courtly propriety, its etiquette, and

its solemn grandeur, grew nearer and ever nearer. Mad days at sea were nearly done now, and adventure was coming to an end. Don Manuel, reclining on his pillows, spoke of duennas; my lady hid a shudder and turned wistful eyes towards Beauvallet. To one reared in the freedom of the New World trammels of the Old would not be welcome. Don Manuel said severely that he had permitted his daughter too great a license. Faith, the girl thought for herself, was pert, he doubted, and certainly head-strong. As witness her behaviour on board the *Santa Maria*. A maid surprised by piratical marauders should have stood passive, a frozen statue of martyrdom. A daughter of Spain had no business to kick, and bite, and scratch, or to brandish daggers and spit venom upon her captors. Don Manuel had been shocked indeed, but knew her well enough to forbear comment. He trusted that his sister would find a strict duenna to govern her. He had marriage plans in mind, too, and hinted as much to her. He would see her safely bestowed, he said, and drew a fine picture of her future life. Dona Dominica listened in growing horror, and escaped from her father's cabin to the free air above.

"Oh!" cried she, "are English ladies so hedged about, and guarded, and confined, as we poor Spaniards?"

They were in colder latitudes, and the wind bit shrewdly. Beauvallet loosened the cloak about his shoulders, and clipped it fast about my lady, so that it fell all about her. "Nay, I'll not confine you, sweet, but I shall know how to guard my treasure, don't doubt it."

She drew the cloak about her, and looked up, wide-eyed. "Do you in England set vile duennas to watch your wives?"

He shook his head. "We trust them, rather!"

Her dimples quivered. "Oh, almost you persuade me, Sir Nicholas!" She frowned a warning as his hand flew out towards her. "Fie, before your men? I said 'almost', señor. Know that my father plans my marriage."

"A careful gentleman," said Beauvallet. "So, faith, do I."

"If you came, indeed, into Spain you might haply find me wed, señor."

A gleam came into his eyes, like a sword, she thought.

"Might I so?" he said, and the words demanded an answer.

She looked away, trembled a little, smiled, frowned, and blushed. "N-no," she said.

Too soon the day came that saw Spanish shores to the southward. Don Manuel braved the cold air on deck for a while, and followed the direction of Beauvallet's pointing finger. "Thereabouts lies Santander, señor. I shall set you ashore to-night."

The day wore swiftly to its close. Dusk came, and my lady watched Maria pack her chests. Maria stowed jewels away in a gold-bound box, and jealously counted each trinket. She could never be at ease amongst these English, but must always suspect darkly.

My lady was seized by an odd fancy, and demanded to stow her jewels with her own hands. She took the casket to the light, and laid its contents out on the table, and debated over them with a look half rueful, half tender. In the end she chose a thumb ring of gold, too large for her little hand, too heavy for a lady's taste. She hid it in her handkerchief and quickly locked up the case that Maria might not discover the loss of one significant piece.

In the soft darkness of the evening she flitted up on deck, a cloak wrapped about her, and her oval face pale in the dim lamplight. The ship made slow way now, the dark water lapping gently at her oaken sides. There was a little bustle on the deck; she heard the Master's voice raised: "Steady your helm!" She saw Beauvallet standing under the light of a swinging lamp, with his boatswain beside him. The boatswain held a lantern, and was peering into the darkness. Far away to the south Dominica could see the little glow of lights, and knew that Spain was reached at last.

She stole up to Beauvallet and laid a timid hand on his arm. He looked quickly round, and at once his hand covered hers where it lay on his latticed sleeve. "Why, child!"

"I came—I wanted—I came to speak with you a minute," she said uncertainly.

He drew her apart, and stood looking down at her quizzically. "Speak, child, I am listening."

Her hand came out from the shelter of her cloak; in it

she held the golden ring. "Señor, you gave me a ring of yours to keep. I—I think you will never see me again, and so—and so I would have you take this ring of mine in memory of me."

The ring and the hand that held it were alike caught in a strong hold. She was swept out of the circle of light cast by the lamp above, and stood face to face with Beauvallet in the friendly darkness. She felt his arms go around her, and stood still, with her hands clasped at her breast. He held her in a tight embrace, laid his cheek against her curls, and murmured: "Sweetheart! Fondling!" Madness, madness, but it was sweet to be mad just once in one's life! She lifted her face, put up a hand to touch his bronzed cheek, and gave him back kisses that were shy and very fugitive. Her senses swam; she thought she would never forget how an Englishman's arms felt, iron barriers holding one hard against a leaping heart. A shiver of ecstasy ran through her; she whispered: "*Querida!* Dear one! Do not quite forget!"

"Forget!" he said. "Oh, little unbeliever! Feel how I hold you: shall I ever let you go?"

She came back to earth; she was blushing and shaken. "Oh, loose me!" she begged, and seemed to flutter in his arms. "How may I believe that you could do the impossible?"

"There is naught impossible that I have found," he said. "You shall leave me for a space, since to that I pledged my word, but not for long, my little love, not for long! Look for me before the year is out; I shall surely come."

A rich voice sounded close at hand. "Where are you, sir? They answer the signal right enough."

Beauvallet put the lady quickly behind him; the boatswain came to them, peering through the darkness.

What followed passed as a dream for Dominica. There was a furtive light dipping and shining on the mainland; she escaped below decks, and saw her baggage borne away, and heard the bustle of a boat being prepared. Don Manuel sat ready, wrapped about in a fur-lined cloak, but shivering always. "He hath compassed it," Don Manuel said in quiet satisfaction. "He is a brave man."

Master Dangerfield came to fetch them in a little while;

he gave an arm to Don Manuel, spoke words of cheer, but cast a regretful eye towards my lady. They came up on deck and found Beauvallet by a rope-ladder. Below, bobbing on the ink-black water, a boat waited, manned by the boatswain and some of his men, and with the baggage stowed safely in it.

Sir Nicholas came forward. "Don Manuel, have you strength to descend yon ladder?"

"I can essay, señor," Don Manuel said. "Bartolomeo, go before me." He faced Beauvallet in the shaded lamplight. "Señor, this is farewell. You will let me say——"

"No need, señor. Let it be said anon. I shall see you safely ashore."

"Yourself, señor? Nay, that is too much to ask of you."

"Be at ease, ye did not ask it. It is my pleasure," Beauvallet said, and put out a strong hand to help him down the ladder.

Don Manuel went painfully down the side with Bartolomeo watchful below him. Beauvallet turned to Dominica, and opened his arms. "Trust yourself to me yet again, sweetheart," he said.

Without a word she went to him and let him swing her up to his shoulder. He went lightly down the side with her, let her slip to her feet in the boat below, and held her still with one supporting hand. She found a seat beside Maria, crouched in the stern, and nestled beside her. Beauvallet left the ladder and gained the boat, stepped past the two women to the tiller behind them, and called a low order to his men. There was a casting off, long oars dipped into the heaving water; silently the boat cleaved forward towards the land.

A crescent moon gleamed suddenly through a rift in the clouds above; Dominica looked round and saw Beauvallet behind her, holding the tiller. He was looking frowningly ahead, but as she turned he glanced down at her and smiled. She said suddenly on a sharp note of fear: "Ah, if there should be soldiers! A trap!"

His white teeth shone between the black beard and mustachio. "Never fear."

"Foolhardy!" she whispered. "I would you had not come."

"What, and send my men into a danger I dare not face?" he rallied her.

She looked at him, so straight and handsome in the pale moonlight. "No, that is not your way," she said. "I cry pardon."

The clouds covered the moon's face again; Beauvallet was a dark shadow against the night. "I have a sword, child. Fear not."

"Rather, Reck Not," she said in a low voice.

She heard the ripple of his gay laugh.

Soon, too soon, the boat's keel grated on the beach. There were men running down to meet them now, men who caught at the boat, and held her, and questioned eagerly, in low, rough Spanish. Sir Nicholas picked his way across the baggage, and between the rowers to the nose of the boat, and sprang ashore, closely followed by his boatswain. There was the quick give and take of question and answer, a sharp exclamation, a subdued babel of voices in a long parley. Then Beauvallet came back to the boat, with the sea washing about his ankles, and gave his hand to Don Manuel. "All is well, señor; these worthy fellows will give you a lodging for the night, and your man may ride into Santander to-morrow to find a coach to bear you hence."

A burly sailor lifted Don Manuel on to dry land; his daughter lay in tenderer arms. She was carried up the beach, held closer still for a moment. Beauvallet bent his head and kised her. "Till I come again!" he said, and set her on her feet. "Trust me!"

✑ Chapter VI ✎

THE *Venture* was left in Plymouth Sound, under charge of Master Culpepper, and her treasure safely stored. She was docked, and would be clean careened before she could put to sea again. Beauvallet stayed some three nights in Plymouth, where he found a sea-faring crony or two, heard what news was abroad, and saw to the bestowal of his ship. He took horse then, with Joshua Dimmock in attendance, and a hired man following hard upon them with led sumpters, and made for Alreston, in Hampshire, where he might reasonably expect to find his brother.

My Lord Beauvallet had other dwellings beside this, but of all this manor of Alreston saw him the most. There was a grim hold in Cambridgeshire, built nearly two hundred years ago by the founder of the house, Simon, First Baron Beauvallet. A left-handed scion of the old house of Malvallet, Simon cleaved for himself a new name and a new title. Under King Henry V, he saw much fighting in France, and when those wars were done, came riding back into Cambridgeshire with a French bride, a countess in her own right, holding lands and a stronghold in Normandy. You might read of this first Beauvallet's mighty deeds in the dreamy chronicles of his close friend, Alan, Earl of Montlice, who occupied the latter years of his life with the writing of his reminiscences. It is a diffuse work, something poetical in tone, but contains much of interest.

Since the days of the Iron Baron the family fortunes had fluctuated. The French County was lost to the English branch very early, for Simon, finding himself continually at loggerheads with his first-born, bestowed it upon his second son, Henry, who was thus the founder of the present French house.

Geoffrey, the second baron, survived the Wars of the Roses, but left the barony considerably impoverished by his vacillations. His heir, Henry, took to wife Margaret, heiress of Malvallet, by which wise alliance the two families were made one. His successors all laid schemes for the family's advancement, but the times were troublous, and it was not always possible to steer a safe course through the varying politics of the day. Thus in this year, 1586, although the house of Beauvallet had by dint of careful marriages planted its roots in many great houses, and become one of the wealthiest in the land, the present holder of the title was only a baron, as his ancestor had been before him.

This Seventh Baron, Gerard, a solid man, had built the new house at Alreston, a noble mansion of red brick, with oak timberings. My lady, a frail dame, complained of the cruel temper of the climate in Cambridgeshire, and was urgent in her gentle way, to be gone from an ancient castle full of draughts and damp and gloomy corners. My lord, inheriting much of his great ancestor's rugged nature, had a fondness for this medieval hold, and saw in the use of oak for house-building a sign of the decadence of the age. He was, so they said, a hard man, with a will of iron, but there was a joint in his armour. My lady had her way, and there arose in milder Hampshire, on lands that had come as part of the dowry of Gerard's grandmother, a stately Tudor mansion, set in fair gardens, surrounded by its stables, its farmsteads, and its rolling acres of pasturage. It was seen that my lord for all his hardy notions had pride in the magnificence of the building. He might speak slightingly of an age of luxury, but he adorned his house with every trapping of wealth, used the despised oak for his panelling, and had all carved and painted to the admiration of his neighbours.

Thither rode Nicholas, on a bright spring day, and came in sight of the square gatehouse, after an absence of over a year. The gates stood wide, and showed a broad avenue stretching ahead, with rolling lawns to flank it, and the high gables of the manor beyond. Sir Nicholas reined in, and sent a shout echoing through the archway. The gate-keeper came out, no sooner saw who called than he hurried forward, beaming a welcome. "Eh, but it could be none other! Master Nick!"

Beauvallet stretched down a hand in careless good nature. "Well, old Samson? How does my brother?"

"Well, master, well, and my lady too," Samson told him, and bent the knee to kiss his hand. "Are you come home for aye at last, sir? The place misses you!"

There was a shrug of the shoulder and a shake of the head. "Nay, nay, the place needs but my brother."

"A just lord," Samson agreed. "But there is never a man on Beauvallet land would not be glad to welcome Sir Nicholas home."

"Oh, flatterer!" Beauvallet mocked. "What have I ever done for the land?"

"It is not that, master." Samson shook his head, and would have said more.

But Sir Nicholas laughed it aside, waved his hand, and rode on under the arch.

A flight of broad stone steps led up from the neat drive to the terrace and the great doorway. There were clipped yews in tubs, and in the stonework above the door the Beauvallet arms were set in a stone shield. Leaded windows reared up slim and stately to either side, built out in rounded bays, with scrolls beneath them of stonework set against the warmer brick. The roof was tiled red, with tall chimney-stacks to either end, and round attic windows set between the many gables. The door stood open to let in the spring sunshine.

Sir Nicholas swung himself lightly down from the saddle, tossed the bridle to Joshua, and went bounding up the steps. Like a boy he set his hollowed hands to form a trumpet for his mouth, and called: "Holà, there! What, none to cry Nick welcome?"

In a moment heads peeped from upper windows. There was a stir amongst the serving maids, a whisper of: "Sir Nicholas is home!" and much preening of stuff gowns and patting of prim coifs. Sir Nicholas might be counted on to give a hearty buss to the prettiest, ignoring my lady's murmured protests.

Portly Master Dawson, steward for many years, heard the shout in his buttery, and made haste to come out into the sunlight. A couple of lackeys hurried at his heels, and Dame Margery, urgent to be the first to greet her nursling. She pushed past Master Dawson as he reached the door, dived under his arm without ceremony, a little wrinkled woman in a close white cap. "My cosset!" cried Dame Margery. "My lamb! Is it my babe indeed?"

"Indeed and indeed!" Sir Nicholas said, laughing, and opened his arms to her. He caught her up in a great hug while she fondled and scolded all in one breath. He was a good-for-naught, a rough, sudden fellow to snatch up an old woman thus! Eh, but he was brown! She dared swear he was grown; but his cheek was thin: she misgave her he was in poor health. Ah, he was a sad wastrel to be so long gone, and to come home but to laugh at his poor nurse! She must pat him, stroke his hands, feel the thickness of his short cloak. A fine cloth, by her faith! all tricked out with points and tassels of gold! Oh, spendthrift! Take heed, take heed! Could he not see my lord coming to greet him?

My lord came sedately out from the house in a gown of camlet trimmed with vair, with a close cap set upon his head, and a gold chain about his neck. My lord wore a cathedral beard like a churchman. He was fair where Nicholas was dark; his eyes were blue, but lacked the sparkle that was in his brother's eyes. He was a tall man of imposing mien, had a grave countenance and a stately gait. "Well, Nick!" he said, with a glimmer of a smile. "My lady heard a shouting and commotion, and straightway saith Nick must be home. How is it with you, lad?"

The brothers embraced. "As you see me, Gerard. And you?"

"Well enough. A tertian fever troubled me in February, but it is happily passed."

"He must needs go into Cambridgeshire to that damp, unhealthy castle," sighed a mournful voice. "I knew what would come of it. I foretold an ague from the start. Dear Nicholas, give you good den."

Nicholas turned to greet my Lady Beauvallet, kissed her hand right dutifully, and so came to her lips. "Do I see you well, sister?"

"Nick!" She blushed faintly and shook her finger at him. "Ever the same swift way! Nay, the hard winter—harder than any I remember, was it not, my lord?—tried me sorely. At the New Year I had the sweating-sickness. Then, at Candlemas, an ague seized me, and was like to have carried me off, methought."

"But the spring comes, and you grow strong with it," suggested Nicholas.

She looked doubtful. "Indeed, Nicholas, I trust it may be found so, but I have the frailest health, as you know."

Gerard broke in upon this lamentation. "I see you bring home that ruffler," he said, and nodded to where Joshua stood in parley with the lackeys. "Have ye schooled him yet?"

"Devil a bit, brother. Joshua! Here, rogue, come pay

your duty to my lord!" He put an arm round my lady's
waist and swept her into the house. "Have in with you,
Kate. The nip of the wind is like to lay you low of a
second ague."

My lady went with him protesting. "Nick, Nick, so
hardy still? Not a second ague, I assure you, but more like
the seventh, for, indeed, no sooner am I raised from one
than another strikes me down. Come into the hall, brother. There should be a fire there, and they will bring wine
for you. Or there is some March beer of two years tun-
ning. Dawson! Dawson, bring—oh, he is gone! Well, come
in, Nicholas; you will be chilled from your ride."

They went through the screens to the Great Hall. This
was a noble apartment with the roof high over their heads
crossed and re-crossed with oaken timbers. Tall windows
were set all round the walls at a height above a man's
head. Between them the walls were covered with panels of
linen-fold. A dais was set at one end, in the bay of the
front windows, with a long table upon it and benches
around. A great fireplace stood in one wall, with logs
burning in it. Above the lofty mantelpiece, supported by
pilasters, my lord's quarterings hung. Rushes, with rose-
mary strewed amongst them, covered the floor; there was
a settle on either side of the fireplace, and some carved
and panel-backed chairs ranged neatly along the wall.

My lady sat down on one side of the fire, and since her
monstrous farthingale seemed to occupy most of the settle,
Sir Nicholas went to the other. "Yes, sit down, dear
Nicholas," she said. "Dawson, will be here anon, and my
lord too, I dare swear."

Sir Nicholas loosed the cloak from about his shoulders
and tossed it aside. It fell over one of the chairs against
the wall, and Margery, peeping round a corner of the
screens, frowned to see the fine thing so rudely used. My
lady caught sight of that puckered face and smiled kindly.
"Come you in, Margery. You will say it is a good day that
sees Sir Nicholas come riding home."

"Good indeed, my lady." Margery dropped a curtsey.
"But a feckless, heedless boy! Ah, is there never one to
school him?" She picked up the cloak and folded it carefully. "Tut, the brave hat upon the floor! Two feathers in
it, i'faith!" She looked a fond reproof at such extrava-

gance. "Heed old Margery, my cosset, and get ye a wife!"

"What need?" Sir Nicholas asked, and disposed his graceful limbs at ease along the settle. "What need while I still have Margery to scold, and a fair sister to shake her head at me?"

"Oh, Nicholas, for shame!" my lady said. "I shake my head? Though, indeed, ye often deserve that I should. Ah, my lord, in good time! Here is your brother says we scold, poor Margery and I."

My lord came to sit beside Nicholas on the settle. "Dawson is gone to fetch the March beer for you, Nick. He is sure it is what you need." He smiled. "It is a rare thing, faith, to see the house turned upside down for a graceless rogue that heeds naught that concerns it."

Sir Nicholas threw back his head, and laughed. "The old tale! I irk you sorely, Gerard, alack!"

"Nay, nay." My lord looked on him with some kindness. "So ye be come home now to stay. . . ."

"Patience, Gerard, patience!" Nicholas said mischievously.

Dawson came in preceding a lackey, bearing the famous beer upon a salver. "Sir, at your pleasure!"

"In good sooth!" Sir Nicholas stretched out a hand for the tankard. "Give you my word I have yearned often for this. My lady, I drink to your better health."

"Ah!" sighed my lady, and shook her head.

My lord took the second tankard. "You will wish to hear news of my Lady Stanbury," he said. "I had a letter from her lord last Friday se'n night, telling me she had been brought to bed of a fair son."

"What, a son at last?" quoth Sir Nicholas, tossing off the rest of his beer. "Marry, I lost count of poor Adela's daughters long since! Dawson, another tankard, man, to drink my nephew's health!" He looked at Gerard. "How doth my sister? Who stands sponsor?"

"Well, very well. I am asked to stand, with my lady, and another. Ye should journey into Worcester to visit them; Adela would be glad of it. You will not have heard that our cousin Arnold is wedded to Groshawk's second daughter? A fair match, no more than fair. The elder girl favoured her mother too much for Arnold, so I heard."

Talk ran a while on family matters; my lady went away presently to see to the preparation of the heir's chamber, and Nicholas must needs be off to the stables to greet old servants, and inspect new horses. My lord went with him, willingly enough.

"There's a Barbary horse might suit you," said he. "Ye shall try his paces. I bought him last Michaelmas, but he is scarce up to my weight, I believe. He should please you: a fiery, impatient brute." He linked arms with Nicholas, and made his brother curb his hasty steps to match his own. "Gently, lad! What's your hurry?"

"None. What hawks do you keep now? What sport?"

"Fair, fair. I was out with my neighbour Selby last Thursday. I let fly my tassel-gentle at a pheasant, discovered in a brake. A rare bird that! I had her from Stanbury when he was here over Twelfth Night; ye shall see her anon. Selby found a mallard, whistled off his falcon. Down she came, twice missed, but recovered it at a long flight. . . ."

They talked of hawking, and of venery, and of the management of the estate. When they came slowly back to the house the sun was sinking behind it in a red glow. Master Dawson met them with a warning of supper. Sir Nicholas' baggage had arrived, and was safely bestowed in his chamber. Sir Nicholas went up the wide stairs two at a time, and found Joshua laying out a doublet and hose of slashed mochado, with netherstocks of carnation silk, and a clean stiff ruff.

A great bed with a canopy of carved wood supported at all four corners by pillars in the form of caryatides, stood out into the room. It had hangings of worked damask, and a Venice-valance. A bow-fronted chest of walnut inlaid with cherrywood stood at the foot of it; there was an armoire in one corner, a second chest bearing upon it a basin and ewer of pewter ware, painted cloths upon the wall, and a thrown-chair by the window. Sir Nicholas flung himself down in this, and stretched his legs out before him. "Off with my boots, Joshua. Where the casket I bade ye cherish?"

"Safe, master; I will bring it on the instant." Joshua knelt, and tugged at the muddied boots. "All goeth merrily at home, sir, as we see. 'What now,' quoth Master

Dawson—he grows somewhat fat on good living, mark you—'What now, do ye stay in England, Master Dimmock?' This is to pry into our affairs, master. I made him a short answer, never fear me. 'It's not for me,' quoth I, 'to divulge what plans Sir Nicholas hath in mind.' He stood abashed."

"I warrant me!" Sir Nicholas said mockingly. "A rare, politic answer, my Joshua. Pray, what are my plans?"

Joshua arose with the second boot in his hand. "Nay, sir, ye have not favoured me with them yet," he said with unabated cheerfulness. "But it was not fit that I should say as much to that fat steward. A swag-bellied, pompous ass, I make bold to say. Yet, master, and I do not speak without reflection, it might suit us well to remain snug at home now."

Sir Nicholas stood up, his fingers busy with the untying of his points. "Further, rogue, it might suit us better to be gone again just so soon as the *Venture* is ready to put to sea."

Joshua's face fell. "Is it so indeed, master?"

The glancing blue eyes looked down at him a moment. "Rest you snug at home. Do I constrain you? I am off on a wild adventure this time."

"The more reason to take me along," said Joshua severely. "If you are to be off again I shall certainly accompany you." He picked up the doublet from the bed, and frowned a stern reproof. "This is to jest, sir. I shall be at hand to keep a watch over our interests. I do not say that I had not as lief be at home, but I shall without doubt go where you go, for that is clearly my fate."

"Like Ruth," said Sir Nicholas flippantly.

In a little while he was descending the stairs again, very brave in his doublet of the French cut, with the high wings to the shoulders, and the embroidered sleeves. He had a fine leg, set off to advantage in stockings of carnation silk, with rosettes to the garters below his knees. The little neat ruff made no more than a stiff cup for his face; my Lord Beauvallet, favouring a wider fashion, called it Italianate, and looked severely.

My lord and his lady were found in the winter-parlour, where supper was spread upon a draw-table. Sir Nicholas came in upon them, splendid in his rich trappings, and

set a small casket before my lady. "Spain pays toll to
beauty, Kate," he said, and looked wickedly under his
lashes at Gerard's disapproving countenance.

My lady knew very well what she might expect to find
in the casket, but chose to dissemble. "Why, Nicholas,
what do you bring me?" she wondered, raising her
watchett-blue eyes to his face.

"A poor gewgaw, no more. There is a length of China
silk in my baggage you might make into a gown, or some
such thing."

My lady had opened the casket, and clasped her hands
in breathless ecstasy. "Oh, Nick! Rubies!" she gasped, and
almost reverently drew forth a long chain set with the
precious stones. She held it in her hands, and looked
doubtfully at Gerard. "See, my lord! Nicholas makes me a
noble present."

"Ay," said my lord glumly. "Jewels filched from some
Spanish hold."

My lady sighed, and put the chain down. "Should I not
wear it, dear sir?"

"Tush!" Nicholas said bracingly, and caught up the
chain from the table, and cast it about my lady's thin
neck. "I've other such toys for the Queen. I warrant you
she will wear them. Heed him not."

"I am sure," said my lady, plucking up courage, "that
what the Queen's Grace does not disdain to wear I need
not."

Gerard sat down in the high-backed chair at the head
of the table: "You will do as you please, madam," he said
deeply.

Supper was eaten in silence, as was customary, but
when the green goose had been taken away, and sweetmeats were on the table, and Hippocras set before my
lord, conversation began again. My lord dipped his fingers
in a gilt basin handed to him by a lackey liveried in blue,
and spoke more genially. "Well, Nick, ye say naught of
your designs. Have you come home to stay?"

"Confess, brother, you are more at ease when I am
abroad!" Nicholas rallied him, and poured Hippocras into
the delicate glass of Venetian ware before him.

Gerard permitted a smile to break his gravity. "Nay,

acquit me. I do not gainsay, though, ye are a mad, roystering lad."

"Swashbuckler, ye were wont to call me."

"Well." My lord smiled more broadly.

"Oh no, I am sure he is sober enough now!" my lady
said in a flutter. "No hard words, I beg! Why he numbers
some thirty-four, thirty-five summers, surely?"

"God a' mercy, do I so?" Sir Nicholas said, startled. He
lifted his glass, and held it up to see the light through the
wine in it. He seemed to be pondering some quaint
thought; my lord saw the corners of his mouth lift a little.

"Time to be done with all this ruffling on the high
seas," my lord said.

Beauvallet shot him a quick look; there was a hidden jest
in his eyes. He returned to the contemplation of his wine.

My lady rose. "You will have much to say to one
another," she said. "Ye will find me in the gallery
anon."

Beauvallet went to hold the door for her. As she passed
him she put out a hand, and smiled vaguely. "Indeed, I
hope you will listen to my lord, Nick. We should be glad to
have you at home."

He carried her fingers to his lips, but would give her
neither yea nor nay. She went out, and he closed the door
behind her.

My lord pushed back his chair a little way from the
table, sat more at his ease, and poured another glass of
wine. "Sit ye down, Nick, sit ye down! Let me know your
mind." He observed the secret jest still in his brother's
face, and knew a feeling of some slight alarm. There was
no knowing what folly Nick might be planning.

Sir Nicholas pulled his chair round a little, sank into it,
with one leg thrown over the arm. His fingers closed
round the stem of his glass, twisting it this way and that.
His other hand played gently with his pomander.

My lord nodded and smiled. "I see you still have that
trick of swinging your pomander. As I remember it never
boded good. My memory serves, eh?" He drank his wine,
and set down the glass. "Thirty-five summers! Ay, my
lady is in the right of it. Thirty-five summers and still
roaming the world. Now to what purpose, Nick?"

Beauvallet shrugged his shoulders. "Oh, to bring rubies home for Kate," he parried.

"It's what I don't like. I'll not conceal it from you. It's very well for such men as Hawkins or Drake, but I would remind you, Nick, that you stand next to me in the succession. To make the Grand Tour is well enough—though what good ye came by from it, God knoweth!"

"Nay, brother," Sir Nicholas protested. "I learned to foil with the point from the great Carranza himself in Toledo! Grant me that."

My lord was roused to an expression of strenuous disapproval. "A pretty ambition, God wot! All this pricking and poking with a barbarous rapier is an invention of the devil himself. An honest sword-and-buckler was good enough for our fathers."

"But not good enough for us," said Beauvallet. "Yet I will engage to worst you in an encounter with your sword-and-buckler, Gerard. I believe I have not altogether lost the trick of it. But for delicacy, for finesse, let me have the rapier!" He made an imaginary pass in the air. "What, you say I learned no good upon my travels? Did I not sit at the feet of Carranza, and after find out Marozzo himself in Venice? Ay, he was old, I grant you, but he had some tricks still to show. Alack, ye have no Italian! Ye should else read his *Opera Nova,* in the which book he carefully explains the uses of the *falso* and the *dritto filo.* No good, ye say? Produce me the man who can worst me with the rapier and the dagger!"

My lord maintained an unyielding front. "Do you count such foreign tricks a gain? What else have you to show for these years of junketting abroad?"

"A rare Toledo blade, brother," returned Nicholas, unabashed. "A blade tempered in the waters of the Tagus, and inscribed with the name of Andrew Ferrara between eight crowns. Yet another such blade, from the hand of Sahagom. What, more? Why, then, a suit of Jacobi armour you yourself did not despise; an acquaintance with our cousins in France; an intimate knowledge of the French, the Spanish, and the Italian tongues—which I think ye lack——"

"The English of my forefathers sufficeth me," said my lord grimly.

"You've no ambition, Gerard," mourned Beauvallet.

"I've no vagrant spirit," said my lord tartly. "Will you never be still? I pass over the Grand Tour; I may pass over even that mad emprise ye set forth on with Drake——"

"A thousand thanks!" Beauvallet's eyes were alight.

"I grant you it was worth the doing," said my lord grudgingly. "Ay, a rare feat, and all honour to you for compassing it."

"Give honour to Drake, where it is due," said Beauvallet, and lifted his glass. "We drink his health! To Drake, the master-mariner!"

My lord drank the toast, but without enthusiasm. "It's very well, but why ye must needs cleave so fast to this same Sir Francis passeth my comprehension."

"Does it so?" Beauvallet said. "But then, brother, you have not sailed the world round in his company, nor learned seacraft of him, nor faced sack, battle and wreck at his side."

"Ye have imbibed unfit notions from him. A voyage round the world! Very well, very well, a feat indeed, and duly we honoured it. Ye brought home a store of riches, moreover, enough for any man. Then was the time to call an end to this wandering fever. But did ye? Nay, ye built your fine ship, and must needs be off again. A madness! A most damnable folly, Nick, give me leave to say!"

Sir Nicholas bowed his raven head in mock contrition. "I cry your pardon, good my lord!"

"Ay, and sit there as graceless as the day ye were first breeched," said my lord, a hint of humour in his deep voice. "Nay, Nick, I speak advisedly. Ye have laid up a goodly treasure, as I know who husband it for you. Treasure come by in a way I like not, but let it go. There is the manor of Basing waiting for any time you choose to go to it. My lady brings me no heirs, nor is not like to. I look to you. What comes to our house if you be slain or drowned? Get a wife, and be done with this roystering!"

Sir Nicholas lifted his pomander to his nose. "Give me joy, brother, I am about to get me a wife."

My lord was momentarily surprised, but he hid it quickly. "In good time. My lady hath her eye upon a likely maid for you. We had thought on the Lady Alison, daughter of Lord Gervais of Alfreston, but there are others beside. Ye might go into Worcestershire for a bride. My sister writes sundry names might please you."

Beauvallet held up his hand. His eyes were fairly brimful now with that secret jest. "Hold, hold, Gerard! I am going to look in Spain for my bride."

My lord set down his glass with a snap that came near to breaking it. He stared under his projecting brows. "What's this? What new folly?"

"None, I swear. My choice is made. Give me joy, brother! I shall bring home a bride before a year is out."

My lord sat back in his chair. "Expound me this riddle," he said quietly. "Ye jest, I think."

"Never less. I give you a new toast." He came to his feet and lifted his glass on high. "Dona Dominica de Rada y Sylva!"

My lord did not drink it. "A Spanish Papist?" he asked. "Do you ask me to believe that?"

"No Papist, but a dear heretic." Sir Nicholas leaned on the goffered-leather back of his chair. With a sinking heart my lord noted the scarce curbed energy of him, the exultant look in his face. He feared the worst. The worst came. "I took her and her father aboard the *Venture* after the sack of the *Santa Maria*. More of that anon. Since she would have it so, and since to that I pledged my word, I set them ashore on the northern coast of Spain. But I swore I would ride into Spain to seek her, and so I shall do, brother, never doubt me."

My lord sat still in his chair, looking up at Nicholas. His face was set. "Nick, if this be indeed no jest——"

"God's my pity, wherefor should I jest?" Beauvallet cried impatiently. "I am in earnest, in deadly earnest!"

"Then ye are mad indeed!" my lord said, and struck the table with his open palm. "Mad, and should be clapped up! Fool, do ye think to ride scatheless into Spain in these days?"

The smile flashed out; Sir Nicholas nodded. "Ay, I think to come out of Spain with a whole skin."

My lord got up out of his chair. "Nick, Nick, what devil rides you? We have no ambassador in Spain to-day. How should you fare?"

"Alone. The stars always fight for me, Gerard. Will you take a wager that I do not come home with a bride on my arm?"

"Nay, have done with laughing! To what a pass has this senseless love of danger led you? Lad, heed what I say! If ye go into Spain ye will never come out again. The Inquisition will have you in its damnable toils, and there is no power under the sun can save you then!"

Sir Nicholas snapped finger and thumb in the air. "A fig for the Inquisition! Gerard, my careful Gerard, I give you *Reck Not!*"

ᴀ Chapter VII ᴋ

To my Lady Beauvallet, discovered in the Long Gallery, Gerard exposed the folly of his brother. He sat him down heavily in a chair covered with gilded leather, and spoke bitterly and long. My lady listened in amazement and distress, but Nicholas wandered down the gallery inspecting such new pieces as my lord had lately acquired, and gave no ear to the discourse.

"If you have more influence than I have, Kate, I pray you use it now," Gerard said. "I grant you he lives but to plague me, but I should desire him to continue to live."

Nicholas raised his head from a close scrutiny of a piece from one of the cabinets. "Whence had you this Majolica ware, Gerard?" he inquired.

"But Nicholas cannot mean it!" my lady said hopefully.

"Prevail upon him to admit as much, madam, and call me your debtor. Prevail on him only to pay heed to sager counsel!"

She turned her head, and saw Nicholas at the other end of the gallery, intent upon Majolica ware. "Good my brother! Nicholas! Will you not tell me what you have in mind?"

Nicholas put back the piece, and came sauntering towards her. "Pottery, Kate, but Gerard denies me an answer. What's your will?"

"God sain you, Nick, can you not be serious even now?" my lord said sharply.

Nicholas stood before them, swinging gently on his toes, with his hands tucked into his belt. A smile lilted at the corners of his mouth. "Here's heat! I've said my say, Gerard, and mighty ill you liked it. What would you have now?"

"Nick, put by this mad humour, and give me a sober answer! Tell me ye did but jest."

"Soberly I tell you, brother, I did not jest."

My lord's hand clenched on the arm of his chair, and he spoke with some force. "It's to throw away your life for a whim. Are you tired of it? Does the thought of death please you so well? Or are ye besotted with success and now think even to succeed in this?"

Nicholas nodded.

"Oh, but Nicholas, this is not like you!" fluttered my lady.

"It's very like him, madam!" Gerard retorted. "Any wild scheme is meat for Nick! I might have known what would come of it! But to think to snatch a wench out of Spain, to bring her home, a foreigner and an enemy, to be my lady one day passes all bounds!"

"Does it so indeed?" Nicholas interposed swiftly. "You're at fault, Gerard. I do but follow the example of the first baron, who also brought home a foreigner and an enemy to be his bride."

My lord glared; my lady stirred restlessly, and hurried into speech. "Of what like is she, Nicholas?"

"Tush!" said my lord awfully.

Nicholas looked down at my lady; a gentler light was in his eyes. "Kate, she is a little lady all fire and spirit, with great brown eyes, and two dimples set on either side the sweetest mouth in Christendom."

"But a Spaniard!" my lady protested.

"Trust me to amend that," he said lightly.

She liked the savour of romance, smiled, and sighed. My lord brought her down to earth again very speedily. "What boots it to ask of what like she may be? Ye will never see her. Nor will ye see Nick again if he goes on this mad quest. That is certain."

Nicholas laughed out. "Marry, only one thing is certain, Gerard, and that is that ye will never be rid of me. I always come back to be your bane."

"Lad, you know well I've no wish to be rid of you. Can I not prevail with you? For the sake of the house?"

Nicholas held up his hand, and showed the lady's thumb-ring upon his little finger. "See my lady's token. I swore on it to reach her. Are you answered?"

My lord made a gesture of despair. "I see there is once more to be no ho with you. When do you look to go?"

"Some three months hence," Nicholas answered. "The *Venture* lies in dock, and will take some time refitting. I must to London within the week to pay my duty to the Queen. I have appointed young Dangerfield to meet me there. I might go thence into Worcestershire to see how Adela does. You will see me home again in a month, never doubt it."

He left Alreston two days later upon the Barbary horse from my lord's stables, with Joshua Dimmock riding sedately behind him, and travelled 'cross country at his leisure until the post road was reached.

"Never at quiet!" Joshua remarked to the heavens. "Court drowning at sea, court foundering in mire upon land: it's all one."

"Peace, froth!" Beauvallet said, and made his horse curvet on the green.

They came within sight of the city late one evening as the gates were closing. "What, the good-year!" Joshua cried, roused to wrath. "Shut Beauvallet out, is it? Now see how I will use these churlish Londoners!"

"No swashbuckling here, crackhemp; we rest at the Tabard."

The great inn showed welcoming lights, and placed her best at Beauvallet's disposal. He stayed only one night, and was gone in the morning over London Bridge to the Devil Tavern in East Chepe, where he had reason to think he might find Sir Francis Drake.

The host, who knew him well, accorded him a deferential welcome, and bustled about to prepare a chamber for his honour. Sir Francis lay at the inn indeed, but was gone forth that morning, mine host knew not where. But there was a dinner bespoke for eleven o'clock, and Master Hawkins would be there—nay, not Master John, but his brother—and Sir William Cavandish, so mine host believed, with some others.

"Lay a place for me Wadloe," Sir Nicholas said, and went out in search of Sir Francis, or any other friend who might chance to be abroad.

Paul's walk was the likeliest place to find Sir Francis; he would be sure to go there to learn what news might be current. Sir Nicholas strode off westwards through the crowded streets, came in good time to the great cathedral, and ran with the clank of spurred heels up the steps.

Merchants and moneychangers no longer congregated in the church, as they had done only twenty years ago, but Paul's Walk was still the meeting ground for every court gallant who wished to show himself abroad. If a man desired to see a friend, or hear the latest news, to Paul's Walk he must go, where he would be bound to meet, sooner or later, most of the notables of town.

Beauvallet came up with a score of young gallants, exchanging Court gossip. His glance swept over these; he clove a way through them, and looked keenly round. Over the heads of two foppish gentlemen who eyed him with disfavour, he saw a bluff, square-set man, with a fierce golden beard, and long grey eyes set slightly slanting in a broad face. This man stood with feet planted wide, and arms akimbo, talking to an elderly gentleman in a long cloak. He wore a peascod doublet, hugely bombasted, and a jewel in one ear.

Sir Nicholas pushed through the crowd, and raised his hand in greeting. The square man saw; his narrow eyes opened wider; he waved, and came to meet Beauvallet through the press. "What, my Nick!" he rumbled. His voice had some strength, as if he were accustomed to make himself heard above wind and cannon-shot. "Why, my bully!" He grasped Beauvallet's hand, and clapped him on the shoulder. "Whence do ye spring? God's light, I am glad to see you, lad!"

Some heads were turned. A gentleman pushed forward, saying:—"Beauvallet, as I live! Save you, Nicholas!"

Beauvallet greeted this friend, and others who drew

near. With Drake's hand on his shoulder he stood bandying idle talk some little while, answering eager questions. But soon Drake bore him off, and they walked back together towards the Devil Tavern.

"What news?" Drake said. "I had word of you in the Main, ruffling still. What chance?"

"Good," Sir Nicholas answered, and recounted briefly some of his adventures.

Drake nodded. "No mishaps?"

"Some few deaths, no more. Perinat came out from Santiago to teach me a lesson." He chuckled, and flung out a hand on which a single ruby ring glowed. "Oho! I took that from Perinat for dear remembrance's sake."

Drake laughed, and pressed his arm. "Proud bantam! What else?"

"A galleon bound for Vigo laden with silks and spices, and some gold. More of that anon. Tell your tale."

Drake had Virginian news, being but just returned from the little colony. He had brought back the colonists, and had much to tell. Talk ran freely, and footsteps lagged. It was after eleven when they reached the Devil, and in an upper room were gathered some half a dozen guests awaiting their host.

Drake rolled in with an arm flung across Beauvallet's shoulders. "Cry you pardon!" he said. "Look what I bring!"

There was some little stir, a cry of "Mad Nicholas, by God!" and a babel of welcome.

There was Frobisher, ready with a quiet greeting; Master William Hawkins, solid, frieze-clad man; young Richard, his nephew, standing beside Cavendish, a courtier among the seadogs; Master John Davys, rugged man, and a scattering of others, most of them known to Sir Nicholas. The rafters rang soon with wild tales tossed to and fro, laughter, and the clink of tankards. Drake sat fatherly at the head of his table, and had Sir Nicholas upon his right hand, Frobisher on his left. Frobisher bent his brows at Beauvallet, and said: "I heard of your coming; there were some men of yours met some of mine at the Gallant Howard. Fine doings! I am advised you sail with women aboard. How now, Beauvallet?"

Drake cocked a wise eyebrow in Beauvallet's direction;

young Cavendish looked as though he would like to hear more, yet hardly liked to raise his voice in this august gathering.

"True enough," Sir Nicholas said lightly.

"Rare work for a sailor," Frobisher said ironically. "A new cantrip, I doubt?"

"You're jealous, Martin," Drake cut in with a deep laugh. "What's the reason, Nick?"

"Simple enough," Beauvallet said, and told it, very briefly.

Drake dipped a sop in his wine, and looked sideways a moment. Frobisher said grimly:—"Beauvallet looks for romance upon the high seas, and makes his fine gesture. I would not sail with you, Beauvallet, for a thousand pound."

"No stomach for it, Frobisher?" Sir Nicholas said sweetly.

"None, beshrew me. What fresh devilment this voyage?"

"Some fine prizes," Drake said. "And a ring from Perinat—for remembrance's sake, Nick, eh?"

"I am a plain man," Frobisher remarked. "Too plain for such doings. Drake and you, Drake and you!" He shook his head over them.

Master Davys let a sudden laugh at this, and began at once to speak of a mooted expedition in search of the North-West passage he so fervently believed in. "Ay, you're a mad runagate, Nick, but there's a place for you with me if you care to venture forth."

At that there broke out a general discussion, some ribaldry, and a gentle twitting of Master Davys' earnestness.

Cavendish, listening bright-eyed to all this discourse, ventured a word here and there, and presently spoke of his own plans. He had three ships fitting out for a West Indian expedition, and was agog to follow brave examples set him. Sir Nicholas wished him God-speed, and drank success to his venture. He found the grave, considering eyes of young Richard Hawkins upon him. He threw him a gay word, and young Richard blushed, and laughed.

"This babe sails with you, Drake?" Sir Nicholas said.

"Well-a-day! I left him scarce out of his swaddling-bands!"

"Ay, ay," Drake said. "All alike, these Hawkins—born to the sea. Did you have speech with old Master Hawkins at Plymouth?"

"Long speech, over a tankard of rare beer. I hear the great John grows greater still, Richard."

"My father talks of war with Spain," Richard said. "He says Walsingham looks keenly for it."

"A cup to the happy day!" Beauvallet said.

Frobisher struck in to inquire of Beauvallet's plans; Master Davys, aroused from a dish of eels, struck the table with his clenched fist, and loudly bade Beauvallet sail with him to the North-West passage.

Beauvallet turned it off with a laugh, and gave Frobisher an evasive answer. Drake looked sideways again.

But it was not until much later, when these two sat alone in the empty room, over a fire of sea-coal, that Drake put his question. Then he puffed at his long pipe, and stretched his massive legs out before him, and looked up at Beauvallet out of his narrow, all-seeing eyes. "What devilment, Nick? Let me have it."

Beauvallet brought his quick gaze up from the red heart of the fire, and looked challengingly. "Why must I needs have devilment in mind?"

Drake pointed the stem of his pipe. "I know you, Nick, d'ye see? You've not given me the full sum of it, but Martin jumped your fine secret for you."

So he had it then, in a few graphic words. It made his jaw drop a little, but it made him twinkle too. "Pretty, very pretty!" he said. "But what now?"

"I shall go to Spain to fetch her," answered Sir Nicholas, in much the same tone as he would have said he would go to Westminster.

At that Drake let out a mighty echoing laugh. "God amend all!" He sobered suddenly, and leaning forward took Beauvallet's arm in a strong hold. "Look you, Nick, ha' done. Art too good a man to be lost."

The gleaming blue eyes met those long grey ones for an instant. "Do you think I shall be lost then?"

Drake twisted his beard upwards, and chewed the end

of it. "Well, you're human." His shoulders began to shake
again. "Ho, pull me Philip's long nose, Nick, if ye see his
Satanic Majesty! You would come safe out of hell, I dare
swear. But how to come into Spain? Your smuggling
port?"

"Nay, I had thought of it, but it's to court exposure. I
must have papers to show at need. The plague is on it we
have no ambassador in Madrid to-day."

"English papers would never serve," Drake said.
"You're frustrated at the very outset. Go to, put the folly
aside."

"Not I, by God! I shall try my fortune with my French
kinsmen."

"God's Death, have you any?"

"A-many. One in particular would be glad to serve me
for old times sake, I believe. The Marquis de Belrémy,
with whom I travelled many leagues on the Continent,
years ago. Ay, and we saw some scrapes together, God
wot!" He laughed softly, remembering. "If he can put me
in the way to get French papers, well. If not—I shall still
find a way."

Drake puffed in silence for a moment. "And a licence
to travel over seas, Master Madman. Letters of Marque
won't serve for this emprise. It's in my mind the Queen
may have other plans for you than to lose you in a
hare-brained venture to Spain."

"Trust me to get a licence. If the Queen will not, think
you Walsingham would be so nice?"

Drake pulled a grimace. "Ay, marry, we know he'd be
glad enough to send a spy into Spain. Beshrew your heart,
Nick, it's madness! Do you hold your life of so mean
account?"

"Nay, but it's charmed. Yourself said so, Drake. Where
lies the Court?"

"At Westminster."

"Then I'm for Westminster to-morrow," said Sir Nicholas.

He came to the palace in the forenoon of the next
day, very bravely tricked out in a slashed doublet, scented
with musk, and his beard fresh trimmed. He had a cloak
of the Burgundian cut aswirl from his shoulders, and
caught up carelessly over one arm. It was not difficult to

gain access to the palace, especially for Sir Nicholas
Beauvallet, who was known to be a favourite with the
Queen's Grace. She had always a soft corner in her heart
for a handsome dare-devil.

Sir Nicholas reached, without difficulty, one of the
Long Galleries to which he had been directed. Some of
the Queen's ladies were gathered here, and many of the
court gallants. He learned that the Queen was closetted
with the French Ambassador, Sir Francis Walsingham and
Sir James Crofts in attendance. This he had from the
Vice-Chancellor, Sir Christopher Hatton, strutting in the
gallery. Hatton gave him a cool, polite greeting, and two
fingers to do what he willed with. Beauvallet let them fall
soon enough, and fell into talk with the elegant and grave
Raleigh, also waiting for her Grace to come into the
gallery. Sir Christopher rolled a fiery eye, and seemed to
withdraw the hem of his garment from Raleigh's vicinity.
At that Sir Nicholas grinned openly. Sir Christopher's
jealousies seemed to him absurd.

He had to wait perhaps half an hour, but he employed
his time pleasantly enough, and very soon drew a shocked
titter from one of the Maids of Honour, who rated him for
a bold, saucy fellow. This he certainly was.

There came a stir at the far end of the gallery; a curtain
was held back, and four people came slowly into the
gallery. First of these was the Queen, a thin lady of no
more than middle-height, but mounted on very high heels.
A huge ruff, spangled with gems, rose behind her head,
which was of fiery colour, much crimped and curled, and
elaborately dressed with jewelled combs, and the like. Still
more monstrous loomed her farthingale, and her sleeves
were puffed out from her arms, and sewn over with jewels. She was dazzling to behold, arrayed in the richest
stuffs, glinting with precious stones. She drew all eyes, but
she would still have done so had she been dressed in the
simplest fustian. Her face might have been a mask for the
paint that covered it, but her eyes were very much alive:
strange, dark eyes, not large, but very bright, and oddly
piercing.

A little behind her, his hand upon the curtain, De
Mauvissière bent his stately head to listen deferentially to
some word she had flung at him over her shoulder. Behind

him Sir Francis Walsingham was folding a scrap of paper, which anon he handed to Crofts, frowning in the background. Sir Francis' unfathomable, rather sad eyes, seemed to embrace everyone in the gallery. They rested thoughtfully on Beauvallet for a moment, but he made no sign.

De Mauvissière bent to kiss the Queen's hand. She was tapping her foot, and her eyes snapped dangerously. Her ladies, being familiar with the signs, knew some misgivings.

De Mauvissière went out backwards, bowing; the Queen nodded, and still tapped with one foot. She was out of temper, flashed an angry glance at her two ministers, and hunched a pettish shoulder.

Walsingham crooked a long finger. His royal mistress must be diverted: not Hatton, not Raleigh, whom she might see every day, would serve. Sir Nicholas Beauvallet was come in a good hour.

"God's Death!" swore her Grace. "It seems I am right well entreated!"

There was a quick step; a gentleman was on his knee before her, and dared to look up, twinkling, into her face.

"God's Death!" swore her Grace again, hugely delighted. "Beauvallet!"

Well, he had her hand to kiss, got a rap over the knuckles from her fan, and was bidden rise up. The storm had passed over; her Grace was happily diverted. Walsingham might hide a quiet smile in his beard; Sir James Crofts could banish his worried frown.

"Ha, rogue!" said her Grace, showing teeth a little discoloured in a smile of great good-humour. "So you return again!"

"As a needle to the magnet, madam," Sir Nicholas said promptly.

She leaned on his arm, and took a few steps with him down the gallery. "What news do ye bring me of my good cousin of Spain?"

"Alack, madam, to my sure knowledge he hath lost three good ships: a carrack, and two tall galleons."

Her bright eyes looked sidelong at him. "So! So! To whom fell they a prey?"

"To a rogue, madam. One named Beauvallet."

She burst out laughing. "I swear I love thee well, my merry ruffler!" She beckoned up Walsingham, and gave him the news. "What must we do with him, Sir Francis?" she demanded. "Ask of me, my rogue, and ye shall have." She awaited his answer without misgiving for well she knew that he was in need of naught, but was come instead to enrich her coffers.

"Two boons, madam, I crave on my knees."

"God's Son! This is churlish-sounding, by my faith! Name 'em then."

"The first is that your Grace will accept of a New Year's gift I am come so tardily to offer—a trifle of rubies, no more. The second is that your Grace will give me leave to travel into France for a space."

That did not please her so well. She frowned over it, and would know more. "I vow I'll give you a place about the Court," she said.

It was his turn to frown. Your true courtier would have smiled, and murmured his eternal devotion. This Mad Nicholas must needs twitch his black brows together, and give a quick unmannerly shake of his head.

"By God, you're a saucy knave!" her Grace said stridently. But she sounded more amused than angered. "What's this? You'll none?"

"Give me leave to travel a while, madam," begged Sir Nicholas.

"I'm minded to box your ears, sirrah!" said her Grace.

"Oh, madam, forgive a tongue unused to speak softly! I had rather serve you with the strong arm abroad than lie idle at your Court."

"Well! well! That's prettily spoken, eh, Walsingham? But I don't need your strong arm in France. Nay, I grant no licence to you. Be plain with me, sirrah!" She saw his blue eyes dancing, and struck him lightly on the arm with her fan. "Ha, you laugh? God's Death, you are a daring rogue! Let me hear it. Speak, Beauvallet: the Queen listens."

"Madam, I'll not deceive you." Beauvallet dropped to his knee. "Give me leave to go into Spain a while."

This startling request fell into an amazed silence. Then her Grace burst out again into her loud laugh, and those at the far end of the gallery envied Mad Nicholas who could so amuse the Queen. "A jest! An idle jest!" the Queen rapped out. But her piercing gaze was intent upon him. "Wherefor, then?"

"Madam, to perform a vow. Grant me so small a boon."

"Grant you leave to throw away your life? What shall that profit me? Do you hear this, Walsingham? Is the man mad in good sooth, think you?"

Walsingham was stroking his beard. He too watched Sir Nicholas, but there was no reading what was in his mind. "Sir Nicholas might haply bring news out of Spain," he said slowly.

The Queen turned an impatient shoulder. "Oh, get some other to do your spies' work, sir! Well, and if I grant this boon, Sir Nicholas? What then?"

"Why, madam, only tell me what you would have me bring you out of Spain?"

Maybe the swift rejoinder pleased her; maybe she was curious to know what he would do. She said gaily:— "Marry, the best that Spain holds, sir. Mind you that!"

Then Walsingham spoke in his soft, cold voice, leading the talk away from this request. Beauvallet was content to have it so. The Queen gave neither yea nor nay, but Sir Francis Walsingham would certainly give a licence to Sir Nicholas Beauvallet for the good intelligence he saw might come of it.

◄◄ *Chapter VIII* ►►

IT was over three months later that Sir Nicholas Beauvallet went riding southwards from Paris towards the Spanish border. There had been some necessary delay at home: treasure to be bestowed at the Queen's pleasure, and his own affairs to look to. He had also to visit his sister in

Worcestershire, and she would not soon let him go. He made a merry month of it there, but told Adela nothing of his plans, and trifled shamelessly with the ladies she brought forward to tempt him into matrimony.

The licence to travel was obtained from Walsingham easily enough. Beauvallet was closeted with this enigmatic man for a full hour, and protested afterwards that the Secretary made him shiver. But it is believed that they were much of a mind in that both would welcome war with Spain.

With Joshua Dimmock, and a fair stock of money against his needs Sir Nicholas came at last to Paris, and inquired for his distant kinsman, Eustache de Beauvallet, Marquis de Belrémy. This nobleman, whom Nicholas had not met since certain riotous days in Italy, when both were in the early twenties, was not to be found at his town house. His servants reported him to be at Belrémy, in Normandy, but Beauvallet heard other news that placed the Marquis farther south, on a visit to a friend. There was nothing to be gained from seeking the elusive Marquis through France; Beauvallet swore genially at the delay, and sat him down to await his kinsman's return. He did not visit either the English ambassador, or the Court of Henri III. For the one, he preferred his presence in France to be unknown; for the other, the fopperies of the French Court were not at all to his taste. He found the means to amuse himself outside the Court, and passed the time very pleasantly.

At the end of a month the Marquis returned to Paris, and hearing of Beauvallet's visit, straightway kicked his majordomo for allowing his so dear kinsman to lodge otherwhere than in his house, and set forth at once in a horse-litter to find Sir Nicholas.

Beauvallet had a comfortable lodging near the Seine. It suited him very well, but Joshua muttered darkly, and saw a Catholic murderer in every convivial guest who came there. Saint Bartholomew's Day was fresh enough yet in a plain Englishman's mind, said he.

The Marquis, a wiry, resplendent personage, no more than a year older than Beauvallet, came tempestuously into his room, and clasped his kinsman in an ecstatic embrace with many suitable exclamations and reproaches.

It was long before Beauvallet could come to his business, for the Marquis had much to say, and much to ask, and many mad memories to recall. But at length the reason for this visit was asked, and then they came to grips. When the Marquis heard that Sir Nicholas wanted a French pass into Spain he at first threw up hands of despair, and cried "Impossible!" At the end of half an hour he said:— "Well, well, perhaps! But it is madness, and it will be a forgery, and you are a good-for-naught to ask it of me!" Within the week he brought the pass, and said only "Aha!" when Beauvallet asked how he had managed to procure it. It gave leave for a M. Gaston de Beauvallet to travel abroad. Beauvallet learned that this Gaston was a cousin of the Marquis, and chuckled.

"But look you, my friend!" the Marquis cautioned him. "Do not stumble upon our Ambassador, for he knows Gaston well, and us all. I caution you, be wary! Ah, but to travel into Spain at all! And with that name! Madness! Unutterable folly!"

"*Basta, basta!*" said Sir Nicholas, and frowned upon the pass.

Now as he rode south it was in his mind that this pass, though it would safely carry him across the Frontier was likely to lead him to exposure at Madrid. He rode in silence, pondering it rather ruefully, but presently he twitched his shoulders as though to cast off these cares, and spurred his horse to a gallop. Joshua, following at a soberer pace with a led sumpter, watched his master disappear down the road in a cloud of dust, and shook his head. "Our last venture," said Joshua, and kicked his horse to a brisker pace. "A plague on all women! Come up, jade!"

They made no great haste on the journey, for Sir Nicholas was loth to part with the horse he had bought in Paris. It bore him nobly, and he cherished it well. They went south by degrees, resting at the inns along the post road, and came at last to a lonely tavern within half a day's ride of the Frontier.

It lay in a squalid village, and was obviously unfrequented by travellers. The last great inn they had passed housed a sick man, whom Joshua was quick to nose out. He got wind of a pestilent fever, and was urgent with his master not to remain. The afternoon was young yet, and the sun warm. Beauvallet consented to ride on.

So they came at dusk to this rude inn, lying a little off the post road. None came forth to welcome them, so Joshua went to kick the door, and raised a shout. Mine host came out, surly-seeming, but when he saw so richly caparisoned a gentleman he lost his scowl, and bowed to the ground. There was a room for the gentleman to be sure, if monseigneur would condescend to this poor abode.

"I condescend," said Sir Nicholas. "Have you a truckle-bed, my man? Then set it up in my chamber for my servant." He swung himself down from the saddle, and fondled his mare a moment. "Eh, my beauty!" He had had her through the Marquis' advice, a fine, fleet black, with powerful quarters, and a mouth of velvet. "Take her, Joshua." He stretched himself, and swore at his stiffness. The landlord set open the door, and bowed him into the low-pitched taproom.

Beauvallet sent him to fetch wine, and seemed to snuff the air. "Faugh!" It was squalid in the taproom, of a piece with the untidy yard without. He went to the window and forced it open to let in the clean air.

The landlord came back with the wine, looked askance at the open window, and muttered a little under his breath. Sir Nicholas drank deeply, and upon the shuffling entrance of an out-at-elbows servant, stretched out his legs to have the high boots pulled off.

He was at supper—a meagre collation which drew sundry pungent remarks from Joshua—when there came the sound of a led horse on the cobbles outside. A moment later the door was thrust open, and a young gentleman came in, very out of temper.

He was dressed richly, but dust lay on his fine clothes. He scowled at Beauvallet, seated at the table, and shouted for the landlord. Upon this worthy's coming the young gentleman burst into a flood of angry talk. His woes seemed to be many. There was, to start with, the excessive dust upon the road which had well-nigh choked him; to go on, there was a sick man at the regular inn some miles back; to crown his troubles his horse had gone lame, the jade, and another must be brought him on the instant.

Having delivered himself of this demand my fine gentleman flung off his cloak, bespoke supper, and sat down on the settle with the air of a thwarted schoolboy.

The problem of horse-flesh was beyond the landlord's solving. He gave his new guest to understand that he had no riding horses in his stables, nor could he tell where any might be found in this hamlet. Monsieur must send to the nearest town, back along the road.

At this monsieur let forth an oath, and declared that he had no time to waste, but must be gone over the Frontier first thing in the morning. Mine host had nothing to say to this, but shrugged sullenly, and turned away. His ear was seized between a finger and thumb. "Look you! a horse, and swiftly!" snarled monsieur.

"I keep no horse," reiterated the landlord. He rubbed his ear, aggrieved. "There are but two horses in my barn, and they belong to this gentleman."

Upon this monsieur became aware of Beauvallet, struggling with a tough fowl. He bowed slightly. Sir Nicholas raised an eyebrow, and nodded in return, wasting little ceremony.

"Give you good-evening, monsieur." The young gentleman tried to conceal his ill-temper. "You will have heard that I have suffered a misfortune."

"Ay, faith, the whole house will have heard it," said Sir Nicholas, and poured more wine.

Monsieur bit his lip. "I have urgent need of a horse," he announced. "I shall be happy to buy one or other of your nags, if you will sell."

"A thousand thanks," Sir Nicholas answered.

Monsieur brightened. "You will oblige me?"

"Desolated, sir! I cannot oblige you," said Sir Nicholas, who had small mind to part with his horses.

This seemed final, to be sure. A rich colour mounted to monsieur's cheeks; he choked back his spleen, and condescended to plead, though stiffly.

Sir Nicholas tilted back his chair, and tucked his hands in his belt. He looked mockingly at the young Frenchman. "My good young sir, I counsel you to be patient," he said. "You may send to the town in the morning, and procure a horse against your needs. I do not part with mine."

"One of these nags!" Monsieur snorted. "I do not think that would suit me, sir."

"And I am quite sure it would not suit me, sir," said Sir Nicholas.

The Frenchman looked at him with evident dislike. "I have informed you, sir, that my need is instant."

Sir Nicholas yawned.

For a moment the Frenchman seemed inclined to burst forth into fresh vituperations. He bit his nails, glaring, and took a quick turn about the room. "You use me ungraciously!" he flung over his shoulder.

"Well-a-day!" said Sir Nicholas ironically.

Monsieur took yet another turn, seemed again to choke back some hasty utterance, and at length forced a smile. "Well, I will not quarrel with you," he said.

"You would find it very difficult," nodded Sir Nicholas.

Monsieur opened his mouth, shut it again, and swallowed hard. "Permit me to share your board," he said at last.

"With all my heart, youngling," Sir Nicholas answered, but there had come a watchful gleam into his eyes.

But the Frenchman seemed to cast aside his evil-humours in good sooth. True, he railed a little at ill-fortune, but was forward with plans for the acquisition of a horse upon the morrow. The plague was on it he could scarce hope to get across the Frontier now for two days. As he remembered the town lay many leagues behind— but he would not complain. He pledged Beauvallet in a brimming cup.

Supper being at an end, monsieur grew restless, complained of the ill-entertainment, pished at the poor light afforded by two tallow candles, and at length proposed an encounter with the dice, if such might chance to jump with monsieur's humour.

"Excellent, well," said Beauvallet, and banged on the table with his empty cup to summon back the landlord. Dice were brought, more wine was set upon the table, and the evening bade fair to be merry.

The dice rattled in the box. "A main!" said monsieur.

Beauvallet called it, and cast the dice. Monsieur rattled

the bones, and threw a nick. Coins were pushed across the greasy boards; fresh wine was poured; the two men bent over the table, absorbed in the game.

It was a merry evening enough. The candles burned low in their sockets; the wine passed freely, and more freely yet; money changed hands, back and forth. At last one of the candles guttered dismally, and went out. Beauvallet thrust back his chair, and passed a hand across his brow. "Enough!" he said, somewhat thickly. "God's me, after midnight already?" He rose unsteadily, and stretched his arms above his head. This made for a slight stagger. He laughed. Cup-shotten!" he said, and laughed again, and swayed a little on his toes.

The Frenchman sprang up, steady enough upon his feet, but flushed, and somewhat wild-eyed. He had not drunk as much as Beauvallet. "A last toast!" he cried, and slopped more wine into the empty cups. "To a speedy journey, say I!"

"God save you!" said Beauvallet. He drank deep, and sent the empty cup spinning over his shoulder to crash against the wall behind him. "One candle between the two of us." He picked it up, and the hot tallow dripped on to the floor. "Up with you, youngling." He stood at the foot of the rickety stairs, holding the candle unsteadily aloft. The dim light flickered over the steps; the Frenchman went up, with a hand against the wall.

Upstairs a lantern, burning low, was discovered. The Frenchman took it, called a good-night, and went into his chamber. Sir Nicholas, yawning prodigiously, sought his own, and stumbled over the low truckle-bed on which Joshua lay peacefully asleep. "God's Death!" swore Sir Nicholas.

Joshua was awakened by a drop of tallow alighting on his nose, and started up, rubbing the afflicted member.

Beauvallet set down the candle, laughing. "My poor Joshua!"

"Master, you are in your cups," Joshua said severely.

"None so deep," said Sir Nicholas cheerfully, and found the basin and ewer that stood upon a rude chest. There was a great splashing of water, and a sputtering, "Pouf!" said Sir Nicholas, towelling his head. "Go to sleep, starveling. What are you at?"

Joshua was for rising. "You've need to come out of those clothes, sir," said he.

"Oh, let be!" said Beauvallet, and flung himself down as he was upon the bed.

The candle went out, but the moonlight shone in at the uncurtained window. It lit Beauvallet's face, but could not keep him awake. Soon a snore disturbed the stillness, and then another.

He was awakened out of a deep sleep by a hand shaking his shoulder, and a hissing whisper in his ear. He came groping out of the mists, felt the clutch upon his shoulder, and of instinct shot out a pair of hands to grasp the unknown's throat. "Ha, dog!"

Joshua choked, and tried to tear apart the gripping fingers. " 'Tis I—Joshua!" he gasped.

The grip slackened at once. Sir Nicholas sat up, and was shaken with laughter. "Ye were nigh sped that time, chewet! What a-plague ails you to come pawing me!"

"Matter enough," Joshua said. "Ha' done with your laughter, sir! Yon Frenchman's crept below stairs to steal the mare."

"What!" Beauvallet swung his legs off the bed, and felt for his shoon. "Cock's passion, that whey-faced maltworm! How learned you this?"

Joshua was groping for his breeches. "I waked to hear one go creeping down the stairs. A step creaked. Be sure I was alert upon the instant! *I* do not fall cup-shotten into a stupor."

"Peace, you elf-skin! What then?"

"Then might I hear the door open stealthily below, and in a moment a cloaked fellow with a lantern crosses the yard to the barn. Ho, thinks I——"

"Give me my sword," Beauvallet interrupted, and made for the door.

"I shall be with you on the instant!" Joshua hissed after him. "A plague on these points!"

Sir Nicholas went swiftly down the stairs, sword in hand, and crossed the taproom in two bounds to the door. Outside in the yard was bright moonlight, and to the right the barn cast a great black shadow. Through the door came the glimmer of a lantern, and the muffled sound of movement.

Beauvallet gave his head a little shake, as though to cast off the lingering fumes of the wine he had drunk, and went forward, cat-like, over the cobbles.

Inside the barn the Frenchman was hurriedly buckling saddle-girths. Beauvallet's mare was bridled already. A lantern stood upon the baked mud floor, and the Frenchman's cloak and hat were flung down beside it. His fingers trembled a little as he tugged at the straps; his back was turned towards the door.

There came a sound to make him jump well-nigh out of his skin, and spin round to face the door. Sir Nicholas stood there with a naked sword in his hand, laughing at him.

"Oho, my young iniquity!" said Sir Nicholas, and laughed again. "Now I think you are shent!"

For an instant the Frenchman stood at gaze, his face all twisted with fury. And Beauvallet set his sword point to the ground, and laughed at his discomfiture. Then, suddenly, the Frenchman sprang forward, tearing his sword from the scabbard, and in his leap contrived to kick over the lantern, and put out its frail light. Sir Nicholas stood in the shaft of moonlight in the open doorway, but all else in the barn was pitch dark.

Beauvallet's sword flashed out before him; he sprang lightly to one side, felt a blade thrust within a hair's breadth of his shoulder, and lunged swiftly forward. His point went home; there was a choked gurgle, the clatter of a sword falling to earth, and a dull thud.

Beauvallet swore beneath his breath, and stood listening, back against the wall, with a shortened sword. Only the uneasy snorting and pawing of the horses broke the silence. He moved forward cautiously, and stumbled against something that lay on the ground at his feet. "God's Body, have I killed the boy?" he muttered, and bent over the still figure.

Across the yard Joshua came running at full-tilt, and bounded into the barn. " 'Swounds! What's here? Master? Sir Nicholas!"

"A plague on your screechings! Help me with this carcass."

"What, dead?" gasped Joshua, feeling in the darkness.

"I know not." Sir Nicholas spoke curtly. "Take you his legs, and help me to bear him out. So!"

They carried their burden out into the moonlight, and laid it down on the cobbles. Beauvallet knelt, and stripped open the elegant doublet, feeling for the heart. A clean-edged wound was there, deep and true.

"Peste, I thrust better than I knew," Beauvallet muttered. "The devil! But the young traitor sought to murder me. What's this?"

A silken packet was in his hand, attached to a riband about the dead man's neck.

"Open," said Joshua, shivering. "Perchance you might learn his name."

"What should that benefit me, fool?" But Sir Nicholas took the packet, and thrust it into his doublet. "This is to ruin all. We must bury him, Joshua, and that speedily. No noise mind!"

"Bury! With your sword?" Joshua said. "The evil hour! Nay, wait! As I remember there are tools within the barn."

An hour later, the grim work done, Sir Nicholas, thoroughly sobered now, came softly back to the inn. He was frowning a little. This was an ill happening, and had gone otherwise than he had planned. Yet who would have thought the young fool would play the traitor so? He mounted silently to his chamber again, and sat down on the bed, while Joshua relit the lantern.

It was set upon the chest. Beauvallet slowly wiped his sword, and returned it to its scabbard. He drew forth the packet from his breast, and slit open the silk with his dagger. Crackling sheets of paper were inside. Beauvallet bent towards the lamp. His eyes ran over the first sheet frowningly, and came to rest on the signature. A short exclamation broke from him, and he pulled the lantern nearer yet. He held a letter from the Guise to King Philip in his hand, but the bulk of it was writ in cypher.

Joshua, inquisitively hovering at hand, ventured a question. "What is it, master? Doth the writing give his name, perchance?"

Beauvallet was looking now at a fair-inscribed pass. "It seems, my Joshua," he said, "that I have slain a scion of the house of Guise."

"God mend my soul!" quoth Joshua. "Shall it serve, master? Shall we turn it to good account?"

"Since these purport to be papers writ to his Catholic Majesty it seems we may turn it to very good account," Sir Nicholas said, poring over the first paper again. "Now, I have some knowledge of cyphers, as I believe. . . ." He looked up. "Get you to bed, rogue, get you to bed!"

An hour later Joshua, waking as he turned on his bed, saw Sir Nicholas seated still by the chest, with a soaked cloth bound about a head which Joshua judged had good cause to ache, and his brows close-knit over the papers. Joshua closed his eyes again, and sank back into slumber. He woke again to broad daylight. Sir Nicholas lay asleep in the big bed; there was no sign of the papers. Joshua dressed softly, and stole away downstairs. He found there a perplexed landlord who was loud in abuse of the young gentleman who had stolen away in the night without paying his shot. Joshua's casual interest in this was well acted. He asked the proper questions, exclaimed piously at such behaviour, and thought privately of the night's work.

In a little while the voice of Sir Nicholas was heard, calling for his man. Joshua skipped upstairs with a tray bearing his master's breakfast.

Sir Nicholas was wide awake, and as brisk as though he had not sat up through the night puzzling over a cypher. His eyes were bright and unclouded; only a damp cloth on the floor bore witness of the night's labours.

Joshua set down a tray, and shook out a clean shirt for Sir Nicholas. "Look you, master, there is a deal of pother below, on account of we-know-what. Where is the man gone? why is he gone? I do not presume to answer, me, but I consider it meet we should make all speed over the Frontier."

"Just as soon as I have broken my fast," said Beauvallet. "See that door well-shut. Now, rogue, give ear a minute." He drank some wine, and broke off a piece of rye bread. "I am become overnight the Chevalier Claude de Guise, do ye mark me?"

"Well, master. I said we might turn all to good account."

"The best. I don't fathom all these papers, and one is sealed fast. But enough to serve, I judge. Matters too high

for you, but ye may know that we travel henceforth as a
secret messenger from the Guise to King Philip. Hey, but
I have meat for Walsingham in this!" He stretched, and
reached out a hand for his shirt. "A great venture, rogue—
the greatest I have been on."

"Like to end in nasty wise," Joshua grumbled. "Secret
messengers, forsooth! Ay, we shall be so secret there's none
will hear of us again."

"An ill jest. This as mad a quest as I have ever known.
Does your courage fail? Turn back then, you have still
time."

Joshua threw out his chest. "Ho, pretty speaking! I
follow to the end. Moreover, it has been foretold that I
shall die in my bed. What have I to fear?"

"On then," said Sir Nicholas, and laughed. "On, and
reck not!"

ᴖᐰ Chapter IX ᐳᴖ

IT was an easy matter to cross the Frontier, armed with
the Chevalier de Guise's credentials. From as much of the
despatch to Philip as he could read, or was not sealed,
Beauvallet had learned that the youthful Frenchman was
some sort of a cousin to the Duc de Guise, and it seemed
probable from so particular a mention of him that he had
not been employed on an errand into Spain before.
Beauvallet did not doubt that he could brave out the
imposture, but he knew that he carried his life in his
hand. One evil chance, one Frenchman in Madrid to
whom the Chevalier was known, and he might expect to
find himself sped. The knowledge made him set his horse
caracolling on the road, never so keenly enjoying life as
when he stood in danger of losing it. He tossed his sword
up in the air, and caught it deftly as it fell. The sunlight
glinted all along the shimmering blade. Between eight
crowns the name Andrea Ferrara was inscribed, and

beneath it a pungent motto:—*My bite is sure*. "A sword
and my wits against all Spain!" sang out Beauvallet, and
whistled a catch between his teeth. Then he fell to thinking
of her whom he went to seek, and the leagues passed
uncounted.

There was time enough for meditation during these long
days upon the road, for it took them close on two weeks
to come within sight of Madrid, a white town perched on a
spur above a vast plateau, looking north over many windy
leagues to the Guadarrama Mountains, and south to the
grand chain that guarded Toledo.

The roads called forth curses from Joshua, struggling
with the led sumpter. Years ago he had journeyed into
Spain with Beauvallet, but he protested that he had forgotten long since how incomparably bad were the roads.
He rode to the rear, and observed all with bright, calculat-
ing eyes. "Naught but sheep!" he grunted. "Enough to
ravage the land. God's Life, but this is a poor country!
Ruin stares us in the face, master, from all sides. Here are
no crops, no snug farmers. Naught but bare rocks, and
dust. And sheep—I forget the sheep, which you would
have thought hardly possible. Why, call you this a road?
Ho, we Englishmen can still teach the Spaniards some few
matters, it seems!"

"Set a guard on that tongue of yours," Beauvallet said
sharply. "Let me hear no talk of Englishmen. Ay, this is a
waste country. Now, how might a runner go at speed, to
the Frontier, let us say?"

"He might not, master, on these roads without foundering. It's a land of the Dark Ages, one would say. Bethink
you of the fair manor my lord has built him in Alreston,
and look on these grim fortresses!" He spoke of a gloomy
castle seen some miles back along the road, and shud-
dered. "Nay, I like not this land. It frowns, master! Mark
what I say, it frowns!"

Over the Guadarrama Mountains they climbed, and
dropped on to the great, parched plateau. They rode league
upon weary league, and at last saw Madrid ahead, and
came to it in the cold of the evening. Joshua shivered on
his horse, and muttered against a climate so extreme. He
was roasted by day, he swore, but when evening fell

Arctic winds arose that were like to lay him low of a
fever.

Beauvallet knew Madrid of old, but found it grown
since his day. He made his way to the inn of the Rising
Sun, lying some paces off the Puerta del Sol. It was not
necessary to caution Joshua again. That wiry individual
ceased complaining as they climbed the steep streets into
the heart of the town, and might be trusted to carry all off
with a bold front. Beauvallet had no fear of unwitting
betrayal from him. French he spoke fluently, if roughly,
and Spanish very fairly. He was not likely to slip into his
own tongue through inability to find words in a foreign
language.

Sir Nicholas bespoke a private room at the inn, and
supped there that evening, waited on by Joshua. "Since it
is very certain that the French Ambassador is not privy to
this correspondence I carry, you will say, Joshua, that I
am travelling for my pleasure. You know naught of secret
documents."

"Master, what will you do with these papers?" Joshua
asked uneasily.

The corners of Sir Nicholas' mouth lifted under the trim
moustachio. "Why, present them to his Catholic Majesty!
What else?"

" 'Sdeath, sir, will you go into the lion's den?" quaked
Joshua.

"I know of only one lion, sirrah, and that one is not to
be found in Spain!" Beauvallet said. "I am bound on the
morrow for the Alcazar. Lay me out a rich suit of the
French cut." He brought out the stolen papers from his
bosom, and laid them on the table. "And stitch me these
safe in a length of silk." His eyes twinkled. "What, do you
tremble still? Cross yourself, and say Jesu! It's in the part."

Access to the Alcazar was not found to be so easy as
access to any of Queen Elizabeth's palaces. There was a
long delay, many questions and the pseudo-Chevalier's
credentials were taken from him while he was left to cool
his heels in the great austere hall.

He sat down on a carved chair of cypress wood, and
looked about him with interest. There was much sombre
marble, much rich brocade, and hangings of Flanders

tapestry depicting the martyrdoms of various saints. A statue in bronze stood at the foot of the wide stairway; there were Turkey carpets on the floor, strange sight to an English eye, so that footsteps fell muffled. Certain, there was no sound in the Alcazar. Lackeys stood graven on either side the great door; sundry personages passed across the hall from time to time, but they spoke no word. There was a courtier, all in silk and velvet; a soberly clad individual whom Beauvallet took to be a secretary; a priest of the Dominican order with his cowl shading his face, and his hands hidden in the wide sleeves of his habit; an elderly man who looked curiously at Beauvallet; an officer of the guard, a hurrying woman who might be a maid of honour.

It was oppressive in the lofty hall; the very hush of the place might have preyed on nerves less hardy than Beauvallet's. Here, to an Englishman, was a place of grim foreboding, of lurking terror. It did not need the sight of that dark priest to conjure up hideous pictures to the mind.

But Sir Nicholas saw no hideous pictures, and his pulse beat as steadily as ever. A false step, and he would never again see England: with a kind of brazen dare-devilry he was confident there would be no false step. In Paris, a month ago, the Marquis de Belrémy had said aghast:— *"Mon Dieu, quel sangfroid!"* Could he have set eyes on his kinsman now he would have been still more aghast, and might have repeated with even more conviction, that Nicholas would sit jesting in hell's mouth itself.

After a full half-hour's wait the lackey came back with a long-gowned, close-shaven secretary who looked keenly at Beauvallet. "You are the Chevalier de Guise?" he asked in French.

Sir Nicholas was swinging his golden pomander. He did not think, from his knowledge of them, that the Guise would rise out of the seats for a mere scrivener. Gravely he bowed his head.

"You have letters for his Majesty?" pursued the secretary.

Again Beauvallet bowed, and knew that he was creating a good impression. Privately he thought: "Our sovereign

keeps men of better blood than this about her, God wot!"
He was very quick to nose out the parvenu.

The secretary bowed in his turn, and held out his hand.
"I will deliver them to his Majesty, señor."

At that Beauvallet raised his black brows delicately.
Maybe he thought it more in the part, maybe it was the
audacity of the man, or a mere curiosity to see this
far-famed Philip, but he said gently: "My orders, señor,
are to deliver these letters into his Majesty's own
hands."

The secretary bowed again. "All goes very well,"
thought Beauvallet, watching him like a lynx, in spite of
his careless demeanour.

"Follow me, señor, if you please," said the secretary,
and led the way up the stairs to a long gallery above.

Down a labyrinth of corridors they seemed to walk,
until they came to a curtained doorway. Beauvallet went
through into a severely furnished chamber, and was left
there to wait again.

More martyrdoms hung on the walls. Sir Nicholas grim-
aced at them, and deplored his Catholic Majesty's taste.
Another half-hour passed; King Philip was in no hurry, it
seemed. Sir Nicholas looked out of the window on to a
paved court, and yawned from time to time.

Back came the secretary at last. "His Majesty will
receive you, señor," he said, and gave back the Chevalier's
credentials into his keeping. "This way, if you please." He
held back the curtain for Beauvallet to pass out, and led
him across the corridor to double doors. These opened at
his scratch upon the solid panels; Sir Nicholas found
himself in an ante-chamber where two men sat writing at
a table, and two guards stood beside the doors. He followed the secretary across the room to a curtained archway; the curtain was swung back by a guard there, and
the secretary went through. "The Chevalier de Guise,
sire," he said, bowing very low, and drew back a little
against the wall.

Sir Nicholas came coolly in, paused a moment as the
curtain fell back into place behind him, and in one swift
glance noted the contents of this bare, cell-like apartment.
There was little enough to note. A chest, an escritoire, a

priest by the window, a table in the middle of the room, and behind it, seated in a high-backed chair with arms, with his foot upon a velvet stool, a pallid man with sparse yellow locks, flecked with grey; and a yellow beard, scant as his meagre thatch; and hooded eyes, sombre and vulturine under the puckered lids.

Sir Nicholas sank gracefully down on to his knee; the plumes in his hat swept the ground before him. "God's my life!" was his irrepressible thought. "The two of us in one small room, and he does not know it!"

"The Chevalier de Guise," repeated Philip in a slow, harsh voice. "We bid you welcome, señor."

But there was no kindliness in the expressionless tone; nor any life in those dull eyes. "There would be less kindliness if he knew how he bade Nick Beauvallet welcome," thought Sir Nicholas, as he rose to his feet.

Philip, sitting so still in his chair, seemed to study him for a moment. It was tense, that moment, fraught with peril. Sir Nicholas stood calmly under the scrutiny; they were not to know how ready to be out was the sword at his side. The moment passed. "You have letters for us," said the slow voice.

Beauvallet brought the silken packet out from the breast of his doublet, came to the table, knelt again, and so offered it.

The King's hand touched his as he took the packet; the fingers felt cold and slightly damp. He gave the packet to the secretary, and made a movement to Beauvallet to rise. "Your first visit to Spain, señor?"

"My first, sire."

Philip inclined his head. The secretary had slit the silken wrapper, and now spread crackling sheets before his master. Philip's eyes travelled slowly over the first page, but never changed in their lack-lustre expression. "I see you are cousin to the Duc de Guise, señor," he remarked, and pushed the sheets away from him on the table's polished surface. "We will look over these matters, and have an answer for you in a week or so." Haste was not a word in his Majesty's vocabulary. He spoke to the secretary. "Vasquez, if Don Diaz de Losa is in the palace you will send to fetch him." He brought his gaze back to

Beauvallet. "Don Diaz will look to your entertainment, señor. Your lodging?"

Beauvallet gave the name of his inn. Philip seemed to consider it. "Yes, it is best," he said. "You are not here officially."

"I give out, sire, that I am travelling for my pleasure."

"That is well," said Philip. "You will contrive to pass the time pleasantly, I trust. Madrid has much to show."

"I have promised myself a ride out to see the great Escorial, sire," said Sir Nicholas, assuming reverential tones.

Some spark of life entered Philip's eyes, enthusiasm into his dead voice. He began to talk of his vast palace, nearing its completion, he said. He talked as one absorbed in his theme, as in a holy matter, and was still talking when Matteo de Vasquez came back into the room. He was accompanied by a stately gentleman of middle years, dressed very magnificently, in contrast to the black-garbed King.

The brief enthusiasm left Philip. He presented Don Diaz de Losa, and consigned the Chevalier to his care. In the wake of this nobleman Beauvallet bowed himself out of the King's cabinet.

It seemed that Don Diaz was in the King's confidence, for he asked none but the most trivial questions. He had a grave Castilian courtesy, and begged that the Chevalier would call on him for any needs he might have. He escorted him through the corridors to a gallery, where a fair sprinking of gentlemen were gathered, and presented him punctiliously to all who were present. The Chevalier was a gentleman from the French Court, travelling to enlarge his knowledge of the world. Thus Beauvallet was sponsored into society. Don Diaz requested his company at a party at his house that evening, Beauvallet accepted without hesitation. He stayed some while in the gallery talking to these grandees of Spain, and presently took his leave. Don Diaz went with him to the hall, and they parted with great politeness.

Joshua was anxiously awaiting his master's return, and heaved a large sigh of relief upon seeing him come in. Sir

Nicholas flung himself into a chair. "God's Death, what a court!" he said. Then he began to laugh. "What a king! what a graven king! If one had but whispered *El Beauvallet* in his ear! Only to see him start!"

"God forbid!" said Joshua devoutly. "Hey, but this likes me not at all!" He looked anxiously. "How long do we remain, master?"

"Who knows? What a tale for Drake! God send I win through to tell it him!"

"God send so indeed, sir," said Joshua glumly.

"Comfort you, knave: in three short weeks the *Venture* will cruise off that smuggling port we wot of, and every night she will creep in towards the coast, and watch for my signal."

"What use if you be clapped up?" said Joshua rather tartly.

"I shall win free, don't doubt it. Hearken, my man, a moment! This plot grows thicker still, and there are pitfalls. If I should fall into one . . ." He paused, and sniffed at his pomander, eyes narrowed and meditative. "Ay. If I be taken, Joshua, remove on the instant from this place, with all my traps. Go look for an obscure tavern against our needs. I shall then know where to find you. When you hear of my death—or if I come not inside ten days—make all speed to that port, and signal with a lantern after dark, as you know how. That's in case of need. Trust yet a while in Beauvallet's luck. Go now, and nose me out the house of Don Diaz de Losa. I visit there this evening. If you can get news of Don Manuel de Rada, call me your debtor."

"A plague on all women!" Joshua said. But he said it on the other side of the door.

Don Diaz de Losa's apartments were crowded when Beauvallet arrived that evening. There was dicing going forward in one room, where a great many young caballeros were gathered, but the function seemed to have more the nature of a cold reception. Magnificent gentlemen strolled from group to group; there were ladies amongst them, not so discreet as had been the ladies of Spain in a bygone age. Serving men in the de Losa livery, each one bearing his master's cognizance offered refreshments on heavy silver trays to the guests. There was wine in glasses of Venetian ware: Valdepeñas from Morena, red wine of Vinaroz and Benicarlo; Manzanilla, lightest of sherris-wine from San Lucar. With these went sweetmeats and fruit: Austrian pomegranates and grapes from Malaga, but other refreshment there was none. To an English taste this might seem meagre, to be sure, in the face of so much ostentatious display. Don Diaz's house had carpets to tread upon, chairs lined with cut velvet, candelabras of wrought silver, a Toledo clock of rare design, hangings of silk and tapestry, but it did not seem to be the Spanish custom to entertain guests with banquets, as would have been done in kindlier England.

There was an oppressive grandeur over all, as though each man were mindful of his high degree, and the canons of polite behaviour. No voice was raised light-heartedly; all talk was measured and punctilious, so that Beauvallet's laugh sounded strangely in this sedate gathering, and men turned their heads to see whence came the care-free sound.

It had been provoked by a gentleman from Andalusia, to whom Don Diaz had made the Chevalier known. This Southerner had a gaiety lacking in the grave Castilians, or the proud Aragonese, and had cracked some joke for the Chevalier's delectation. They stood chatting easily enough, so easily that Don Juan was moved to congratulate the Chevalier on the excellence of his Spanish. No doubt the señor had been in Spain before, or had at least Spanish friends?

Beauvallet owned to a Spanish friend, and said that this one had enjoyed the acquaintance of Don Manuel de Rada y Sylva. Had he the name aright?

"Ah, the late Governor of Santiago!" Don Juan said, and shook his head.

The golden pomander was held to the Chevalier's nose. Over it his eyes were watchful. "I had thought to present myself to him," Beauvallet said.

"You have not heard, señor: Don Manuel is dead these three months. A strange tale!"

"Dead!" Beauvallet said. "How is that?"

"The West Indian climate, señor. Treacherous! ah, but treacherous! But there was more to it: a tale to take one's breath away!"

"But let me hear it, señor, of your kindness!"

The Southerner spread out his hands. "Have you in France heard of a certain English pirate? One named El Beauvallet?"

"Assuredly!" Sir Nicholas' eyes danced. "Who has not heard of him? The scourge of Spain I have heard him called. Am I right?"

"Very right, señor. Alas! They say the man uses witch-craft." Don Juan crossed himself, and was swiftly imitated. Sir Nicholas' black lashes hid the laughter in his down-cast eyes. When he raised them again they were grave, if you could discount the merriness that must always lurk at the back of them. Don Juan, absorbed in his tale, did not notice it. "He sacked and sank the ship that bore Don Manuel home, and—you will scarce credit it—took Don Manuel and his daughter aboard his own vessel."

"So!" Beauvallet raised politely surprised eyebrows. "But wherefor?"

"Who shall say, señor? A mad whim one would sup-pose, for one can hardly credit such a man with chivalrous intent. They say he is mad, who have had traffic with him. But he had the effrontery, señor, to put into a port of Spain, and there to set Don Manuel ashore!"

"You astonish me, señor," said Sir Nicholas. "I suppose he bore off the daughter to England, this famous free-booter?"

"One might have expected it, but no. Dona Dominica took no hurt, though her father died soon after his land-ing. She is under the guardianship of her good aunt, Dona Beatrice de Carvalho."

"Thank you for that information," thought Sir Nich-olas, and made a mental note of the name. Aloud he said: "But this is a wonder that you recount, señor! To escape unhurt from the clutches of so desperate a villain as this Beauvallet!" His shoulders shook ever so slightly.

A gentleman standing close to them turned his head and looked keenly. He bowed to Don Juan, and again to the Chevalier. "Your pardon, señor, but you spoke a certain name. Has that freebooter been taken at last?"

Don Juan made the introduction, but it was Beauvallet who answered. "Nay, nay, señor! Surely he bears a charmed life? I have heard men say so."

"As to that, we shall see, señor," said the newcomer.
"You have set eyes on him, maybe?"

"I have seen him, yes," Sir Nicholas answered. The
long fingers that swung the pomander gently to and fro
never quivered. "In Paris, where he sometimes visits."

Don Juan displayed a lively curiosity. "Is it so indeed?
And is he as mad as they say? They tell us, who have had
dealings with him, that he is a man with black hair who
laughs."

White teeth gleamed for a moment. "Yes, he laughs,
señor," said Sir Nicholas. A chuckle came, they little knew
how audacious. "I dare swear if he stood in this room
surrounded by his enemies at this moment, he would still
laugh. It is a habit with him."

"One hardly credits it, señor," the stately gentleman
replied. "There would very soon be an end to his laughter." He bowed slightly, and passed on.

Don Diaz came up at that moment, and laid his hand
on Beauvallet's arm. "I have been searching for you,
Chevalier. I would present you to a countryman of yours:
your ambassador, M. de Lauvinière."

Not by the flicker of an eyelash did Beauvallet betray
how unwelcome this courtesy was to him. Danger
crouched before him; he went smiling towards it: Beauvallet's way!

Don Diaz led him across the room, and spoke in a soft
undertone. "It is judged best, señor, that no secret should
be made of your visit to Madrid. M. de Lauvinière might
then suspect. I need not warn you to be on your guard
with him. There he stands, near the door."

The Frenchman was a man with grey hair and a hook
nose. His eyes were deep-set, and he looked piercingly.
Upon Don Diaz's presentation of the Chevalier he bowed,
and looked with a keenness that probed deep. "A cousin
of the Duc de Guise?" he said. "I do not think . . ." He
frowned a little, and his eyes never wavered from
Beauvallet's face. "But I claim the very slightest acquaintance with the Guises."

Therein lay a certain safeguard, thought Beauvallet. It
was not to be expected that a member of the Court party
would be on terms of friendship with the great Guise
family.

"I am a distant cousin of the Duc's, monsieur," said Sir Nicholas.

"So?" De Lauvinière looked still more searchingly. "Of what branch of the family, monsieur, if one may ask?"

It would not do to hesitate. "Of the junior branch, monsieur. The Duc is my cousin in the second degree."

"I have heard of you, monsieur," the ambassador said. "I had thought you were a younger man. Do you make a long stay in Madrid?"

"Why no, monsieur, I believe not. I have a desire to visit Sevilla and Toledo."

"Ah yes, you should certainly journey south," nodded de Lauvinière.

A lady came up on the arm of her husband to claim his attention. Beauvallet drew back thankfully. Had he been vouchsafed a glimpse of a postscript added to de Lauvinière's letter home, and despatched upon the morrow, it might have shaken his nerve.

"I should be glad," wrote his excellency, *"if you would discover what age man is the Chevalier Claude de Guise, cousin to the present Duc. Let me have what news you can hear of him, in especial of what like he is, of what height, and of what lineaments. Your assured friend, Henri de Lauvinière."*

ᴄ⟨ Chapter X ⟩ᴄ

In bed next morning Sir Nicholas sipped a cup of chocolate and gave ear to his servant. Joshua had the news he wanted, and imparted it after his own fashion as he laid out his master's dress. A bottle of wine with the landlord of the Rising Sun had loosened a tongue that dealt much in gossip. Who so clever as Joshua Dimmock at finding out information? Let Sir Nicholas be at ease: the lady was found.

"In the guardianship of her aunt. I know," Sir Nicholas said.

Joshua was put out. "Ay, so it is, and Don Manuel dead these three months. The lady inherits all—all!"

"That does not concern us," said Beauvallet. "She cannot carry her lands to England."

"True, master, very true. But here is somewhat you may not have heard. Her espousals are talked of."

Sir Nicholas yawned. "They will be more talked of yet," said he.

"Master, the tale runs that she will wed her cousin, one Diego de Carvalho."

"So-so!" said Beauvallet. "Early days to talk of betrothals yet. Cousin, eh? That means a dispensation, or I'm much at fault."

"You mistake me, sir: nothing is yet done. These are rumours." He laid a finger against his nose. "This gives to think, master. I learn that the Carvalhos are as poor as may be. Nothing to gape at there, you say. True; there seem few enough nobles here with coins to rub together. Curious, curious! And yet so much pomp! We do not use that way in England. Under my breath I say it; have no fear of me. Perpend then, master. What if this aunt—her name is Beatrice, for your better information—hath made a little plot to possess herself of all this wealth?"

"Very possible," nodded Sir Nicholas. "And a bribe to the Church to hasten the dispensation."

"Certain, I think, master. These priests! If what one hears be true!"

"What do you learn of Don Diego?" demanded Sir Nicholas.

"Little to the point, sir. A creature of no weight, as it seems to me. These Spanish caballeros! Foh, match me a young Englishman, say I! Well, he is prodigal: all young men are so. It's to say nothing. He does what all springalds do in ruffling it about the town. For the rest I learn that he is accounted well-looking, rides comely, knows how to handle a bilbo, hath elegant accomplishments by the score. You nose out a fop. I do not gainsay it, for so it appears to me. He need not concern us."

"He might concern us very nearly," said Sir Nicholas. "What else? Is the father of this fine sprig alive?"

"Surely, master, but here again I would say, a creature of no account. As I read our host's talk—in his cups he waxes a thought garrulous. Strange sight in one so prim!— he lies beneath his good lady's thumb." He made a descriptive gesture. "So! By all I can understand that is a lady of odd manners, sir. You would say an original. We shall doubtless know more anon. They have estates somewhere to the north of Burgos, as I apprehend, but at this present, sir, they stay, all four, at their house in Madrid. This I have found, off the Plaza de Oriente. While you slept, master, I have been about the town a little. Some fine buildings, to be sure, and a quantity of Popish Churches—enough to turn a man's stomach. The house of the Carvalho you may find easily. There is a wall grown with a vine at the back, and, as I judge, a garden upon the inner side." He rolled a knowing eye. "Thought I, we may find a use for that. Further, master, there is to be a ball given this day week at that house, in honour of our Diego's birthday. This is much talked of, for it seems these Spaniards do not give them often. All the world will be there."

"Then so must I," said Beauvallet, and sprang out of bed. "Now how to make the acquaintance of the Carvalhos?"

"Walk on the Mentidero, master," Joshua advised. "It is still the haunt of your Court gallant, as I hear. You might compare it with Duke Humphrey's Walk at home— to its disadvantage, mark you!"

"A happy thought," said Beauvallet, pulling on his netherstocks. "I might perchance come up with my friend of last night."

The Mentidero was a raised walk along the wall of the Church of San Felipe el Real, which stood at the entrance to the Calle Mayor. Here came the wits of the day, and the courtiers, to exchange gossip, to talk the latest scandal, to exhibit a new fashion in cloaks, or a new way of tying a garter. Under it were a score of little booths, where one might buy such trifles as a pair of embroidered gloves for a lady, a loveknot, or an ouch of wrought silver. Across the Calle Mayor lay the Oñate Palace, with the rough side-walk beneath where painters showed their pictures to attract the Court. The market lay in the centre of the Calle; there were water-carriers gathered there, and the scene was busy and noisy. Round about were shops, and here and there a coffee-house, where one might meet one's cronies.

The gentleman from Andalusia was found upon the Mentidero, and professed himself charmed to meet the Chevalier again. Sir Nicholas joined him in his strolling up and down, and came at length to his business with him. In default of Don Manuel, whom he had hoped to meet, he would desire to present himself to Don Manuel's worthy brother-in-law. Yet he was uncertain how this project might be effected, since he could claim no acquaintance with the Carvalhos.

The matter was very easily arranged. Don Juan de Aranda would himself present the Chevalier any time he should choose. He might meet Don Diego de Carvalho this very morning, if he wished, since Don Diego was abroad, after his usual custom, upon the Mentidero. They had passed him a while back, talking to de Lara and young Vasquez.

They turned, therefore, and began to walk slowly back the way they had come.

"I understand Don Diego to be a very proper caballero," Beauvallet remarked. "The only offspring, I believe?"

"True, señor." Don Juan was a little reticent, and it struck Beauvallet that he had no great admiration for Don Diego. Presently he nodded, and spoke again. "There is Don Diego, señor: the smaller of the two."

A slight young gentleman was lounging gracefully ahead of them, exchanging languid conversation with another, just as elegant. Don Diego was very dark, with black brows, almost meeting over the bridge of his nose, and full, curved lips. He wore a jewel in the lobe of his left ear, was very generously scented with musk, and twirled a rose between one very white finger and thumb. A flat velvet hat with a plume in it was set on his curled head at an angle; his ruff was large and edged with lace, and his short cloak was lined with carnation silk.

Sir Nicholas looked, and said afterwards that he had an

instant itching in his toe. Be that as it may, he went forward very pleasantly, and upon Don Juan's introduction, made his best bow.

The bow was returned. As Don Diego straightened his back he found a pair of very bright blue eyes looking into his. The two men seemed to measure each other; it is probable that each conceived an instant dislike for the other, but each hid the uncharitable emotion.

"The Chevalier is travelling amongst us for his pleasure," said Don Juan. "We are all resolved to show him the true Spanish hospitality that he may carry a good tale of us home with him to Paris."

Don Diego smiled politely. "I hope so, señor. But the Chevalier comes at a bad season; the amusements draw to a close, and we all think of the country, just so soon as the Court moves to Valladolid." He looked at Beauvallet. "A pity you did not come a month ago, señor. There was a bull-fight might have interested you: I believe you do not have them in France. And an *auto da fé* as well. There was a great press of people," he said pensively. "One turned faint at the heat and the smell of the common people."

"Did you indeed?" said Beauvallet sarcastically. For the life of him he could not control that disdainful curl of the lip. "What I have missed!"

"Yes, I fear we shall see no more such sights yet a while," said Don Diego regretfully. His wandering gaze came back to Beauvallet. "I regret I was not at de Losa's house last night, where I was told I might have had the felicity of meeting you." He bowed again.

"My loss, señor," said Sir Nicholas. "I looked for Don Manuel de Rada, known to me through hearsay, and—alas!—heard the sad news of his death."

"Alas indeed," Don Diego answered. But it did not seem to Beauvallet that this sentiment came from the heart.

"I shall do myself the honour of waiting upon your father, señor," said Beauvallet.

"My father will count himself honoured, señor. Do you stay long in Madrid?"

"Some few weeks, perhaps. No more, I believe. But I

detain you." He stepped back, doffed his cap again, and
bowed. "I shall hope to see more of you, señor."

"The pleasure will be mine, señor," returned Don Diego.

On that they parted. Later in the day Sir Nicholas
sought out his sponsor, Don Diaz de Losa, and had no
difficulty in getting from him a letter of introduction to
Don Rodriguez de Carvalho.

"All goes merrily," he said to himself, as he walked
back to the Rising Sun. "Enough for one day, I think.
Patience, Nick!"

Upon the morrow he made his way to the Casa Carvalho, and was fortunate enough to find Don Rodriguez at
home. If he had hoped to see Dominica he was disappointed. No glimpse of her could be obtained, though he
sharply scrutinised the windows that gave on to the *patio*
as he crossed it behind the lackey.

He was ushered into a dusky library that looked out on
to the walled garden Joshua had discovered. Volumes in
tooled leather lined the room; there were several chairs of
walnut, tortuously carved, a Catalan chest, with flat pilasters upon its front and sides, and an escabeau over against
the window.

Don Rodriguez came in presently with de Losa's letter
open in his hand. He was a lean man of middle age, with
eyes rather too close-set to be trusted, Beauvallet thought.
They shifted here and there, never resting for long on any
one object. His mouth bore some resemblance to his son's,
but there was weakness in the lines about it, and a kind of
petulant uncertainty in the slightly pouting underlip.

He received the Chevalier kindly, and said a great deal
that was proper on the sad subject of his brother-in-law's
death. His sighs were gusty, he shook his head, cast down
his eyes to the floor, and meandered on in his talk of the
exigencies of the West Indian climate.

Beauvallet was becoming impatient of this tedious exchange of futilities when they were interrupted by a sound
on the gravel walk outside. The long window was dark-
ened, and there was the gentle hush of a lady's skirts.

Sir Nicholas turned quickly, but the lady who stood
looking in was not Dominica. She was a large woman,

built on flowing lines, and dressed very richly in an embroidered gown of purple mochado. Her hair was extravagantly coiffed, her farthingale brushed the window-frame on either side as she came through, and her ruff stood up high behind her head. She was certainly handsome, and must have been lovely before increasing years made her stout. Her mouth was faintly smiling, and her eyes, almond-shaped under weary eyelids, smiled too. The hinted smile betokened a sort of compassionate amusement, as though the lady looked cynically upon her world, and found it foolish. She moved as one who would never hurry, and in spite of her ungainly farthingale she walked with a certain lazy grace.

"Ah, Chevalier! My wife—Dona Beatrice," Don Rodriguez said. He addressed the lady with a hint of fluster in his voice as though he stood in lively awe of her. "My love, permit me to present to you a noble stranger to Madrid—M. le Chevalier de Guise."

The disillusioned eyes ran over Sir Nicholas; the smile seemed to deepen. Dona Beatrice held out a passive hand, and appeared to approve Beauvallet as he bent over it. Her voice was as languid as her carriage. "A Frenchman," she remarked. "I had ever a kindness for a Frenchman. Now, what do you make here, Chevalier?"

"Nothing but my pleasure, señora."

It seemed an effort to her to raise her brows. "Do you find pleasure in Madrid?" she inquired. She went to a chair and sank into it, and began slowly to fan herself. "I find it unbearably fatiguing."

"Why, señora, I find much pleasure here," Beauvallet answered.

"You are young," she said, in extenuation. "And French. So much vigour! So much enthusiasm!"

"Plenty of food for enthusiasm in Madrid, madam," said Sir Nicholas politely.

"Ah! But when you attain to my years, señor, you will realize that there is nothing in the world to feed enthusiasm."

"I shall hope to preserve my illusions, madame."

"It is far better to have none," drawled the lady.

Don Rodriguez, hovering solicitously about his spouse,

smiled deprecatingly. He found himself in constant need
to temper her oddities by this fidgetty, excusing smile.

"Let us talk in your own tongue, Chevalier. I speak it
very indifferently, but it is a polite language." She spoke it
very well.

"My love, the Chevalier had hoped to find your poor
brother. We have been speaking of his sad death."

She answered without taking the trouble to look at him.
"Why sad, señor? One must hope he has found repose. So
you were acquainted with my brother, Chevalier?"

"No madame, but I knew a friend of his once, and I
had hoped to present myself to his notice upon that score."

"You would not have found him at all entertaining,"
said Dona Beatrice. "It is far better to know me."

Sir Nicholas bowed. "I am sure of it, madame," he
said, and was inclined to think he spoke sooth.

"I must have you come to my ball on Friday evening,"
she announced. "It will be very painstaking and very dull.
You shall solace my boredom. I suppose you must meet
my son." She sighed and addressed Don Rodriguez.
"Señor, Don Diego is somewhere at hand. Pray send for
him."

"I have already had that pleasure, madame. I met your
son upon the Mentidero yesterday."

"Ah, then you will not want to see him again," she
said, as though she perfectly understood. "You need not
send, señor."

Sir Nicholas bit his lip. "On the contrary, I shall be
charmed, madame."

Her eyelids lifted for a moment. He thought he had
never seen eyes so curiously cold, so cynical, yet so good-
humoured. "Señor, send for Don Diego," she sighed.

In a minute or two Don Diego came in, and with him
the scent of musk. He was very punctilious in his manner
towards Sir Nicholas, and while the two men spoke together his mother lay back in her chair watching them
with her omniscient smile.

"You will see the Chevalier at your ball, my son," she
said. "My dear Chevalier, how remiss I am! I did not tell
you that it is in my son's honour. His anniversary. I forget
which, but no doubt he will tell you."

"It can be of no interest to the Chevalier, señora," said Don Diego, annoyed.

"I shall hope to have the felicity of meeting your niece, madame," said Beauvallet. "Or perhaps she does not go into public yet?"

Don Diego looked cross; Dona Beatrice continued to fan herself. "She will be present," she said placidly.

It struck Beauvallet that both father and son looked sharply at her, but she gave no sign. He rose to take his leave, kissed her hand, and was ushered forth.

When the door had closed behind him Don Diego gave a pettish shrug of the shoulder, and flung over to the window. "Why must you invite him for Friday?" he asked. "Are you so enamoured of him? He walks abroad as though he had bought Madrid."

"I thought he might amuse me," his mother replied. "A very personable man. It is most entertaining to see you at such a disadvantage, my son."

Don Rodriguez expostulated at this. "My love, how can you say so? Diego is a proper caballero—the properest in Madrid, I dare swear. His air, his carriage——"

"Very exquisite, señor. I have never seen him otherwise, and I fear I never shall."

"I do not profess to understand what you would be at, señora," said Don Diego, with a half-laugh.

She got up out of her chair. "How should you? You should live in a painting, Diego; a painting of soft lines and graceful attitudes. I doubt the Chevalier would ever stay still in it." She went out, chuckling to herself.

Father and son looked at each other. "Your mother has a—has an odd twist in her humour," said Don Rodriguez weakly.

"My mother, señor," said Don Diego tartly, "likes to be thought enigmatic. She said that Dominica would be present, but will she?" He opened the little comfit box that he carried, and put a sweetmeat into his mouth. "If she consents it will be for the first time."

"Leave her to your mother. She—she is a very remarkable woman, Diego."

"Likewise is my cousin a very remarkable self-willed chit," said Don Diego. He licked his fingers and shut up the box. "She is as cold as ice," he said impatiently. "Bewitched. A scornful piece that wants schooling."

"Bethink you, it is very soon after Don Manuel's death for her to be thinking of bridals," Don Rodriguez said excusingly. "You would maybe do well to deal gently."

"Do I not deal gently?" The sneer was clearly marked now. "And while I stay supplicating she but grows the colder, and every caballero in the town is eager to hazard his luck. She is like to be off with another if this continues. Or her uncle de Tobar will take a hand in the game, and try to get her for that overgrown fool, Miguel. Oh yes, she hinted that she might write to him! A vixen!"

Don Rodriguez murmured a vague expostulation. "I don't think it, I don't think it. She has no mind to wed yet, and your mother hath an eye on her. Belike you do not go well to work with her."

"I will use her more hardly if this coldness endures," said Don Diego. His eyes glinted, and Don Rodriguez looked away.

"Leave it to your mother," he advised feebly. "It is early yet to despair."

There was some excuse for Don Diego's ill-humour. He had a very pretty cousin, heiress to great wealth, marked clearly by heaven to be a bride for him, and the devil was in it that the girl must needs flout him. Such a thing had never happened to him before. He was at first incredulous, then sullen.

As for Dominica, there was a good reason for her refusal to fall in with the wishes of her family, had they but known it. How should a maid think of Diego who had lain trembling in Beauvallet's arms?

Since those mad days at sea much had happened in her life. She found herself bewildered, undaunted, certainly, but wary. Her father came home only to die, and he left her in the ward of his sister Beatrice. She discovered that she was wealthy, mistress of large estates in the south: a rare matrimonial prize, in effect. She was gathered under her aunt's ample wing, and knew not what to make of that lady.

There was no gainsaying Dona Beatrice's kindness, but there was more to her than mere indolent good humour.

Dominica had not been long under her roof before she discovered that her uncle, even her cousin too, were puppets, whose strings were pulled by Dona Beatrice. She suspected that she also was to be a puppet, and lifted her chin at the thought. Dona Dominica, accustomed for many years to be mistress, did not take kindly to a subordinate position, nor could she stomach the strict rule under which well-born maidens lived in Spain. She let it be seen that she had a will of her own, and tossed up her head to face wrath. None came; no one had ever seen Dona Beatrice put out. She blinked her sleepy eyelids, and continued to smile. "Charming, my dear, charming! It suits you admirably," she said.

Nonplussed, Dominica stammered: "What suits me, aunt?"

Dona Beatrice made a little gesture with her fan. "This display of spirit, my dear. But it is wasted, quite wasted. Show my poor son these flashing looks: I am much too old to be moved, and far too lazy."

Dominica, aware even then of the family's designs, chose to come into the open. "Señora, if you mean me for my cousin's bride, I think it only fair to tell you that I will have none of him, so please you."

"Of course I mean you for his bride," her aunt said calmly. "My dear, pray sit down. You fatigue me sadly."

"I had guessed it!" Dominica said indignantly.

"It was not very difficult to guess," said Dona Beatrice. "But we shall not talk of bridals yet. Decency must be observed. I have often thought how absurd is this to do we make over death, but it is the way of the world, and I never go against custom."

"Señora—I do not like my cousin enough!"

Dona Beatrice was not at all disturbed. "No, my love, I had not supposed you did. I find him very lamentable myself, and I bore him. But what has that to do with marriage? Do not make that singular error of confusing liking with marriage. It has nothing to do with it."

"I choose to think it has, aunt. I could not marry where I did not love."

Her aunt yawned behind her fan; she looked amused, tolerant. "Be advised by me, my dear, and be rid of such

notions. Marry for convenience and love at discretion. I
assure you, these things smoothe themselves when one is
married. As a maid you are bound to be prim. It is all
very different when you are comfortably established."

Dominica started, and could not forbear a giggle. "Do
you advise me to wed my cousin, señora, for the sake of
taking a lover afterwards?" she asked, half-shocked, half-
entertained.

"Certainly, child, if you wish. Only pray use discretion.
Scandal is very odious, and there is never the least need to
incur it if you observe care in these little affairs. You have
only to look at me."

Dominica did look at her, almost aghast. "Aunt!"

"What is it now?" inquired Dona Beatrice, lifting her
eyes for a moment. "You did not suppose that I married
your uncle for love, did you?"

Dominica felt herself to be young and foolish, at a
disadvantage. "I did not know, señora, but for myself I do
not mean to wed my cousin. He is—he is—in short,
señora, I do not care for him."

Her aunt only looked at her with the tolerant amusement she found so galling, and would say no more.

But the matter was not to be so easily allowed to slide.
Don Diego's attentions became more marked; he was
impervious to rebuffs, just as his mother was impervious
to argument. Dominica felt Beauvallet's signet ring lying
snug in her bosom, and turned a shoulder on Don Diego's
advances.

She would look at the ring sometimes when she was
alone and remember how it had been given to her, and
what words had gone with it. She had been induced to
believe then, under the influence of that dominant person-
ality. Even now when she conjured up Beauvallet's image
before her mind's eye, and saw again his laughing face,
and the turn of his dark head, a little of that belief would
come stealing back to her. It could not long endure.
There, upon the high seas, anything had seemed possible;
here in grave Spain it was as though that swift romance
had only existed in her imagination. She had only a ring
to remind her of its reality; if her heart still cherished its
secret hope, her brain rejected it, and knew Beauvallet's
coming to be an impossibility.

Perhaps he had forgotten; perhaps he was even now teasing some English lady in the way he had used to her. Yet he had said: "I shall not forget," and he had not been jesting then.

She wondered what her aunt would say if she knew but the half of it. Anyone else, Dominica thought, would be horrified, but she could not imagine Dona Beatrice roused to so strenuous an emotion. Probably she would laugh at the romance; she who had had lovers enough in her day might even sympathise with her niece, but it was very certain that she would not see in the brief idyll a bar to marriage with Diego.

Dominica had been careful from the outset to hide that piece of the past from her aunt. She showed an admirable indifference to Beauvallet, knowing that such an attitude would be the least suspicious. She said that she thought his powers overrated: he was nothing beyond the ordinary, to be sure. It was not caution made her so reticent, for she could not think that she would ever see Sir Nicholas again, but she had a dread of letting her aunt into her confidence. Dona Beatrice was like a snail, she thought, trailing a sticky poison in her wake. What she touched she soiled; all virtue was made to seem a little foolish; all vice was merely smiled upon.

She shocked her niece from the first, most of all upon the question of religion. When it appeared that Dominica went too seldom to Mass Dona Beatrice spoke of the omission, and told the girl that it would be wise to attend regularly.

Dominica, hardly knowing how she dared, perhaps stung by the placid tone her aunt assumed, hinted at reformed notions. She was startled by Dona Beatrice's attitude, startled, and certainly shocked.

"I dare say, my dear," had said Dona Beatrice. "But it is most foolish to brandish such ideas abroad. You may be as heretical as you please to yourself, but pray do not let Frey Pedro get wind of it. Talk such as this leads to an unpleasant sequel. Respect the forms of religion, I do beseech you."

This, from a seemingly devout Catholic! Dominica had expected censure, had steeled herself to meet denuncia-

tion. But a calm recommendation to her to play the hypo-
crite seemed to her depraved beyond words. She looked
indignantly at Dona Beatrice, but ended in obeying her.

Chapter XI

WHEN she first heard of the projected ball to be given in
honour of Don Diego's birthday Dominica pleaded her
mourning state, and said that she could not be present.
She had a suspicion that this ball, surely unsuitable for a
man's anniversary, was planned to lure her from her
fastness. Maybe it was to serve as a prologue to her
betrothal. She would not be present.

This decision drew a sigh from Dona Beatrice. "My
dear, you are very teasing," she complained. "In Spain
girls do not say I will, and I will not to those set in
authority over them. Do me the favour to give way with a
good grace."

"You cannot think it seemly, señora, for me to be
dancing so soon after my father's death."

"I do not think it at all seemly for you to stay moping
in your chamber," replied Dona Beatrice. "We will set all
in train to have a new gown made for you. There is
naught so enlivening to the spirits as a new gown, believe
me. But I do not think you should wear colours yet. A
cut velvet might do very well."

"I do not mean to be present," repeated Dominica.

"Or a pure white taffeta," mused Dona Beatrice. "We
must consider it."

"Aunt!"

"Well, child? Oh, are you still tilting your chin at me? I
take it very unkindly in you then. Oblige me by being
present on this one occasion, and let us say no more about
it."

"I am sorry that you think me unreasonable, señora," Dominica said stiffly. "But if I obey you in this, you will expect me to obey you in—other things."

"Marriage," nodded her aunt. "It makes no odds, my dear. Whether you come to the ball or not I am still desirous to see you wed. You cannot suppose that the care of a niece is at all pleasing to one of my indolence."

"Show me, then, another suitor!" flashed Dominica.

Dona Beatrice picked up her fan. "Now I had thought you cleverer than that," she said. "How should we benefit by another suitor for you?"

The brown eyes looked sternly. "In a word, aunt, you covet my possessions! And so we have the truth at last!"

"Naturally, child. What did you suppose?" said Dona Beatrice, unruffled. "We find ourselves in deplorably straitened circumstances, and you come as a gift from heaven, one would say."

Dominica looked round at the opulence of the room. "One does not immediately perceive your poverty, señora."

"Certainly not," said Dona Beatrice. "We all maintain a good appearance. But show me the man who is not impoverished to-day for all his outward pomp!"

"I think," said Dominica forcibly, "that Spain is a hateful country, and the people—corrupt!"

"Very corrupt," agreed Dona Beatrice. "An age of loose-living. I remember when I was a girl a Spanish lady was the model of decorum. It is all very different now, and much more amusing. I believe that we become a byword."

"I wonder, señora, that you are content to be so!"

"To be a byword? What odds? As for our corruption, what would you, when the King keeps his grandees away from the affairs of state, and encourages them to waste their substance?" She shrugged. "I observe, and I am content to smile."

"So it seems," said Dominica. "Yet you can leave smiling to lend yourself to an odious scheme to marry me to my cousin. Well, I will not wed him. Never! You will see, señora, that I mean what I say."

"I don't doubt it, my dear. You are a very charming girl, and you have wit—a little. But when you put your wit against mine, you must lose."

"When you find, señora, that my wits have won the day——"

Her aunt rose. "I shall have a lively respect for you, my dear. Cut velvet and your pearls. I will see to it."

Well, in the end Dominica gave way, and not quite from a sense of duty. Her aunt's attitude had given her pause; that placid, smiling dame frightened her: there was no gainsaying it. She guessed that she was required to appear in public to give the lie to a world that might possibly be saying that the Carvalhos kept her cooped up against her will. There was her uncle on the mother's side, one Miguel de Tobar, who had two likely sons of his own, and might conceivably have designs upon her himself. One suitor was as distasteful as the other, but it might serve to play off Tobar against the Carvalhos, Dominica thought. She began to scheme and ponder, weaving her toils. She was afraid of Dona Beatrice, ay, but she would fight her, for all that, and find joy in it. She put a finger to her lips, bit the rosy tip, and looked this way and that, frowning at fate. Policy dictated an end to her seclusion. She must go into the world, and nose about for a deliverer. Tobar would serve to alarm the Carvalhos; she had very little intention of carrying it further than that. She had had letters from him, guarded enough, to be sure, but sufficiently plain in their purport to tell her that she might call on him and find a ready answer.

An end to this moping, then. She got up briskly, with a little toss of the head, as though she would be free of a curbing rein. She would go to this ball, but dance she would not. She would wear what was put out for her to wear, and show herself a martyr to tyranny.

But velvets and love-knots, pearl-sewn lace, and the fashioning of a corsage must necessarily interest a young lady, and when tailors were busy she abandoned the attitude of martyr and asserted herself. She would have the neck cut so, and the kirtle of such a silk, and there should be crystals sewn on her ruff. She harried the tailors, and sent her maid—not Maria, now, who had left her to marry a hopeful young groom, but an older woman, sour-faced and silent—bustling to find a certain point-lace that was laid by.

When the day came she was secretly glad that she was to be at the ball. A maid cannot weep for ever, and to say truth, she was heartily sick of her seclusion. The new gown pleased her; her pearls looked remarkably well about her slim neck, and her hair under its silver net was dressed to her satisfaction. It was a pity her cheeks were so pale, but she would have none of her aunt's rouge-paste. Let the whispering world see her pale and wan, and draw what conclusions it liked. Nor would she by any means carry a very pretty fan of pink feathers, sent to her with her cousin's compliments.

"This trifle," says my lady, mighty haughty, "this fan, which pleases me not at all, you may have, if you like, Carmelita. I do not want it."

"Señorita, it is the fan Don Diego gave you," old Carmelita reminded her.

"Is it so?" Dominica held it up and turned it this way and that. "I do not like it. Take it if you will, or give it to your niece." She tossed it aside, and would have no more to do with it.

She went downstairs presently, a snow-maiden, trying to look sadly martyred. She found her aunt in the great hall, with Don Rodriguez at her side.

He was ready to take Dominica's hand and fondle it. He could never be at ease in her presence. Her large eyes looked too straightly, nor would she ever give him any help. She thought him a poor creature, and despised him accordingly. If he were to play the villain, then a' God's name let him play it boldly, and put a brave face on to it! A villain who was yet a man would not infuriate her near so much as this man who was a villain against his kinder nature.

He complimented her now, and said that he was glad indeed to see her amongst them, and looking so beautiful.

Dona Beatrice, almost overpowering in apple-green silk, with pink embroideries, and an ornate headdress, looked her over critically. "Yes, you are very well," she said. "We shall have serenades beneath your window, I suppose."

One could not be proof against such flattery. Dominica dropped a demure curtsy, and said she was glad she pleased her good aunt.

There came an interruption to drive the dawning smile out of her eyes. Don Diego came into the hall from the ballroom, and bowed with great flourish.

Dominica looked at him with warm indignation in her face. Whether of intent or not, and she was very sure that it was of intent, he had chosen to array himself in white to match her. He wore pearl-coloured Venetian hose, embroidered cunningly with pale pink and a paned doublet to go with them. His points had silver aiglets; his ruff was stitched with silver, and was so large that it looked like a dish through which he had stuck his head. He had a rapier with a jewelled hilt at his side, a single ruby drop in one ear, and he carried a pure white rose in his hand.

Dominica looked him up and down, and gave the tiniest of sniffs. Her aunt's soft laugh sounded behind her. "What a pretty caballero!" said Dona Beatrice. "Where, oh where could one find a prettier?"

Don Diego chose to ignore this tribute. He came up to Dominica with the smile she so much disliked, and kissed her hand. "Fairest cousin! I salute you! In my honour, this ball? Nay, rather in yours, the loveliest lady in Spain." He released her hand, and held out his rose. "A white rose to match you, sweet cousin."

"I should be loth to deprive you of it, cousin."

He came closer. "Only give it me again when the ball is ended. I shall wear it next my heart then. Let me pin it on your bosom. Roses should bloom together."

She drew her skirts away. "Keep your rose, cousin. You tease me to no purpose."

He lowered his voice. "Still so cruel! Still so cold? You who sets hearts flaming!"

"God send a shower to quench them," she said and moved away to her aunt's side.

She stayed there for a long hour while guests arrived and were announced. All were strangers to her; she had to be presented again and again. To her annoyance Don

Diego stood upon her other side. It must look as though they were betrothed already, she thought, and was careful never to turn in his direction.

The hall become crowded; already they were dancing in the ballroom beyond. Dominica's foot tapped the floor involuntarily. Diego saw it, and came possessively close. "Dare I hope for the honour of leading you out, sweet cousin?" he murmured.

"I hope you dare not," she answered smartly. "I do not dance to-night." She made a movement as though to bid him stand further off. "Pray go and lead out some other lady," she said.

Above the sound of the rebecks, above the subdued chatter of guests gathered in the hall, sounded the steward's voice. There was a stir at the door. "M. le Chevalier de Guise!" called the steward, and bowed in this late arrival.

Dominica looked towards the door, wondering who the Frenchman might be. A knot of gentlemen gathered there parted to let the newcomer pass. There was a quick, decided step; no Frenchman came in, but Sir Nicholas Beauvallet, as though upon his own quarterdeck.

Dominica almost let fall her fan; the breath caught in her throat, she stood staring, first pale, and then red, and through the mad riot in her brain ran only one clear thought: He has come! He has come! He has come!

Across the hall he came, with that graceful, careless step she knew so well. He was brave in silk and velvet, with a neat, small ruff such as he had always worn clipping his throat about. He had a hand laid lightly on his sword-hilt and his eyes looked straight at Dominica. She saw them fearless, with a kind of mocking challenge in their blue depths, as though they would signify "Well, did I not say I would come?" Everything in her responded to the daring of him. Ah, what a man! Ah, what a lover for a girl! what a brave, laughing lover!

He was close now, bowing to her aunt.

"Ah, so you have come, Chevalier," said Dona Beatrice, giving him her hand. "We shall talk a little, but later on. Let me present you to my niece, Dona Dominica de Rada y Sylva. This gentleman, my dear, is a French-

man strayed by some good chance into Spain. The
Chevalier de Guise."

Dominica, still hardly daring to trust her eyes, saw his
hand held out, and knew his gaze to be upon her. She put
out her own little hand, and his long fingers closed over it.
She looked down at his black head as he bent to kiss her
hand; she thought if she spoke her voice must betray her
agitation.

It was a real kiss pressed on her hand, no formal brush
of the lips. He stood straight again, and released her slight
fingers. "Señorita, I am enchanted," he said. "But Dona
Beatrice is wrong: I did not come by chance into Spain. I
had a set resolve to journey here."

Her long lashes fluttered downwards. She knew herself
to be blushing. "Indeed, señor?" she said faintly.

"Such an odd resolve!" commented Dona Beatrice.
"What can you hope to find here to amuse you?"

Dominica looked up to see his eyes crinkle at the
corners. He addressed himself to Dona Beatrice, laughing-
ly. "Oh, I come on a quest, dear señora," he said. Then
he seemed to become aware of Don Diego, upon Dominica's other hand. "Well-met, señor! I give you joy of your
anniversary." The mockery in his eyes deepened. "But
you are bridal, señor! bridal!"

Don Diego stiffened, but a moment after shrugged
slightly at this deplorable lack of formality. "My attire
does not like you, Chevalier?" he said disdainfully.

"On the contrary," said Sir Nicholas gaily, "it reminds
me of my own nuptials, which draw close."

Dominica's hand, slowly waving her fan to and fro,
faltered a little. What a game to play with fire! Oh, he was
mad indeed, divinely mad!

"I felicitate you," said Don Diego. "Permit me to find
you a partner for the *coranto*."

Sir Nicholas turned. "I shall crave the hand of Dona
Dominica," he said.

Don Diego spoke before she could reply. "My cousin
does not dance, señor."

"How foolish!" said Dona Beatrice, turning her head.
"Let the Chevalier lead you out, my dear. There are no
men to rival Frenchmen at dancing."

"If you will dance, cousin, let mine be the honour of leading you out," said Don Diego.

Sir Nicholas had taken her hand; the pressure of his fingers was insistent. "Ah, but I was before you, Don Diego," he said.

Don Diego looked angrily, and took a quick step forward, as though he would snatch Dominica's hand from its resting place. His rose dropped unheeded to the ground. "Cousin, I understood you would not dance!"

"You have let fall your pretty flower," Sir Nicholas pointed out gently.

Don Diego turned with an ugly look in his face, forgetting his duty to a guest. His angry stare met an amused glance from cool blue eyes that did not waver. Sir Nicholas still held Dominica's hand, but one eyebrow was quizzically raised, as though to say: "Do you wish to quarrel? Say but the word!"

Dona Beatrice interposed to put an end to an awkward moment. Her fan brushed Dominica's shoulder. "Be advised by me, my dear, and go with the Chevalier. Resolutions are made to be broken only."

Don Diego seemed to recollect himself. He recovered his *sosiego* and bowed. "I am less fortunate than the Chevalier, cousin. I shall ask for your hand later in the evening."

"As you please, cousin," Dominica sent a fleeting glance upwards to Beauvallet's face and dropped her eyes again. Obedient to the pull on her hand she went with him across the hall to the ballroom.

"God pity me, I have borne a fool!" sighed Dona Beatrice. "You do not go well to work, my poor son."

"She did it to flout me!" he said hotly.

"If she did it promises very well," she replied. "But when a man like the Chevalier craves a boon there are few women will not grant it. For where he craves he might take, look you."

"He is insufferable!" Diego said. "My sword itches to taste his blood."

Dona Beatrice smiled more broadly. "I dare say the Chevalier has some skill with swords," she said. "I do not think—no, I do not think that you would be well advised to send him a challenge."

Don Diego stayed glooming a moment. "One would think you wanted her to go with him," he complained.

"I did," said his mother imperturbably. "The girl saw a very personable man, with more charm in his lightest smile, my poor son, than any other here to-night. She was tempted to be forsworn, and I bade her go. Had I intervened for you she would not have danced at all. Now you are sure of her, for she cannot refuse, having danced once."

In the ballroom Dominica had little opportunity to speak to Sir Nicholas. She dreaded lest some overheard phrase might betray him; for the first few steps of the dance she could only look up eloquently into his face. They drew together a moment, and she whispered:—"You have come! How could you dare?"

"Had you not my word, little doubter?"

They drew apart again; another couple was too close to allow them to say more. The music stopped; Sir Nicholas was bowing, and Don Diego was possessively at Dominica's elbow.

She lived through another hour in a fret. Don Diego stayed close at her side; she could only watch Beauvallet across the room, and long to be alone with him. It seemed she would never find the opportunity, but presently her cousin's attention was claimed, and he had to lead another lady out to dance. Dominica cast a quick look round, saw her aunt at the other end of the room, and drew back behind the ample form of a portly dowager. She slipped along the wall then to where heavy curtains hung, shutting off a small antechamber. Knowing Beauvallet's eyes to be upon her she went through, and stood breathlessly waiting.

The curtains moved; he was before her. She went to him in a little run, with both her hands held out, and her eyes full of happy tears. "Oh, to see you again!" she whispered. "I never thought it possible!"

He gathered her hands in his, and held them clasped against his breast. "Softly, my heart! This is dangerous work." His voice was quick and decisive for all he spoke so low. "I must have speech with you alone. Which way looks your chamber?"

"To the garden. Ah, Nicholas, I have wanted you!"

"My fondling!" His hands pressed her closer. "Does your woman sleep with you?"

"Nay, I am alone." She looked wonderingly up at him. him.

"Set a lamp in your window when you judge all to be asleep, to give me a sign. Can you trust me?"

"Ah, you know! You know I can trust only you. What will you do?"

"Climb up to you, sweetheart," he answered, and smiled at her face of amazement. "What windows look out that way?"

"My woman's—my cousin's closet—some servants."

"Good." He kissed her hands. "Expect me then when you show a light. Patience, my bird!"

He released her, and stepped back. The curtains parted for a moment, and he was gone.

The rest of the evening passed in a bewildered haze for her. She was conscious only of Beauvallet's presence, but he did not come near her again. Her cousin besought her to dance with him again, and when she would not, stayed by her, teasing her ear with his soft speech.

"Who was the Frenchman?" she asked. "The Chevalier. Is he of the Ambassador's court?"

"De Guise! No, my dear cousin, the Ambassador owns him not. Some idle traveller swaggering abroad. I trust he will soon be gone from us. It was no wish of mine that he should be invited here to-night. A trifler, no more."

"You do not like him, cousin?" she said, looking sideways.

He raised those expressive shoulders. "An arrogant Frenchman who bears himself as though he would snap his fingers in one's face! No, I do not like him, cousin."

A gleam of mischief shot into her eyes. "It is to be hoped he will not snap his fingers in your face, cousin," she said demurely.

"I should have but one answer, Dominica." He touched his sword-hilt. "I do not think the gay Chevalier would return to France."

ᴄ❨ *Chapter XII* ❩ᴄ

IT seemed an age before the house was quiet, and all
lights put out. Dominica sent her sleepy tirewoman away
as soon as she came up from the ball. The woman made
little resistance, she could hardly keep her eyes open,
and was glad to be sent back to bed. Dominica let
her unlace her gown, and put away her jewels. She put on
a loose wrapper, and laid another log on the fire. As
ill-luck would have it her aunt came in to bid her good-
night, and stayed to talk over the ball. She professed
herself thankful that the affair was over; it had been very
dull, she thought, and the Chevalier de Guise was the only
relief she had had from utter boredom. Dominica, very
much on her guard, stifled a yawn, and allowed the
Chevalier to be well enough.

"Do not lose your heart to him, my dear," remarked
her aunt lazily. "Frenchmen are sadly fickle, and I believe this one is betrothed already."

"Yes, so he said," Dominica answered. An imp of
malice prompted her to add:—"So my cousin need not be
jealous of him, señora."

"Diego is too much in love with you to forbear jealousy
of any man who looks twice at you," said Dona Beatrice,
a hint of cynicism in her voice.

"Or is he in love with my money?" asked Dominica
sweetly.

"Very much, my dear. We all are." Nothing, it seemed,
could disturb Dona Beatrice's composure. She got up out
of her chair and tapped her niece's cheek. "No more of
this seclusion, child. You will show yourself abroad a
little, and remember that we shall soon leave this tiresome
town for a little quiet and peace."

Dominica's eyes were cast down, but the breath was

stayed in her throat. "Very well, señora," she said submissively. "But do we leave Madrid indeed?"

"Shortly, my dear. We shall go north to Vasconosa as soon as may be, and we hope that Diego in the country will like you better than Diego in town."

Dominica dropped a curtsey. "I don't think it, señora."

"No? But you can try to, my dear." Dona Beatrice went out with her slow tread, and a minute later a door shut in the distance.

Dominica sat down by the fire to wait. Presently she heard her aunt's tirewoman pass by her door to the stairs that led to the servants' quarters above. Don Rodriguez, coming up from downstairs, called a good-night to his son, and went into his room. But Don Diego must needs go into his closet, and stay there for what seemed an interminable time to his impatient cousin. At length he came out, and went across the hall to his bedchamber. Dominica heard him speak sharply to his man, and shut the door with a snap. There was silence for a while, and then the same door opened and shut again: his servant had put Don Diego to bed at last.

The man's footsteps died away on the stairs, and silence settled down on the house. Still Dominica waited, counting the slow minutes. She went presently to her door, and softly opened it. All was dark in the passage. Holding her gown close about her that no rustle might betray her presence she stole down the short corridor to the upper hall. A bar of light beneath one of the doors showed that Don Diego was still awake. Dominica stayed where she was, motionless against the wall. In a few minutes the light disappeared. She crept back to her chamber, put more wood upon the fire, and went to arrange her curls in the mirror. When she judged that Don Diego had had time to fall asleep she went out again into the passage, and this time took the precaution of listening at her tirewoman's door. She heard a snore, and was satisfied, knowing how very hard to wake was Carmelita. Flitting silently in her stockinged feet she reached the hall, went ghost-like to three doors, and at each listened intently. She must be sure, very sure, that the whole house slept before she signalled to Beauvallet, for he came to certain death if he should be discovered.

No sound reached her straining ears; she crept back to her room, stealthily shut the door, and little by little turned the key in the lock. It went home with a click that seemed to din through the stillness. She stayed, breathing fast, her ear to the crack. No answering stir sounded; nothing but the grating of a mouse nibbling at the wainscoting somewhere down the passage.

She left the door then, and went to the window, and parted the heavy curtains that hung over it. Holding her lamp in her hand she stepped out on to the little semi-circular balcony.

Moonlight flooded the garden below, and the trees cast ink-black shadows on the ground. From out the shadow a shadow moved; she saw Beauvallet cross the garden, and raised her free hand in a little welcoming sign. He was beneath her balcony now; she had to lean over to see him. How he would contrive to climb up she did not know, but that he would manage it somehow she was very sure.

He made surprisingly little work over it. A climbing rose gave him foothold. He came up swiftly and silently, braced a foot against the iron pipe that ran down the side of the house from the rain-gutter, seemed to measure the distance with his eye, and threw himself forward.

Dominica stretched out her hand involuntarily to help him, but he caught the rail of the balcony, and the next instant had swung a leg over it, and was beside her.

Neither spoke a word. Sir Nicholas had an arm about Dominica's waist, and led her into the room, his other hand laid lightly across her parted lips. She set the lamp down on the table while he closed the long windows and drew the curtains over them.

He turned, a moment looked at her, and opened his arms. Dominica went into them in a little run, and felt them close tightly about her.

"My heart! My dove!"

She could only say: "You have come! You have come! It is you, really you!"

"Had you not my word?"

"How could I believe? How could I think that you would dare—even you? Oh, *querida*, why have you come?" Her hands tugged at his shoulders. "There's death lurking in every corner for you!"

"I have played many games with Death, fondling, but the dice always fell my way. Trust me."

"Mad!" she whispered. "Mad Nicholas!"

He kissed her. For a while she was content to lie in his arms, but presently she said on a sigh: "Folly, oh folly! I have brought you to your death!"

"Nay, nay, I came of mine own free will, as I swore I would—to make an Englishwoman of you." He made her look up. "How now, my heart? Will you go with Mad Nicholas?"

She tried to hide her face. "It is not possible. You know it is not. God knows how you are here, but you must go quickly, quickly! You could never escape with me to burden you."

"Give me a plain answer, fondling. Will you go with me?"

She evaded him. "I have been so unhappy," she said pitifully.

"You shall never be so again, I swear." He held her away from him. "Will you trust me further yet? Will you put your life in my hands?"

She looked up into his eyes, her own troubled and questioning. He had taken her by storm; he was a lover from a fairy-tale, and she had longed for him, and dreamed of him, but now that he spoke so urgently, and looked so keenly, she realised all that it would mean to her if she gave herself to him. He was a stranger and an Englishman, and if he won out of Spain a strange land and a strange people awaited her. She loved him, but how little she knew of him! A girl's fears shook her; she looked searchingly, peering for the future, and the colour ebbed in her cheeks. He awaited her answer; she thought how bright his eyes were, how compelling.

"Nicholas—you could not understand," she faltered. "I am so alone. I do not know—"

"I do understand," he answered instantly. "I love you. Trust me!"

Her fingers sought his. "You will be good to me?" she said in a small voice.

He smiled. "I will never beat you," he promised.

At that she smiled too, but fleetingly. "Nay, do not jest, do not laugh at me!" she said.

He raised her hand to his lips and kissed them. "On my soul," he said, "I've only the one ambition left; to care for you."

She nestled back into his arms. "If we could! If we only could!"

"What, doubting still?" he rallied her. "What do you fear, little faint heart?"

"To lead you to your death," she said. "How can I not fear it?"

"Nay, nay, 'tis I shall do the leading," he smiled. "Have faith, O Lady Disdain!"

"Not that!" she protested, but a smile trembled on her at the old memories the name conjured up.

His arm was hard about her shoulders. "Do you love me?" he asked, and his eyes compelled an answer from her.

She looked up. "Do you not know that I do—doubter?"

He swooped then, and kissed her almost before she was aware. Holding her close still he asked her with the teasing note in his voice:—"Shall I make an Englishwoman of you after all, my bird?"

She nodded. "Only take me away," she said. "Take me away from here! Anyway!"

For a moment he held her closely embraced, cheek to cheek. Then he let her go, brought her to the fire, and made her sit down on the faldstool before it. He stirred the smouldering log with his booted foot, and it fell apart, and the flames sprang up. "Do they seek to wed you to that pretty cousin of yours?" he asked abruptly.

"I hate him!" she said. "I have told my aunt I will never, never wed him, but she—Nicholas, you do not know her! She smiles, and nods, and agrees with me, but she is like a rock! She frightens me, Nicholas. She is so quiet, and it is like a fate pursuing one! Yes, I am afraid, I!"

"No need," he said. "Remember I am near you, and take heart. Now how to spirit you away?"

"How did you come?" she said. "In the *Venture*—that fishing village?"

"Nay, over the border, openly, with letters to King Phillip," he replied.

She gasped. "Are you a wizard, then? Tell me, how!"

"Very simply, child. My luck, no more. I fell in with a secret envoy to the King, and him I slew perforce, and came on in his place. But to get you to the coast is the problem now. It is a-many weary leagues, and the hunt will be up then in right earnest. Barful, barful!"

She sat straight on the faldstool. "Nay, but listen, Señor Nicholas! We leave Madrid soon now—I do not know when, but soon. Dona Beatrice told me so to-night, and hoped I might like Diego better in the country than I do here. We go north, to Vasconosa, near Burgos. I do not know when, but Dona Beatrice would wish it to be soon."

"God 'ild her, then! What keeps her?"

"Diego, I think. Oh no, she does not care for him, but of what use to take me into the country if he be not by? And he hath engagements still, and will not go till they are done."

"Fiend seize the princox!" Beauvallet said. "North of Burgos? It will serve, it will serve."

She looked eagerly up at him. "It is not more than a day and a night from the coast, but they will watch me close. Can you do it, Nicholas?"

"Surely, surely, sweetheart. Have no fear. The *Venture* will lie off that port you wot of, and if the luck holds we may make it safely." He went to the window, and drew back the curtain a little way. "It is growing light, child. I must be gone." He came back to her, and took her hands. "Leave me to find a way, chuck. Only let me have a sight of you, and a word with you at need. I lie at the Rising Sun if you should want me, and Joshua is with me to bear a message. I have been about this town a little, but in no house do I meet you. You lie close, love."

"I would not go out. That's over now. I shall go with my aunt to Don Alonso de Alepero's house on Monday. Will you be there?"

"I can arrange it," he said. "Expect to see me in this house as soon as may be. This aunt of yours seems to have a fondness for me." He bent, and kissed her hands. "Now fare thee well, my heart, and fear naught."

"Only for you," she said.

"Fear for me when you hear of my death," he smiled.

"Not till then." He held her close a moment. "Keep Diego at arm's length, my lass," he said, twinkling, "or I might be tempted to out sword and thrust him there."

"Oh, you must be prudent!" she said urgently. "Promise me! He hates you already; he said to-night almost as much."

"God save his puppyhood!" said Sir Nicholas lightly. "Am I to be in a sweat for fear of Master Puke-Stocking? We shall come to grips yet, he and I. I can snuff out a fight with the best. He's hot for it." He bent to kiss her lips. "A last goodnight!"

She gave it, clinging to him. "You must go—yes, you must go. Oh, my love, I love you!"

ᕮᗩ *Chapter XIII* ᗡᕭ

IT was not perhaps surprising that in so short a time the gay Chevalier de Guise made some noise about the town. He had the trick of it. To be secret, to lie close, seemed to be no part of his design. His credentials were good, Losa's patronage carried him whithersoever he listed, and he used it to the full. There was scarcely anyone in Madrid who had not heard of the Chevalier, few who had not met him. From the Court came no sign. Philip must ponder his reply, annotate the despatch, sleep upon it, lay it aside to ponder it yet again. Those who sought to hurry the Catholic King did so to their own despair. He would do nothing without carefully weighing it; if his brain worked slowly he at least was not aware of it. He was methodical, plodding, infinitely conscientious, and he prided himself upon his cautious judgment.

For Philip to be dilatory up to a point suited Sir Nicholas very well, since, as he saw it, nothing could be done in his affair while Dominica still lay at Madrid. If Philip delayed too long, however, he would have to employ another messenger to carry his answer back to the Guise.

Sir Nicholas would be very well pleased to get that answer
into his own hands, for it promised to be interesting to an
English Protestant. Walsingham would be glad of it, but
Sir Nicholas had no notion of serving Master Secretary to
his own plan's undoing. There was food enough for Walsingham in the Guise's cyphered letter, a copy of which
was safe in Beauvallet's possession. It concerned one Mary
Stewart, unfortunate lady, at present a state prisoner in
England, and certain illuminating schemes for her future
as compiled by his Majesty King Philip, and the Duc de
Guise. Fine doings there! Enough to make Master Secretary's hair stand on end.

For the rest Sir Nicholas went junketing about the
town, and by the way gleaned some useful information
likely to interest not only Walsingham, but Sir Francis
Drake too, and not less the Lord Admiral, Howard of
Effingham. There was a fleet building in Cadiz harbour;
Sir Nicholas made copious mental notes of the size and
strength of those tall galleons, and even toyed with the
notion of travelling south to see for himself.

His behaviour during this period provoked nervous
qualms in Joshua Dimmock, who declared himself to be a
meacock creature, and shivered from time to time. He
had reason for his qualms, for he had good cause to know
that never was Beauvallet so reckless as when he played
with danger on every hand. "Master," said he, "is there
never one who suspects?"

"Ay, the French Ambassador," Sir Nicholas answered.
"One of his satellites hath been set to question me—very
cleverly, so he thought."

"God's me! this is to undo all! And you said, mister?"

"Oh, I gave him a bountiful answer, be sure," was all
he could get from Sir Nicholas.

On Monday evening Dominica was to be seen at the
Alepere house, off the Calle Mayor. When Sir Nicholas
could escape from the amiable clutches of her aunt, he
made his way to her side, ousted an admiring caballero
from his place of vantage there, and proceeded, to all
appearances, to pay his court to her.

Don Diego, watchful in the background, was swift to
interpose his presence, but got little by that.

"Ah, my bridal friend!" said Sir Nicholas, very urbane.

"You are come in a good hour, señor. Dona Beatrice is inquiring for you. You shall not let us keep you."

"My mother, señor?" said Don Diego, glaring his disbelief.

"Your mother, my dear friend. You are loth to leave us, I perceive, and I should be flattered but that I respect the charms of this lady to be the true cause." He bowed to Dominica.

"I cannot suppose, señor, that my mother's need of me is urgent," said Don Diego, colder still.

"I am sure you underrate yourself," returned Sir Nicholas.

Don Diego looked furious, but did not see how he might remain. "I am obliged to you, Chevalier," he said, mighty sarcastic. "I do not permit myself to forget that you are a visitor to Spain." There was a good deal of meaning to this. Dominica stirred uneasily, and shot a quick look up at Sir Nicholas.

The mobile eyebrow was up; Sir Nicholas waited. Don Diego met his look for a moment, then bowed ceremoniously, and walked away. They understood one another well enough: what the tongues were not permitted to say the eyes said fully.

"Oh, folly!" Dominica breathed. "Why anger him? To what purpose?"

Sir Nicholas was watching Don Diego go across the room. "I am certain I shall not leave Spain until that paraquito and I have measured swords," he said thoughtfully.

"Señor Nicholas, I do not think that I was ever afraid until I met you," Dominica said. "Why will you do these things?"

He looked down at her. "What, afraid for me? Let be, child; there's no need."

"You run on your fate!" she insisted.

He laughed inpenitently. "I had liefer do that than run from it, sweetheart," he said. "What news for me?"

Her face clouded. "Not as we had hoped, Señor Nicholas. The King puts off his removal to Valladolid, and we wait upon him. My uncle is in attendance till then, you see. But I think I could contrive a little." She looked up inquiringly.

His eyes were warm with amusement. "Let me hear your plot, little contriver."

"Then do not laugh at me—robber," she retaliated. "Don Miguel de Tobar is coming to town, and he is my uncle upon my mother's side, and I am very sure that he would like me for his son Miguel." She nodded wisely and compressed her lips.

"How she is sought after!" marvelled Sir Nicholas. "Surely it needs a robber to win her."

A dimple quivered. "Maybe, señor. Now I think it would not suit my good aunt to have me throw myself upon Don Miguel's protection, for he has influence with the King, and he might well get an injunction to have me away from the Carvalhos. I think, Señor Nicholas, that if I were to talk roundabout a little they would be very glad to bear me away to Vasconosa, out of reach of Don Miguel. And there marry me, doubtless, but you will be at hand."

"Be very sure of it. Weave your toils, fondling, but walk warily, for I misdoubt me that aunt of yours hath the seeing eye."

Her eyes sparkled with mockery. "A word out of your own mouth, Señor Pirate—trust me."

At his mother's side Don Diego learned with little surprise but considerable annoyance that she could not remember to have inquired for him. She seemed amused when she heard how he had been sent off. "The rogue!" she said, and chuckled.

"This cousin of mine who will not think of espousals!" said Don Diego. "She is willing enough to have that French ruffler whisper honeywords in her ear. Mark you that!"

"Of course she is," agreed Doña Beatrice. "I have no doubt he is very adroit. If you were more of his complexion, my son, you might make better speed with her."

Don Diego made what speed he could next day, when he offered Dominica his hand and his heart, and spoke his piece in passionate terms. She saw her opportunity in this, and was quick to seize on it. Don Diego was bidden take both hand and heart elsewhere; he pressed his suit more ardently, dared to attempt a kiss. She whisked herself out

of his hold, flew into a royal rage, and flounced away to
find her aunt.

Dona Beatrice was confronted by Flaming Indignation
in a charming form, and blinked at it.

"Señora!" broke out Dominica, panting over it. "I
have to complain of my cousin! I thought you had understood me very well when I told you that I had no mind to
wed with him, yet to-day I am to be teased, it seems, by
his demanding of my hand, and more beside! Ah, more
indeed!" Her eyes flashed sparks, her tongue darted its
rage. "Your son, señora, dares to lay hands on me! I am
to be mauled like any kitchen-wench! I! I say it is not to
be borne, señora, nor will I bear it. This is no way to go
to work with me. You must learn, señora, and your son
with you that I am not to be so entreated, no, not I! And
if you will not learn, then my uncle of Tobar shall hear of
it. What, am I—Rada y Sylva!—to have easy kisses thrust
on me, hateful fondlings, unmannerly hugs? No, señora,
no!" Her cheeks flew storm signals; she had her hands
clenched hard at her sides.

Dona Beatrice put by the book of poems she had been
reading, but continued to fan herself. She watched closely
under her weary eyelids. "Well, you are in a great heat,"
she remarked. "But what is all this to the purpose? If you
do not like Diego's kisses my advice to you is that you
wed him with speed, for if he is at all my son he will very
soon cease to want what he may have for the mere asking."

Real anger leaped up; my lady seemed to grow taller
with it, a very goddess. "This is to insult me! Nasty talk,
señora! Shameful talk! Well, my uncle is coming to
town, as I hear, and in a good hour! Do you think,
señora, that he will approve your plans for me? Do you
think it indeed?"

"I do not," said Dona Beatrice patiently. "I think he
has some little plans of his own for you, my dear, but,
believe me, they differ in only the one particular from
mine, that he would change the name of your bride-
groom."

"Señora, be assured of this, that any bridgegroom were
less distasteful to me than your son!" said Dominica.

"You have not seen young Miguel de Tobar," her aunt

reminded her. "I concede you Diego is not a Chevalier de Guise, my dear, but he is far preferable to Miguel."

"The Chevalier de Guise!" cried out Dominica hotly. "What is the Chevalier de Guise to me? You do not put me off, señora! I will have a plain answer from you: will you seek another bride for my cousin?"

"I thought we understood one another better, my dear," complained Dona Beatrice. "Of course I shall not."

"Then my uncle shall hear of it, señora. You force me to it. If he thinks that I am content to serve the interest of Carvalho he shall know that it is not so."

Dona Beatrice went on fanning herself; her smile broadened. "How foolish of you to warn me, my dear!" she remarked. "You should not let yourself be in such a passion. You show me your defences, which is quite ridiculous of you. I fear you will never win in a battle of wits with me. Now had you curbed your temper, my dear, you would have carried out this plan of yours in secret, and discomposed me sadly. I should certainly have respected you." She picked up the book of poems again, and began to find her place in it. "Of course you will be away from Madrid by the time Tobar enters it."

Dominica knew those sleepy eyes watched her still. There was no saying what Dona Beatrice suspected, what traps she might be laying. The girl let her eyes fall, bit her lips, moved a hand amongst the laces at her bosom as though she were agitated. Her wits against her aunt's? She was very content to set them up for battle; played her little comedy better even than she knew. "Aunt!" She pretended to seek for words, put her hands together as though she would clasp them, moved them apart again. Her eyes lifted; she tossed up her head. "And I will still find means to let him know how you use me!" she cried. "You may do as you please, señora, but you will not induce me to wed with Don Diego!" She judged that to be enough: there had been sufficient childish petulance in her voice to satisfy her aunt. She flung round on her heel, and ran out.

Dona Beatrice went on reading her poems. At dinner, some hours later, she spoke to her husband in a slow, lazy voice, and with a glance of amusement at Dominica. "I

find, señor," she said, "that these heats tax me too much.
Madrid becomes insupportable."

Don Rodriguez was all solicitude at once, wondering
fussily what might be done to relieve the lady. She broke
into his talk. "I have a simpler remedy than these of
yours, señor. I shall go to Vasconosa ahead of you." She
paused, and pulled a dish of sugar-plate towards her.
"To-day is Tuesday," she remarked. "Shall we say a week
from to-day?"

Don Diego looked sharply; Dominica kept her eyes
down. She judged from her aunt's faintly derisive tone
that she had ascertained the date of Tobar's arrival in
Madrid. She could have wished it had been nearer, since
every day Sir Nicholas spent in Madrid added to his
danger. There could be no peace for her while he stayed.
A grim fear stalked beside her; every day she dreaded to
hear of his capture; every time she saw him his very
carelessness brought her heart into her mouth. There was
a price to be paid by the lady who was loved by Mad
Nicholas.

He came that evening to wait on Dona Beatrice. It
seemed he had an assignation with her; she had lent him a
Romance, and he came to give it back to her, and stayed
on talking French with her.

His audacity passed all bounds, Dominica thought. She
withdrew towards the window, and looked severely when
he flung a compliment, like a challenge, at her. She bore
herself like a maid whose primness was shocked; only he
was to know that her reproachful look was to reprimand
his recklessness, not his gallantry.

She wondered whether she dared tell him that she was
to leave Madrid that next week. While she sought in her
mind for a phrase that should seem innocent enough, her
aunt took the words out of her mouth.

Having got the information he wanted Sir Nicholas
soon took his leave. There was some idle play between
him and Dona Beatrice; Dominica had to bite her lip to
keep from smiling. Sir Nicholas humoured Dona Beatrice
to the top of her bent, whispered his audacities into her
receptive ear, and showed his watchful lady very plainly
that he knew well what way to use with her sex. But even

as he devoutly kissed Dona Beatrice's large white hand he shot a rueful, laughing look at Dominica, as though to deprecate her silent reproof.

He came to take his leave of her; she was on tenter-hooks at what his mad humour might prompt him to say or do, and curtsied very stiffly. She would not look at him as she held out her hand. It lay in his, held firmly, but he did not kiss it at once. His voice sounded, brimful of teasing mischief. "But how she is cold!" he said.

She tried to draw her hand away; she was near to boxing his ears.

"My dear Chevalier, you have shocked my niece," said Dona Beatrice, amused. "She is unused to your French ways. We do not go to work so hardily in Spain."

"Have I shocked her? Will she not look at me, and smile at me as she knows how?"

At that her eyes lifted. She had no smile for him, but a straight look, a little fierce. She saw the laugh dancing in his eyes, and dropped her own again. "I fear she is very angry with me," said Sir Nicholas sadly. "She frowns, alas! I think if she had—let us say, a dagger—to hand, I were sped."

Her hand quivered. "You are pleased to jest, señor."

He bent his head, and kissed her fingers. "Señorita, my heart is under your feet."

"Chevalier, Chevalier, you are a trifler!" said Dona Beatrice. "A moment since I had thought it was under mine."

Dominica got her hand free at last. Sir Nicholas turned to Dona Beatrice. "Ah, madame," he said, "you are severe. But I have so many hearts."

She laughed. "Ungallant, I protest! And is there ever a one among the many that will be true, I wonder? Oh, these Frenchmen!"

"Only one, madame," said Sir Nicholas meekly.

She raised her brows, willing to be entertained. "Ah? To whom this one?"

"Madame, to my betrothed," said Sir Nicholas. "She hath it all."

She shrugged at that. "Why, it's very dutiful, señor, but I wonder what you will say—a year hence?"

Dominica turned her back, and looked out into the garden.

"Oh, it is of so faithful a disposition, madame, I am very sure I shall but repeat myself. But I shall still have a heart to lay in—admiration—at your feet." Upon which he took his leave, not before it was time, thought Dominica.

Her aunt began to talk of the coming journey to Vasconosa.

But there was to be another traveller bound thitherwards of whom she knew nothing. Back at the Rising Sun again Sir Nicholas studied such maps as he could come by, and conned the road as best he might. Joshua Dimmock, watching, took heart again, and said darkly to the coat he was folding that the sooner they were off upon this journey the better it would be for them. "Yet," said he, brushing dust from a pair of hose, "I must ask myself, what if the *Venture* be not there? With the General not on board it is to be questioned whether she may keep safe in Spanish waters. Ay, there's a rub." He eyed his master's abstracted profile, and sighed. "We may make marks upon a map, I grant you, and mutter of stages, but I hold, and mark me well, that we may not be sure of a happy issue. I had rather than fifty pounds I were snug at home. It needs not to tell me that we shall make that smuggling port. I make bold to say that we may do that in spite of all these bisson Spaniards. But how if we come upon this port, and find no ship awaiting? Ay, then we are shent. We spend the remainder of our days in Spain, and they will not be many, I warrant me! All to hang upon the *Venture*, and the *Venture* sailing without her General! Ah, the whole emprise is very barful."

Beauvallet looked up. "Peace, chewet! What ails you?"

"This ails me, master, that you have not the means to be avised of the *Venture's* being in these waters."

"Am I so often disobeyed then?"

"Nay, I do not say that, sir, nor would I doubt the good faith of Master Dangerfield, but I say, master, that he is not Sir Nicholas Beauvallet, and he may well fail."

"Oh, croaker! You bring up objections cut and longtail. You're bird-eyed, man, and see danger in every corner. Diccon has as cool a head as you may wish to see, and has my orders to go upon beside. I don't fear for aught there. What, would my men fail me when I was in need?"

"Nay, nay, but if you fear naught there, master, what is it you do fear?"

"To say truth," Beauvallet answered. "I mislike the look of yon French Ambassador."

"For my part, sir, I mislike that popinjay cousin of your lady's. If he is not of a mind to pick a quarrel with you I do not know the signs when a man will be in fighting humour."

"God held him, then!" Beauvallet said, and bent again over his map. "My lady goes to Vasconosa on Tuesday next. Now, it is in my mind that we will attend her on that journey."

"Ay, and then, master?"

"God's Death, man, how do I know who have not seen the place. We shall carry her off, and to the coast. Ask me more when I know more."

"I fear a mischance," Joshua said sadly. "This runs too smoothly for a coil of yours, sir."

Beauvallet folded his map, and put it safely away. There was a look in his face that Joshua had seen there once or twice before. "Fear what you will," said Sir Nicholas, "and let come what may. I tell you, by this hand, I will reach Vasconosa, and have my lady away before she has slept two nights in the place!"

⚜ *Chapter XIV* ⚜

DON DIEGO, accompanying his parents and his cousin to an evening party at the house of Don Luis de Noveli suspected his cousin of going only to meet the Chevalier. His mother was more than weary of these suspicions, and would lend them no ear. "My dear Diego," said she, before they had left the house. "The Chevalier shocks

Dominica far more than he fascinates her. I regard the
coming of Tobar with more misgiving."

"We shall have her fast at Vasconosa by then," he said,
"and the knot may well be tied before he can act. I would
not put it beyond her to be off with that tricksy Frenchman, if only to spite us all. I tell you, señora, he was at
her side more than half the evening at de Chinchon's
house last night, paying his court to her."

"How well you play the jealous lover!" admired his
mother. "I never knew you had it in you to hate anyone
as you hate this conquering stranger. It is most entertaining."

There is no doubt this young man had conceived a very
violent dislike for Sir Nicholas Beauvallet, and was at
increasingly little pains to conceal it. Maybe those blue
eyes mocked too openly. Don Diego knew himself for a
very exquisite caballero, and it was evident Sir Nicholas
had no such notion of the matter. Sir Nicholas had a curl
of the lip that offended; he laughed for no apparent reason, and bore himself as though there were few whom he
considered worth the snap of a finger. His careless eyes,
with the laughter half stayed in them, looked quizzically,
as though he would say, "do you want to fight me? Well, I
am ready for you, but I shall not wait upon you." He
went abroad with a light, swinging stride, as though he
were very much at home, and the very carriage of his neat
head betokened arrogance. Don Diego burned to let a
little of this proud blood.

He felt all his suspicions confirmed when he saw that
the Chevalier was present at the gathering. Since his mother refused to pay any heed to his suspicions he determined
to keep a close watch on Dominica himself, and stayed as
near her as he might all the evening. She bore this as best
she might, and hoped that Beauvallet would not come
near. He was quite capable of coming to her out of sheer
devilry, she thought, and when she caught his eye across
the room she put all the warning she could into her look.
He made a grimace, but for once was obedient to the
pleading in her eyes. She had scolded him well for his
behaviour at the Casa Carvalho when she had met him
last night. She told him that such dangerous work brought
her heart up into her mouth, and he had kissed her

fingers, and sworn he was a villain to alarm her. That was
all very well, but Dona Dominica had realized by now
that her lover was not only headstrong, but took a wicked
delight in tempting long-suffering Providence. But it
seemed her words had had some effect, for he kept aloof
from her now. He was in his gayest mood. How could she
help watching him, dreading disaster?

She had a feeling of foreboding; maybe it was due to
her cousin's unwelcome presence beside her, and the
knowledge she had that he too was watching Beauvallet,
with scowling hatred in his face. She tried to be rid of
him, but he stuck close and she saw that he suspected her
of wanting to have Beauvallet beside her. She was rescued
at last by her aunt, who presented her to a prim girl who
had said she would so much like to meet the lady who had
been captured by the notorious pirate.

Sir Nicholas was within earshot, and what must the
prim girl do but ask a score of questions about El
Beauvallet. Dona Dominica answered as briefly as she
might, afraid every moment that Sir Nicholas' merry humour would break out. Out of the tail of her eye, as she
told her eager listener that she had not been brutally used
by the demon-pirate, she saw the smile lilting on his lips,
and knew that he was listening.

"Oh, señorita, it was a miracle!" said the prim girl
fervently. "But tell me, what is he like, this terrible
man?"

"Indeed, señora, there is very little to tell," said Dominica, impatient. "He is a man like other men. I observed
nothing remarkable in him."

"I had heard," said the girl, rather disappointed, "that
he was very handsome, and we know that he is daring."

"He is well enough," said Dominica. "I think you in
Spain have made too great a figure of him. He is nothing
above the ordinary."

The black head turned; to her horror she saw that that
left eyebrow had flown up. God send the man Beauvallet
was talking to suspected nothing! She turned her shoulder
resolutely. Was this a time to send a jesting look at her?

The prim girl, baulked of excitement, began to talk of
Santiago, and asked more questions. Dominica was rescued at length by Don Rodriguez, who put a hand on her

arm, and smiled at her in the deprecating way he used. "There is one present, dear child, whom you would be glad to meet, perchance. One who was lately at Santiago, and whom I think you know." He lowered his voice mysteriously. "In ill-odour just now, alas, but you will not regard it," he said, leading her across the room. "He lost his ship—but you would know all that, for it must have chanced before you came home." He was making for a group by the door, unconscious of the rising tide of foreboding in his niece. "One cannot but feel for him, but he has been much blamed. In ill-odour at Court, my dear, so you will be wary of how you speak of such matters."

A chill was spreading over her. "Who is it?" she said levelly.

"Did I not say? It is Don Maxia de Perinat, child. He who was sent to chase El Beauvallet, and—and failed. He tells me that he knew you and your poor father." He coughed, and went on hurriedly. "Of course you will not mention the disaster."

Perinat! Perinat in Spain, and in this very house! Perinat, whom she had last seen wild-eyed and stuttering, raving of an English devil who laughed, and cracked a jest in the heat of battle. Every instinct strained to shriek the news to Beauvallet, and tell him to go, go before this looming peril could catch him up. Involuntarily she turned her head to seek him in the crowd. She saw only the back of his black head, the width of his shoulders. And then, while her thoughts raced, she was aware of Perinat bowing over her hand, and offering condolences for the death of her father.

She shook off the gathering numbness that threatened to overcome her, and forced herself to answer, to go on talking, to keep him by her at all costs, away from Sir Nicholas, so unconscious at the other end of the room of this imminent danger. She hardly knew what she said; her mind was casting this way and that for the means of warning Beauvallet. She stood before Perinat, with a forlorn hope of shielding Beauvallet from his notice, and for the only time in her life was glad to see her cousin approaching. She presented him to Perinat at once, hoping that they would fall into conversation and give her time to slip away to Sir Nicholas' side.

Don Diego was bowing; Perinat had a polite word for the son of an old acquaintance. And then, in a momentary lull, came the sound of Beauvallet's gay voice, crisp and clear, and fatally carrying.

Perinat's head was jerked up instantly; he broke off in the middle of a sentence. "*Madre de Dios*, I should know that voice! What witchcraft is this?" he said hoarsely.

Dominica began to talk feverishly, but she was not heeded. Perinat had stepped quickly forward, and was staring at Beauvallet's profile, like one who could not believe his eyes.

Sir Nicholas was talking to his Andalusian friend. Numb with horror Dominica saw the characteristic movement of the back-flung head, and heard the gay laugh that could never be forgotten.

"Ah!" The sound, hardly more than a gasp, came from Don Maxia. His hand was fumbling at his sword hilt. "*Sangre de Dios,* am I in my senses? Do I dream? *El Beauvallet!*"

The name was shouted. Sir Nicholas swung round of instinct, but in this was nothing singular. There was scarcely a man present who did not spin about at the sound of that dread name flung across the room.

Dominica saw the quick glance sweep the group by the door. Sir Nicholas saw Perinat standing livid and staring, but only the veriest flash of recognition came into his eyes.

Don Rodriguez was bewildered, as was everyone, but found his tongue sooner than the rest. "What do you say, Perinat? Are you mad? Who—what——?"

"It is he! It is Beauvallet—Beauvallet's self, I tell you! *Sangre de Dios,* do I not know him? Have I not cause? Shall I ever forget that face, or that laugh, body of God! Ah, dog! ah, villain! At last, at last!"

The startled whisper, "*El Beauvallet, El Beauvallet!*" ran round the room; Perinat's shaking hand pointed straight at Sir Nicholas. Amazed faces peered; those near Beauvallet fell back suddenly, and more than one hand felt for a sword hilt. Only Sir Nicholas stood unmoved, an eyebrow raised in mild surprise, a look of interrogation on his face.

"But—but that is the Chevalier de Guise!" someone said in a dazed voice. "How should El Beauvallet be in Spain?"

"I tell you it is he! I, Maxia de Perinat, who have fought with him hand to hand!" Perinat's words seemed to jostle one another. "Lay hands on him! Will you let him escape? I swear on the Cross it is El Beauvallet!"

"Perinat's misfortunes have turned his brain," whispered the Andalusian.

Dominica stepped forward a pace. "Why, what are you saying, Don Maxia? That is not Beauvallet!" Her voice was perhaps unnaturally calm. "I should know, surely. This man is certainly not he."

There was a movement behind her; Don Diego's hand gripped her wrist. "Ah, jade, I have it at last!" he said fiercely. "This is El Beauvallet, this flaunting Chevalier, and he is your lover!'

There was a buzz of excited whispering. Someone moved to the door, as though to guard it. Beauvallet's voice cut through the subdued babel. "God's life, I am flattered!" he said, and even in the midst of her sick terror, Dominica could exult in the cool amusement in his tone, and worship the iron nerve that could keep him careless and mocking still. "Do you take me for El Beauvallet, señor?"

"Jesting dog of a pirate, are you not he? Ah, dare you look me in the face and say you are not he?"

"What need? This is moon-madness, señor, or you are cupshotten. If I were Beauvallet, what in God's name should I hope to make here?"

"I believe him!" Don Diego was at Perinat's side. "There is more to this Chevalier de Guise than we know. I will tell you what you hope to make, pirate! You hoped to snatch my cousin away. I see it all now, but you shall go to perdition on my sword's point first!" He dragged his sword from the scabbard as he spoke, and sprang forward.

There was a hiss of steel, the glint of candlelight on a blue, shimmering blade. Beauvallet's leaping sword was out, a true piece from the hand of Sahagom of Toledo. Don Diego's thrusting point was caught on the swift blade and beaten aside. Beauvallet sprang back to the wall, and stood facing his assailant. Dominica saw the gleam of white teeth as he smiled.

"Well, gentleman, well? I wait you. Is there any other will come to Don Diego's assistance? If I am El Beauvallet it will take a-many and a-many!"

"Stand back, stand back, this is for me!" Perinat cried, and thrust Don Diego aside. "Measure your sword with mine yet once again, pirate! Do you remember how the deck was slippery beneath your feet? Ha, do you remember, dog?" He snatched at his dagger, and bore down on Beauvallet, a weapon in either hand.

"Hold off your madman," said Sir Nicholas. "Perchance I may do him a mischief. So-so, señor! Gently, then, and keep your guard!" He saw Don Diego advancing on him from the side, and shifted to face him, holding Perinat at check.

Noveli, master of the house, was shocked out of his stupefaction, and rushed forward, pulling out his sword.

"What, more?" said Sir Nicholas. "Oh, brave! I am well-matched indeed."

"Hold, hold!" Noveli cried, and beat up the swords. "What, are you crazy, Perinat? Put up, young señor, put up, I say! This, in my house! Shame! Shame on you both!"

"Seize on him!" Perinat gasped. "Seize on him, I tell you! Will you let him go, you fools? It is El Beauvallet!"

Beauvallet stood leaning lightly on his rapier, and laughing as though he found the situation irresistibly amusing. "Peace, Señor Graybeard, I am here still!"

"He laughs at you! See how he mocks!" Perinat cried, almost beside himself. "Put my words to the test! Call the guard! Call in the guard!"

Diego put up his sword. "Yes, let the guard be called in," he said. "We will sift this to the bottom. Ho, there! Call in the guard!"

Noveli turned quickly. "Do you give orders in my house, Don Diego?"

But many voices took up the cry. "Yes, let the guard be summoned! Let the matter be looked to, Noveli! If Perinat is mistaken the Chevalier will pardon it. If he speaks sooth—nay, have in the guard!"

Noveli looked uncertainly at Beauvallet, torn between his feelings as a host, and his suspicions. Behind Beauvallet was a phalanx of men watching for the least sign of an attempt to escape. And Beauvallet held his sword between his hands, and laughed.

"I should send for the guard, señor," he said.

"Chevalier, you will pardon such seeming rudeness," Noveli said, seriously put out.

"With all my heart, señor," Beauvallet answered lightly. His glance flickered to Dominica's face of despair; his hand went to his beard, and for an instant a finger lay across his lips. He saw her eyes fall, and knew that she had understood.

Someone had sped forth to call the guard. Sir Nicholas turned his head, and seemed amused to see so many gathered between him and the door. "God's my life, you hold this Beauvallet a desperate man, do you not, señors?" he said.

Perinat put up his sword. His first wild passion had died down; he spoke calmly now, but with great bitterness. "Desperate indeed must you be to dare come into Spain," he said. "You have made a jest of me, and of others, Beauvallet, but he who laughs last may laugh the longest."

Beauvallet's eyes glinted. "The last laugh, señor, is certainly going to be mine," he said. "You say that I am Beauvallet, but there is one yonder who says I am not, and it seems she should know."

"She does know!" Don Diego said, ignoring a warning look from his mother. "You cannot fool us thus, dog!"

"Enough of that!" Again Noveli intervened. "This is for other interrogation than yours, Don Diego. Hold your peace, I command you! If we do you an injustice, Chevalier, I hope you will be kind enough only to laugh at us."

"You may be sure of it, señor," said Sir Nicholas. "We shall all laugh." Again his glance flitted to Dominica's face. "Let no one be ill at ease. This affair will have a happy ending, don't doubt it." There came a stir by the door, and the clank of spurred heels. "Aha, the guard!

Now by my faith you count El Beauvallet a dangerous
fellow! As I live, the Guards of Castile, and a round
dozen of them!"

He was surrounded. The lieutenant, who wore a face of
incredulous wonder, bowed stiffly. "Señor, I regret, I
must ask you for your sword." It was presented him, hilt
foremost. "Señor, be good enough to go with us."

"With the greatest pleasure on earth, Señor lieutenant," said Beauvallet. He looked towards the Andalusian. "Don Juan, it seems I may have to forego my game of
trucos with you tomorrow, and maybe some other engagements I had made. Accept my apologies. But all the other
engagements that I have for later dates shall certainly be
kept. Señor, lead on!"

He went out, close-guarded, but his voice echoed still in
Dominica's ears: "The engagements that I have for later
dates shall certainly be kept . . . shall certainly be kept."

⤳❧ Chapter XV ❧⤳

JOSHUA DIMMOCK, prowling in the shadows outside the
Casa Noveli, saw enough, and more than enough to set
him fingering his dagger. Certain, it itched to be out, but
"Yarely, my man, yarely," Joshua cautioned himself.
"One man at large is better than two caged."

It was his habit to lurk near whatever house Sir Nicholas stayed in. He was laughed at for his pains, but laid
a finger to his nose. "I look for trouble," quoth Joshua
Dimmock. "I don't wait to have it brought to my notice."

It seemed he had good reason. The gentleman who
went running out to fetch in the *ginetes* from the barracks
hard by little knew how nearly he ran on death. The
dagger was out, a wicked blade, long and razor-edged;
Joshua, guessing from the sound of turmoil within what

evil fate had chanced, guessed also this flying gentleman's errand. To stab him where the neck joined the shoulder would be easy enough. Ay, and then what? Joshua put up his dagger, snatched so instinctively from its sheath. No way to get Sir Nicholas off, that.

He bethought him that he had maybe let his mind jump at conclusions; drew farther into the shadows, and waited. He saw the *ginetes* come; they passed so close he might have touched one. They went into the house, and came out again soon with Sir Nicholas Beauvallet in their midst.

"Ay, I beagled it out well enough," Joshua muttered. "Now what?" He saw Sir Nicholas walking briskly between his guards, heard him say something to the lieutenant, and laugh. "He goes fleering to death!" groaned Joshua. "Mocker, mocker! Will you not look your fate in the face and know yourself sped at last? But this is to tax idle circumstance." He pulled himself together. "Up, mother-wit! No time for mourning, this." He peered towards the open door of the house, where two lackeys stood talking excitedly together. "I see the first step of my way. Now to sound these hildings." He withdrew a little way, came out from the shadow of the wall, and went towards the Casa Noveli at a brisk trot. "What's here?" he cried out. "Guards at your place! Who was't? Strange doings!" He became the epitome of curiosity, and got his answer.

"*Madre de Dios!*" one of the lackeys said. "They say it is the pirate, El Beauvallet!"

"Jesu!" Joshua fell back, and crossed himself. "That fine gentleman? Do you make a jest of me? How should such a thing be, pray you?"

The first man shook his head hopelessly; it was his companion who answered, as he prepared to go indoors. "Why, there's Admiral Perinat within, foaming like a mad dog." He jerked his thumb over his shoulder. "He it was who cried out on the Chevalier."

Joshua wanted no more. The lackeys went in, remembering their duties; Joshua went speeding towards the Puerta del Sol.

He was in time; no guards had come yet to the Rising Sun to ransack his master's baggage. He slipped in at the back entrance, waited for a cook-maid's back to be turned, and so got him upstairs unseen.

He did swift work there. Doublets, hose, boots, shirts were flung from the chest by the window, some of them stowed away pell-mell into a pack, the rest left to lie on the floor.

"Here we play the knavish servant," Joshua encouraged himself. "What it is to have a head on one's shoulders!" He found Sir Nicholas' strong-box, and forced it open with the point of his dagger. "Ay, thus it goes. We take the money, and some few papers we may need, and leave the box to tell of our thieving. Ha, what's this? He unfolded the Chevalier de Guise's pass. "Softly, Joshua, that should be found, for I think we have no more need of it, and it may very easily help Sir Nicholas. We must be supposed to have searched in vain for it." He looked around him, saw a loose mandilion he had pulled out of the cupboard, and caught it up. "In the pocket, I believe. Lie there then, and I hope they may find you." He tucked the pass into an inner pocket, and hung the coat up at the back of the cupboard. "Ay, we sought it, and found it not. It may serve you yet, master." He came away from the cupboard. "Cheerly, Joshua! all will be well yet. Now to stow these clothes away." He packed as much of Sir Nicholas' raiment as he could carry with him, hid the jewels about his own person, and nipped out to get such of his own traps as he should need. Still there came no sound of guards approaching to seize Beauvallet's papers. Joshua spied from the window, listened, heard only the voice of a tapster below, and drew in again to finish his work. Two neat bundles stood ready upon the floor, but this did not seem to be enough for Joshua Dimmock. He went to work to create more havoc, and succeeded very fairly. A small chest he had emptied he chose to lock, and then break open. He tossed an old doublet into it, a pair of stocks, a riding boot. "Ay, that is the way it goes. The naughty knave to rifle his master's chest! Master, you may live to thank God you have me for your servant yet." He stood back, and surveyed the litter. "A rare gallimaufry, by my faith! What more? God's light! The sword!" He slapped his forehead, and darted to unearth the weapon from the depths of the cupboard in the wall. Out it came, that blade from the hand of Ferrara, delicate, flexible, with straight quillons, and a knuckle-bow of two shell shapes, chased with gold. "*My bite is sure!*" quoth Joshua. "I warrant me!"

Downstairs the inn was quiet, for it was late into the evening now. Joshua might have got away with none to see his flight, but chose instead to stumble into the sleepy tapster. He executed a well-feigned start, and let fly a French oath. "*Sangdieu!*" A ducat was pressed into the tapster's hand. "You do not see me," said Joshua. "Eh?"

"I see you very plainly," said the tapster, agape.

"That is not how it runs. Look you!" He took the tapster's ear between finger and thumb, and whispered. "Word's brought my master's clapped up. Do you take me now? Well, he will be free soon enough, I suppose, but I'll not be here to see it." He looked slyly. "There's a little farm in Picardy, and a rare wench to be won—if a man had the means." He patted the money-bags slung about his waist; indeed he fairly staggered under the weight of them. "I don't let opportunity slip, Mother of God!"

The tapster was bemused. He twisted his ear free. "What's this? Your master clapped up?"

"Some idle talk of his being El Beauvallet. Ho-ho, a very likely tale! Think I, it's some enemy has put this on him, for he's known the length and breadth of France for a Guise. But these are not matters for me. I'm for the Frontier, and a good riddance to a bad master!"

The tapster was left to blink after him. He shook his head making nothing of all this mysterious talk, and yawned, and wondered what o'clock it might be. Joshua got clear away while he was still wondering.

There was one other who was concerned in this capture, one who had also a part to play, and was warily mindful of it. The party at Noveli's house broke up swiftly, but not before many guests had crowded round Dona Dominica to hear what she might have to say.

In her heart was despair, for the hawk was snared, but she could still do what she might to aid him. Courage mounted; she set to fanning herself, and forced her pale lips into a smile of incredulity. "Señors, I have no more to say than what I have said. If this man is El Beauvallet

he is changed indeed since last I saw him. I grant you a
like colouring, but for the rest—*Madre de Dios,* if you
but knew the pirate, and had heard his abominable Spanish!" She tinkled a laugh, became aware of her aunt close
beside her, and turned. "Well, señora, your poor
Chevalier is fallen upon an evil hour indeed!" She sank
her voice. "Perinat——" She looked significantly, and
touched her forehead. "Ever since he lost his ship he has
been—strange in the head on this one subject." She
nodded wisely.

Don Diego made as if to speak, but his mother interposed. "I have not been so entertained for many a long
day," she said. "I am for my bed now. I suppose we shall
hear more of this in the morning. Come, my dear. Do you
follow us, Don Diego?"

He waved them away; he had still much to say, and
was burning to say it. "Presently, señora. Do not wait
upon my coming."

Dona Beatrice led her niece to make her curtsey to their
hostess.

There was a battle to be fought now, harder than the
skirmish that had just passed, Dominica knew well. As
they jolted homewards in the bumping coach Don Rodriguez was left to talk as he pleased. Dona Beatrice lay
back against the cushions, and allowed him to run on. He
exclaimed, wondered, surmised to his fidgetty heart's content, and his niece put in a word where she might.

They reached the Casa Carvalho. Dona Beatrice went
with her niece up the stairs, and followed her to her
chamber. Dominica had herself well in hand. Now for the
battle! now for the setting up of wits against wits!

Dona Beatrice sank down into a chair by the window.
"So that is it!" she said, amused. "What a daring lover you
have, my dear! Yes, I was hoodwinked. I must be getting
old." She shook her head over it.

"Heaven, señora, are you too besotted then?" asked
Dominica scornfully.

"Make no mistake, my dear," said Dona Beatrice placidly, "I wish him all success. Diego was in a rare taking,
was he not. Yes, many of them there had a fine scare
to-night. Cry Brava, El Beauvallet! But I think I will
have you away into the country." She smiled. "A very

charming romance, my dear. A pity it can come to naught."

Dominica pressed her hands to her temples. "You make my head to reel!" she complained. "I love a pirate? God save you, señora, what next will you put on me?"

Dona Beatrice nodded. "Very well played, my dear. You have more head than I give you credit for. But you need not be so careful now. I have no wish to see your hero perish. No, none whatsoever, I assure you. I have nothing but respect for a man of such daring. I wonder how he contrived to come by those papers of his? It would make a rare tale, I do not doubt. Alack, I am not like to hear it." She sighed. "But for you, my child—you must be got away with all speed."

"Why must I?" Dominica blinked at her. "Am I in peril, señora, because your infamous son accuses me of having a pirate for my lover?"

"Yes, was it not foolish of him? Madness!" agreed her aunt. "He has no head. Enough, one would say, to bring the familiars of the Inquisition to our house to-morrow. That, my dear, is one reason why you should be got away, and swiftly wed. We shall give the lie to suspicion of heresy against you. No doubt, if his papers are in order, as I dare say they may be, El Beauvallet will be set at large. Faith, a man who would take his life in his hand right to the heart of Spain might even contrive to snatch you from under my nose! Well, child, all honour to him if he can compass it, but you shall not expect me to lend him my aid."

"If his papers are in order," Dominica pointed out, "he will stand proved to be the man he says he is, so what fear?"

"Ah, but I too have brain. I see much now that—I confess—was hidden from me before." She smoothed the heavy silk of her dress. She was still smiling, still imperturbable. "Such a personable man—to be a pirate. I do not blame you at all, my dear. You made rare work of it aboard that ship, did you not? It is all most enlivening. For you I admit a pang or two. It will pass, and you will remember that you have had more romance than comes to most women in this weary world. But we shall leave Madrid. Certainly we shall leave Madrid."

"As you please, señora, but you give me no good reasons."

Dona Beatrice picked up her fan. "I will give you one you may perceive to be good, child. If you stay here you may haply be examined. Now I do not want that."

"I am very willing, aunt. I can but say what I have said."

"King Philip and the Holy Inquisition," said her aunt gently, "are not nice in their methods of obtaining information. Enough harm has been done already without you becoming suspected to be a heretic." She rose, and went with her languid step to the door. "We will have you safe married, my dear, and think out some tale against our need. As I see it, my child, you cannot better serve this bold lover of yours than to give the lie in such a way to those who suspect you and him."

The attack was renewed again next day, by Don Diego now, curbing his anger. He pressed marriage on his cousin, hinted his father might intercede for El Beauvallet, besought her to wed him at once, and trust to his good offices to help Beauvallet.

These were blundering tactics; Dominica curled her lip at them and him. Well she knew that once his identity was proved no power under the sun could save Beauvallet. The Holy Inquisition would step in and claim him; it was not necessary for Don Diego to tell her that she would see her lover burned at the stake. She knew it, had faced the horror squarely, and would not now change colour. Desperate need lent her courage, and agility of mind. She never hesitated, never blanched, could still laugh her scorn. "This is very kind, cousin!" she said tauntingly. "And if the unfortunate gentleman were indeed El Beauvallet and beloved of me no doubt I should avail myself of your offer." Oh, but her tongue had a sting in it still! She watched him flush, and bite his lip. She curtseyed. "But I have no interest in the Chevalier de Guise, my good cousin, and I doubt he does not stand in need of my help."

He took her wrist and shook it. "You think you hoodwink me? You think I do not know that fellow for what he is? Well, you shall see him burn!"

She smiled disdainfully. "Shall I so? I think it is you,

my cousin, who will know yourself for a fool before many days are out. Loose my wrist. You will get nothing by this usage."

He left her, sought out his mother. He was in a fret, biting his nails; he flew out upon her coolness, and was urgent with her to have the girl away at once.

Dona Beatrice regarded him blandly. She seemed amused by his agitation, and set her finger at the root of it. "One would say, my dear Diego, that you went in considerable fear of this Englishman."

"I do not fear any man, señora, but this devil——" He crossed himself. "There's witchcraft at work! You have not talked with Perinat. He tells me—in league with the devil, señora! What, could he have come otherwise into Spain, or sunk so many good ships of ours? We know El Draque to employ evil arts, and this man was trained under him."

"Witchcraft?" said Dona Beatrice. Her shoulders shook. "I wonder if his arts will bring him off from that prison?"

"You speak very lightly, señora. You cannot appreciate the dangers of our situation. While that man is alive, and my cousin still a maid, we may not know a moment's peace! At any time he might even be released! Have you thought of that? Perinat has little credit; his word may not serve against the fiend's papers. What, are we to have him loose amongst us, and you'll sit smiling?"

"I was never more in smiling humour," she remarked. "To see you so disturbed, my son! I owe the pirate a debt of gratitude, it seems. And you were within an ace of biting your glove in his face!"

"And would do so still!" he said sharply. "Make no mistake, señora, if he and I stand up together with a sword apiece I shall know what to do. If I fear aught it is his wiles, his devilish cunning! A man may not fight against witchcraft. Horrible sin! Deadly danger!" Again he crossed himself.

"Do you look to see him waft off Dominica in a cloud of smoke?" she inquired. "I find you ridiculous, Don Diego."

"Maybe, maybe. It is easy to sit contemptuous, señora, but you have had no dealings with the man."

"I have had some pretty traffic with him. He is a very bold rogue, and I had ever a fondness for such men. Moreover"—her fan waved rhythmically—"I like the merry look he has. A proper man, when all is said. I shall be sorry if I hear he comes not off."

"You will be sorry!" he ejaculated. "Oh, señora, will you lead my cousin to him, and say 'God bless you, pirate, take my niece?' "

"You are a fool to ask me," said his mother composedly. "I dare say I am as much his enemy as you are, but I have this gift, my son, that I can respect my foes. You may conjure up what nightmares of witchcraft you please; I shall not be in a heat for that. I am sure the man would laugh if he could hear you."

He pounced on that. "Yes, señora, yes! And will you tell me that it is not Satan who prompts him to laugh? Will you tell me that a mere man laughs as this warlock does when he faces death, and sees the dead all about him? Perinat could tell a tale!"

"I make no doubt he could," agreed Dona Beatrice. "I pray I may not have to hear him. I would stake my life all the magic this man uses is the magic of courage, and the arts you and others such as you have endowed him with. He takes a galleon: witchcraft! you cry. He sacks a town: more witchcraft! He comes into Spain on an errand of romance: foulest witchcraft of all! swear you. Well, I will tell you what I think, and I believe I am not a fool. He is English, therefore a little mad; he is a lover, therefore reckless. If he laughs it is because he is of those sort of men who will laugh though they die for it. There is all his magic." She yawned. "I dare say he will laugh as he goes to the stake, as I fear he will go. You fatigue me, Don Diego, and put me out of all patience with myself that I bore a fool."

"Very well, señora," he said hotly. "It's very well! But will you take my cousin into the country?"

"Certainly," she said.

"At once, señora, with what speed you can make!"

She raised her eyelids momentarily. "I shall leave Madrid for Vasconosa on Tuesday, as we have concerted, my son."

"Folly!" he cried, and took a turn about the room.

She lay back upon the day-bed, completely at her ease. "Do you think so?" she said mildly. "Maybe I see more clearly. All Madrid knows that I leave for Vasconosa on Tuesday. What do you suppose Madrid would think if I was off in a sudden start? There is only one thing that can make me put forward my departure, and that is the coming of Tobar. Pray you go harry your father with those fears and spare me." She shut her eyes as though she would go off into a doze.

He checked, pondered it, and said grudgingly: "I had not thought of that."

"No," she said, not troubling to open her eyes. "You lack the habit of thought, I believe. I wish you would leave me; you disturb my *siesta* to no purpose that I can see."

"I pray you may not be disturbed by anything more disastrous than my presence, señora!" he said. "You choose to sneer and think yourself wiser than us all, but I will tell you this—I shall warn my father if that devil escapes from his prison he must send the King's men hot-foot after him to Vasconosa!"

"By all means," agreed the lady. "Go and warn him at once."

ᴀ Chapter XVI ᴇ

UPON the morning following the strange arrest King Philip was disturbed at his orisons by a secretary made over-bold by the amazing news. He must needs, forgetful of time and place, blurt out to his master that El Beauvallet was taken prisoner. King Philip made no sign at all, but went on with his prayers.

The secretary flushed scarlet and drew back. King Philip finished his prayers and went his stately way to his cabinet.

He sat down at his desk there, placed his gouty foot upon the velvet stool, and pondered a document. A note was laboriously written in the margin. King Philip laid down his quill and raised his hooded eyes to the secretary. "You said something," he stated, and folded his hands tranquilly before him.

Vasquez, still discomposed, told the news badly. "Sire, El Beauvallet was captured at the house of Noveli last night!"

Philip thought it over for a moment. "That is not possible," he said at last. "Explain yourself."

The tale came tumbling out then, garbled, of course, but sufficiently arresting. Vasquez had it from Admiral Perinat that the Chevalier de Guise was none other than El Beauvallet, the terrible pirate. The Chevalier, then, was laid by the heels, and there were men in the ante-chamber craving an audience with his Majesty.

Philip blinked once, but seemed unmoved. "The Chevalier de Guise," he said slowly. "His papers were in order," he announced heavily. He looked calmly at Vasquez. "Does he admit it?" he inquired.

"No, sire, I believe not. I believe—I am sure—he sent at once to the French Ambassador to demand his protection. But Don Maxia de Perinat—"

Philip looked at his folded hands. "Perinat is a bungler," he said. "One who blunders once may blunder twice. "This seems to me a foolish tale. I will see M. de Lauvinière."

The French Ambassador came in a moment later, unhurriedly, and made his bow. His countenance was a little troubled, but he made no haste to come to his business. Compliments passed, an idle word on some idle matter. At length Philip said: "You have come upon some urgent business, señor. Let me hear it."

The Ambassador bowed again. "I have come upon the strange business of the arrest of the Chevalier de Guise, sire," he said, and paused as though he hardly knew how to proceed.

Philip waved one hand slightly. "Take your time, señor," he said kindly. "I perceive that you are troubled. You may trust me with your whole mind."

This was to set the Ambassador at his ease. De Lauvinière, knowing the King of old, inclined his head with a slightly ironic smile. The irony went unnoticed. "Sire, the Chevalier has sent, as a subject of France, to claim my protection," he said bluntly. "I am indeed troubled. I have to understand that he has been arrested on suspicion of being no less a person than Sir Nicholas Beauvallet, the sea-robber. My first impulse, sire, was to laugh at a charge so absurd."

Philip put his finger-tips together, and over them watched the Ambassador. "Continue, señor."

"The Chevalier, sire, very naturally denies this. His papers are in order; I cannot find from anything that I hear that there is any proof to substantiate the charge than Don Maxia de Perinat's word. I have seen Don Maxia, sire, and I must humbly confess that although he speaks as a man altogether convinced, I cannot deem his conviction to be sufficient evidence against the Chevalier. Moreover, sire, it appears that a certain lady who has taken prisoner by this same Beauvallet not so many months ago utterly denies that this man is he."

"I had not supposed it possible, señor, that El Beauvallet could be in Spain," said Philip calmly. "You come to request his release."

The Ambassador hesitated. "Sire, this is a very strange, a very difficult matter," he said. "It is no part of my desire to act hastily in it."

"Rest assured, señor, we shall do nothing without careful consideration," Philip said. "Do you identify the Chevalier?"

Again there was a momentary hesitation. "I cannot do that, sire. I am not over-familiar with the members of the house of Guise; I have never, to my knowledge, met this man. But from what I know of the family I did from the first moment of seeing him suspect that this man might not be what he claimed to be. It is in my mind that the Chevalier de Guise should be a younger man than this, nor can I trace any resemblance to the Guises in his countenance."

Philip weighed that. "It might thus chance, señor," he said.

"Certainly sire. I may well be mistaken. But upon my first meeting with him I wrote into France to discover more of him. The answer to my letter must be awaited before I can state whether this man is the Chevalier or whether he is not. I have come here today, sire, to request you, very humbly, to be patient a few weeks, to hold your hand, in effect, until I receive the answer to my letter."

Philip nodded slowly. "We shall do nothing unadvisedly," he said. "We must think on this. You shall hear more of our decision, señor. Be sure we should be loth to proceed against a subject of our cousin of France."

"I have to thank your Majesty for your courtesy," de Lauvinière said, and bowed over the King's cold hand. He was ushered out of the cabinet, and passed through the antechamber without delay. Perinat tried to stop him and shot an eager question, but de Lauvinière answered evasively, and passed on.

The King would not see Don Maxia de Perinat. "It does not need for us to listen to Don Maxia," he said coldly. "He will make his deposition to the Alcalde at a later time. We will give audience to Don Cristobal de Porres."

Don Cristobal, commander of the Guards of Castile, Governor of the great barracks where Beauvallet was imprisoned, was awaiting the King's pleasure in the anteroom. He was a man of some forty years of age, dark and tall, with a grave countenance and a thin mouth half concealed by his black mustachio and the pointed beard he wore. He came in very promptly, and stood just inside the door, deeply bowing. "Sire!"

"We have sent for you, señor, to inquire into this matter of your prisoner. I do not immediately understand why the *ginetes* were called in."

"The Casa Noveli, sire, is hard by the barracks," Porres answered. "A gentleman came in hot haste with the news that El Beauvallet was captured, and my lieutenant, Cruza, perhaps acted without due reflection. I have held the man in ward against the hearing of your Majesty's pleasure."

Philip seemed to be satisfied, for he said nothing for a moment or two, but gazed with apparent abstraction before him. Presently he brought his eyes back to Porres' face, and spoke abruptly. "Let search be made in his baggage," he said. "We shall require you to keep the Chevalier under surveillance, Don Cristobal, until such

time as we make known our further pleasure. If he travels
with a servant—" he paused. "It might be well to interrogate the man."

"Sire——!"

Philip waited.

"It was judged expedient, sire, to send early this morning to the inn where the Chevalier lodged. I do not know
sire, if this was agreeable to your Majesty, but in consideration—the charge was of such a nature—there was a
fear——"

"Compose yourself, señor."

"In short, sire, acting a little on Don Maxia de Perinat's
advice, I caused search to be made through the
Chevalier's effects, and sent to apprehend the servant,
deeming it a measure your Majesty would approve."

"You acted precipitately," said Philip. "These things
are not done without good advice. Continue."

"I ask your Majesty's pardon if I did wrongly. When
my men came to the inn they found the—the Chevalier's
baggage strewn about, his chests and strong box broken
open and empty. His money was gone, his jewels, a sword
of Ferrara make, the best of his dress—in short, sire, a
seeming robbery, committed by the servant, who had
fled."

"Who had fled," repeated the King. "But continue,
señor."

"This we thought a suspicious circumstance, sire, but
upon question the tapster at the inn confessed to having
had speech with the servant last night, when he was
evidently making his escape. The man says that he was
something merry in his bearing, talked of his good fortune, and said that if his master was laid by the heels it
was a good riddance to him, and he was not one to be
slow to catch at opportunity."

"Possible! Possible! said Philip. "Yet this might well
be a ruse. We have to consider all points, Don Cristobal.
What said the Chevalier?"

Don Cristobal smiled rather ruefully. "The Chevalier,
sire, exhibited a very natural anger, and—in fact, sire, he
demands—he is high in his tone—that strict search should
be made for the fellow. He would have us send after the
man to the Frontier, for he is left penniless. The

Chevalier, sire, was particularly enraged at the loss of his sword. He started up, sire, and demanded to know whether the servant had made off with this piece, and upon being told that it was not to be found, he seemed like to fly into a very real passion. The next thing he asked, sire, was whether his papers too, were gone, and it seemed to me—I was watching him closely—that he showed great relief when I could assure him that they were safe."

"Ah, the papers were left?" Philip asked.

"They were discovered, sire, in the inner pocket of a mandilion. I judged that the man had overlooked them in his haste. A wallet was found on the floor with a few odd bills in it, but nothing more. The Chevalier's linen was overturned as though the servant had sought amongst it for something, and we found sundry other articles of raiment."

"Let these be taken to the Chevalier," said Philip. "This is a delicate matter, señor, needing our careful judgment."

There was the sound of a softly opened door behind him. A man came into the room from some inner room behind Philip, a man in a priest's gown. Philip's thin lips parted in a smile that showed teeth that were yellow and rather pointed. "You are come opportunely, Father."

The priest had gone unobtrusively to the window, but he turned at Philip's words, and came nearer to the King's chair. He was Father Allen, an English Jesuit, never far from Philip's side. "You have need of me, sire?"

"I may have need of you, Father," Philip answered cautiously. "There is a man held in ward, Father, who is accused of being the freebooter, Beauvallet."

"I have heard something of this, sire, from Frey Luis."

"Do you know this Beauvallet, Father?" asked Philip directly.

"I regret, sire, no. I knew his father by sight, but the sons by hearsay only."

"A pity." Philip's smile died. He regarded the opposite wall for a while. "I do not see what El Beauvallet does in Spain," he said, and awaited enlightenment.

It came from Porres. "The tale is very strange, sire, almost incredible. It is said—by the lady's cousin—that

El Beauvallet came into Spain to carry off Dona Dominica de Rada y Sylva."

Philip looked at him. It was plain that such a mad exploit was beyond his Catholic Majesty's comprehension.

Father Allen spoke from behind the King's chair. "Beauvallet had no need to come into Spain if that had been his purpose."

Philip nodded. "That is true. This is a very foolish tale," he said. "Moreover, it is impossible for such a man as El Beauvallet to enter Spain."

"As to that, sire"—Father Allen lifted his shoulders— "there might be ways of compassing it, if the man were bold enough."

A new voice spoke from the door behind Philip. "A man in league with the powers of darkness could do it." A monk of the Dominican order had come in quietly. His scowl partly shaded his face, but his eyes shown dark and intense. He came farther into the room. "I have thought on this, sire." He sighed heavily. "Who can say what such a man might do?

The faintest hint of a contemptuous smile flitted across Father Allen's lips, but he said nothing.

"Consider, sire, what dreadful errand this man may have come upon," insisted Frey Luis in a hushed voice.

Philip brought his gaze round to the Frey. "What errand?" he asked, puzzled.

"Sire, how shall we say that El Beauvallet would hesitate to seek the life of even your Majesty?" Frey Luis folded his hands in the wide sleeves of his habit and fixed his eyes on Philip.

Phlip moved a paper on his desk. His brain turned this over and detected a flaw. "If such were his errand, Frey Luis, he would have made the attempt when I saw him in this room with only yourself present," he said.

"Sire, who knows in what cunning ways Satan goes to work?"

Don Cristobal interposed. "I do not think that this man is such a one, sire. I could more readily believe, from what I have seen of the man, in Don Diego de Carvalho's explanation."

But King Philip was not at all inclined to believe in it.

His matter-of-fact mind discarded it as the wildest of suppositions. "A test might be made," he mused. "A simple Mass, perhaps."

Don Cristobal coughed. The dull eyes travelled to his face. "You were about to say, señor?"

"The Chevalier, sire, has made the suggestion himself."

Philip looked at the Jesuit. Father Allen spoke smoothly. "That is clever of him," he said. "But you should know, sire, that it is not so long since the Beauvallets were of the True Faith. It is almost sure that this man would pass such a test triumphantly."

Frey Luis spoke again. "There are tests the Holy Inquisition would impose that would be harder to pass. We have to think of the soul, sire. Let this man be given over to the infinite compassion of the Church."

Philip laid his hand on the table. "A heretic of any nation, Frey Luis, belongs to the Church. I am not so undutiful a son of Christ as to withhold from the Church any heretic, be he a notorious pirate or a peaceable burgher," he said austerely. "As an enemy of Spain El Beauvallet should be judged by the secular arm, but I have to think of the soul, which must be saved at all costs. The Church demands him."

"Your Majesty is a faithful son of the Church," Father Allen said. "That is well known. Humbly I would suggest, sire, that the charge of heresy be strictly followed up."

There was a short silence. Don Cristobal stood patiently waiting by the curtain that hung over the doorway. The King's eyes were veiled; he seemed to brood, like some sated vulture. What thoughts passed in that tortuous mind even Father Allen could not guess.

"There is as yet no suspicion of heresy," the King said at last. "We must remember, Father, that we have to deal with a subject of France."

Father Allen bowed his head and stood back. The matter was plain enough now. Philip had no wish to offend the French King upon so trivial a matter, nor did he want his own secret dealings with the Guises to be made public. He would not run the risk of the Chevalier de Guise disclosing these dealings, Father Allen knew well.

Frey Luis, no Jesuit, but a priest with one single aim, one obsession, did not read the King's mind so acutely, nor, had he been able to appreciate Philip's difficulty, would it have weighed with him. His faith was simple, and burned like a consuming flame; earthly considerations he would never consider. "The Inquisition claims him," he said. "There may yet be time to rescue his soul from the depths to which it has sunk."

The King gave only half an ear to this. "We gain nothing by haste," he said. "You assume, Frey Luis, that this man is indeed El Beauvallet. I am not so easily satisfied. I have listened to wild tales; they do not convince me."

"The Holy Inquisition, sire, is tender above all things and infinitely just," said Frey Luis earnestly. "It does not leap to conclusions, and there can be nothing to be feared at its hands by a true son of Christ. If this man be the Chevalier he could raise no objection to appearing before a tribunal appointed to sift him."

Philip listened in silence. "True," he said meditatively. "There could be no objection. A son of the Church would not flinch from such a test." He paused and frowned. Much was revealed in such tests, he knew very well; perhaps more in this instance might be forthcoming than would be agreeable to his Catholic Majesty. The King saw clearly that this was yet another case that went to prove the truth of his maxim that nothing should be attempted without mature reflection. His frown cleared. He repeated his former observation. "We gain nothing by undue haste. If the man is proved not to be the Chevalier de Guise, I shall know how to act. Until such time as I shall receive intelligence from M. de Lauvinière, the Chevalier shall be kept in ward." He turned to Porres. "This will be your charge, señor. You will treat the Chevalier with all consideration, but let him be kept in guard." The frown returned. "He must be used with strict courtesy," he said slowly. "He will appreciate the grave difficulties of our situation. But we would not have him in the least degree rudely entreated."

Don Cristobal was a little puzzled. "Pardon, sire, is he to be a prisoner, or may he go abroad?"

Such bluntness was little to Philip's taste. His frown deepened. Father Allen interposed. "Sire, if this man should be Beauvallet you cannot guard him too securely."

"True," the King said. "We have to think of the safety of our realm. You have some apartment, señor, in which he might be safely bestowed? Some room from which no exit is possible? We do not speak of prison cells."

"Yes, sire, he is in such a room now, pending your pleasure."

"There is no need to put indignity upon one who may well be proved innocent of the charge proffered against him," Philip said. "A lock should suffice, and a sentry outside. You will see to it, señor. We shall hold you responsible for the Chevalier's safety and well-being. You will remark his bearing, and report to us the least sign of an attempt to escape."

Don Cristobal bowed. "I shall obey your Majesty in all my best," he said, and bowed himself out of the closet.

✑◄ Chapter XVII ►✎

No word came from the Alcazar to summon Dominica to answer an examination. Don Rodriguez, uneasily awaiting such a summons, brought back word first that the Chevalier was to be held in ward pending the arrival of word from France; second, that his Majesty had spoken no word concerning Dona Dominica; and thirdly, that Don Miguel de Tobar had started for Madrid sooner than had been expected, and was likely to arrive within the next few days.

Dona Beatrice was unwillingly roused to action. Sighing over it, she said that it was all very fatiguing, and not a

little tiresome, but if suspicion did not rest on Dona
Dominica there was no reason why they should not leave
Madrid upon Saturday.

Dominica heard this with dismay. God knows what she
hoped for by remaining in the capital; she hardly knew
herself, but to journey north so many leagues out of sight
or sound of Madrid filled her with despair. To stay could
do Beauvallet no good. True enough, but how could one
go, knowing him to be in such danger?

She said never a word, but bowed her head slightly and
tried to look indifferent. She was far from that ideal state.
While she was borne off north God alone knew what
might be done to Beauvallet. She had heard that those
who fell into the clutch of the Inquisition were sometimes
never heard of again. She fell to trembling and to silent
prayer. Her own fate seemed no longer to be a matter of
moment. Listlessly she observed a certain quiet satisfaction in her cousin's demeanour which she supposed could
betoken no good, but it seemed no longer to signify. If
Beauvallet died they might do with her as they would.

Don Diego left Madrid a day ahead of his mother and
cousin. Dominica heard of his plans without change of
countenance, but his mother drawled: "You do not ride
with us?"

He answered very easily that he would go before to
have all in readiness against their coming to Vasconosa.
He could not but think that the Carvalho guards would be
protection enough for their equipage.

Dona Beatrice looked at him with narrowed eyes,
seemed to consider him, but said only: "You are not very
gallant, my son."

His departure was watched by one of whom he knew
nothing. Joshua, anxious to get speech with Dominica,
haunted the vicinity of the Casa Carvalho, and saw Don
Diego set forward that Friday with his valet and two
lackeys with led sumpters. Joshua's sharp nose smelled
mischief. He lounged against the sun-baked wall and
picked his teeth, but his ears were on the prick and his
eyes sharp beneath the slouching brim of his hat. A chance
word let fall by one of the lackeys strapping a pack to the
sumpter disclosed their destination. There was little need
of it; Joshua had been in small doubt. He watched Don

Diego mount and gather up the reins; heard him admonish the lackeys to press forward at speed; and saw him ride off. Joshua drew his own conclusions.

"Ay, go swiftly, villain!" he apostrophised Don Diego. "Waste no time, for you will have Mad Nick behind you, never doubt it! Cullion and coystrill! Oh, an eater of broken meats, a very pungent rascal! It would do one's heart good to slit the villain's nose. I shall suggest it to my master in due course." He heaved a sigh. "Master, as I see it, you would do well to break out of ward swiftly. Here's roguery afoot. If I can but get speech with my lady and know what they will be about! A plague on all women!"

An hour of patient loitering rewarded him. Dominica at last appeared, accompanied by her maid, and bound, as Joshua had hoped she might be, to hear Mass at a neighbouring Church. She cast a passing look at him where he lounged, but it was unrecognising. As well it might be, for there was little trace of swaggering Joshua in the sober, clean-shaved personage she saw. He wore a buffin gown as might some needy clerk; gone were the ambitious mustachios, gone the beard that Sir Nicholas was wot to call his *pique de vent,* gone, too, the strutting carriage. A meek individual followed my lady at a discreet distance to Church.

She chose an unoccupied bench at the back of the Church. Joshua waited until old Carmelita was bowed over her rosary, devout and unseeing, then slid on to the bench and edged gradually closer to my lady.

Her eyes were open, looking straight before her. She became aware of Joshua and turned her head. She was inclined to be angry at his encroachment: that he saw by the spark in her eyes. He looked fully at her, laid a finger to his lips and beckoned her surreptitiously nearer.

She did not know him; she stiffened; her look should have abashed him. He was at a loss; he dared not move nearer to her lest the maid should be roused from her devotions, or the lady withdraw. He looked imploringly, and she turned her shoulder. A hasty glance round him showed him only a few people busy at their prayers. He bent his head and whispered: "Lady, *Reck Not!*"

His quick eyes peeped up at her; she had heard; she was looking keenly at him now. Again he made that little

beckoning movement. She let fall her missal, bent to pick
it up, and in the doing of it shifted her position till she
was close beside him.

He pretended to mumble prayers, telling over the beads
of a rosary. "Lady, you do not know me. I am Joshua
Dimmock. My beard is off. What of that? Caution! Caution!"

She stole a glance at him, met the upward flash of his
shrewd grey eyes. Recognition sprang into her own. She
bent her head and put her clasped hands up to hide her
face. "You! Oh, what do you know?"

"He is in ward. Courage, señorita! I am here to discover what plans are laid for you. Does Tuesday hold
good yet?"

"Saturday," she whispered back. "To-morrow. He sent
you? You have contrived to get speech with him?"

"Nay. Be of good heart, lady, and keep faith. He will
break free yet."

She gave a long sigh. "I have led him to his death."

Privately Joshua was in complete agreement with her.
"It was noticeable," he said later, "that she seemed to
have little idea of having led me thitherwards. But I let
that pass."

For all his secret convictions, vicarious dignity would
not permit him to let the lady think that she had had any
hand in this escapade. His answering whisper contained
some austerity. "I have yet to learn, señorita, that my
master is led by aught save his own inclination. Let it go.
I am avised of your movements; it but remains for me to
get speech with Sir Nicholas."

Her eyes flickered to his face. "Is it so easy? Can you
do it?"

"It will not be easy," said Joshua severely, "but certainly I shall do it. Be of good cheer; trust me, and trust my
master. No more of this. Dangerous dealing!" He edged
away along the bench, and she was left to her seeming
prayers.

She was oddly comforted by this talk with Joshua. He
spoke with an assurance he was far from feeling, but she
was not to know that. She might doubt still, but she now
had hope, for if Joshua, who knew Beauvallet so well,
could be sanguine, she too, might expect a happy issue.

He was not perhaps so sanguine as he chose to appear, but for the timorous man he declared himself to be, he was very cool. A squalid tavern in the meaner part of the city now housed him; if he could but get a sight of his master he would have only one regret, and this the loss of his brave mustachios.

"Alack!" he told himself mournfully. "I who was, I believe, a personable man, now look like some starveling scrivener." He spat into the kennel. "So much for that. It boots not to bewail my lost mustachios; they are very decently interred. The loss of a fair beard I can better support; one may call it a fortune of war. But the mustachios are another and more serious affair. Something of the cock of Beauvallet's own, I apprehend. I wore them with a good grace. A plague on all shaven lips! But this is to talk more and no more. I do not repine." He walked on towards his lodging. "Now what, I must ask myself? Do you come out of that stronghold, master? Nay, we must admit it to be an impossibility." He threw out his chest and strutted a little. "Ha! A word we do not know. We maybe have some few wiles left that they may still blear the eyes of these Spanish dawcocks." He abated his pace and abandoned the swagger. "Yet I own myself to be very pigeon-livered in this matter. You may say I had his word he would escape if he were taken. Maybe we brag a little—a very little." He shook his head slightly. "Master, if I knew of a way—but I make no doubt a way will present itself to me. I must lie close, as I am bid, and keep good watch. To do else might be to o'erset deep laid schemes. Courage, Joshua!"

The question of Dominica's departure next occupied his busy mind. He scented mischief there, bristled at it like a dog, and shook his fist at an imaginary Don Diego. "Mark me well, we will carbonado you finely yet, Master Hemp-Seed! Sir Nicholas, you would do well to let your guards taste of your mettle at once, for I mislike the complexion of this whole matter. Let us consider. How long might a coach take to reach Vasconosa? The roads are bad. True, but we have had no rain, and there will be no mud for the coach to founder in. They are to change horses, as I learn, at every stage. Ten days, maybe, swift going. For a man riding hard, as we might ride? Ah, that is another

and very different affair." His pace quickened. "There is
the question of horses. We must go privily to work and
discover at what stages one can buy nags upon the road.
The plague is on it, I have had to abandon Sir Nicholas'
fine mare. Now, if Sir Nicholas were to appear of a
sudden, as I believe he may do? What will be his cry?
Horses, Joshua! True. And how shall we answer? Certain,
it is meet that I lay out some money on a couple of good
nags to be in readiness. Ah, what it is to have a head!
Master, if I but knew where you lie, and how they use
you!"

He would perhaps have been comforted had he known
that Sir Nicholas lay in a very fair apartment, and was
most courteously used. He might have all he wanted for
the mere asking.

Don Cristobal came to visit him each day, and was at
pains to be polite. It was from him that Sir Nicholas
learned of the messenger sent off to France to inquire
more particularly into his identity. When he heard that he
gave an irrepressible laugh. Certain, the net was closing
in. Don Cristobal understood the laugh to imply no more
than a scornful amusement, and did not wonder at it. His
attitude throughout was of painstaking civility. The difficulties of his position were felt keenly by him, and he was
anxious that—in the event of the Chevalier coming off
triumphant—his prisoner would have no cause to complain of his treatment in ward.

He had many talks with the Chevalier, and the more he
saw of him the more convinced he became that Perinat
had made some ridiculous mistake. Don Cristobal could
not conceive that a man who knew himself to be in such
danger could wear so care-free a countenance, or could
crack light-hearted jests at every turn. Some signs of
unease there must surely have been had the man been El
Beauvallet indeed. He ventured upon one occasion to
hope that all would go well for the Chevalier, and hinted
at the Inquisition, watching Beauvallet keenly as he
spoke.

He got nothing by that. The black brows flew up in a
kind of artless surprise; the smile only grew the more
amused. "*Sangdieu!*" said Beauvallet in mock alarm. "I
hope so, too!"

It was very evident that he had no doubts about it. Don Cristobal felt that he had passed another test satisfactorily.

The Chevalier soon requested that he might be allowed some exercise. Don Cristobal had to admit this to be a reasonable desire, and made arrangements to grant it. Beauvallet was permitted the indulgence of walking in the courtyard for an hour each day, closely attended by the two guards who waited on him.

There was more to this request than a mere desire for exercise. Sir Nicholas, hurried to the barracks at night, had as yet had no opportunity to take in his surroundings. To walk in the court would give him a chance to get a plan of the building in his mind, which was necessary to a man whose brain was busy all the time with schemes for escape.

He knew already, from a glance out of his chamber window, that his prison was upon the first floor. His window overlooked a quiet street that was flanked on the opposite side by a blank wall. He wasted very little time here. Even if the bars across the window had been weak enough to pull out, the room was too high above the ground for a man to attempt the drop. Escape did not lie that way.

When his guards came to escort him out to the court he found that his room gave on to a stone corridor, or cloister, with tall open arches overlooking a paved courtyard. The barracks seemed to enclose this court in a square, and as far as Beauvallet could see the corridor ran right round, with doors opening off it upon the inner side. A quick glance up and down as soon as he came out of his room discovered a spiral stairway to the left, set in the width of the wall where the corridor turned at right-angles to run along the south side of the court.

The guards directed Beauvallet away from this stair, and went with him down the long corridor to the further corner, and round on to the north side. Sir Nicholas judged the length of the corridor to be as near ninety or a hundred feet as made no odds. On the north side was a large stairway, evidently the principal stair in the building, coming up from the arched gateway to the soldiers' quarters.

They went down it, and Sir Nicholas found himself in the open courtyard, with the sun beating down upon him. To the north an arch led to the street. There were sentries on guard there. To one side of this arch was the stairway down which he had come; to the other was a closed door.

They paced slowly round the court. The ground floor owned just such another corridor as was found on the floor above. There was another storey, Sir Nicholas ascertained, but the corridor was enclosed here, and had windows set, perhaps, eight feet apart all round the square, each with its little semi-circular balcony, so typical of the Spanish house. Above was the flat roof and the chimney-stacks.

Sir Nicholas continued his promenade between the two guards, and chatted amiably with them, as his custom was. They had eyed him in round-eyed wonder at first, and had been suspicious of him, seeing under his gay exterior a very dreadful pirate, but those feelings had not lasted long. It was the opinion of the guards that the pleasant gentleman was being wrongfully imprisoned. He never gave the least sign of a wish to escape, was merry in his talk, and, in their eyes, was too much of a gentleman to be an English sea-robber. They were quite willing to talk to him, and saw no harm in his questions. He displayed a casual interest in the Guards of Castile, and was surprised to hear how many of them were gathered in this place. However, it was no wonder, he supposed and looked round him appreciatively. "I dare swear you might house an hundred more in a place of this size."

"Why, señor, if it comes to the pinch, more than that," one of the soldiers told him. "There are rooms up aloft"—he nodded towards the second storey—"that stand as bare as my hand."

The other man was inclined to cavil at this. "Not many more," he said. "There are the stables, and there have to be rooms set aside for stores. The place is not so big as would seem, señor." Why, the armoury alone, over yonder, takes up a great space, and no men housed there, and you have the guard-room as well upon this level."

"But you might surely house an hundred upon one side of the building alone," objected Sir Nicholas. "Four sides

—nay, I forget: the gateway takes away from one side. Three sides, then, all fit to house an hundred men."

"Nay, nay, there are the Governor's quarters to consider," said the guard.

"Ah, of course!" said Sir Nicholas blandly. "I had forgot that he lived here." He looked rueful. "I give him joy of it. For my part, I find it a dreary place."

"Well, señor, you are unfortunate," he was told. "The Governor does well enough, with a very pretty garden to walk in and a score of fine rooms, I warrant you."

Sir Nicholas began to talk of something else. The disposition of the Governor's quarters and the whereabouts of his garden was all he wanted to know now, and he would go his own way to work about that. He complained of the scorching sun, and brought his walk to an end. When Don Cristobal came to visit him later in the day, and inquired whether he had taken his exercise, Sir Nicholas thanked him, but believed that for the future he must confine his walks to the corridor.

"I find it rather too sunny, señor. Heyday! I would M. de Lauvinière's messenger mght bestir himself a little." He observed Don Cristobal's troubled look, and smiled. "Nay, do not look so worried, señor. I must be content with the corridor, and this grim incarceration cannot last for many weeks."

"Why, Chevalier, I should be loth—certainly the sun beats down very hotly. I do not think there could be any objection to your walking in my garden for a space every day. I will arrange for it."

"But this is too kind, señor! Indeed, I shall take no hurt in the corridor. I should not like to trespass into your garden," Beauvallet said.

"No trespass, señor. Consider it agreed upon. I am held responsible for your well-being, and I am assured his Majesty is anxious to make this unfortunate time as pleasant for you as maybe. Is there aught else I may do for you?"

Beauvallet seemed to consider. He drew some coins from his pocket, and looked at them with a grimace. "Lay that fellow of mine by the heels, señor, and I shall be much your debtor. But I believe I have enough to buy me some few things. Of your kindness, señor, some book to help while away the time. I do not know whether I am permitted to write to my friends?"

Don Cristobal hesitated. "With the greatest reluctance, señor, I should feel myself bound to glance at any messages you may wish to send out of this place."

"Oh, you may read all my papers with my very goodwill," Sir Nicholas told him.

"I will send you some ink, then, and paper," Don Cristobal promised, and withdrew.

Upon the following morning Beauvallet was escorted to the Governor's quarters, by the stairway he had gone down the day before, and through the door he had noticed on the opposite side of the arched gateway. This led into a large hall, furnished very richly with fine hangings and chairs of Italian *intarsia* work. Across the hall a door gave on to a walled garden shaded by trees, and through this they went.

Beyond the wall Sir Nicholas judged that there was a street as on his opposite side of the building. The wall was high, but rough upon the inner side, with one or two espaliers trained up it. If a man had the help of a rope he might make shift to scale that wall; at a pinch he might make the attempt without assistance, but with indifferent hope of success. There seemed to be no other way into the garden than through this one door.

Sir Nicholas studied the outside of the building closely. Here were no barred windows, and the side of the house was grown over with a thick wistaria. A man penetrating into one of the upper rooms on this side of the building might climb down the wall by the aid of that wistaria—if it held. So much Sir Nicholas decided; it was little enough. He went back presently to his prison and sat down by the window to write an innocent letter to his Andalusian acquaintance.

It might have been noticed that the Chevalier nearly always sat by the window, and very often stood looking out on to the street. His guards made nothing of that. There was little enough to see in the street, but the poor gentleman had nothing else to interest him, to be sure, until the Governor sent him a selection of books to read. Even then a gentleman cannot be reading all the day.

Sir Nicholas, watching the street below, did not at first

recognise his swaggering servant in the clean-shaven, demure individual who strolled slowly along on the opposite side of the road. But his attention was held by the apparently idle glances this clerk-like person cast up at the barracks as he came, and he knitted his brows a little.

Joshua was opposite his window now, and again looked up. The puzzled frown vanished from Beauvallet's face; he lifted his hand, and Joshua saw him.

Joshua cast a glance behind him. There was no one in sight. He stood still, showing a joyful countenance. Sir Nicholas passed a hand over his beard, caressed his mustachio tips, and affected an intense grief. But his shoulders shook.

"Ho!" said Joshua softly. "This is pretty treatment, God wot! Nay, then, master, have done! Is this the time to make merry? It sorteth no good at all. God be thanked you are safe, and in spirits, as it would seem! What, will you be fleering still?" He shook his head severely. "I may say you are incorrigible. Now I must tell you some few things. And how?" He saw a man turn down the corner of the street, and bent as though to take a stone from his shoe. After that he walked on until the man had rounded the corner, and then came swiftly back. It would not do to shout to Sir Nicholas, that was certain. He put his head on one side and debated. The street was still empty when he came opposite to Beauvallet's window again, and he began to indulge in a piece of pantomime for his master's benefit. Don Diego was portrayed by a mincing step, a sniffing at an imaginary flower, and a flourishing bow. Sir Nicholas grinned and nodded. Joshua made believe then to throw himself upon a horse, and to ride off at full speed.

The play ended he looked up inquiringly. Sir Nicholas was frowning. He drew a large V in the air, and cocked up an eyebrow. Joshua nodded vigorously, and made beckoning signs as though to bid his master make haste.

That Sir Nicholas understood more or less what he meant to convey was easy to see. He signed to Joshua to go, and himself fell to pacing the floor of his room.

If Dominica had gone already to Vasconosa, as Joshua's play would seem to indicate, with Don Diego hard on her heels, it looked as though there was mischief brewing. Sir Nicholas had been content to lie in his prison till Tuesday, or even later, for there was nothing to be gained by breaking free while Dominica still lay at Madrid. On the contrary, there was all to be lost. Once out of prison he must lose no time in getting out of Spain; there would be no time then for waiting upon his lady's movements. But this new development changed the complexion of the affair. Sir Nicholas sat down on the edge of his bed and began thoughtfully to finger his beard. " 'Ware Beauvallet, if you see him at that trick!" would have said Joshua Dimmock. But the Guards of Castile were not so familiar with Sir Nicholas Beauvallet's ways.

His brain began to shape plans, twisting and scheming. If he failed in his attempt he must stand self-convicted as El Beauvallet. He knew what to expect then. He shrugged his shoulders and lifted his pomander to his nose.

Sniffing at it he evolved his plan. It was sufficiently desperate to appeal to that lively sense of humour in him. "Come, Nick!" he apostrophised himself. "Let us take *Reck Not* for our watchword yet once again. It has not been known to fail us yet. But I am sorry for that sentry."

By which it may be seen that Sir Nicholas counted the sentry outside his door a dead man already.

He moved to the table, and wrote three lines to Joshua. They were quite simple.

"Be ready to-morrow evening with a rope outside the wall on the opposite side of the building to this. When you hear my whistle, cast it across and hold tightly."

This, he twisted into a screw and put away in his bosom. Upon the following morning Joshua walked down the street again. The screw of paper went fluttering down from Beauvallet's window, and was swiftly pounced on.

Joshua went back to his tavern strutting light-heartedly.

⌒⊰ *Chapter XVIII* ⊱⌒

EVER since the first day of his imprisonment Sir Nicholas had been waited on always by two men. Never one came without the other, and although, gradually, this precaution had become little more than a form it was still observed. Sir Nicholas pulled a wry face over it. Truly they held him to be a desperate man since they kept a sentry outside his room, and dared not send a single armed man to take his meals to him. Well, they were right, but he thought he had successfully lulled their fears. For his escape to have the smallest chance of success one of those men must be got out of the room. All hung on that; if one man could not be induced to leave the room torture and the fire awaited Sir Nicholas, as he very well knew.

He had chosen his time carefully, and knew that he could trust Joshua to do his part. Every evening at dusk supper was brought to Sir Nicholas from the Governor's kitchens. The cook was at pains to please the unwilling guest, for there was still enough money left in Beauvallet's pockets to provide a sufficient incentive. The cook, receiving a double ducat, sent with a compliment, vowed the Chevalier was a true gentleman, and devised subtleties for his delectation.

Upon the day chosen by Sir Nicholas for his attempt at escape, his two gaolers came a little late with his supper. One of them, the senior, had charge of the key of his room, and always locked the door punctiliously upon the inside when he entered, and continued to hold the key in his hand while his fellow set covers on the table and lit the candles.

Sir Nicholas had a high-backed chair with arms and a velvet seat to sit in, but he was not sitting in it when the two soldiers entered. He was standing near the window, leaning his shoulders against the wall, and whistling a cheerful tune to himself.

"I thought I was to be starved," he remarked, and came lounging over to the table and sat himself down on the arm of his chair, idly swinging one foot.

The chief gaoler smiled indulgently. "No, no, señor. It is only that the cook spoiled one of the dishes—or rather, I should say, that one of the scullions, left to stir it, let it burn a little—and the whole had to be made again."

The other man was busy shaking out a cloth and spreading it over the table. Sir Nicholas sniffed the air. "Well, it hath a very savoury odour," he said. "Let us see the *chef d'œuvre.*"

The knife was set, a bottle of wine placed carefully beside the cup at Beauvallet's elbow, and a shining cover lifted with a flourish

"Marvellous!" said Sir Nicholas. He still sat negligently on the arm of his chair, sideways to the table. "Present my compliments to the cook." He stretched out his hand for the bottle, while the soldier took salt and pepper from the tray he had brought, and put them on the table. He poured out a cupful of the wine, and raised it with a little laugh. "Tell the cook I drink his very good health!" he said, and made as if to toss off the wine. But that fine gesture was stayed before he had done more than taste it. The cup left his lips; he pulled a grimace. "My very dear friends!" he said. "What's this? Do you seek to poison me? What have you brought me here?"

The soldiers stared at him. "*Madre de Dios,* señor, there is no thought of poisoning you!" said one of them, shocked.

Sir Nicholas smiled. "I did but jest. But you have brought me a very vile potion, none the less. Let me have another bottle, my good fellow. Take this away."

The chief frowned upon his subordinate, shifting the blame from off his own shoulders. "Dolt! Take up the bottle! What, do you bring the señor bad wine? Pardon, señor! an oversight. The cup, fool! Take away the cup and bring a clean one back!" He hustled his protesting fellow towards the door.

"It was you chose the wine," grumbled the unfortunate.

"You confused the bottles," the other said hastily. "Get you gone, get you gone! Will you have the señor's supper grow cold?"

"You have the key," his subordinate pointed out. "I did not confuse the bottles, I tell you. You yourself——"

"A'God's mercy, have done!" struck in Sir Nicholas curtly. "I care not who made the mistake so long as you bring me a fresh bottle."

"On the instant, señor!" his gaoler assured him, responding instinctively to the voice of authority. He unlocked the door, pushed the wine-bearer out, and slammed the door again behind him, once more locking it.

Sir Nicholas' lashes drooped over his eyes, hiding the sudden gleam in them. The departing soldier had not taken the key with him. "Put the cover over this very choice dish again, my man," said Sir Nicholas.

"Certainly, señor!" The man picked it up and came all unsuspecting to the table.

Sir Nicholas' hand had left playing with his pomander; his foot had stopped its gentle swinging, and the toe of it was firm-planted on the floor. The soldier bent to put the cover over the dish on the table.

Even as his hand left the cover, and he was about to step back, Sir Nicholas made his spring, a clean, lithe spring, noiseless and sure. Before the soldier realised what had happened a pair of iron hands were choking him into insensibility, and he was half-flung, half-lifted backwards on to the bed behind him. Sir Nicholas' knee was over his dagger; he could not reach it. He could make no sound; he could only tear fruitlessly at the merciless fingers that were grasping his throat. His eyes started horribly, glaring up into Sir Nicholas' face: the last thing he was conscious of was the brightness of the blue eyes above him and the grim smile that curled Sir Nicholas' lips.

Sir Nicholas' hands left the bruised throat; he stepped to the table, caught up the napkin laid ready there, and tied it expeditiously round the unconscious man's mouth. The dagger was drawn from its sheath, the key picked up from the floor where it had fallen. Holding the dagger in his right hand, Sir Nicholas went with a firm tread to the door, fitted the key in the lock, turned it, and opened the door.

Outside the sentry stood, leaning on his halberd. Some instinct must have warned him of danger, for even as the door opened he turned his head sharply to see who came. He had only time to let out a startled cry, but that second's mischance brought an oath to Beauvallet's lips. The dagger went home between neck and shoulder, and the sentry seemed to crumple up where he stood.

But the one cry, shrill as it was, was like to ruin all. An answering shout sounded, and from the main stairway a man came running.

Sir Nicholas wrenched the dagger free, and was gone in a flash towards the south side of the building. His intention had been to get round on this side to the Governor's quarters, but now, with the alarm given, and men running to the pursuit, this was clearly impossible. He bounded up the spiral stairway at the junction of the corridors, and found himself in a similar passage to the one below, except that it was walled in, with embrasured windows over which hung heavy curtains, giving on to the court below. A cresset hung at the top of the stairs, and threw a feeble light; there was another in the middle of the corridor to his left.

Below there was the sound of running feet, shouts, and the clatter of pikes. Sir Nicholas sent a quick look round, and his eye alighted on a stout oak chest standing against the wall. He stepped quickly forward; there was a heave and a thrust, and the chest went crashing down the stair on top of the foremost man who was running up. The chest jammed tight on the turn of the stair; there was a furious oath, clatter, and confusion. The first of the pursuers went tumbling backwards into the arms of the man behind him, who, in his turn, lost his balance under the sudden impact and fell heavily.

Sir Nicholas laughed out at that, and having seen his chest securely wedged, turned. He had not the least idea what he was going to do next, and he rather thought that he was trapped, but his eyes were fairly blazing with sheer joy of action, and a smile of amusement was on his lips.

Footsteps and voices sounded on the main stair at the other end of the quadrangle. Sir Nicholas stayed, poised on his toes, waiting to see which way these pursuers would come. They rounded the far corner of the eastern corridor, where he stood, some three or four soldiers running with halberds levelled. Sir Nicholas sprang to the left, and was off down the southern passage, making for the Governor's quarters on the western side.

He had almost reached the corner when he checked suddenly, and cast a quick glance round him for some way of escape. Ahead of him, down the western corridor, perilously close, was coming the thud of heavy feet, running fast. He was indeed trapped.

Another moment and the men behind him would have rounded the corner, and would have him in view again. Sir Nicholas made for the end window on this side, slipped into the embrasure, and drew the heavy curtains to behind him.

The window opened on to its little railed balcony; Sir Nicholas stepped out, soft-footed, and cast a glance down into the court below. It was too dark to distinguish forms, but he could hear voices, and knew that there were soldiers gathered there.

He thrust the dagger through his belt, tested the iron railing a moment with his hand, and peered through the gloom for the first balcony on the western side. He could just distinguish it. One moment he measured the distance; then he set his foot on the railing and came lightly up with a hand on the wall to steady himself. Judging by the sounds, the men running down the western corridor had now reached the corner. Sir Nicholas gathered himself together and jumped like a diver, head first for the next balcony. His hands just caught its railing; he hung there a moment, panting, put forth a great effort, and hoisted himself up. He had a leg over the rail in a minute, and the next instant he had disappeared in at the window.

He found himself in a deserted passage. Down the corner along which he had come were pelting the soldiers; in another moment they would collide with the other party whom Sir Nicholas had first seen. There would be more talk of witchcraft after this night's work, thought Sir Nicholas, and grinned appreciatively. Each of those converging parties were convinced they had the escaped prisoner trapped; they were very shortly to discover that El Beauvallet had once more lived up to his reputation, and this time had vanished, to all appearances, into thin air. El Beauvallet kissed his fingers in the wake of the zealous guards, and made for the first door he could see.

It was unlocked. He went in cautiously, and found himself in an empty bedchamber, poorly furnished, and with one small cresset lamp burning over the mantelpiece. It was probably some tirewoman's chamber, he thought. He closed the door softly behind him, and went to the window. It stood open, looking on to the garden. Sir Nicholas swung one leg over the sill, feeling for a foothold. The wistaria brushed his leg; he found a branch, swung the other leg over, caught at the thick tendrils, and went sliding, scrambling down to the balcony immediately below, upon the first storey. The wistaria tore away from the wall, but he reached to safety. He had one leg over the balcony rail, one hand feeling for a hold on to the creeper, when there came a noise to make him draw back quickly.

The door leading into the garden from the hall below was flung open; there was the flare of torch, and a voice said clearly: "Two of you keep guard lest he try to escape this way."

Without a moment's hesitation Sir Nicholas slipped in at the open window behind him.

The curtains were slightly parted, and a soft light shone through. Sir Nicholas, keeping against the dark background of the curtain, peeped in. The room was empty; Sir Nicholas went in and pulled the curtains to behind him.

"God's Life!" he muttered ruefully. "Where am I now?"

He stood in a large bedchamber, which was furnished in a massive style, with a great four-posted bed hung with curtains of velvet, a chest of inlay work, a table, chairs, and a hanging cupboard against the wall. There was a door opposite the window and even as Sir Nicholas went towards it footsteps sounded outside, and a hand was laid on the latch. Sir Nicholas drew swiftly back to the bed and slipped behind the heavy curtains.

The door opened; someone came in with a quick step, went to the table, and pulled a drawer out in it. There was a rustle of paper; Sir Nicholas parted the curtain and saw a man standing with his back to him, hurriedly turning over papers in the drawer. He was cloaked, and wore a large capotain hat with a drooping plume in it. At his side, hitching up the long folds of the cloak, hung a rapier.

Inch by inch, cat-like, Sir Nicholas came towards him. A board creaked suddenly under his foot; the cloaked man turned sharply, and as he turned Beauvallet's fist shot out. The man fell without a sound, and Sir Nicholas saw that he had knocked out no less a personage than Don Cristobal de Porres, Governor of the Guards.

"God save the mark, my noble gaoler!" said Sir Nicholas, and stepped over Porres' prostrate form to the door. He shut it, cast a quick glance at the limp figure, and went to the bed. With one eye watchfully upon the Governor he slit the fine brocade coverlet into strips with his dagger, and came back to kneel beside the still form.

"Nay, but I am sorry for this, my poor friend," he said, and stuffed one of his strips into Don Cristobal's slack mouth. Another, torn across was tied hastily round to keep the rude gag in place. He unclasped the cloak from about Don Cristobal's neck and the gleaming collar of the Golden Fleece met his eyes. Off it came; Sir Nicholas gave a tiny chuckle. "My dear friend," said he, "I believe this may stand me in very good stead. You shall not grudge it me." He fastened the collar round his own neck, unbuckled the baldrick that held the Governors rapier, and neatly bound the unfortunate man's ankles and wrists. As he tied the last knot Don Cristobal stirred, and opened his eyes. They fell on Beauvallet, seemed bewildered at first, and then as full consciousness returned, furious.

"I know, I know," said Sir Nicholas. "I am sorry for it, señor, but you will admit I am hard-pressed." His eyes twinkled. "A churlish return for all your kindness, Don Cristobal, and I would not have had you think El Beauvallet so ungrateful a dog." He saw the look of consternation leap into the Governor's face, and laughed. "Oh

yes, señor, I am El Beauvallet." As he spoke he was
buckling the baldrick about his waist. "Señor, I must
stow you away. Keep my sword in exchange for this of
yours; it is a rare blade, and you may say with truth
that you were the only man who ever took aught
from Nick Beauvallet against his will. Now, señor, if you
please." He had opened the door of the cupboard, and
now he bundled Don Cristobal into it, and shut the door
upon him. He picked up the cloak, fastened it about his
shoulders, and disposed its ample folds about his person.
The Governor's lace handkerchief and long cane lay on
the floor; Sir Nicholas gathered them up, set the broad-
brimmed hat well over his eyes, thanked God for a beard
and a pair of mustachios very like Don Cristobal's, and
walked to the door. As he laid his hand on the latch there
was a scratching on one of the panels, and a man's voice
called: "Señor, the coach waits."

"In a very good hour!" thought Sir Nicholas. "God
send I may brazen this out. I thank my luck that the light
is behind me. Forward, El Beauvallet!" He opened the
door, and went calmly out into the passage.

A servant stood there; Sir Nicholas could not see his
features plainly in the dim light of the passage, and hoped
that his own were as well hid. He closed the door behind
him, and motioned the servant to go before. The man
bowed, and went ahead at once.

Along the passage they walked to the stairs at the end.
The servant stood aside there for Sir Nicholas to pass. Sir
Nicholas went down the stairs unhurriedly and crossed the
hall at the bottom.

The front door was held open by a lackey, who stared
to see his master coming so unconcernedly. He ventured
to speak. "Señor—the lieutenant has just gone into the
library in search of you. You have not heard, señor—the
prisoner has escaped!"

Sir Nicholas raised the handkerchief to his lips and
coughed. Through the cough he said in as fair an imitation
of Don Cristobal's voice as he could assume: "He is taken.
The sergeant has my instructions."

He went past the lackey as he spoke, but he knew that
the man was surprised, perhaps even suspicious, and there

was not a moment to be lost. A coach with plumes upon the roof and curtains hung at the sides stood waiting. He got in. "I am late. Drive fast."

The coachman was agog with excitement. "Señor, the prisoner——"

"The prisoner is safe!" said Sir Nicholas. "Drive on!"

The coachman gathered up the reins; the horses' hooves clattered on the paving-stones, the coach moved slowly forward under the arch towards the open gates.

The lackey at the door ran after. "Señor, the lieutenant——"

"To hell with the lieutenant!" said Sir Nicholas. "Drive on!"

The coach rumbled out of the gate and turned at right angles into the street.

The lieutenant, Cruza, hurrying out of the house, was just in time to see it disappear round the corner. "What— the Governor!" he cried.

The lackey rubbed his perplexed head. "Señor, the Governor would not wait. He sounded very hasty, and unlike himself."

"The Governor would not wait?" Cruza stared uncomprehendingly.

There came a shout from within. "Stop that man! Stop that man! The Governor is here, gagged and bound! *Stop that man!*"

"*Sangre de Dios,* he is away!" cried the lieutenant, and went bounding out through the archway. "For your lives after that coach!" he shot at the sentries. "The prisoner is in it! Off with you!"

But when two labouring soldiers came up with the slow-moving coach there was no one inside. El Beauvallet had vanished.

ᴐᴀ Chapter XIX ᴒᴄ

OUTSIDE the wall that enclosed the Governor's garden
Joshua waited, safe in the shadows. He had a coil of rope
in his hand, and had hitched his dagger round so that he
might easily come at it. He shivered from time to time,
started at small noises, and was finely scared by a maraud-
ing black cat. Recovering from this fright he watched the
cat slink off, and was moved to shake his fist at it. "What,
you doxy! You'll creep up to give me a fright, will you?
You may thank my need for quiet that I do not spit you
on the end of my knife." The cat disappeared over the
wall. "Ay, over you go, featly as you please, upon your
naughty business," said Joshua bitterly. "If a man might
get over that wall so easily I should be the better pleased."
He set himself to listen again, but could hear only the
rustle of the light wind through the trees. "Can he make
it?" muttered Joshua. "I do not doubt, no, but I confess I
shall be the more at ease when I see you safe beside me,
master. Ha, what's this?"

He listened intently, heard the sound of voices on the
other side, but could not catch what was said. A door
slammed, he heard the gravel scrunch under a heavy boot,
a sound as of a grounded halberd, and a murmur of voices.

Dismay consumed him; he was in a fret to be gone
from his post, to be up and doing, at least to know more.
If Sir Nicholas had broken free he could never escape this
way, with men posted in the garden. And how to warn
him? Joshua wrung his hands in impotent despair. "God's
me, God's me, this is to ruin all! I am in no doubt now
that you have broken free, master, but why so slow? Ah,
why, why? You will walk into this trap. This is not Mad
Nick's way to let others be before him. What mischance?
Trapped, trapped!" He looked right and left. "To warn

you—think, Joshua, think! I am no loose-living cat to go jumping walls." He bit his nails in a frenzy, glanced up at the wall, shook his head hopelessly. "Naught to do but to wait. But if he hath broken loose what makes he there? Will he fall upon these men in the garden? What, weaponless to pit his strength against I know not how many men with pikes? And here stand I mammering! Nor dare do else!"

He stood still, listening, sweating, dreading at once the sound of a capture in the garden, and the approach of some loiterer, or, worse, a guard in the street.

He stiffened suddenly, and peered into the darkness. A light step sounded, approaching fast. He began to walk away down the street, as though bound upon some errand.

The footsteps were coming closer, rapidly overhauling him. He stole a hand to his dagger, and went steadily on his way. If this was a guard he was coming on his death.

He was overtaken, felt a grip on his shoulder, and spun round, dagger out. A hand caught his wrist in mid-air, held it clamped hard. "Death on thy soul, Joshua! learn to know your master!" hissed Sir Nicholas.

Joshua almost fell to his knees. "Master! Safe! safe!" he whispered ecstatically.

"Of course I am safe, fat-wit. Put up that knife. A horse is all my need."

"Said I not so!" Joshua was moved to kiss his hand. "Said I, what will be my master's cry? Why, what but Horses, Joshua! They are hard by, sir, saddled and ready."

"God 'ild you, then. Lead me to them. The hunt is up in good sooth, and we must win clear away to-night." He gave a little chuckle. "A rare night's work! Where's my lady?"

"Gone these four days, master, and that squirting ahead of her." Joshua led him down a side-alley, walking fast. "I had speech with the noble lady, and bade her be of good cheer, and keep faith. Then I saw her leave Madrid with the old lady, and learned they were to waste no time upon the journey. I warrant I have been about the town a little! How came you out of that hold, master?"

He was told, very briefly, and rubbed his hands over it. "Ay, that is the way it goes. Ho-ho, they have our measure now, if they had it not before! But I submit, master, that we have to consider a little. Having lost their prisoner what will they do?"

"Send hot-foot to the Frontier, and the ports," said Sir Nicholas.

"True, master, and we take the Frontier road as far as Burgos." He shook his head. "Still very barful. But we will not be amort. We have the start of them, and they will not look for us at Vasconosa. Tarry here awhile, sir. No need to show yourself." He had stopped at a street turning. "I go to fetch the horses."

He was back soon with two fine jennets, each with a light pack strapped to the saddle.

"Boots, man!" said Sir Nicholas. "Have you my sword safe?"

"Never doubt me, sir!" said Joshua complacently, unbuckling a pack. "Your boots are at hand. I have thought of everything. I am not one to be bestraught by disaster." He unearthed a pair of top-boots, caught up the shoon Sir Nicholas had kicked off, and stowed them away.

The long boots were pulled on, the spurs swiftly fastened. Sir Nicholas vaulted lightly into the saddle. "On then, my Joshua!" He laughed, and Joshua saw that his eyes were alight.

"A race for life this time!" he said, wheeled about, and drove in his heels.

The two sentries came panting back to the barracks, and to Cruza, feverishly awaiting them. "Gone, señor!" they gasped.

"Fools! Dolts! He was in that coach."

"He was gone, señor."

Cruza fell back. "Holy Virgin, witchcraft!" He hurried in to where his superior waited. Don Cristobal, unbound now, shaken, but composed, received him with a questioning lift of the brows.

"Señor, he was not in the coach when the guards came up with it. It is witchcraft, foul devil's work!"

Don Cristobal smiled contemptuously. "If you would

say we have been finely tricked you speak nothing but the truth," he said acidly. "Would he sit still in the coach to await capture? Turn out the guard!"

Cruza shot an order to a goggle-eyed sergeant, waiting close by. "Senor, can it be that it is El Beauvallet indeed?"

Don Cristobal slightly rubbed his bruised wrists. "He did me the honour of telling me so with his own lips," he said. He moved to the table, and dipped a quill in the inkhorn. "One man to take this writing to Don Luis de Fermosa, to request him to order out the alguazils to search the town. The prisoner cannot have gone far."

Cruza wrinkled his brow at that. "Señor, will he not make for the Frontier?"

Don Cristobal dusted his paper with sand, and read it over before he answered. As he folded and sealed it he said calmly:—"He must procure a horse for that, Cruza, and we know that he has no money." He gave the paper into his lieutenant's hands, and turned to his valet. "A hat and a cloak, Juan."

The valet hurried away. Cruza ventured another question. "Señor, where do you go?"

"To the Alcazar," replied the Governor. "To learn his Majesty's pleasure in this matter."

Access to Philip was at first denied him. The King was private in his closet, and would see no one. A word in the King's valet's ear produced the required effect. That privileged person went off in a hurry, and presently Don Cristobal was summoned to the presence.

The news had been told Philip, but he displayed his habitual equanimity to Don Cristobal, deeply bowing before him. He let his apathetic gaze run over the Governor, but said nothing.

"Sire"—Don Cristobal made the shortest work he could of it—"I have to inform your Majesty, to my shame, that my prisoner has escaped."

Philip folded his cool hands. "This is a very strange thing that you tell me, Don Cristobal."

The Governor flushed. "I do not know what to say, sire. I am myself overwhelmed."

"Compose yourself. When did the prisoner escape?"

"Not an hour ago, sire. He overpowered the guard who

brought his supper to him, stabbed the sentry without; by some means unknown to me slipped through the hands of two parties of guards who thought they had him trapped between them, and by means equally unknown to me reached my own chamber. I, entering and knowing nothing of the affair, was taken by surprise, sire." His hand went unvoluntarily to the bruise on his chin. "The prisoner struck me down, sire, before I was aware, and when I came to myself I was gagged and bound upon the floor. The prisoner put on him my hat and cloak, my insignia of the Golden Fleece, my sword, and thus disguised, sire, went down to the coach that waited to take me to the house of a friend. My lieutenant, suspecting some mischief, sent after the coach hotfoot, but when the guards came up with it the prisoner had vanished."

Silence fell. The lids dropped over Philip's eyes, hiding whatever chagrin or anger he might be feeling. After a pause he raised them again. It was characteristic of him that he chose to dwell upon one of the smaller points of the matter. "This would seem to show that he is El Beauvallet, by his own confession," he said weightily.

"Sire, the prisoner spoke his name out boldly to me. He said, sire, when he took my sword from me, that I might keep his in exchange, and boast that I was the only man who ever took aught from El Beauvallet against his will."

There was another pause. "He must be captured," said the King at length, and struck a silver handbell at his side.

"Remembering, sire, that he has no money wherewith to buy him a horse, and must therefore be hiding in Madrid, I sent at once to Fermosa to request him to search the town."

Philip inclined his head. "You did well, señor."

A man came in, and stood attentively at the King's elbow. Philip was already writing a laborious memorandum. His pen moved unhurriedly. He remarked without raising his eyes from the paper: "Yet so desperate a man as this might not hesitate to steal a horse. A runner must be sent to the Frontier."

From what he had seen of Beauvallet Don Cristobal did not think that he would hesitate for a moment. "With submission, sire, I would suggest that a runner be sent to the ports, in especial Vigo and Santander."

"Runners will be sent at once," said Philip calmly, "to all the ports with orders to the Alcaldes to apprehend this man. But we shall do well to remember, Don Cristobal, that we have to do with one who has evil arts at command."

Whatever doubts Don Cristobal might cherish as to Beauvallet's supposed wizardry he merely bowed his head respectfully.

Father Allen, until now a silent listener over against the window, came forward. "Your Majesty has forgotten that there is the servant to be reckoned with."

The King's brain did not work fast, but it never forgot. "The servant fled, Father," he said positively.

Father Allen bowed. "So we were led to believe, sire."

Philip had to digest this. A shade of annoyance crossed his face. "I cannot think that I have been well-served in this," he said, and motioned to the secretary to write at his dictation.

The various despatches were at last ready; messengers were to ride to the Frontier, and to any port of size. Through the length and breadth of Spain would run the news that a famous pirate was at large. Philip leaned back in his chair with a thin-lipped smile of satisfaction. "He will run into a net," he said with unwonted urbanity. "We shall presently draw the strings tight."

This was all very well, but there were others who did not share the King's optimism. Perinat, when he heard next day of the escape, fairly danced with mortification, and predicted disaster to the awestruck circle.

"To hold him and to let him slip through the fingers!" raved Perinat. "He should have been shackled and handcuffed, and never left! What do you know of him? Nothing! I knew, ah, I knew! but I was not heeded. Oh devil and fiend! oh warlock, you are away yet once again!"

Noveli cut into this impassioned outburst. "He cannot get away. Every port will be stopped, and none allowed to set sail on any vessel. The Frontier will be barred before he can reach it, and even if it were not you forget that he has no pass."

Perinat pointed a prophetic finger. "You may stop the ports, you may bar the Frontier, but he will slip through your guards, and laugh at you as he does so! Ah, to have had him, and to let him go!" His fierce gaze swept the group. "The ports! the Frontier! Why came he into Spain? Heard you not the true reason from Carvalho's lips? Where is Dona Dominica de Rada?"

"Why, on the road to Vasconosa," said someone. "But——"

"Then let the King send there for him!" said Perinat. "And still he will be too late! The villain's away, I tell you!"

Another gentleman came to join the group, one whose eyes were restless and uneasy, and whose fingers twitched rather nervously. Don Rodriguez de Carvalho, on whom the news had fallen like a thunderbolt, was in a sorry case. Sharing to the full the popular dread of El Beauvallet, he did not know what to do. He feared for his son's life, he feared for his niece's safety, and he dared not divulge Beauvallet's probable destination for fear of implicating Dominica, and seeing her and her wealth swallowed up by the Holy Inquisition. He came now, fussy and fidgetting, to hear what was being said of the escape, and was in time to catch Perinat's last words.

Perinat pounced on him at once. "Ah, in a good hour, Carvalho! Tell me, will not this pirate be after your niece?"

Don Rodriguez looked startled. He stammered:—"I do not think it—I cannot suppose it. She was resolute in denying him. Maybe we mistake—what should El Beauvallet hope to make in Spain?"

"He is self-declared," interposed Aranda. "That evening when I first met him he dared to speak his own name! Do you remember, Losa? He said that if El Beauvallet stood where he stood then he would still laugh. What impudence! What daring! One gasps at it."

Perinat, obsessed by the one idea, brushed this aside. "You waste time! The King should be told of this. It is for you, Carvalho, to warn him."

Don Rodriguez hesitated and was lost. "If you think it wise, señors ... But I cannot agree with you. I cannot suppose that my niece would suffer him. She is headstrong indeed, but she does not forget—in short, señors, if El Beauvallet seeks her indeed it is against her will."

"Against her will when she declared she knew him not?" burst out Perinat. "The girl's besotted!"

Losa lifted a finger to silence Perinat. "I think that the King should be told that Dona Dominica de Rada is on her way to Vasconosa, and that El Beauvallet may well be on her heels," he said.

"Well, señor, well. . . . If you do not think it is to waste his Majesty's time," Don Rodriguez said unhappily.

He went to the King, and found Don Cristobal de Porres there, announcing failure to find El Beauvallet in Madrid. He blurted out his mission as best he could, and was at pains to tell the King that he himself was no believer in the wild tale.

Philip gave it his slow consideration. The first thing he said was:—"If this is so it casts grave doubts on Dona Dominica's faith. This must be looked into. Why was I not told that Dona Dominica had left Madrid?"

Don Rodriguez made haste to say that he had come with the news the instant he had heard of El Beauvallet's escape.

Followed a lengthy conference. Slowly, methodically Philip pieced the whole thing together in his careful head, and when that was done turned to Porres, who was fretting to set matters in train. "We shall entrust this charge to you, señor," he said.

Don Cristobal bowed. "I thank your Majesty. I will have a party ride north at once. Give me leave to withdraw, sire!"

Philip waved him away; the Governor kissed his hand, went out sedately backwards, but once clear of the King's closet wasted no time.

A party of guards was despatched within half an hour, with orders to spare neither themselves nor their horses, but at all costs to reach Vasconosa ahead of El Beauvallet. Changes of horses they must have, and could get easily enough at the various post-stages; or if none were to be had there they were on the King's business, and might commandeer what mounts they pleased. Cruza, burning to capture the man who had slipped so easily through his fingers, was sent in charge of the little party, and swore to bring the pirate back in bonds. There would be little rest allowed to Cruza's men on this wild ride north.

◅ Chapter XX ▻

THE big coach that bore Dominica away from Madrid pushed northwards with what speed it could make. Four horses dragged it, and these were changed at every post. For a lady of such natural indolence Dona Beatrice moved swiftly when she chose to move at all.

The coach was decked with plumes upon the roof, hung with leather curtains that could be fastened at will, and fitted with padded seats of red velvet. The body was of the newest kind, slung on stout leather straps, which helped to ease the discomfort of the journey. It was roomy enough to accommodate not only the two ladies, but their tire-women as well, and a number of packages and bags. Behind it came lackeys with led sumpters; beside it rode guards of the Carvalho household, decked out in their master's livery, making a brave show of it on this journey through the country. Dominica, listlessly regarding this cavalcade, reflected that if her aunt feared to be overtaken by El Beauvallet she had a very ample guard to protect her from this one man.

Changes of horses had been bespoken beforehand at each stage. None but the strongest Flemish horses were harnessed to the equipage, and these great powerful beasts drew them rapidly on their way.

The post-road was full of pot-holes, and deep ruts, hard-baked by the sun; at times it was a mere track across the plain, at others it became a rocky mountain pass, where the number of horses had to be doubled to drag the coach up. They slept at inns along the road, but the coach never stopped until it was too dark to go farther, and it was off again betimes in the morning. When Dominica wearily asked the reason of such insensate haste her aunt only smiled, and said:—"When I rouse myself to undertake such a disagreeable journey as this, my dear, I waste no time over it."

The lady beguiled much of the tedium of the journey by sly references to Beauvallet, left behind them. She veiled her words, out of consideration of the listening tirewomen, but Dominica was never in any doubt as to her meaning.

Dominica, jolted and bumped in her corner of the coach was not at a loss for suitable answers. They came out very pat, and had an edge to them. Dona Beatrice chuckled softly, and pinched the girl's cheek, not at all ruffled.

This cat-and-mouse play was not to be borne. Dominica made a bid for freedom, and announced her wish to ride part of the way. To sit in a bumping, lurching coach, she said, day upon day, irked her sorely. With her aunt's good leave she would have a horse saddled for her on the morrow, and ride for at least an hour or two.

"How restless you are, my dear!" remarked Dona Beatrice. "By all means do as you please. Young blood cannot be still? But I do not know that it is at all seemly."

"There will be none to see me, aunt, and I have not been used to be cooped up," Dominica said.

"True," agreed Dona Beatrice, and disposed herself to slumber.

On the morrow it was so ordered. Dominica came down from her chamber at the inn in riding-dress, fully prepared to fight for the privilege she claimed. However, there was no need. Dona Beatrice merely said that it was a pity Don Diego was not there to act as escort, and told a groom to stay near his young mistress.

Dominica carried a heavy heart in her breast, but could still enjoy this spell of exercise and of freedom. There had been little enough riding for her since she had come back to Spain. She remembered long gallops at Santiago, and knew a little of the same joyous feeling of freedom as she had had there. She rode well, had no fear, and led the groom a fine chase at a full gallop. She reined in at last, flushed and wind-tossed, breathed her horse a moment, and went cantering back to meet the lumbering coach.

Her aunt had had the curtains drawn back, and greeted her with a quizzical look. "You are a very Diana, my dear. Were you riding to escape from me?"

Dominica tucked an escaped curl back under her French hood. "No, señora, I doubt it would be of no avail," she said frankly.

She came presently to sit in the coach again, but thereafter it was understood that when my lady willed it so she would ride, and there was always to be a horse procured for her.

Away from her aunt's side she had leisure to indulge her thoughts. They could not be pleasant. Not even Joshua's stout optimism could allay her fears. She felt herself to be a traitress, flying from Beauvallet in his hour of need, yet Joshua had seemed to think she did well to go, and indeed what could she do by remaining, even had it been possible? If they had chosen to interrogate her she would have fought with all her woman's wit for Beauvallet, but they had not chosen. Oh, if she were a man she would fight for him in other ways than that! Her eyes kindled to the thought, and her hand clenched on her whip.

If she could believe that Sir Nicholas would escape she might play with the fancy of him in pursuit, even now as she rode from him. She imagined him hard on her heels, spurring on and on, riding down this stately equipage. She could imagine how his sword would flash out, how he would snatch her up, and ride off with her, laughing, triumphant. She had to shake the tears from her eyes; the gay lover was caught and prisoned, and would no more come riding to win her.

They came within a stage of Vasconosa upon the tenth day. The labouring lackeys swore softly against such haste. "One would say the devil was on our heels."

Dominica overheard the phrase. If Sir Nicholas had been behind they would be very sure the devil was on their heels, she thought.

There was a stream to be forded; the coach lurched down the bank, and the shallow waters lapped round the wheels. Dominica's horse chose to jib at the stream, sidled, and backed, but was forced on. She went through, climbed the slope beyond, and reined in to await the coach. There was some trouble over this; the wheels sank into the mud of the streambed, and the great horses strained in vain. The men were all about the coach, pushing, gesticulating, arguing. It was decided to rope two saddle horses to the coach.

There came a thunder of hooves to the north, behind Dominica. She turned her head, and saw a troop riding towards her, *ventre à terre*. Her eyes narrowed in surprise; the horsemen came nearer, and she saw masked faces. She cried out in swift alarm, wheeled her horse about, and went quickly down the slope to where the coach still stuck in the stream. "Bandits!" she said. "A troop of masked men! Get to horse!"

The men left their task of extricating the coach. Two of the guards sprang into the saddle at once; the coachman got out his musket.

Dona Beatrice leaned back at her ease. "Did you say bandits, dear? I can hardly credit it."

"Masked men, señora. I know not, but I misliked what I saw."

Dona Beatrice looked round at her bodyguard, and yawned. "Well, and if you did, my dear, we have guards enough to give them a fine scare. Do not be alarmed."

"I am not alarmed," said Dominica with dignity.

The troop appeared over the top of the slope, cloaked men, with gauze masks covering their faces. A shot sounded, there was a flash of steel; the bandits came scrambling down the slope to engage with Dona Beatrice's bodyguard.

Dominica thought there were no more than six of them, but she could not be sure in the *mêlée*. Her heart beat fast, but there was something about this battle that made her draw her brows together, and look frowningly. There were pistol shots, but no man was wounded; swords flashed, but no man was cut down.

Dona Beatrice's fan stopped waving. Her eyes were narrow all at once, and behind them her brain was moving quickly. She sat forward with a hand on the side of the coach, watching this odd fray.

Dominica knew a sudden, inexplicable fear. She

brought her horse up close to the coach. "Señora,—aunt—
what is this?" she asked urgently.

"That is just what I am asking myself," said Dona
Beatrice calmly. "If these men are brigands they act as no
brigands did that I ever heard of."

A couple of the masked men spurred up to the coach; a
hand seized Dominica's bridle. She slashed at the masked
face with her whip; the leather thong cut the mask across,
and revealed an unshaven chin, a thick nose, and the fast
rising weal of the whip-lash. The whip was wrested from
Dominica's hands. She cried out to her guards:—"To me!
To me, cravens!"

They were sheepish, laying down their arms, as though
worsted in the fight. Yet there was not a man among them
who had taken a hurt.

Dominica drove her heel in hard, struck at the hand on
her bridle. Her horse plunged forward, but her captor
jerked it up. "Help me, cowards!" Dominica cried furiously.

Dona Beatrice had half risen from her seat as though
she would descend from the coach. She sank slowly back
now, her eyes fixed under their drooping lids on a masked
horseman who stood a little apart from the rest. She
watched him turn his head to give an order to one of the
men. She could not hear his voice, but she had no need to
hear it. A woman should know her own son.

Her hand felt for her fan. Thoughtfully she looked at
her niece, being forced on up the slope. A very infamous
proceeding. She was surprised that Diego should think of
such a scheme. Her shoulders shook slightly; meditatively
she bit one finger-nail. Should she put a stop to it or no?
She had no doubt that a word from her would subdue
Don Diego, but should that word be spoken? This was a
crude performance, by her standards, but she admitted she
could have thought of no surer way of reducing her niece
to obedience.

She slightly raised her ample shoulders in a gesture of
fatalism. Let Don Diego do as he chose; a girl never liked
a man the less for being shown the strong hand. She
turned her attention to her screaming tirewoman. "I beg
you will be quiet," she said. "We are not attacked, and
you do no good by that screeching."

Old Carmelita pointed a shaking finger. "Señora, señora, they bear off the señorita!"

"I am not blind," said Dona Beatrice. "I can do nothing to the purpose. Pray you be calm."

The masked riders had closed round Dominica; in another moment they were over the brow of the slope, and had gone out of sight.

One of the guards came to the side of the coach, pushed on by his fellows, and mumbled something inarticulate.

"I suppose you to know what you are about," said Dona Beatrice sharply. "Pray do not think me a want-wit. What did Don Diego pay you for this piece of work?"

The man was put out of countenance, shifted uneasily from one foot to the other, stammered an unmeaning answer.

"You are a fool," said Dona Beatrice. She had resumed her fanning. A movement of the fan beckoned the coachman forward. "Where is my son taking Dona Dominica?" she asked languidly.

"Señora—it—I do not know," said the coachman.

"You would be better advised to speak the truth," said Dona Beatrice.

The coachman looked at her, and seemed to think she might be right. "Señora, to the lodge."

"Ah!" said Dona Beatrice. "Who else is there?"

"Señora, none but Luis, the valet."

"You shock me," said the lady. "I think you had better set yourself to pull the coach out of the stream."

⚓ Chapter XXI ⚓

THE riders hedged Dominica closely about, and struggle as she might there was no withstanding the insistent drag on her bridle. She fought desperately to rein in her horse, but the bridle was wrenched from her straining hands. A

cut across the quarters made the frightened animal bound
forward. Dominica leaned forward in the saddle to strike
passionately at the man who led her. He laughed, bade
her be still, and pressed on.

She was sobbing with rage, quite powerless, but ready
almost to fling herself from the saddle rather than be
carried on thus ignominiously. "Who are you?" she
panted. "What do you want with me? Answer me,
you!"

No one replied to her question; she looked round wildly
at the masked faces; the blank gaze told her nothing. She
looked ahead then, to note the way they went, and found
that they had left the road, and were pressing on up a
slight hill, towards wooded country.

They had to check their pace; there were boulders in
the way, and overhanging tree-branches above their
heads. A rough track led through the forest; as far as
Dominica could ascertain they were striking north,
towards Vasconosa.

A man pushed forward, and came to ride on her other
side. Dominica stared at him, saw an elegantly gauntletted
hand upon the rein, and smelled the sweet scent of musk.
It was not fear that seized her then, but a cold fury that
almost bereft her of speech. She struggled for words,
rejected what came, and said at last in a voice redolent of
scorn:—"You may unmask, my heroic cousin. I have your
measure now."

He gave a slight laugh, and put up his hand to remove
the mask. "Fairest cousin, well-met!" he said, and bowed
to her over the saddle-peak.

She spoke through shut teeth. "Unless I am much mistaken, señor, you will not say so for long."

"I am sure you are much mistaken, sweet cousin," he
returned, and laughed again.

She pressed her lips together, and rode on in silence.
After a while Don Diego leaned towards her, and took her
bridle from the man who held it. "Let me be your escort,
child."

"I appear to have little choice, señor."

They rode on ahead of the troop. "You drove me to it,
Dominica," Don Diego said softly.

She gave a short laugh at that. Now she could despise

him to the full. A man who would apologise for his villainy, whine at it! "Holy Virgin!" she ejaculated. "Is that your excuse, cousin?"

"My love for you!" he said, flushing at the contempt in her voice.

"A rare love, by my faith!"

"It brooks no hindrance. I am desperate for you. You shall not think harshly of me."

"I shall not think of you at all," she replied. "You are of no account."

His brows drew close over his nose. "I shall show you otherwise, Dominica."

She yawned.

"You scorn me," he said, "but I love you. You have flouted me, given me sharp words, and cold looks, but I have you now by the strong hand."

Her eyes flashed; her lips curled. "The strong hand! Yours!" She flicked at it with her glove. "My God, I could match you a strong hand which would put yours to shame!"

He coloured. "You betray yourself, Dominica. Was Beauvallet's hand so strong then? Did it keep him from capture, and will it keep him from the stake?"

She looked disdainful. "You rave. You are ridiculous. Mother of God, but you sicken me!"

"You will not long say so," he answered.

"What, am I to be rid of you then? I give thanks for a happy deliverance."

He sneered at her. "Who shall deliver you, señorita? Your fine Beauvallet, so neatly caught and prisoned? You will grow weary of waiting for him, believe me."

"I do, very easily, señor," she returned lightly. "But I make no doubt the Chevalier de Guise would be happy to serve me were he free."

"Very clever," he said, "but I sprang your secret the night he was taken. Why persist in this pretence?"

She shrugged. "If you have a maggot in your brain, cousin, I see no reason why I should share it." She turned her head. "I suppose this to be a plot of my aunt's?"

"Dear cousin, give honour where it is due. The plot is mine alone."

"You amaze me, señor. I had not thought you possessed the stomach for so hardy a deed."

"I am not so spiritless as you think, perhaps," he said quickly. "If you are happy to be with freebooters you should like this exploit."

"Given any other man to be the abductor, señor, I might," she conceded.

He jerked his shoulder up. "You gain nothing by such talk, cousin."

They rode on in silence, farther into the forest to a ride Dominica recognised. She was being taken to the old hunting-lodge belonging to the Vasconosa estate. It seemed to her a crowning insult that he should dare to take her to a house not five miles from where her aunt lay. She fairly gnashed her little teeth over it, and her cheeks flew colours of rage.

They drew up before the door. He lifted her down from the saddle, and, looking round, she saw that the troop had dispersed, only one man remaining to take their horses. Ignominy upon ignominy! She guessed the men to be hildings employed upon the estate, and could imagine what chuckles and sly looks were passing between them at her expense. Anger consumed her; there was no room for fear.

Luis, Don Diego's valet, had come out, bowing to them. He held the door wide; she hesitated a moment, and then brushed past him into the hall of the lodge.

Diego, following her close, found her tapping her foot by the table. "Dearest cousin, you are surprisingly beautiful when you are enraged," he told her. "There is a chamber prepared for you upstairs. I regret I have no tirewoman to offer you, or any change of raiment. But you will find such things as you need, and you have only to call, and Luis will bring you what you ask for."

"Your consideration passes belief, cousin," she said. "I do not purpose to make a long stay, I thank you. I shall be glad to know what you intend by me."

The valet went discreetly away to the kitchens. Dominica was left facing her cousin, straight and stiff in the middle of the hall.

"I intend marriage, child, as I think you know."

"Is this the way you woo in Spain, señor?"

He came closer. "It is the only way to use with such a wild maid as you, Dominica."

"You are doomed to disappointment, señor. It is no way to use with me."

He smiled. "You are tired from your long ride, and these alarms you have sustained. Come, child, cry a truce, and let me lead you to your chamber! When you have reposed yourself a little we will talk."

She ignored his outstretched hand, but turned towards the stairs. She had need to collect herself, to marshal her defences. She saw that she stood in great danger; she would need all her wits about her to evade it, and she was indeed shaken. Moreover, while he thought her safe upstairs she might contrive to escape, she thought. Dona Beatrice might stand back and allow her son to do his worst, but Dominica was fairly sure she would not take a more active part in this villainy. If she could win to her side she would be safe enough.

This hazy idea was soon put to rout. Don Diego, ushering her into a chamber upstairs that gave on to the little garden at the back of the lodge, displayed a key. "You will forgive the discourtesy, dear cousin, but I must lock you in. I will come to fetch you to dinner in an hour, if it please you!"

She would not trust herself to speak; her breast heaved. She turned sharply on her heel, and walked into the room.

The door was shut behind her, the key grated in the lock.

She stood still until she heard the stairs creak under Don Diego's retreating footsteps. Then she went in a little dash to the window, and flung it open, and looked out. It was unbarred, and for a sufficient reason. There was no need of bars, for the wall of the house fell sheer to the ground some twenty feet below. No friendly creeper afforded a foothold, nor even a rain pipe. To jump from the window would mean broken limbs, and maybe worse. She stayed panting by it, her fingers gripping the ledge till the nails showed white. It was of no use though to rage, and grind her teeth. Escape did not lie that way.

She turned away from the window, and came back into

the room, and took stock of her surroundings. A great bed stood out from one wall, hung with curtains of red damask; arras of tapestry covered the walls; there was a chest, a chair, an escabeau, a table with carved legs, a mirror hung above a second chest, whereon stood a basin and an ewer of silver.

The mirror showed a tempestuous lady, wrath in her face; her hair dishevelled under the French hood, her habit dusty and disordered. Dominica poured water into the basin, and bathed her face and her hands slowly, abstractedly. A cake of soap was to hand, delicately scented, a towel. She stood rubbing her fingers dry, and looking at her reflection in the mirror, thinking, thinking.

An hour later, Don Diego scratched on the panel of the door. A cool voice bade him enter; he found his cousin seated by the window, her hands folded in her lap, the picture of maidenly resignation. But he knew her too well to suppose her resigned; it did not need the steely flash of her eyes as she raised them to tell him that his cousin was prepared to give battle.

He bowed to her. "Dearest cousin, supper awaits you. May I lead you down?"

She rose at once, and came to the door; she even allowed him to take her hand. They went in silence down the stairs and across the hall to a smaller parlour, panelled with mulberry wood. Covers were laid upon a draw-table; Luis stood deferentially waiting behind one of the chairs. She was handed to it, and sat down with what composure she could muster. The curtains had been drawn to shut out the fading daylight, and a cluster of candles on the table lit the room. Outside the silence of the country seemed to enfold the house. Dominica felt very alone, and had to fight down a rising wave of panic.

"Rude fare, dear cousin, I fear me, but you will forgive it. Luis is an unaccustomed cook."

She inclined her head. The food was well enough; she supposed this was Don Diego's way of telling her that there was no one but herself and him and Luis in the house. Superfluous information, she thought.

He poured wine into her glass. "Will you take some of this wine of Alicante, cousin?"

She looked up quickly, puzzled and searching. The words were oddly familiar, stirred a chord of memory. Her mind flew back; she stared at Don Diego, but she saw instead a laughing face, with eyes of deep wind-swept blue. . . .

"Do you suppose, señor, that your daughter will take wine from my hands?" . . .

A tremor shook her. Her eyes shut for a moment, as though to hold the brief vision. She opened them again, and the *Venture's* stateroom slid back into the past. "I thank you, cousin," she said quietly, and picked up the cup with a steady hand.

She ate sparingly, drank less, and answered in monosyllables Don Diego's easy flow of talk. Sweetmeats were at last set on the table, and some ripe pomegranates from the south. Luis withdrew, and they were alone.

She pushed back her chair a little way from the table, and turned her gaze towards Don Diego. "Cousin, I await your explanation."

He lifted his cup in a silent toast. "It is contained in the one short phrase, my dear. I love you."

"You have an odd way of showing me, señor, that you love me. May I not rather suppose that you love my possessions?"

He frowned at that; he had not his mother's frankness. "They are as nothing beside your charms, Dominica."

"I fear you flatter me, cousin."

He leaned towards her, stretched a pleading hand across the table. "Let us not bandy idle words to and fro, Dominica. Believe I am mad for you!"

"It does not strain my credence to believe you mad, señor."

"I am mad, yes, but for love of you. No, let me speak! You do me wrong when you think me anxious only to possess your wealth. I do not deny that was my first thought. But I did not know you then; you had not cast your divine spell over me. I would wed you were you penniless." He saw that she was about to break in on this, and hurried on. "There seemed to be no way but this. I took the straight, swift road to my desires. You shall not blame me for that. You are angry now, outraged; I see your eyes flame. Think but a little and you will pity me, understanding my seeming madness!"

"I might pity your folly, señor, but pity will not work on me to wed with you," she said.

"Dominica!" He tried to take her hand, but it was swiftly withdrawn. "I should be loth to use force. You shall learn to love me, even if you hate me now. Put this English pirate out of your head——"

"Oh, God's mercy, señor, still harping on that fairy tale?" she exclaimed. "You put me out of all patience?"

"He is sped," he insisted. "There is no escape for such as he. Set him aside; forget him."

She looked at him fully now, almost sternly. "Señor cousin, you talk without meaning, but if the Chevalier de Guise were my lover, and he El Beauvallet, I would be faithful to him though he died and I faced death because of him."

An ugly look leaped into his eyes. "You speak very strongly, cousin. There are some things harder to face than death."

This was coming to grips at last. Battle was joined, and she was glad to have it so. Anything were better than his lovemaking. "Cousin," she said, clenching her hand on the table. "I am no milk and water maid for your ravishing. I tell you again that there is no power under heaven will make me marry you."

He leaned back in his chair, nonchalant, keenly watching her. "Bethink you of your fair name, Dominica," he said gently.

"I care nothing for it."

"No?" He smiled. "Brave words, but you have not thought on it yet, sweet cousin. You show me no mercy, no kindness. Should I then show you any?"

"I make no doubt you would not," she said swiftly. "But if you think to wring consent to marriage out of me by such means, you are mistaken, and have not my measure."

He lifted the wine-cup to his lips, sipped, and held it still, his elbow on the arm of his chair. "I can ruin you, my dear," he said. "If you go from here unwed you can never show your face abroad again."

"Do you not think, señor, that if I had to choose between marriage with such as you and a cloister I would not choose the cloister?"

It was plain that he had not thought of that. He set the cup down with a snap, staring at her from under suddenly frowning brows. After a moment he hitched up his shoulder in the way he had, and gave a short laugh. "Idle words!"

"Try me, and you will see, señor."

He poured more wine, but he did not drink. "You think I do not know what heretical notions you hide," he taunted her.

She kept her countenance. "All that is past. I am a true daughter of the Church, nor could you prove me other. The Church would receive me, and my wealth too, be you very sure."

"You do not know what you say." He drank deep, and set the cup down. "This is to work on me, no more."

"You live in a fool's paradise, cousin. There are no lengths to which I would not go for the purpose of frustrating your foul designs. Why, what does the world hold for me that I should cling to it? I am alone, amongst enemies, for such you and my aunt have shown yourselves to be."

"There is El Beauvallet," he said, and looked intently to see whether she would change colour.

She cast up her eyes, but answered patiently. "I humour your whims, cousin. If the Chevalier de Guise were El Beauvallet, and my lover, what would be left to me now but a cloister?"

He sneered at that. "Oh, methought he could burst all bars and bolts, this famous pirate!"

"I suppose you thought so indeed, cousin, since you fled Madrid in such haste," she said tartly.

He showed his teeth a moment. "Do you imagine these holiday terms serve you, señorita? I would be gentle with you, but you drive me to harsh measures. You are besotted; you do not know in how dire a state you stand. The hour grows late already, my cousin, and there is only Luis in the house. I warrant you he will not hear a cry for help."

She was afraid, desperately afraid, but no sign of it

appeared in her face. "You will let your desires ride you to your own undoing, cousin. Work your will on me: you will lose my substance."

He sprang up. "By God, woman, you are shameless!" he said violently. "Is this the bold spirit the New World breeds? Do you hold your honour of so small account? Out on you, I say!"

"Do you then hold my honour in so great account?" she asked contemptuously. "Was it your care for it induced you to bear me off to-day?"

He began to walk up and down the room, kicking a joint-stool out of his way. She sat still, watching him, and courage soared high. He was irresolute. She knew herself to be the stronger of the two; she could hold him off for a while yet.

His thoughts raced; he shot a quick look at her as he passed in his impatient stride. She was sitting straight in her chair, hedged about by a flaming barrier of resolve. She was strung up; events had marched too swiftly to allow her girl's imagination to sap her courage. In a dim way he realised this. Stealing yet another look at her rigid face, and the dark eyes that burned in it, he could picture her very clearly following out her threat. He had her in his power; he could work his will on her, but some instinct told him that she was in too exalted a mood to capitulate.

He was honestly shocked by the attitude she chose to take up. It had been unforeseen; it took him so much by surprise that he was thrown out of his stride. She sat like a goddess, fearless and invincible. So much he could see.

He went on with his pacing, biting his finger-nails now, as he always did when he was put out. He knew something of women; he had had dealings with a-many and a-many, but this girl was out of his ken.

He reflected. Her uplifted mood could not last; she was no goddess, but a girl strung up to a pitch of abnormal excitement that would die. He made up his mind to wait, to allow anticipation to wear down her courage.

He came to a halt opposite her. "We will see how you feel in the morning, my cousin," he said. "Let the night bring sager counsel. You are over-wrought, and I would not hurry you, nor do I wish to constrain you by force.

But mark me well! To-morrow night, if I have not your promise to wed with me, you will not find me so gentle. If you will not have me with the Church's holy tie you shall have me without it. You have a night and a day to make up your mind whether you will be wife or mistress, but one or the other you shall be. That I swear!"

Some of the tension went out of her. She let her eyes fall that he might not see the relief in them. Much might happen in a night and a day; there was hope still.

She rose. "Then I desire to retire to my chamber, señor, with your good leave," she said.

ᴄᴀ Chapter XXII ᴾᴄ

OF that mad ride through Spain Joshua never afterwards spoke without a shake of the head, and a gesture of incredulity. "You ask me how we compassed it?" says he. "I will tell you very simply, I do not know. We were out of Madrid featly enough, none saying us nay. Why should they? My master wore the collar of the Golden Fleece about his neck, a fine gaudy thing, to rank with our Garter, so I believe. That weighed with them, I warrant you. If any speered after us, why, we were on the King's business, and you may believe we tarried not to see how they stomached that.

"We rode through that first night without drawing rein. I thanked Jupiter—a very potent planet in my affairs— that there was some faint moonlight, else had we been shent. Past some town—you would not know it, and nor did I—clouds came up, and we were left to flounder among the ruts and the boulders. As I remember, we lost the road twice between that stage and the next. I was near to breaking my head against low-hanging tree-branches, lost, then bogged in some swamp. 'How fares your honour?' sings I out into the darkness. 'Merrily, merrily!'

calls Sir Nicholas back to me. What can be done with such
a mad-wag? We were casting about to find the road,
stumbling here, foundering there, with all Spain hunting
us to the rearward. But 'Merrily, merrily! quoth Sir Nicholas, and I doubt he thought so. Did he lose the road?
What matter for that? Trust him to nose out the north; it
was enough. The dawn came up, and a sharp wind with
it, enough to cut me in two. I was never more glad of the
daylight. We struck the road—God's light, there was little
enough to choose between it and the open country!—
pushed on, the horses nigh done. My nag went lame: small
blame to him. We fetched up at the next stage, walking the
last league. You may be sure we had put a-many between
us and Madrid.

"My head was a-nod, and my eyes full of dust. What
matter for that? 'How fares your honour?'—'Excellent
well,' quotha, as though he were upon a day's hunting.
Ay, and a hunt it was, and he the hart. Yet I do not deny
he hunted too, a quarry of his own, and maybe gave more
thought to that than to the hounds behind him. So did not
I, but I own myself to be a very meacock creature,
besides which the salt fell towards me in an unlucky spill at
that inn, and such a happening cannot be regarded as
fortunate. For all that I kept a good heart. There was a
certain prophesy made concerning me which led me to
suppose I was not destined to die upon a gallows, or at
the stake. Moreover, if you go upon a venture with Mad
Nicholas you had best leave fear behind you.

"We stayed but to break our fast at the stage. Maybe
they looked curiously at the inn. As I remember, there
was a weasel-beaked fellow mighty sprag to beagle out our
business. He made little by that. We ate but a running-
banquet there; no sleep for us yet, by your leave. A
mouthful snatched, a cup or two of wine to slake our
throats, and away we went again. I remember I bestrode a
leathern-mounted Almaine—a devil to ride, but a devil to
go. Sir Nicholas had a Barb under him, a fine fleet beast,
but mine would have gone for double the distance. Let
that pass. We went at full stretch, no rest for man or
beast. Thus it is to go abroad on Sir Nicholas' affairs. But
I do not complain. 'God save you, sir!' cry I, and I was
reeling in the saddle. 'Will you ride till Doomsday?' We

drew rein then, at the next stage. 'We have a fair start of them,' says my master, stretching up his arms. 'I'm for bed.' I warrant you I dropped where I stood, and so slept.

"It was all of a piece. We suffered a check here, an ill-chance there. At one stage there were no nags to be had. We wasted a matter of six hours; precious time if you are hunted men. But Sir Nicholas carried it all off with a high hand. I shivered to hear him, but it served, it served. He had not been master of a ship's crew for naught, do you see? We took what horses we would, scattered the ducats here and there. Did a man refuse to sell? A murrain on the fellow! if he would not sell in all honesty he must be robbed. To speak sooth, when it was thus shown him he would, in the general way, sell. Our need? Why, we went upon the King's business. Did they ask for proof? We waved a folded paper in their silly faces. (It was an inventory of some shirts and other matters sent to the washer woman, I believe, but they were not to know that.) It sufficed. Our errand? Why there was a dangerous pirate let loose, a very fiend in human shape. Who was this one? Ho, who but El Beauvallet himself! What a stir was there! We were off whiles the dizzards chattered over it.

"We suffered a bad check somewhere south of Burgos. There was not a horse to be had that was not full of windgalls, or past cure of the staggers. We lay up at an inn—a very noisome hole it was, but we took little account of that. It was there we came near to our undoing, but it passed, it passed. There came the sound of a horse ridden hard. I could see the watchful look in my master's eye; he bore a fidgetting sword in his scabbard those few minutes, nor was my dagger restful in its sheath. A man went by our inn in a cloud of dust. When it cleared he was away, but I know the look of a soldier, do you see? He was rocking in the saddle: well he might if he had o'ertaken us! For we had not gone at a jog-trot, as you may imagine. He was not on our track. Nay, nay, unless I am mistaken he was bound for the Frontier. We might have stood in his path and mowed at him; he would have paid no heed. All his orders were to stop the Frontier pass. For that matter I believe we might have declared ourselves all along the way, and had better service. The common folk make a

hobgoblin of my master, and fear him like the plague—
the grandees not far otherwise, from all I could observe.

"Well, we made it in seven days, and might have made
it in less, I believe, but for that check south of Burgos.
Odds lifelings, but I was glad to leave the post road
behind us at Burgos, and strike north-west to Vasconosa.
It was to shake off the hounds, you understand, for those
that went not to the Frontier would make Santander, as
we judged, and that lay to the east of us. A wild, mad
journey, and a miracle that we came off, say I!"

Miracle or not, they did indeed come to Vasconosa at
dusk upon the seventh day. There was some sort of an inn
there, but little else in the village but a few hovels, and the
Great House.

Joshua did good work there while Sir Nicholas washed
the travel-stains from his person, and changed his dress.
He was trimming his beard when Joshua came up to his
room. Joshua came strutting, and looked wisely.

"We have beagled out some new matters, so please you,
master. The Great House we have seen, and I learn the
family came in late last night. Nothing's to be heard of
them yet. We may easily come at the house; there are a
dozen ways through the gardens, and no guards save at
the gatehouse, and the stables. Naught to fear, they think.
Why no, if they had not El Beauvallet stalking them."

"What of our road?" interrupted Sir Nicholas, combing
his beard to a point. "Could you discover the way?"

"Never fear me, master. There will be some 'cross
country work to be done yet, over the hills, but we may go
on a fair track, so I understand, as far as Villanova. You
ask me how I might find this out without betraying matters not for the tapster's ears? Very simply, sir. I am loud
in my complaints that there is no road but the one in these
parts. In the south, say I, we are better served. That put
our dawcock on his mettle, I warrant you. 'Ho!' says he,
'I'd have you know there is the road that runs to join the
post-road a matter of ten miles to the east of the Great
House, and another which runs past the hunting-lodge in
the forest to Villanova."

"We found Villanova on the map," said Sir Nicholas.
"What is this hunting-lodge?"

"Be sure I asked, master. It need not concern us, being

no more than a summer-house that yon popinjay, Diego, uses for his sports. More sports than you might think, master, I dare swear. It lies a matter of five miles from here, and the track comes out not a hundred yards from this inn. I have conned it. Now it seems to me, master, if you are to steal your lady away, I had best have the horses tethered in the spinney hard by the Great House, and so make that track as speedily as may be possible." He saw that Sir Nicholas had put on a clean ruff, and plucked a poking-stick from out his doublet. "So please you, sir, we will poke out the folds of the ruff a little. Will you have me procure a third horse with a lady's saddle?"

Sir Nicholas frowned into the mirror. "I dare not take the risk," he said after a moment's thought. "We want no questions asked, no tongues set wagging. I'll have my lady up before me as far as to Villanova." He glanced out into the fast gathering darkness. "Dark enough for me to venture," he said. "Can you find that track at need, my man?"

"I have it safe in my head, master." Joshua put up the poking-stick. "But I would know, sir, what plan you have in mind."

Sir Nicholas rose up from his chair. His eyes twinkled. "Marry, so would I know, Joshua," he said frankly.

Joshua shook his head severely. "This is no way to go to work, master. What, do you think to have the noble lady away this night with never a plan in your head?"

"I know not. I've a-many plans, but I move in the dark, my friend, and I have need to nose about a little. Maybe I shall get her off to-night, if opportunity serves; maybe I shall hold my hand a while. We will take the horses in case of need. See a fresh pair saddled, and tell what lie leaps most readily to your tongue."

Joshua prepared to depart. "I shall take leave to say, master, that a man has to be nimble-witted to keep pace with you," he remarked, and went out.

Sir Nicholas did not inquire what lie had been told when he came down twenty minutes later. Joshua had two good horses at the door, and the landlord seemed satisfied. Sir Nicholas swung his cloak over his arm, and sallied forth.

They had not far to go to the spinney Joshua had located. It ran on a low wall, crumbling and ivy-grown, which shut in the gardens of the house they sought. The wall was easy enough to come over. The horses were tethered in a thicket, a hundred yards or more from the road. Sir Nicholas set a hand on the low wall and vaulted lightly over; Joshua climbed after him.

They found themselves behind a yew hedge that bordered a paved walk. There were openings cut in it, and through one of these they went, to the pleasaunce.

Ahead of them the house loomed up in the darkness; they could see a light burning through an open window on the ground-floor, and another in a room above-stairs. For the rest there seemed to be no sign of life in the house, or else the windows were shuttered.

"Stay you in the lee of that hedge," Sir Nicholas whispered. "I am off to see what is to be seen." He slipped past, and was across the pleasuance before Joshua could expostulate; bareheaded, a hand on his sword hilt.

Joshua saw him reach the window of the house, and lost him then for a space. Evidently he was making a reconnaissance of those dark windows. Joshua shivered and drew his cloak more closely about him.

There was no sound behind the shuttered windows, nor any light discernible. The place seemed to be strangely quiet, or else this side of the house was not much inhabited. Sir Nicholas stole along until he stood beneath the one unshuttered window. Flattening himself against the wall, he peeped cautiously in.

The window stood wide to the cool evening air; the room seemed to be a sort of winter parlour, very elegantly furnished. In a chair half-turned from the window sat Dona Beatrice de Carvalho, reading from a gilt-bound volume.

Sir Nicholas considered her for a moment. Then with a little shrug of fatalism he set his hands on the sill and noiselessly swung one leg over.

Dona Beatrice, yawning over her book, heard a tiny sound, the click of a scabbard against the stone wall. She turned her head towards the window, and for once was startled out of her composure. She let fall her book.

"I give you a thousand good-morrows, señora," said

Sir Nicholas pleasantly, and came gracefully into the room.

Dona Beatrice recovered herself. "My dear Chevalier!" she drawled. "Or should I say my dear Señor Beauvallet?"

"But were you in doubt?" said Sir Nicholas, one eyebrow up.

"Very little," she said. She lay back in her chair, placidly regarding him. "You are a remarkably bold man, señor. I protest I like you. But what do you hope for here?"

"To be frank with you, señora, I am here to carry off your niece," said Sir Nicholas. He walked to the door, opened it, and looked out into the passage. There was no sign of anyone stirring. He shut the door, and came back into the room. "And if your charming son is at hand I shall be happy to cross swords with him," he added.

She gave a low laugh of pure enjoyment. "You are delightful," she assured him. "But do you think I shall sit quiet while you perform these deeds?"

He smiled disarmingly. "Why, as to that, señora, I am afraid I shall have to use you rather roughly," he said. "It is not my custom to war with women, and I should be loth to have you think me a brutal fellow, but I fear I shall have to tie you up and gag you." The smile grew. "Be at ease, I shall not hurt you."

She was perfectly at her ease. "Holy Virgin, a desperate man, I see! What possessed you to come in at this window, Señor Beauvallet?"

"It was the only one that stood open," he replied lightly.

"You might have chanced on my son, señor, instead of me."

"I had rather hoped that I might," agreed Sir Nicholas. "I am out of luck."

Her eyelids drooped. "Yes, señor, you are out of luck; more so than you know," she said.

"Am I so, señora?" The blue eyes were watchful now.

"Sadly, I fear. You will have to be content to talk to me. I confess I could not have hit upon a more entrancing way of spending this tedious evening. You see, I am alone in the house but for my servants."

"You astonish me, señora," said Sir Nicholas, politely incredulous.

"Pray you search the house if it will set your mind at rest," she invited. "I am a creature quite without guile. This is a most amusing situation, do you not find?"

Sir Nicholas sat down on the edge of a small table near at hand. He began to play with his pomander, but his eyes never left the lady's face for all they were so careless-seeming. "It is unexpected," he admitted. "But then, as you no doubt know, señora, my genius lies in dealing with the unexpected. Where, dear lady, has your son taken Dona Dominica?"

She was prepared for that. "Rather, señor, he has gone in search of her. Yesterday, not ten miles from here, our equipage was set upon by brigands, and my niece carried off."

"Brigands is exactly the word I should myself have chosen," nodded Sir Nicholas, dangerously sweet. "I understand now why you are in so much agitation, señora. A grievous thing to have your cherished niece carried off." His voice changed; he let fall his pomander, and Dona Beatrice saw that the laughing eyes were like twin swords. "Come, señora!" he said briskly. "Give me credit for some little measure of wit! Where has he taken her?"

"My dear Señor Beauvallet, if he had taken her you would surely not expect me to tell you," she pointed out.

Sir Nicholas' brain was working swiftly now. "I think you have told me all I need to know," he said. "There is a certain hunting-lodge not five miles from here, is there not?"

The faintest shade of alarm, or perhaps it was only of annoyance, crossed her face. It was enough for Sir Nicholas, watching like a hawk. "My thanks, señora." He stood up. There was no smile in his eyes now; they were blazing, and the fine mouth was set hard.

"You know more than I do, señor," she shrugged.

He stood looking down at her for a moment; she gave a little laugh, and looked away. "I know," said Sir Nicholas softly, "that I shall have rid the earth of a very knave when I rid it of Don Diego de Carvalho. As for you, señora——" He broke off, and threw up his head, intently listening. The sound of horses, approaching fast, was heard. He took a quick step forward, and before she could move had a hand hard clamped over Dona Beatrice's mouth, the other gripping her shoulder. There was a sound of trampling round at the front of the house, and at that moment Joshua's alarmed face peeped over the window-sill.

The black brows lifted interrogatively.

"Master, master, King's men!" whispered Joshua.

He nodded briefly. "Rip me up your cloak. Quick, man!" His hand left Dona Beatrice's shoulder, and flicked the handkerchief from the sleeve of his doublet. Without ceremony he forced it into the lady's mouth. Not afraid, but cynical still, she was able to admire in a detached way his coolness, and to reflect that she could hardly recognise him now for the same man who had ruffled it so gaily in Madrid. He had a ruthless look now; there would be quick death for any who crossed his path to-night.

Joshua threw his torn cloak into the room. A thunder of knocks on the front door in the distance set him shivering again. "For God's sake, master——!"

Sir Nicholas answered never a word. With swift, sure movements he twisted one of the strips of cloth tightly round Dona Beatrice's gagged mouth and tied it. Another encircled her body, pinning her arms to her sides. She made no resistance; over the bandage her eyes looked mockingly. If the King's men were at hand now El Beauvallet was doomed.

There was a hurry of footsteps in the passage, servants were running to the front door. Sir Nicholas bent, passed the third strip around the lady's wide skirts, and hobbled her tightly.

"In the King's name!" The peremptory voice reached the parlour; evidently the front door was open now.

Sir Nicholas smiled grimly. "Now, señora!" he said, and lifted her up bodily. She was no light weight, but he carried her easily to the window. Her eyes no longer mocked; they looked startled now, for this was indeed the unexpected.

"Take the lady!" said Sir Nicholas, and lowered her into Joshua's arms.

"Beshrew your heart, master!" whispered Joshua, stag-

gering under the burden. "Are you mad in very sooth?
Come away, sir! For the love of God come swiftly!"

"I come," said Sir Nicholas, and climbed lightly over
the sill. He dropped to the ground, lifted his prisoner from
Joshua's straining arms, and carried her off over his shoulder across the dark pleasaunce to the low wall, and the
spinney beyond.

"We are sped! we are sped!" almost moaned Joshua.
"And you lug the wrong lady off with us! What now,
master? Whither?"

"To that hunting-lodge," said Sir Nicholas through his
teeth. "We shall leave the wrong lady in the spinney. I do
not think they will look for her there in a hurry." He
dumped Dona Beatrice down on the wall, climbed over,
and lifted her up again. She was carried to the thicket
where the horses stood, and set down in the middle of it.
Sir Nicholas untied his horse and gathered the bridle in his
hand. A moment he looked down at Dona Beatrice, glaring up at him. "Señora," he said, "do not repine at the
discomfort of your situation. Had you been a man I
should have killed you."

ᘒᕲ Chapter XXIII ᕬᘓ

THE track through the forest was found, and Beauvallet's
horse leaped forward under the spur. Joshua, pressing up
close, looked anxiously into his master's grimly smiling
face. "Master, what is it?" he said fearfully.

"Don Diego has had my lady shut up in the lodge since
yesterday," said Sir Nicholas curtly.

Joshua's jaw dropped. He could understand now why
Sir Nicholas wore his killing look. This was ill news; the
very worst that could have befallen. His stupefaction
passed; righteous wrath sprang up. "Ah, villain! ah, crackhemp! If we slit not your weasand for this!"

They galloped on down the track. To either side the great trees reared up, ghostly in the darkness. The road was good, a grassy ride cut through the woods. "Well for us it was, for we did not pick our way daintily, look you," says Joshua.

Sir Nicholas caught his horse up on a stumble, and turned his head. "Hard-pressed now, my Joshua," he said, and shook the sword in his scabbard slightly.

"In my opinion, master, there is naught new in that," said Joshua philosophically.

"How many men, by your reckoning?"

"Enough to do our business," said Joshua dryly. "But having dumped the fat lady in the spinney—I allow it to have been politic, upon reflection—and so shut her mouth, we may yet win clear away."

"I don't think it," said Sir Nicholas calmly. "They may waste time in searching for her, but if I read this villainy aright every hilding on the estate will know where Dona Dominica lies, and send the guards hotfoot after me there."

Joshua spoke in a voice of alarm. "Save you, master, save you! do you lose heart? For if that is so at least then I know we are shent."

The answering laugh reassured him. "Oh chewet, do you not know when I am in fighting humour?"

"I should indeed, sir," acknowledged Joshua. "I make bold to say I find you dangerous at this present. There will be broken heads and slit gullets yet."

They rode on in silence, stirrup to stirrup. Presently Beauvallet spoke again. "I may have to lead the chase astray a little," he said. "Do you ride off with my lady by the northwest road to Villanova, and there await me. You mark me?"

"Master, do you tell me to desert you?" said Joshua, offended. "That is not very likely."

He caught the well-known gleam in Beauvallet's eye. "Oho!" said Sir Nicholas softly. "Do you command here, my friend? Now I think you will do as I say, or it may be the worse for you."

"Pretty treatment, master, by my troth!" said Joshua. "Well, go to: I do not deny you are the General."

"If we are overtaken," said Sir Nicholas, ignoring this

stricture upon his ruthless methods, "as I have little doubt we shall be, ride with my lady hotfoot to Villanova, and there await me. Is it understood?"

"Well, master, well. And if you come not?"

"By this hand I shall come!" said Beauvallet. "What, do you fear for me? Know then that I was never more in the mood to try a throw with death."

"That I may very easily believe, sir, and I may add that it does not set me the more at ease," said Joshua. He peered ahead and reined in to a walk. "Softly, now! What's here?"

A house loomed up ahead, approached by a wicket-gate giving on to the track. There was a low building some three hundred yards farther on: stables, Joshua guessed.

Sir Nicholas slipped from the saddle, and twitched the bridle over his horse's head. "This should be the place. Follow me now." He led the way off the track into the gloom of the forest. The moss-grown floor muffled the sound of the horses' hooves; they skirted the house, and came round to the back of it, under cover of the trees. The horses were swiftly tethered to a young sapling. Sir Nicholas unbuckled his sword-belt, and drew the shining blade clear of its sheath. "No need to take this to hamper me," he said, and left the scabbard on the ground. He scanned the back of the house, and saw a lighted window on the upper storey. "Aha, my bird, do you lie there?" he said. "We shall see anon. Now I am for you, Don Diego de Carvalho!"

They went quickly round to the front of the house. Joshua had his long dagger out, and followed silently in Beauvallet's grim wake. Sir Nicholas went boldly now, the naked sword in his hand, and hammered on the door of the lodge with its chased hilt.

"God's my life, we stalk on our fate now!" muttered Joshua, aghast at these high-handed measures.

They heard footsteps approaching inside the house, rather hesitantly. Sir Nicholas beat again on the door, an imperative summons, and Joshua took a firmer hold on his weapon.

The footsteps came nearer; the door was opened a few inches, and Luis, the valet, looked out. "Who knocks? What do you want?"

Joshua's arm slid lovingly round his neck; the point of his dagger pricked the man's throat. "Nay then, my cosset, no sound out of you, or you are sped," he said softly.

The man's eyes stared at him, his lips moved soundlessly.

"Truss him up," said Sir Nicholas, and passed into the lodge.

There were candles in sconces upon the walls; the stairs ran up to one side, to the other a door opened hastily. Don Diego came out, a snatched-up sword in his hand, a look of quick alarm in his face. "Let none enter!" he said sharply, and then started back. "Jesu!" he gasped, blanched and shaking. His eyes were wide and staring, looking fearfully. In the doorway stood El Beauvallet, tall and straight, fiendishly smiling, like avenging doom wafted thither by most dreadful witchcraft.

The candlelight flickered along the blade of El Beauvallet's sword. He held it between his hands, and bent the supple steel to a half-hoop. Don Diego's fascinated eyes saw the white teeth gleam. "One has entered," said Sir Nicholas. He came into the hall, purposeful, a stalking terror. "I have the honour of presenting myself to you, señor, in my true guise." He stood in the middle of the hall now, feet wide planted. "I am El Beauvallet, Don Diego, and I come to seek a reckoning with you!" His voice rang out; his beard jutted dangerously.

Don Diego was backed against the wall. "Witchcraft! witchcraft!" he muttered, and the sword trembled in his hand.

The chin was upflung, the gay laugh rang amongst the rafters. "Ha, do you think so indeed, villain?" He let his blade straighten with a quivering snap, and shook it in Don Diego's face. "Come, pigeon-livered hound! Here are no arts but my sword to yours. Or will you have me spit you where you cower? Come, choose quickly! Death waits for one of us twain to-night, and I am very sure it is not for me!"

Away up the stairs Dominica knelt behind a locked door with her ear pressed to the crack. She heard the ringing laugh, and it was as though joy flooded her whole being. For a moment the world stood still, then she sprang

to her feet, beating on the door with her clenched fists.
"Nicholas! Nicholas! I am here, locked in!" she
shrieked.

He heard her voice and threw up his head. "Cheerly,
my bird, cheerly!" he called. "I shall be with you in a
little!"

She leaned against the door, sobbing and laughing at
once. Might she not have known that he would come, and
come in time, too.

Downstairs in the hall Don Diego had recovered from
his first daze of horror. The colour came back into his
cheeks. He tore his dagger from its sheath, and crouched,
facing Beauvallet. "Dog of a pirate! You shall speed to
hell this night!"

"After you, señor, after you!" said Sir Nicholas blithe-
ly, and caught the thrusting rapier point on his blade.
There was a scuffle of daggers, steel clashed against steel,
and Don Diego sprang back, disengaging over the arm.

Sir Nicholas drove him rigorously; they circled a little;
there was a lunge, and a dexterous parry, the flash of an
upthrust dagger, scurry of blades, and the quick shifting
of light feet on the wooden floor.

Don Diego fought furiously, lips drawn back in a snarl-
ing grimace, brows close knit. He lunged forward to the
heart, was parried by that lightning blade from the hand
of Ferrara, and recovered his guard only just in time. Sir
Nicholas was on his toes; the laugh was back in his eyes,
and on his lips; larger issues were forgot in the present joy
of battle. He had made no idle boast to his brother when
he had said he was a master of the art of foiling with the
point. Don Diego had thought himself no mean swords-
man, but he knew himself outmatched. This man, sprung
on wires; this devil who laughed as he lunged, had a
dashing skill that brought Diego face to face with death a
dozen times. He was fighting for very life, and he had
thought to run through his opponent almost at once.

"Laugh, laugh, dog!" he gasped, beating aside that
flickering blade for an instant. "You shall laugh soon in
hell!"

"Go warn them there of my coming, señor," said Sir
Nicholas gaily, and seemed to quicken.

The fight grew more desperate; Don Diego was losing

ground, and knew it. It was all he could do to keep that dancing sword-point at bay, and ever he fell back before it. The point quivered to his throat, he sprang back, was forced on farther still, hard-breathing, sweating, but fighting every inch of the way.

Faintly in the distance came the thud of galloping horses. Joshua's voice called urgently: "Master, master, make an end!"

Don Diego thrust viciously to the heart. "You shall go hence—shackled!" he gasped.

The steel blades hissed together; one of them snaked out in a straight lunge, driven by a strong wrist. *"My bite is sure!"* quoth Sir Nicholas, and wrenched his sword free of the deep wound.

Don Diego's weapon fell clattering; he threw up his hands with a choking sound, and pitched forward on to his face.

The thud of the horses' hooves was drawing nearer; Sir Nicholas was down on his knee, turning Don Diego over. The black eyes were glazing fast, but gleamed hatred still. Sir Nicholas felt in the elegant doublet, found the key he sought, and sprang up.

Joshua ran in. "Trapped, trapped!" he cried. "They are hard on us!"

"Round with you to the back!" Beauvallet answered instantly. "Wait beneath my lady's window, and when I send her down to you, off with you!"

Joshua made a gesture of despair and ran out. Plainly to be heard now were the galloping hooves.

Sir Nicholas went bounding up the stairs. "Where, my heart, where?" he called.

Her voice led him to the door. He fitted the key into the lock and turned it, listening to the thunder of hooves drawing closer and ever closer.

The door was open, and Dominica sobbing on his breast.

"You are safe?" he asked urgently.

"Safe! Safe!" she answered.

"God be praised!" He put her quickly aside and strode to the bed. The heavy quilt was flung off, the sheets snatched up and knotted. "The chase is hard upon me. I

must let you down through your window, my bird." He
jerked at his knot. The horses were at hand, and trampling
now as they were pulled up outside the lodge. Sir Nicholas
reached the window, "Joshua?"

"Ready, master!" came the stealthy whisper.

He turned. "Come, fondling! Trust me to let you safely
down."

She let him lift her on to the window-ledge, but her
hands clung to him. Downstairs blows were being rained
on the shut door. "But you? But you?"

"Never fear," he said. His voice was cool and reassur-
ing. "Twist the sheet about your hands, so, and hold fast,
child. Brave lass! Are you ready?"

Clinging tightly to her improvised rope she was lowered
over the sill, hung dangling on the end of the sheet, and
was let down into Joshua's ready arms. He set her down,
caught her hand, and led her away at the double across
the garden to the hedge that shut it off from the forest.

"Hist, bist for your life!" he breathed. "Do as I bid
you, mistress, and not a word out of you!"

Behind them the guards were in at the door of the
lodge, stumbling over Don Diego's body.

"Ah, he has been here, the villain!" cried Cruza. "He is
here still! Search the house!"

Upstairs Beauvallet tore the key from the lock of Dominica's door, and fitted it in again on the inside. He pulled
the door to behind him just as Cruza came bounding up
the stairs, a drawn sword in his hand.

"Well met, Señor Cruza!" said Beauvallet cheerfully,
and held a sword and dagger ready.

Cruza sent a shout echoing through the house. "To me!
to me!"

The men came stamping up the stairs. "Why, what a
pack of you!" said Sir Nicholas, amused.

"Yield you, señor!" Cruza cried. "You are outmatched!"

"Yield?" said Sir Nicholas. Up went his comical eyebrow. "God's Son, Cruza, do you know who I am?"

"You are El Beauvallet, and I have sworn to take you!
We are six to your one. Yield, yield!"

"You will be forsworn, good señor. I am El Beauvallet, so the odds are fair enough. Now who will take Nick Beauvallet?" He looked inquiringly, and wondered whether Joshua had got Dominica away yet.

"Insolent dog!" Cruza dashed in with levelled sword. "On to him, and take him alive!" he cried.

Sir Nicholas' blade swept a circle before him. He laughed and shook the sweat from his eyes. "Alas, alas, for vain ambition! So-so! What, winded, my man?" A guard fell back with a slash across the forearm. Sir Nicholas beat down a big double-edged sword, and slipped his dagger-hand behind him, feeling for the handle of the door.

The Toledo blade bit shrewdly and sure indeed. Cruza staggered as the point went home in his shoulder, and recovered again. "Alive! I want him alive!" he gasped out.

Sir Nicholas' fingers had found the door-handle, and turned it now in one quick movement. The door was flung open; he sprang back, fighting his way, sent the foremost guard sprawling with a wound in the breast, and slammed the door home behind him.

Cruza threw himself upon it, thrusting with all his might. "Quick, fools!" he cried, and heard the key grate the lock. "Two of you down into the garden, under the window!" he jerked out. "Break down this door, you others! Break it down!"

Two of the guards went running down the stairs and round to the back; the rest set their shoulders to the door. The lock gave under the weight, the door flew wide, and the guards were in.

The room was empty. An overturned chair lay asprawl by the window; a casement swung open on its hinge, and the curtain beside it was rent from end to end.

With one accord his men followed Cruza to the window and tried to crane out. From the arras behind the door Sir Nicholas slipped out, kissed his fingers silently to the backs of the guards, and was off without a sound across the upper hall to the stairs.

He went down in a series of bounds, reached the hall, and stepped over Don Diego's body to the door. A beam of light cast through the opening showed him a guard standing to the horses' heads. He went forward in a rush

then, and his sword-hilt took the guard on the chin almost
before he was aware, and sent him sprawling in the road.
Sir Nicholas caught a bridle, vaulted into the saddle, and
stood up in his stirrups.

"Come then, ye dogs!" he cried. "Follow El Beauvallet
if ye dare, and take *Reck Not* for the word!" He wheeled
about as the two guards came dashing round the corner of
the house, and galloped off down the way by which he
had come, eastwards towards the Frontier.

ᗞᗴ᎒ Chapter XXIV ᗞᗴ

THE horse he had snatched was a fleet curtal bay, and
responded readily enough to the clap of heels to his
flanks. Sir Nicholas held him on his course with a hard
hand, heard behind him shouts and the trampling of the
horses he had cut loose by his sudden onslaught on the
guard who held them, and pressed on. The noise died
away, only the pounding of the bay's hooves on the track
now broke the stillness.

Where the track came out on the post-road a crowd was
gathered, peering and listening. The news of the guards'
coming and the prey they sought had spread through the
village; there were assembled now some peasants, a-gape,
and servants of the Carvalho estate, fingering staves. Lanterns bobbed and twinkled amongst them, but the moon
was coming up, and a faint grey light already made the
lanterns superfluous.

Sir Nicholas saw what awaited him, and rode down into
the small crowd like a thunderbolt. There was a surge
forward to cut him off, a flurry of agitated shouting, and
the scurry of feet, and the bay horse was amongst them.
Confusion reigned, some trying to fling themselves out of
the way of the plunging hooves, others striking wildly at
the lithe figure atop of the maddened horse. The bay was

rearing and snorting with fright, wrenched aside to evade a murderous blow from a club, backing into a group of peasants, who gave precipitately, gripped by an insistent pair of knees. Sir Nicholas' sword flashed aloft, wielded like a flail. He forced a way through, the serfs falling back before his irresistible path, tumbling over one another in their haste to get away from this demon's reach. The hand on the bridle was slackened, the bay horse was away, ridden hard to the south, towards the track that led eastwards to the Frontier.

There were men on the road, dotted here and there, stragglers hurrying to see the capture of a pirate; they sprang aside instinctively to give place to the mad, runaway horse that bore down on them, and saw in the gray light a straight rider with a naked sword in his hand. Some crossed themselves, some yelled in alarm, but no one offered El Beauvallet hindrance.

The road to the east was found; Sir Nicholas forced the bay in to a more sober pace, and turned down the track. By the shout that was raised behind him he knew that his way was marked. The villagers might be trusted to direct the soldiers aright. Sir Nicholas settled down to a canter, feeling his way, as it were, along the track. The ground seemed level enough, grown over here and there with sparse, shifting turf. To either side scrubby bushes were scattered, with a few trees rearing up amongst them.

Behind came gradually the muffled sound of the pursuit. Sir Nicholas spurred on, mile upon mile, left the road for the flat pasture-land that ran beside it, and galloped on, the sound of his flight deadened by the soft earth. The curtal horse shook his fine head a little, feeling a race in the air as the hand on his bridle slackened, lengthened his easy stride, and took hold of the bit in good earnest.

The trees grew more thickly now, oaks, Sir Nicholas guessed, and presently a black wall seemed to rise up ahead. The track curved slightly, and plunged into a great forest of oak trees. The branches, in full leaf, shut out the moonlight from the depths of the forest; only the track was faintly illuminated where the silver light filtered through the almost interlocking branches.

Sir Nicholas reined in, head up and ears straining,

listening. Faintly, very far away, came the sound of horses on the road.

He swung himself down from the saddle, passed a hand over the bay's steaming neck, and led him into the dusk of the forest.

The horse was restless and fidgetting, but a gentling hand stilled him after a while. He stood quiet, stretched down his neck, and began lipping at some fallen leaves on the ground.

Nearer and nearer, like approaching thunder came the sound of horses on the road, ridden desperately. Up came the bay's head; the ears went forward. Sir Nicholas' hand slid to the satin nose; the pursuit sounded closer still, and Sir Nicholas' long fingers gripped tightly, checking the imminent whinny.

The riders swept up and past; they were so close Sir Nicholas could hear the horses' hard breathing and the creak of the saddle-girths. He held tight to the bay's nose, and waited for the soldiers to pass.

They were gone in a moment, riding close-wedged, hell-for-leather. In a little while all sound of them had died; they were away, making for the Frontier road, and it would take a deal to stop them with their dogged purpose firm in their minds.

Sir Nicholas relaxed his grip on the bay's nose and laughed. "Oh, ye bisson fools!" he said. "Ride on, ride on: ye will have but a cold welcome at the end. So, boy, so!" He led the bay back on to the road, mounted again, and set him at an easy canter along the track towards Vasconosa.

Dominica, tossed up on to a horse before Joshua, clung tight by the saddle-bow, and tried to speak. Joshua's hand covered her mouth imperatively; he struck off through the wood at a walking pace, making westwards.

As soon as he judged it to be safe he bore round a little to meet the track again, came upon it some quarter of a mile beyond the lodge, and kicked his horse to a gallop.

Dominica tried to see his face. "No, no, back, I say! back! What, will you leave him? Coward! Oh, base! Back to him, I implore you!"

Joshua torn with anxiety, sore at his enforced flight, was in no humour to be patient. "Rest you, mistress, we must make Villanova."

She leaned forward to tug at the bridle. "You are leaving him to be slain! Turn, turn! Oh, dastard, cur, craven!"

"Ho! Fine holiday and lady terms these!" said Joshua, bristling. "Know then, mistress, that were it not for you I would be beside Sir Nicholas now, and had liefer be there, God wot! A plague on all women, say I! What, do I bear you off for my pleasure? Out, out, señorita! These are my master's orders, and an evil day it is that hears him give such ones. Let go the rein, I tell you!"

Her fingers were on his bridle hand, clinging, cajoling. "No, no, I did not mean it, but turn, Joshua! For the love of God, set me down and go you back! I will lie close, I will do as you bid me, only go you back to aid Sir Nicholas!"

"And get a broken head for my pains," said Joshua. "My master's an ill man to cross, señorita. Nay, nay, we who sail with Laughing Nick must do as we are bid, come weal, come woe. Content you, he has his plans well laid, I warrant you."

Words tumbled from her lips. She begged, stormed, commanded and coaxed. "I am not the worth of his life!" she said again and again.

"Well, I doubt there would be a fine reckoning between us if Sir Nicholas heard me agree with you," remarked Joshua. "Therefore I keep a still tongue in my head."

"God knows what I said or did not say upon that ride," he afterwards recounted. "Maybe my mistress and I bandied some hard words to and fro, but I bore her no malice, nor did she ever after hold it against me. Which is something remarkable in a woman, I hold."

No sound of pursuit came after them; Joshua allowed his horse to slacken the pace somewhat, and presently drew in to a steady trot. Dominica was quiet now, but her face looked pinched in the moonlight. Joshua, himself not much lighter-hearted, was moved to offer words of comfort. "Cheerly, mistress, we shall have Sir Nicholas with us this night."

She turned her eyes towards him. "How can he fight all those men single-handed?"

"Mark me, if he does not fob them off with some trick," said Joshua stoutly. "Maybe you did not believe that he would break free of that prison, señorita, but he did it. Keep a good heart." He saw her clouded eyes. "By your good leave, mistress, and with respect, I would say that El Beauvallet's lady should wear a smiling face."

She did smile, but faintly. "Yes, she should indeed," she answered. She bit her lip. "I saw him for so fleeting a moment!"

"Patience, mistress; I am bold to say you will hear the bustle of his coming in a little while."

They came to Villanova past ten o'clock at night and fetched up at the inn. "More lies!" said Joshua. "Leave all to me, lady." He lifted her down from the saddle and proceeded to create a stir. "Ho, there! Room for the noble señora! What, I say! Landlord!"

A portly individual came out of the lighted tap-room and stared in amazement at Dominica. She reflected that she must look oddly enough, riding over the countryside at such an hour without cloak or hood or even horse.

"The good-year!" cried out Joshua, voluble. "Eh, me, but this has been an evening's work! A chamber for my mistress, and supper on the instant! The noble señor follows us close."

The landlord's eyes slowly ran over Dominica. "What's this?" he said suspiciously.

Dona Dominica stepped forward; she, too, could play a part. "A chamber, landlord, and at once," she said haughtily. "Do you keep me standing on the road?"

Joshua bowed his lady into the inn. "Brigands, man!" he shot over his shoulder. "A party of three, and my lady's horse shot under her. Ah, what an ill-chance!"

"Brigands? Jesu preserve us!" The landlord crossed himself. "But the señor?"

"Oh, be sure my master is on the villains' heels!" Joshua invented. " 'What,' cries he, 'shall this go unpunished?' The rogues made off with our sumpters, and nothing will do but my master must give chase, leaving me to get the gracious señora under cover. Oh, a very fire-eater!"

Dominica interposed in the voice of one accustomed to command. "A bed-chamber with your best speed, host, and supper against Don Tomas' coming."

Her tone had its calculated effect. She was evidently a lady of quality, and as such the landlord bowed to her. That he was suspicious, however, was plain.

"And well he might be!" said Joshua Dimmock. "An unlikely tale, I grant you, but by this time I was grown barrer of lies, an uncommon thing in me."

Dona Dominica was shown upstairs to a chamber of fair size and appointments. She sank into a chair, and said pettishly for the benefit of the landlord: "It was you who should have chased those knaves, Pedro." She hunched a shoulder. "Don Tomas is too impetuous. To send me off so, and himself to tarry!" She became aware of the puzzled landlord. "Well, fellow, well? What do you want?" she demanded.

He bowed himself out, assuring her that supper should be provided against her lord's coming. A glimpse of a double ducat negligently fingered by Joshua decided him to keep his suspicions in abeyance. Double ducats were not so plentiful in this village that a man could afford to run the risk of losing one.

Joshua nodded briskly, and made a significant gesture of a down-thrust thumb. "We shall do very well," he said. "Now, señorita, with your good leave I shall go get the pack from off my nag's back. I must hope that Sir Nicholas brings on his own jennet, for the most of his raiment is upon it, and I can very plainly hear him calling in the morn for a clean shirt and a clean ruff too."

He took Beauvallet's coming so much for granted that Dominica began to feel that he would come indeed. She laughed, and looked down at her tumbled riding dress. "A clean ruff for Sir Nicholas! Pray you, what will you do for me who have no clothes at all but what you see me in?"

Joshua shook his head. "A very pungent question, señora, I allow. This should have been looked to. But thus it is ever when my master is in this humour! I doubt he will have lost his pack and that scabbard beside. But there is never any ho with him. Reck Not! Ah, do I not know it? In we dash, and if we come off with our skins you may say it is a miracle."

He went down to collect his pack, to see his horse stabled, and fed, and to order a rear-banquet for the lady. She was served in her chamber, and the covers left on the table against Beauvallet's coming. The landlord had by this time very little doubt that he entertained noble guests. What their mysterious errand was he could not guess, though he was inclined, saving only the incomprehensible absence of the master, to suspect an elopement. But Joshua's demeanour alone convinced him of the quality of the lady he served. None but a great noble's man, thought the landlord, would show such a high hand as Joshua's. There must be a cold capon prepared against his master's coming. What, had he no better wine than this poor stuff? Let him make haste to his cellar and fetch up a bottle of the best he had. Where were the suckets? Was my lady to sit down at table to naught but a scraggy fowl and a neat's tongue? Out upon him! The landlord should learn that a lady of his mistress' standing was not to be so used.

He waited upon Dominica himself, and was inclined to be severe with her when she showed so little appetite. She looked up at him with large, frightened eyes. "He does not come," she said.

"Patience, patience, señorita, he is not a bird!" said Joshua testily. "If he got away he was to lead the Guards off on a wrong scent towards the Frontier. It would never do to have them on our heels, mistress, for you cannot ride as we might have to in such a strait."

"I can ride very well if I am allowed," she said meekly.

Time wore on. A last few loiterers in the tap-room went off homewards; candles were snuffed below stairs, and the inn grew quiet. Joshua had bespoken a chamber for his master, and a fire to be lit in Dominica's room, judging with some shrewdness that its friendly crackle and glow would do more to comfort her than any words of his.

She sat by it trying to keep her courage up, and from time to time looked anxiously at Joshua. She would not have him leave her; she would not hear of going to bed for all his pleading. He might bully and override her in most things, she said, but he could not make her rest until she knew Sir Nicholas to be safe.

"I shall take leave to say, señorita, that there is a long

day ahead of you, and you would do well to get what sleep you may."

"I will not!" she said, her old spirit rearing up its head. And there the matter rested.

It was close on midnight when they heard the sound of an approaching horseman. Joshua lifted a finger, and threw out his chest. "Ah, señora, ah! What said I? Ho, trust Beauvallet!" He went to the window and pushed it open.

Dominica was on her feet, clasping her hands. "It may not be. It may be a soldier in search of me. I cannot think . . ."

The horse was reined in under the window. "Holà, there!" rang out Beauvallet's voice. He looked up at the front of the inn and saw Joshua craning from the window. "God's Death, Joshua, what makes you there? Come down and let me in!"

Dominica sank back into her chair, almost stunned with relief. Joshua was making for the door. "Ay, ay, thus it goes," he said. "Briskly, recklessly, with never a thought to who may be listening. Ah, madcap!" He went out, and Dominica heard him clatter down the stairs and draw back the bolts of the door below, shouting to the awakened landlord as he did so that all was well. Then a light step sounded on the stairs, the door was opened, and the next instant Dominica was folded in Beauvallet's arms.

⚜ Chapter XXV ⚜

THEY were up at cock-crow next morning, and away upon their long ride north just as soon as they had broken their fast, and procured fresh horses.

Dominica felt herself to be moving in a dream; events had marched so swiftly that she was dazed by them. She

awoke to hear Joshua scratching on her door, and for a
moment imagined the previous day's wild work to be a
figment of her fancy. But Joshua's voice, unmistakably his
brisk voice, was bidding her rise up, and she knew herself
to be living in no dream.

Breakfast in the small parlour, leading off the tap-room
downstairs awaited her. She found Sir Nicholas there, neat
as ever, and because she was suddenly shy and tongue-tied
she could only give him her little hand to kiss, and say in
a voice that tried to hide her shyness: "Ah, Señor Nicholas, I see you have that clean ruff Joshua spoke of, so I
suppose you did not leave your pack behind."

He flung up a hand. "A' God's Name, let me hear no
more of that pack!" he said in comic dismay. "I have
heard of little else from that tickle-brain behind you since
my coming last night."

She looked round at Joshua's disapproving face. Joshua
pulled out a stool for her from under the table, but fixed a
wintry look upon Sir Nicholas. "Ay, master, no doubt it is
very well to talk in such careless wise, but I shall take
leave to say that to throw away a new doublet of murry
taffeta and a pair of stocks broidered with gold quirks
about the ankles, not to make mention of a set of silver
aiglets and a pair of trunk hose scarce worn, passeth the
bounds of prodigality."

"Peace, froth!" said Sir Nicholas, and sat him down
opposite to his lady at table. His eyes smiled at her across
the covers. "It is in my mind, ladybird, that we have not
sat at table together since you were aboard the *Venture*."
The twinkle deepened. "Do you remember that you were
loth to take wine from my hands?" He picked up the bottle at his elbow and regarded it with uplifted brows. "You
might well be loth to take this from me," he remarked.
"What is it, Joshua?"

"Scarce potable, I allow," said Joshua gloomily. "A
very vile drink, sir, but what would you?"

Dominica's tongue became loosened. She must tell Sir
Nicholas of the curious fancy that had come to her when
Don Diego offered her wine of Alicante, and when that
was done she found she had left her shyness behind
her.

The horses were saddled and ready. As Dominica set her foot in Beauvallet's hand she looked saucily at Joshua, and said: "Now, Joshua, you shall see whether I can ride hard or no."

She showed her mettle that day; she had done with fears and doubts. While she rode with Sir Nicholas at her side there could be nothing to alarm her. She had doubted that he would not reach Madrid, and he had done so; she had been sure that he could not escape from prison, and he had escaped; she had feared that he would not survive yesterday's grim work, and here he was, safe and gay as ever. She could never again doubt his extraordinary faculty of coming off safe from seemingly hopeless traps.

There seemed to be no peril now. Joshua might sniff the air, and keep an ear cocked to the rearward, but Sir Nicholas, leading the way over the hills, was care-free and merry. So, too, would his lady be, then.

The long journey taxed her powers to the uttermost, but she would not admit her weariness. She sat as straight as she could, laughed at the bad road, swore she was very well content, and had no wish to rest her limbs. They lost the way; why, it was part of the adventure, and her Nicholas would soon find it again; her horse stumbled on a craggy mountainside and nearly came down with her: let them not worry, she was safe enough; the sun was scorchingly hot: why, she was used to a hot clime, and would take no hurt.

Joshua was moved to admiration. "With good leave," he said, "I may remark that the señorita bears herself like an Englishwoman."

"This is to praise you, child," said Sir Nicholas, amused.

She nodded and laughed, and grew pink. "I shall very shortly be one, Señor Pirate, shall I not?" she said, and peeped at him.

His hand closed on hers. "My heart!"

They had to travel 'cross country where roads failed them, and this meant slow going for the most part, for the way was very rough, and they had need to study the rough plans Sir Nicholas had made. The shadows were lengthening long before they came within sight of the sea, and Joshua began to fret. He pushed up alongside to gain Beauvallet's ear. "Master, we shall never make it in time," he whispered.

Dominica caught the whisper. "Then let us press on," she said. "We must have Señor Nicholas away to-night without fail."

That made Beauvallet laugh, and even drew a smile from Joshua. This, however, he quickly suppressed. "The señorita speaks wisely," he said. "Rare to junket about Spain singing catches as though we were at Alreston, but I would take leave to remind you, master, that you are a hunted man."

"Oh, wind-bag," said Sir Nicholas genially, "if I could make better way be sure I should. Broken knees won't serve us. We shall make that port this night."

Make it they did, but later than they had hoped for, losing their road in the darkness, and only finding it again after much casting about. Dominica swayed in the saddle, upheld whenever it was possible by a strong, tireless arm, but when she heard Joshua swearing amongst the boulders she could still laugh, though it was but a weary, would-be valiant little laugh.

They saw the lights of the tiny port ahead; Sir Nicholas snuffed the air. "I can smell the sea," he said. "Courage, my bird!"

Her head drooped against his shoulder. He made a movement to summon up Joshua upon his other side. "Walk warily now," he said in a low voice. "If word was sent to the ports to stop our passage, those at Santander will know very well where to look for us."

Joshua started. "God's me, I had not thought of that! Ay, they would remember how you landed there."

A drowsy voice spoke from Beauvallet's shoulder. "Oh yes, they would never forget. We stayed with the Governor of Santander the day after you set us ashore, and I would you could have heard him."

Sir Nicholas looked significantly at Joshua. Joshua stifled a groan, and shrugged. "A posse of soldiers, I dare swear. I might have guessed we were not yet out of the trap." He looked up at the cloudy sky. "What o'clock? Nay, how shall we say? It but remains to find no ship awaiting. What, would she stay right through the night? One cannot suppose it. She will sniff the dawn at hand and be off."

"Dawn, stock-fish?" said Sir Nicholas. "If it is past eleven you may call me a dolt."

"I have a better regard for my skin, master," said Joshua, with dignity.

They gave a wide berth to the cluster of cottages that formed the port, and picked their way cautiously down the hill towards the sound of the sea lapping on the shingle. It was very dark, and the ground was strewed with rocks and hillocks and patches of stones. Sir Nicholas reined in his horse and turned in the saddle to speak to Joshua. "We make nothing by this. We shall do best to tether the nags and go on afoot."

Joshua nodded and slid down from the saddle. Sir Nicholas was on the ground, and already lifting Dominica down. Her legs almost gave way under her; she staggered and caught at his hand. He would have lifted her in his arms, but she shook her head. "No, no, I would rather walk. I am only so stiff."

They went forward, Joshua close behind them with the lantern he had bought that morning in Villanova. Somewhere below them the waves were breaking gently on the beach; the ground shelved steeply towards it. Sir Nicholas stopped. "Light the lantern, Joshua," he said softly.

Joshua knelt to open it. He looked up. "Master, a cloak to hide the light."

Sir Nicholas swung the cloak from his shoulders and held it round both Joshua and the lamp. Joshua was busy with his tinder-box; a spark flared, and the wick caught.

Dominica felt numb with fatigue still. She sank down on a convenient rock and watched Joshua tending his lamp under cover of the cloak. The wash of the sea sounded like a lullaby; she wondered whether, somewhere to the north in the velvety darkness the *Venture* lurked. They seemed so alone in the world in this silence of the night that it hardly seemed possible. Down by the huts men might be stirring, but here on the shelving stony ground all was silent, hushed by the sea.

Sir Nicholas looked keenly round, peering through the darkness. For as far as he could see there was no one abroad. Come what might, the signal must be given. He took the lamp from Joshua and held it high above his head. Then he dipped it quickly, and cloaked it while a man might count twenty. Again he showed it, and yet a third time.

There was a pause. "Oh knaves, if ye be not there!" muttered Joshua. "Oh, Master Dangerfield, I do not trust you!"

Away to the north out of the blackness shone a pinpoint of light three times. The *Venture* had answered the signal.

"Ha, true men!" said Joshua in high fettle. "I would wager young Master Dangerfield against an hundred!"

His wrist was clamped hard. "Silence, man!" hissed Sir Nicholas, and threw up his head to listen.

Joshua stiffened like a dog. To the west of them had come a shout, muffled by the wash of the sea.

"God's Death, they've posted a sentry on the look-out!" muttered Sir Nicholas, and pulled his long dagger from its sheath.

Joshua had his head under the cloak blowing out the lantern. Heavy footsteps were approaching at a jog-trot. Sir Nicholas went forward into the night noiseless and swift.

A man loomed up out of the darknes with a levelled halberd. He was on to Beauvallet before he realized it, and went down with no more than a groan as the dagger struck home.

"Ha, neatly done " said Joshua, not above a whisper, and with complete satisfaction. He put up his own weapon, which he had snatched out as he ran after his master.

But in the distance another cry sounded, as though a fellow-soldier answered that first call.

Sir Nicholas was back at Dominica's side wiping his dagger. "More of them," he said grimly. "The Governor of Santander has my compliments." He swept Dominica up into his arms. "Lie still, fondling," he said. "Naught to fear yet awhile. Down to the beach, Joshua, and on your life no sound!"

He was off into the darkness as he spoke. Joshua crept after, murmuring to himself. "Naught to fear, forsooth!

Well-a-day, well-a-day! and we with the whole pack like to be on us at any minute now! The fiend seize these stones!"

They were halfway down the steep hillside, skirting rocks, slipping on loose stones. Above, on the higher ground, came the crack of an arquebus fired into the air.

"Ha!" muttered Joshua. "That may be a signal to the rest of the pack, but I warrant it will bring our men on fast! I shall die in my bed yet. Courage, Joshua!" He felt level sands under his feet, and quickened his steps to come up with Sir Nicholas, lost in the darkness. Behind, on the high ground, footsteps were running and voices could be heard calling to one another. From the huts to the west came also a stir. Lights showed bobbing on the path above. The hunt was up.

Dominica was set on her feet by the water's edge. Sir Nicholas wrenched his fretful sword from the scabbard, watching those moving lights as they came nearer, wobbling down the slope, outlining the forms of armed men.

The soldiers were casting about now from the looks of it. In the glimmer of the few lanterns Beauvallet could see them peering and searching with halberds levelled. There was but a handful of them, but enough to settle the account of two Englishmen; and from the huts, along the path upon the hill, more were coming to their assistance.

Joshua had waded out into the water, striving to catch the sounds of oars. He came back and touched Beauvallet's arm. "To the right, master, I think."

Sir Nicholas took Dominica's hand and followed. The faint sound of oars grew more distinct; others beside themselves had heard it. From farther up the beach came a shout of command, and a surge of some four or five men towards the water.

"Row, ye devils, row!" groaned Joshua, fairly dancing with impatience.

The soldiers were slipping and stumbling over the shingle; from the dark water came a lusty shout; they could hear Dangerfield's clear voice raised: "Pull, sluggards, pull!" Then the richer voice of the boatswain came to them, chanting in imitation of a waterman: "Heave and ho! rumbelow!"

It was a race now grimmer than any that had been, a race between the boat cleaving desperately through the water and the soldiers pelting down to cut off the fugitives. Joshua stayed peering out to sea to spy the boat, but Sir Nicholas had his back turned, and waited, drawn sword in hand, to check the rush from the land.

The splash of oars was close now; another moment and Joshua saw the boat come nosing shoreward. Behind him the foremost of the soldiers had run on his doom, and Sir Nicholas' sword was red. But now lusty seamen were wading ashore, jostling each other to be the first to reach land, and the air was rent by solid English oaths. The handful of soldiers on the beach drew back. They had courage enough, but lacked a leader, and it was plain that a sprinkling of soldiers could not hope to stand against this troop of bloodthirsty seamen. They fell back then and sent up a mighty yell to warn their comrades that there was need of haste. But the party from the huts was not yet at hand, though it was coming with all possible speed to the rescue.

"Ha, rogues!" shrieked Joshua. "In a good hour!"

"Beauvallet and spare not!" sang out the boatswain, and reached the sands with a splash and a bound. "How fares your honour?"

"Rarely!" laughed Sir Nicholas.

Master Dangerfield was at his elbow. "My God, sir, you have made it!" he cried, and grasped at Beauvallet's hand.

There was a fight in the air, all around the murmur of it. "Ho, Spanish Papishers!" a voice growled. "Now see what comes to those who chase our Nick!"

A second voice bawled out cheerfully: "Ay, have at 'em, lads!" and there was a surge forward up the beach.

Sir Nicholas was only just in time to stop it. "Back, ye rogues!"

The rush was checked but there was dissatisfaction abroad. The *Venture's* crew had been spoiling for a fight all this past fortnight of weary waiting; the excuse was provided, the men were elated, and it was felt that those who had the temerity to harry the *Venture's* commander needed to be taught a lesson.

"What, not one blow, sir?" said the boatswain reproachfully.

Sir Nicholas was amongst his refractory crew. "Back dogs! Man me that boat!" He beat them back with the flat of his sword. "By God, I will have you all in irons if you man me not that boat!" he swore cheerfully.

There was a chuckle, a concerted move seawards; daggers were slid home in their sheaths. Somewhere near her Dominica heard a rough voice say appreciatively: "Ho-ho! The General's back amongst us! I'm for the boat."

They manned the boat. They were disappointed at this tame ending, but it was held to be unhealthy for a man to go against the General's orders. His ungrateful behaviour upon being rescued by his faithful crew rather pleased them. Easy to see Mad Nick was himself still! There was a cheer raised.

The bulk of the soldiers were pelting down the slope of the steep hill now. Sir Nicholas lifted Dominica high in his arms and waded out last of all to the boat.

The crew became aware of the lady, and let another cheer. Many hands were eager to receive her into the boat, foremost amongst them those of Master Hick who had once had his face roundly slapped by her. She stood unsteadily, a hand on one fustian shoulder, the other lost in a great paw.

Sir Nicholas climbed into the boat and waved farewell to Spain. "Give way!" he commanded, and the long oars dipped in the water.

Slowly they drew away, until the lanterns on the shore receded in the distance, and the last sounds from Spain died.

Dominica crouched in the stern, stole her hand into Beauvallet's. His fingers closed over it; he looked down at her, and she caught the flash of his white teeth. "Safe, now, fondling."

She nodded and sighed her content. Behind her, at the tiller, young Dangerfield spoke bashfully. "And a warm welcome for you aboard, señorita, be sure."

She smiled at him, but was too tired to speak. The boat cleaved on through the dark water until the tall sides of the *Venture* reared up before it, and they heard excited voices, and saw the light of a lantern dangled over the side.

"Safe? Have you brought the General off?" shouted the Master anxiously.

The crew let as hearty a cheer as they could for their somewhat winded condition, and something very like a yell of triumph went up from those aboard the *Venture*.

Dominica was carried up the rope ladder and kissed at the top. "Welcome, my bride!" Beauvallet said in her ear, and set her on her feet.

Men seemed to surge around them, questioning, congratulating. There was some display of thanksgiving, not unmixed with many a "Said I not so?" apparently addressed to those who had doubted Sir Nicholas' ability to dupe all Spain.

Beauvallet shouldered a way for himself and his lady through this excited crowd with a laugh and a jest flung carelessly. Dominica found herself confronting a small neat gentleman whom Sir Nicholas clapped on the shoulder. "Save you, Master Capper!" he said. "I have work for you, as I promised."

"Sir Nicholas,"—the neat man wrung his hand—"I count this escape as not less than one of God's miracles, and a sign to these Spanish Papists—a veritable Sign! What may I do to serve you?"

"You may marry me, Master Parson," said Sir Nicholas Beauvallet.

EPILOGUE

"And so we came off," says Joshua Dimmock, sure of the last word. "You say a miracle? Ho, we do not count such trifles as miracles in my master's service! Yet I allow it to have been a feat, and do not look upon my own part in it as contemptible. Sir Nicholas owned himself to be somewhat in my debt: a very unusual thing in him, I may say. However, we had some talk together whiles I was trussing his points that next day in his cabin, and 'Joshua, my man,' says he, 'be sure you are a rogue and a wind-bag, but I owe you some thanks for this month's work.' This was very acceptable to me, as you may be sure, not less so than a certain token that went with it. I wear it upon my finger to this day. Ay, a rare stone: it came out of the Indies.

"But I run on. Sir Nicholas having said as much, and more, and maybe puffed me up a very little in mine own esteem—for I took no account of certain holiday terms such as toss-pot and hempseed that went with his words, these being no more than the genial way he uses—he did me the honour to inform me that he was to be married that morning.

"A rare morning's work, I warrant you! with the crew grinning and looking slyly—until I spoke with them. It was enough. I was become a man of some account, which was not marvellous.

"There was Master Dangerfield at that bridal, the ship's Master, our surgeon, and myself. Be sure I was bidden, and rightly so, for setting aside some other small matters, I was so near to being my mistress' tirewoman in those last few days as makes no matter. A very mettlesome lady, that; I do not deny it. She was married in her riding-dress, for she had none other, and a strange sight it was to see the bride so shabby and the groom so point-de-vice. But I regret that murry taffeta doublet and the new trunk hosen. However, let it go. You may say my lips are sealed as to that lost pack, for there was that other pack I was bound to leave behind at that smuggling port. I warrant you Sir Nicholas made merry work over that: I bore all with a patient countenance.

"I talk more and no more. The marriage over there was some feasting, and the crew, in high fettle. We made all speed for Plymouth Sound, but I doubt my master and mistress cared little when they came there.

"At Plymouth I bestirred myself a little, as I know how, bought some slight matters for my lady, which she was pleased to approve, and call me a proper tirewoman, and set about the ordering of horses and a coach. My lady stayed aboard till she was ready. She was in no case, says she, to show herself to England. Yet I never saw her own herself put-out by the loss of her wardrobe. She took all as it came, and made merry over it, and I am bound to say I was very much her servant before that voyage was over.

"We pushed on to Alreston in rare style, my lady in the coach, Sir Nicholas riding close beside, and myself a little behind. My lady must needs have the curtains drawn back to look about her on our countryside. So he would have it known, but my reading of the matter is that she wanted to look upon my master. And he upon her, God wot!

"You may be sure our home-coming fetched up a rare gallimaufry at Alreston. There was never a one there had thought ever to see Sir Nicholas again. I believe my lord mourned him already as one dead. But in we swept at the gates, up the avenue to the house, and fetched up there with something of a flourish. It is our way. The good-year! We had the whole household about us in a trice, and I make so bold to say that I have never before or since seen my lord in such taking of joy. For he is not one of those who wear the heart upon the sleeve, as the saying is. He had not done wringing my master's hand and hugging him about the shoulders when Sir Nicholas puts him off and begs leave to present his lady-wife. A rare thing it was to see my lord's jaw drop! 'What!' quotha. 'You have never brought her off, Nick?'

"Sir Nicholas handed my mistress out of the coach. I warrant you he looked proudly, with that gleam of the eye and that cock of the pointed beard we all know. Well he might throw up his chin! She was a very lovely piece—with all proper respect I say so, be it understood.

"She was colouring up finely, and holding tight to my master's hand. She felt herself stared at, and maybe feared they might look coldly at her. But my lady had the word then. 'Oh, my dear!' cries she out, and took my mistress into her arms and well-nigh wept over her. You ask me why she should do so? I am bound to say I do not understand these women's coils. She bore my mistress off into the house, and that was the last I saw of them until the dinner-hour.

"My lord had me in then to the winter-parlour. It was pretty to see my mistress, pranked out in a gown of my lady's, lisping her broken English to my lord, and ever and anon looking to Sir Nicholas to give her a word she needed.

"My lord was pleased to speak me very comfortable words, which had not often been his wont towards me. I had a fat purse from him at a more convenient time, but at this present he gave me thanks for having brought his brother off safe. You may lay your life my master let out a laugh at this, but my mistress gave me a rare smile, and vowed my lord had reason. When I consider, I must allow he had. But modesty forbids me to dwell on this.

"What more? Little enough. We were off to London not so long after, and I leave you to judge what Sir Francis said when he heard our tale. I speak of Drake, the Admiral; you will have heard of him, maybe. What my master told Master Secretary is a matter not revealed to me. Suffice it that lean Walsingham rubbed his hands over it. Of that I am assured.

"As I remember, the Court lay at Nonesuch, and thither we went. I warrant you the Queen's Grace fairly crowed to see my master back, and, as I heard, thought it a rare jest he should lay down Don Cristobal's Golden Fleece at her feet.

" 'Is this the best that Spain can show, rogue?' says she. She hath a merry, boisterous way when she is in the humour.

" 'Why, no, madam,' says my master, and brings her up his lady. 'This is the best, madam, and such I present her to you: your Grace's newest subject.'

"Maybe she was not so well pleased with that. I have heard it said that her Grace never liked to see a personable man wed. Be that as it may, she could not well turn pettish now. My mistress had a hand to kiss, and got a tap on the cheek from her Grace's fan. 'How now, mistress?' says her Grace. 'Do you shackle my bold mad Beauvallet?'

"After which she had very little more to say to my lady, but kept my master beside her a full hour, telling her how it had fared with us in Spain.

"In my opinion, the affair passed off better than might have been hoped for, considering her Grace's high temper.

"We were off soon after to Basing, where you see me now. Ay, we lie snug enough, and if you remark that I am become a personage of some note I am not to deny you. I do not say that my master shows this to the world, for that is not at all his way, but I am bold to tell you that I am very indispensable both to him and to my mistress. Which is not at all to be wondered at, I hold! But we have never found a pair of stocks with gold quirks about the ankles to match with those we lost at Vasconosa, and I cannot but deem the throwing of them to the winds, as it were, a very wanton piece of work. But thus it is always upon Sir Nicholas' affairs."

BRING ROMANCE INTO YOUR LIFE

With these bestsellers from your favorite Bantam authors.

Barbara Cartland

☐	20746	VIBRATIONS OF LOVE	$1.95
☐	20747	LIES FOR LOVE	$1.95
☐	20505	SECRET HARBOR	$1.95
☐	20235	LOVE WINS	$1.95
☐	20234	SHAFT OF SUNLIGHT	$1.95
☐	14922	PORTRAIT OF LOVE	$1.95

Grace Livingston Hill

☐	20189	THE TRYST	$2.25
☐	24533	BLUE RUIN	$1.95
☐	14769	TOMORROW ABOUT THIS TIME	$1.95
☐	20044	CHRISTMAS BRIDE	$2.25

Emilie Loring

☐	20829	KEEPERS OF THE FAITH	$2.25
☐	20285	NO TIME FOR LOVE	$1.95
☐	20501	THERE IS ALWAYS LOVE	$1.95

Eugenia Price

☐	22583	MARGARET'S STORY	$3.50
☐	22798	BELOVED INVADER	$2.95
☐	20727	LIGHTHOUSE	$2.95

Georgette Heyer

☐	22762	THE CONVENIENT MARRIAGE	$2.50
☐	22508	LADY OF QUALITY	$2.50
☐	22934	BEAUVALLET	$2.50

Buy them at your local bookstore or use this handy coupon:

Bantam Books, Inc., Dept. RO, 414 East Golf Road, Des Plaines, Ill. 60016

Please send me the books I have checked above. I am enclosing $_____
(please add $1.25 to cover postage and handling). Send check or money order
—no cash or C.O.D.'s please.

Mr/Mrs/Miss_____

Address_____

City_____State/Zip_____

RO—2/83
Please allow four to six weeks for delivery. This offer expires 8/83.

HISTORICAL ROMANCES

Read some of
Bantam's Best
in Historical Romances!